MOLLY WITHERS
and the Golden Tree

KENT ALLAN REES

First published as *Princess Molly and the Golden Tree*
in Canada in 2007 by Golden Tree
ISBN 978-0-9784979-0-3
This edition published as *Molly Withers and the Golden Tree*
in Canada in 2009 by Magic Hat Press
Copyright © Kent Allan Rees 2009
Second Ed. Revised.
Magic Hat Press
ISBN: 978-0-9784979-1-0
Second Edition Text: Kent Allan Rees © 2009
Second Edition Editor: Alethea Spiridon © 2009
Second Edition Book Layout: Lindsay Shewfelt © 2009
Second Edition Cover Layout: Lindsay Shewfelt © 2009
Second Edition Cover Art: Scott Duncan © 2009
Second Edition Professional Photo: Waverly Wyld © 2009

www.mollywithers.com

PRINTED AND BOUND IN CANADA

I offer my warmest appreciation to Andrea for helping me find my feet, Carole for her patience and ubiquitous behind the scenes support, Jeff for his wisdom and friendship, Jenny who fell in love with *Molly* before anyone else, Lindsay for her cover design and book layout genius, Mrs. Harvey for encouraging the *writer's craft*, Ramona for her editing, creative contributions, and belief in this message, Rick for the incredible website, Waverly for her wonderful photos, and my parents Anne and Cyril, for their unconditional love.

For those who have found this real Magic
and for Ramona who showed it to me first.
May leagues of angels whisk you away to
a land of Dreams come true.

Chapter One
-A Girl In Majestica-

By all accounts, King Alfred is a wise and warm hearted man who loves his people very much. By his side, through all things thick and thin, is his loving wife, Queen Claire. Together, they have transformed their small village into one of the largest, wealthiest, and most peaceful kingdoms in all the known lands. They call it Majestica, and because the king and queen well remember their humble beginnings, they are frequently seen socializing with all their devoted citizens.

Majestica is hidden in the middle of a vast forest where certain trees, called ticklers, grow so wonderfully tall that even on bright, sunny days it is no easy task to see the very tops. The soil supporting the ticklers' massive, bulging roots is the darkest brown imaginable, almost black, like chocolate cake, and it is so rich that it produces the plumpest food to be found anywhere. Majestica's grapes are the size of plums; plums the size of apples; apples the size of grapefruit; grapefruit the size of turnips; and turnips the size of watermelons. The watermelons often reach fifty pounds and are so filled with juice, they cause a proper soaking when carelessly sliced. Not to be outdone, the average pumpkin is much, *much* larger with the very largest on record measuring in at exactly four thousand pounds. It took a team of seven maidens to scoop out the innards to make the pies (all three hundred of them), and you can be certain each pie turned out sweeter than honey.

Speaking of honey, it should be noted that the Majestican bumblers haven't any stingers for they are never angry. The flowers grow so thick that walking through them is like wading through water. So it goes that the nectar from these blossoms flows continuously, thereby preventing any competition and aggression amongst the bees, who, if you look closely enough, go about their business with the happiest smiles you have ever seen.

Majestica's clear and cool streams are all over-stuffed with cheeky trout who jump and wink when they do not want to be caught. Countless birds sing in the trees, and all manner of wildlife fills the forests. Yes, to be sure, Majestica is as beautiful as can be described: a place still free from the dark Fear that has taken root in so many other kingdoms.

Now, the keepers of Majestica are none other than the Knights Triumphant and, not unlike the bumblers, these knights have no need to carry swords. Violence and war is not yet known to Majestica. Instead, the knights are renowned for their wisdom and great feats of strength. They can run like deer, pull wagons like horses, and swim like fish. More importantly, they care deeply for their fellow human beings, and this is why they were selected by King Alfred himself. Whenever confronted with hostility from neighbouring kingdoms, the Knights Triumphant make peace through negotiation alone.

They wear the finest and lightest armour for decorative purposes only, and wave glorious red and white flags. You'll see them at their best during the many festivals, or while performing for local charities. They are always smiling, always generous, and always impressing the rosy ladies – even girls like eleven-year-old Molly Withers who pretends she is not yet interested in princes.

At first blush, Molly appears average in every way, but past the hustle and bustle of Town Centre, through all the nearby forests, and beyond the outer reaches of Majestica, Molly is known quite well in *very* private and *very* powerful circles. From softly spoken whispers to dark debates, the word is spreading – *Molly Withers knows the Magic of the Universe!*

Only thing, Molly doesn't believe she knows any magic. Nor is she aware of how special she is. Instead, Molly mostly seeks solitude, playing and singing in the woods and open fields that surround her very small home. She also chases the fairies knowing that she may never catch one, as it is true no mortal in the history of mortals has ever been able to catch one. Sure there are stories of people catching *other* fairies in *other* magical kingdoms, but no fairies are as quick and clever as the Pinkleton Dimple fairies of Majestica. These fairies, with their baby's breath dresses, deep dimples, and rosy little cheeks, can disappear and then reappear quicker than a blink. Some Majesticans claim to have seen the same fairy in two spots at the same time!

Despite their sometimes arrogant nature, Molly can't help but love the Pinkletons' perfect little wings. Most of the time, their wings are that certain shade of green which can only be seen in the spring when leaves are first coming into bloom. But, if the fairies happen to cross the path of a female Unicorn, or if they happen to hear a pleasant song, their wings turn a golden hue. They can't help but turn: like someone's cheeks turning red when embarrassed. To see a fairy, all you need do is walk among the flowers where they snooze their days away. Or you could just use your ears, for although they certainly are tiny creatures, their snores rival the roar of any hungry lion.

As much as Molly loves spending time running through the forest, so too does she love curling up with one of her books under her favourite tree. And what a tree this is. The trunk is thick, thick, thick and to walk all the way around would take you a full minute. Now a minute is not a long time compared to so many things, but how many trees do you know that would take a minute to walk around? Compared in height to the ticklers, though, it is quite a bit shorter, shaped much like a mushroom, and surrounded by a soft, springy bed of very special clovers. Each clover has four and a half leaves, you see, which make them perfect to wish by.

Often alone, it is here Molly comes to read stories of dragons and knights, wolves and grandmothers, and genies and their magical lamps. She imagines these characters come alive for her, and if she isn't careful to close her books quickly, they will leap off the page and escape into the forest. Molly also imagines that her tree is a gateway leading to a world of leprechauns where voices echoing from deep within its stump speak of rainbows, hidden treasures, and fat pots of gold.

Her favourite stories, though, are fairytales that end with princes falling in love with simple country girls and then marrying them as the entire kingdom cheers with joy. Of course these are her favourites because she so longs to have someone take her away from her poor, dull life, and tell her that there is *real* magic left in the world. It's not that the simple spells of the Pinkletons aren't appreciated, but Molly wants to see and feel something so magical that it would change her life forever, something that would give her all that she could ever want. Something as wonderful as the Golden Tree of Truth.

Molly has read several books on the Golden Tree, but she's always been left with more questions than answers. Whether it is fact or fiction remains to be seen, and where in the world this tale first began, no one knows for sure. But according to legend, this Tree, with its delicate golden leaves, has the ability to answer any question imaginable. One popular version of the tale alludes to the famed wizard, Engelbert the Great, who used his unparalleled wizardry to devise a magical seed. One cloudless night, or so the story goes, he planted this seed where no one would ever think to look. Supposedly, the trunk and branches grew on the very spot, but it did not produce a solitary bud for a full three years. It is rumoured, however, that three years to the day after it first sprouted, Engelbert the Great returned to the Tree and discovered it was full of golden leaves. He was so delighted that he cast upon it another spell to protect it: should anyone happen to find the Tree and steal even one of those golden leaves, it would shrivel up and die.

Now, whoever took the leaves would be rich, but the secrets of the Universe would be lost forever. Molly knew very well what *she* would do if she were to find such a Tree. What was a bit of knowledge compared to a lifetime of riches? Yes, Molly spent many a day poring over old cobwebbed books in the town's library hoping to come across a clue that would tell her if the Tree really existed, and if it did exist, then *where?*

After one such excursion to the library, Molly was collecting cabbage grass for dinner from Stankwater Swamp, and as was often the case, the ever annoying Charlie Gregg was in attendance. Charlie was a little older than Molly. He was scruffy, with chestnut brown hair, blue eyes, and a scattering of freckles on his cheeks which he did *not* like because he felt it made him look like a boy. But a boy he was, and as boys are wont to do, Charlie enjoyed teasing girls. One of his favourite victims, of course, was Molly Withers.

Being long overdue back home and desperate to finish her chores, Molly was more agitated than usual when Charlie began to inflict his torments. She wished she could make him go away with a little spell of her own.

'Frickity frumpity frog, be gone you mangy dog!'

Charlie did not disappear as Molly did not know any real spells, but he did look comical now covered in some cabbage grass Molly had launched at him. Charlie calmly removed the wet leaves from his head, as though he was quite used to Molly throwing things at him. He then reached into his pocket, retrieved two familiar flint stones, and struck them together. *Spark!* Neither Molly nor Charlie nor the barking bulldog frogs noticed that a *something* was watching them from behind a fallen tree.

'You shouldn't be here, you know,' said Charlie while making another spark.

'And why is that, Charlie?' asked Molly standing knee deep in muck, with more muck all over her arms, and some muck on her cheeks as well. 'You're not scared, *are you?*'

'Uh – *no*,' Charlie faultered.

Whatever was watching them from the cover of the dark woods stepped on a branch and it made a very distinct *snap*. Charlie looked in the direction of the sound, but saw nothing except the dark rotting trees and a murder of crows shooting to the sky, declaring *cawww, cawww, cawww*. Almost protectively, Charlie took a few steps closer to Molly who didn't care if the whole woods came crashing down. She needed to get this done before it was suppertime so her parents would not be mad. She had already spent too much time in the library, and further procrastinated in the swamp chasing the bulldog frogs, and skipping rocks.

Molly's parents, William (who was a carpenter) and Annabelle, were loving, but they had no time for Molly's imagination and her talk of magic and fairytales. Yet, that's not to say Annabelle had never chased fairies before. She often did as a child. Annabelle had also read under the same tree as Molly, and once claimed that she too heard voices inside that thick trunk. But, somewhere along the way, like so many parents of their generation, Annabelle's childhood magic was replaced with work and so called *maturity*.

'Molly, I don't know why you're here, anyway. It stinks something awful. Besides, everyone's by the orchard getting ready,' said Charlie, hoping to change the subject, and it was a good choice too. Tonight was All Hallows Ball and he knew Molly loved it.

She loved it almost as much as Christmas. She loved watching the knights and their games of incredible strength. She loved how there were skeletons fashioned out of old dry cornstalks that looked so scary you'd swear they were real. She loved how the Pinkleton Dimple fairies cast spider spells so that the entire apple orchard was covered in magic webs that shot little sparks of colour when you passed through them. She loved the Ball's singing competition. She loved Grandma Jones' world famous candy apples which were much larger than grapefruit. She loved the glowing pumpkins and had already carved hers three days prior. The other girls her age, who had not outgrown this grand tradition, carved happy faces, or kitten faces, or, heaven forbid, pony faces, but Molly's pumpkins were always frightfully ghoulish. Whatever the matter at hand, make it dark, or old, or scary in any way, and Molly would love it.

The most pleasing part of All Hallows Ball, though, was the outrageous costumes. Molly cherished the idea of having one night a year when she could pretend she was someone else – *anyone* else for that matter. If she had the means to be whomever she wished, Molly would have dressed up as a fairy princess, for she knew only the daughter of a king or queen could ever be a princess in this world.

Despite all these wonderful things, though, Molly replied: 'I am not sure if I am going this year.'

One eye remained on Charlie, spying his response.

'Too bad. Looks like you are going to miss Priscilla singing,' said Charlie, still pondering the cause for the snapping in the woods. 'Everyone knows she has the prettiest voice in all Majestica. Looks like she might win the Majestica music award this year, too.'

'Prissy!' Molly shouted. She was disgusted with what Charlie had just said. 'Prissy! Prissy! *Prissy?* Why she is only...what?'

'First off, her name is Priscilla. She doesn't like being called Prissy. Secondly, she's my age, thirteen, which makes her only two years older than you. Everyone is going to be there to see it too. The youngest girl to win – ever!' said Charlie being sure to emphasize the 'ever' because he knew Molly loved to sing, and he knew that Molly wished to win this singing contest just as much as she wished to be a princess.

Now there can be no doubt that Priscilla had a fine voice. She always had the best singing instructors to give her lessons and she could afford it because her parents were none other than King Alfred and Queen Claire. Priscilla had the best of everything. Her clothes were all handmade by her very own seamstresses who used only the finest of materials. She owned a prize show pony which won the admiration of all the schoolgirls. She even had her own falconry which daily drew an audience of boys eager to see them feed. Though Priscilla thought handling dead furry critters was disgusting, almost nauseating, she loved attention from boys so much she'd take piles of lifeless mice out to the falconry and throw them straight up in the air for the falcons to catch and devour.

Priscilla also had her own stable and tack shop, as well as an endless fenced in area where she rode any number of her thoroughbred horses. And, as if all these things were not enough, Priscilla was also blessed with very fine looks. Her long blonde ringlets bounced prettily as she walked and her big blue eyes along with her perfect smile always made the boys fumble their words as if their mouths were stuffed full of marshmallows.

Molly recalled all this at once in a sudden flood of emotion. She seriously wondered whether or not she would enjoy All Hallows Ball this year. It was not as if she hated Priscilla, but she knew very well that Priscilla would brag endlessly if she were to win, and *that* might be unbearable.

'I guess I'd win too if I were as rich and as pretty as her,' Molly uttered more to herself than to Charlie.

'Well, I don't really care who wins,' said Charlie. 'I can't wait to see the Knights Triumphant competing in their games. Knight MacDonald is going to have a tug-o-war tonight with Brut, the king's horse! I bet MacDonald wins too! Someday, I'll win a tug-o-war contest with a horse, and not just any horse, either. I am going to out tug a big hefty Clydesdale and then I'll be asked by the king to be his number one knight!'

Charlie made one final spark with his flint stones and then skipped up the path towards home, singing all the way until he and his voice faded in the distance.

'Charlie the Knight Triumphant has won again. Oh yes, what a knight is Charlie. Oh yes, oh yes, oh yes.'

Molly was not amused. Knight or no knight, Priscilla or no Priscilla, singing contest or no singing contest, she was now very late gathering the cabbage grass and she knew her mother would be worried and her father would be angry. In fact, Molly was so late she presumed she would be punished. What if her parents decided not to let her go to All Hallows Ball? Even if Priscilla was going to win the award, Molly wouldn't miss this night for the world – not really.

With two pails of cabbage grass, Molly left Stankwater Swamp behind. She left the lily pads, the bulldog frogs, the dark woods, and the *something* that retreated into the scummy water as soon as she was out of sight.

Not long after, Molly burst through the rickety front door of her family's small home declaring: 'I've got the cabbage grass for the stew, Mom, but I had to fight off Pinkletons to get it home as quickly as I did.'

Molly rushed past her mother who was standing over a washbasin, and poured the greens out onto the counter.

'It was so awful,' continued Molly. 'There must have been thirty, no, fifty of them buzzing around my head all at once. Half were pulling at my hair, while the other half were emptying the buckets, and the other half were tying my shoelaces together so I couldn't chase them. They stole what I first gathered so I—'

'Three halves?' her mother interjected. 'Why, that is a terrible amount of fairies, isn't it? Good thing there wasn't four halves or you may have not made it to the Ball tonight at all.'

Annabelle knew Molly was telling a fib.

'You know, Charlie came by while you were out,' Annabelle continued. 'I told him you were doing your chores as you ought to be doing and I also told him that you wouldn't want to be late for supper, as you surely would not want to be late for the Ball considering it comes but once a year.'

Annabelle couldn't help, but smirk.

'Funny little fellow, that Charlie,' Annabelle said. 'You always tell me you don't like him whatsoever, and he always seems to seek you out. Perhaps he found you down by Stankwater, did he? Must have been dreadfully awful to fight off all those fairies and Charlie, too. I suppose it's a blessing you made it back here in one piece.'

Molly stood there, embarrassed her story was so flawed. Three halves? Honestly. But, she was pleasantly surprised her mother was in good spirits. Perhaps she wasn't going to be scolded after all. This pleasant thought stayed in her head only briefly, however, as her father came steaming through the front door covered with wood chips.

He was a big, solid man who hadn't lost any of his youthful strength. When he smiled, everyone around him smiled, but when he was angry, his eyes lost their brown warmth and turned a filthy red. This was a man you would not cross for any amount of lep-rechaun's gold. He would sputter and curse the most awful things when mad, and still he had one of the warmest hearts in a man. It was obvious he too had lost the youthful magic he once took for granted.

Like so many others, William came to believe the only way to prosper was to work hard all the time. He also came to believe that not everyone could be wealthy and not everyone could do what he or she wanted and not everyone was meant to lead and that most were doomed to a life of servitude. After telling himself these things over and over and over again, he had come to believe that life is *supposed* to be this way. All those cloudy thoughts came thundering through the door with William and he was not remotely happy, standing there wheezing and coughing.

'Fancy that. Molly has finally returned with the cabbage grass after only five short hours. By the time they are cleaned, and by the time we eat, and by the time we have cleared away from supper, and by the time we have brought in wood from outside, and by the time we have fed the chickens and cleaned their coops and by the time we sweep, and by the time—'

'And by the time she does all that,' Annabelle interrupted, 'Molly will have missed the Ball.'

Annabelle was nervous to cut him off like that, but she took a quick breath and continued.

'Now, I can think of no better punishment than to make her go to the Ball straight away and have her applaud that young Priscilla as she wins the Majestica Music Award,' said Annabelle hoping to trick William into allowing her to go, but he wasn't a fool. He stammered a bit more, stomping around the kitchen, muttering mild profanity to himself.

'And when it is all over,' Annabelle pressed, 'she can clean the orchard with Miss Sullivan and ask to bring home some leftovers.'

Now this brought a slight smile to William's face. He relished the thought of free food, but moreso, he wanted Molly to learn the importance of hard work. She needed a role model; someone who could show Molly how to have a better life than he had growing up. Maybe Gabrielle Sullivan was just the person to do this. Even though there were several bizarre rumours that Gabrielle sought the company of witches; even though some said she was not a mortal at all, but a spirit; even though she had an uncanny way of predicting the weather; and even though no one knew where she had disappeared to for seven years after retiring, there was no denying she was a very wise and well respected teacher. Perhaps Gabrielle *would* take Molly under her wing, and teach her the value of schooling and *hard work*.

William turned to face Molly who still hadn't said a peep since he entered the house.

'You be sure to find Miss Sullivan and you listen to everything she has to say. Be sure to help her clean the orchard, and don't forget to ask to bring home anything you think we can use,' he said to Molly whose head had withdrawn inside her body like a scared turtle.

William then retrieved his pipe from his dusty trousers and returned to his wood shop outside.

Molly turned to her mother and saw that Annabelle's subtle smile had already passed. It was not replaced by anger, but rather a tiny bit of sadness. It was the sadness that crept in every time she got a headache, and yes, Annabelle received more than her fair share of headaches. Molly felt guilty knowing that her mother always seemed to get a headache when things in the house were stressful, and Molly believed that things were mostly stressful because of the way she misbehaved.

Annabelle reached into her apron and retrieved a ten cent piece which she offered to Molly.

'Now, you take this and enjoy yourself,' said Annabelle handing it to Molly. 'I know it's not much, but it will at least buy you a candy apple.'

Molly took the coin reluctantly knowing her parents did not have any extra money. She also knew that a ten cent piece would not be enough to buy a candy apple as candy apples have been at least twenty-five cents for no less than three years. But, she wouldn't tell her mother this – not to save the world.

'Sorry I was late, Mom. Can I really go?'

Annabelle smiled and Molly was off lickety split to get washed and changed for the night. One full year had passed and it was time, once again, to experience the splendour of All Hallows Ball, apples or no apples.

Chapter Two
- *Grandma Jones' World Famous Candy Apples* -

It didn't take Molly very long to get ready. When supper was finished and the kitchen tidied to her father's satisfaction, she was out the door before he had a chance to change his mind. Once outside, the panicky feeling within her began to subside and her spirits brightened. Everyone was making their way to the great apple orchard, and what costumes they all wore! Mrs. Beatty was dressed up like a beetle (for the sixth year in a row). She was a short, very round woman who found humour in addressing herself as *Beatty the Beetle*. Though the costume was tattered and the saying overdone, you could not help but be drawn in by her laugh.

Mr. Hawkins was dressed up as a knight. He had rigged something up beneath his costume (perhaps on suspenders) which made him look like he was riding a horse. In front of him projected the horse's head, with a flowing mane made from unravelled ropes. The horse's front legs had been carved from wood; the horse's back legs, though, were Mr. Hawkins' own legs and this rounded out the illusion.

Further up the path was Mr. Orwell, the science teacher. He was an odd sort of man with a rather thin frame, untidy hair, and thick, crooked glasses. He, too, seemed partial to the same costume every year, and though no one knew what he was supposed to be, he was happy to show it off. For legs, he had two lengths of chimney pipe from a woodstove which were hinged at the knee so he could walk. His feet were hidden by silver painted boxes. His arms were covered with anything and everything metallic. There were forks, spoons, knives, nails, and even some silvery fishing lures. He also wore an ancient suit of armour which he must have worked at very hard to restore the shine. In the middle of the belly plate was a hole which held a tiny lantern with red glass. When he walked, the light inside flickered enough to make the lantern look like it was blinking. Finally, atop his head was a pot for a hat. Some kids threw chestnuts at him just to hear the *ting* sound, and this infuriated him. He'd turn to them and say: *'Don't anger Machine Man.'* Whoever, or whatever, Machine Man was, Molly didn't care. It was amusing to look at.

Up a little further from him was Mrs. Harvey, the English teacher. There was no finer teacher and woman at the school than Mrs. Harvey. She was dressed up as a witch, but not like the mean witches of Wesdenburgh. Instead, she was very much a happy, joyful, playful sort of witch, the kind who would only use spells to bring a smile to someone's face. She and Molly had a special bond, and it was likely because Mrs. Harvey was one adult who still possessed the magic of childhood. It was also Mrs. Harvey who first showed Molly's class a mighty tree nicknamed Gidot where the Pinkleton Dimples congregated every hundred years to announce their new queen. Though the tree had died years ago, when the Pinkletons sat upon its branches, their green wings made it look as though it was full of leaves.

By the time Molly shook the image of Gidot and the Pinkleton Dimple fairies from her mind, she was not far from the great apple orchard. There was already a swarm of people jostling to get a special treat outside the main entrance: Grandma Jones' world famous candy apples. A little closer, and Molly could see dear old Mrs. Jones herself handing out apple after apple – shiny, huge, and as red as could be.

'Come an' get 'em while d'ems drippin'! Grandma Jones' world famous candy apples here! No need to frown, dearie,' Grandma Jones added, glimpsing Molly. 'There's 'nuff here fer everyone. Only t'irty-five shiny coppers! Only t'irty-five dull coppers!'

Molly's heart sank. They were even more expensive than last year. Molly felt the ten cent piece burning in her pocket. Grandma Jones peered into her eyes. Molly was embarrassed, though she had done nothing wrong. She hurried past the glaring Mrs. Jones, but bumped into someone quite solid.

'Miss Sullivan!' said Molly.

'By all means, please just call me Gabrielle,' replied the mysterious woman.

'Sorry about that. Wait. It's a good thing I...bumped into you. I was only allowed to come tonight if I helped you clean up afterwards.'

Molly looked up at the tall, full-of-life woman standing in front of her. She was beautiful with her healthy frame, bright eyes, and warm smile. Everything about her said *woman*, and she caught the eye of most single men walking by.

'Allowed to come providing you helped me?' enquired Gabrielle. 'Sounds rather curious, Molly Withers.'

Molly didn't know very much about Gabrielle except that she used to be a teacher, had retired and then vanished from Majestica for seven years. After returning, many people hounded Gabrielle for answers, but without success. Whenever asked where she had gone and what it was she was doing, Gabrielle simply replied: 'I was away *learning.*' Shortly after returning, Gabrielle formed the Ball Committee and that was that. Eventually, people stopped asking her questions.

Molly never noticed before how kind she looked, nor did she notice how big she looked. Not a cake-and-ice-cream-eating sort of big, but as if she took up more space than her actual body. It was as if there was something coming out from her making her seem larger than she really was.

'I was late collecting cabbage grass,' confessed Molly, 'and I was only allowed to come if I helped clean up because there are always leftovers and my parents would appreciate anything I might be able to bring home...if that's okay with you.'

'Of course, of course,' said Gabrielle with a smile. 'I look forward to finally having the pleasure of your company. There are things I have been most anxious to tell you.'

Molly was confused. How did Gabrielle know who she was? Half the teachers didn't remember Molly's name, and here was this retiree saying it as if she had known Molly all her life. It didn't make much sense.

'But there's a full night left before we start any of that,' said Gabrielle, 'so I will see you after the music award is handed out. Does that suit you?'

Merely being in this woman's presence lifted Molly's spirits. It just felt right. Even if it were not punishment, Molly would have gladly spent more time with Gabrielle. What had she *learned* when she was away all those years? And, what was Gabrielle so anxious to tell a little girl whom she had never spoken to before? Was it of great importance? *No,* Molly reconsidered. It was likely nothing more than Gabrielle trying to find new recruits for the clean up crew.

'Sounds great,' said Molly, still hearing Grandma Jones behind her singing the praises of her candy treat.

'Good,' replied Gabrielle. 'Now, why don't you turn around and get yourself one of those apples? I can see that you want one.'

'I can't afford it,' answered Molly, suddenly deflated. 'I only have a ten cent piece to spend tonight.'

Gabrielle smiled once again and Molly figured this woman spent all her days smiling.

'I want you to turn around and take a good look at Mrs. Jones and everything happening around her,' said Gabrielle to Molly, who followed the instruction, but didn't understand why she was forced to stare at something she couldn't have.

'Now, what do you see?' asked Gabrielle.

Molly couldn't see anything out of the ordinary.

'I see kids coming and going. They arrive with at least thirty-five cents, and leave thirty-five cents poorer, but with a gigantic apple to show for it.'

Molly's back was against Gabrielle, and she felt Gabrielle's hands squeeze her shoulders gently.

'Is there nothing else?' asked Gabrielle.

Molly looked harder, but the harder she looked, the more she could see countless children coming and going with smiles as big as the apples themselves.

'I see other rich children all getting what they want, and I don't think it's fair!' exclaimed Molly.

Gabrielle did not respond and there was a moment of silence. Molly felt bad. It wasn't that she begrudged the other children, but she sensed a bit of familiar jealousy swelling up within her. Yes, she knew she was prone to jealousy and she knew it wasn't a great feeling, but she also knew she couldn't help it at times.

'Perhaps there is another way,' suggested Gabrielle. 'Try this. Close your eyes and picture yourself with one of those apples. Feel the weight of it in your hands, the warm candy running over your knuckles, the sweetness upon your tongue. Experience it in your mind for a few moments, then have another look and tell me what you see.'

Molly closed her eyes and tried to clear her mind. As instructed, Molly imagined what it would be like to sink her teeth into one of those fine apples. She pictured the sweet, sugary candy dripping down the stick, running over her knuckles and making a beautiful mess. She imagined it shining in the half light of this spectacular evening. After a few moments of concentrating very hard, Molly *could* feel the weight of it in her hands and it was quite heavy. She could almost taste it.

After imagining all this, she opened her eyes, expecting to see the events as they were before, but something had happened. The whole scene had changed, if only slightly. It was quieter – peaceful even. She could still see the constant stream of happy children, but she noticed something else. She noticed every once in a while Grandma Jones dipped one of those mighty apples and turned away from those lined up in front of her, yet, when she turned back to face them again, the apple was gone!

Molly strained to understand. She waited a few more moments and it happened again. This time, though, Molly noticed a grubby looking boy behind Grandma Jones scurrying away into the crowd with a candy apple. In fact, there were several different children behind Mrs. Jones getting apples. They were delivering small bushels to her, and every time they did so, Grandma Jones rewarded them with one of her famous treats. Molly swung back to a smiling Gabrielle.

'I can get an apple if I bring her a bushel, can't I?' Molly asked excitedly.

'Yes,' answered Gabrielle, 'I am sure of it.'

Molly's breathing quickened with this happy thought. It had been years since she'd had the pleasure of eating one.

Gabrielle placed her hands once again on Molly's shoulders and looked into her eyes.

'You know, Molly, if you can hold in your mind what you want long enough, you shall have it.'

This very important sentiment floated past Molly without being fully absorbed, but no matter – she would be reminded of it again soon enough.

'Thanks,' said Molly. 'I'll see you later!' and she was off to fetch a bushel, and enjoy one of Grandma Jones' world famous candy apples.

All Hallows Ball had begun – officially.

Chapter Three
- *All Hallows Ball* -

Molly relished every bite of her apple as she entered the Ball and then paused to take a good look around. Before her was a large field only ever used for special events. The grass beneath her feet was flat and soft, and there was positively no dirt around at all. This was noteworthy as Molly could always find dirt when she tried. In the middle of the field was a large tent with a stage for the band and the singing contest. Molly saw Priscilla there, barking orders at the committee, probably to have things rearranged to suit *her*.

The entire field was crowded with people dancing to the music and everyone wore a costume. Molly reflected that the only people who were not there were her parents. For one reason or another, they had chosen to stay at home more and more as the years crawled by. But no matter, Molly was there, and that was enough, if even she was the only one without a costume.

Molly loved how this event always took place in the fall and she loved how it was held at night. As she looked around at the decorations, she realized the Ball Committee had outdone themselves this year. Ten foot high posts set ten feet apart surrounded the entire perimeter of the field to mark its boundary. Unlike other years, atop each post was an extremely large jack-o-lantern carved and glowing bright. From where Molly was standing, the impaled pumpkins looked like a string of orange lights.

At the far end of the field was the forest's edge, but not much was happening there. Some of the boys were daring each other to venture into the woods, past the glow of the lights, but very few lasted more than a couple of minutes before becoming absolutely petrified. Charlie was there egging the other boys on, but no matter how far or how long the others stayed, Charlie ventured further and remained longer.

To the right of Molly was the orchard itself and it went as far as the eye could see. As lovers walked hand in hand and as children darted around playing tag, Molly saw the distinctive shape of the fairies' magic webs bursting and crackling softly upon being touched, like mini fireworks.

To the left of all the excitement was a cornfield. During daylight hours, Molly could walk through the corn forever. Now she could never explain why, but at night things were very different and she always felt uneasy passing it. Perhaps it was the way the moon accented the leaves so that the whole field shimmered like ripples on a midnight sea. Or maybe it was the way the wind swept through the field, the leaves tickling and tapping each other, making sounds not unlike critters running across a church floor. Or perhaps, just perhaps, it was because the corn was planted in not-so-perfect rows. You could stand directly in front and see down one or two rows at a time. To the left and to the right, though, you could see nothing. She realized that as sparse as a cornfield appeared, you could easily hide from someone who was quite close by. Handy if you were being chased, but terrifying to think of someone chasing *you*. A Morrukk, for instance, one of the scary tribesmen from Nordenburgh, could have been staring at Molly that very moment from only a few feet away, and she wouldn't have known.

As Molly's imagination gained momentum, she stared harder and harder. She noticed a few feet in that two or three stalks were not swaying like the others. It looked unnatural. What would prevent them from moving? Harder she stared, and finally the stalks moved, but not as Molly expected. They parted. Something or someone was there, watching her.

'Gotcha!' shouted a voice, as Molly was suddenly seized by strong hands. Molly screamed and jumped with fright, only to hear a horrible laugh from behind. She spun round to face her assailant and saw Charlie dressed vaguely like a knight. Because she'd been daydreaming, she hadn't noticed him sneak up behind her. Instantly dismissing the cornstalks' odd behaviour as mere imagination, she stepped towards Charlie to kick his shins, but she thought better of it. Molly had a theory about Charlie, and she wanted to test it.

'Charlie, there you are. My mother pointed out earlier that you have a funny way of seeking me out, and here you are again. Is there something you want to tell me?'

There was the softest sound in the cornfield, and the few awkward stalks began to sway just like the others. Molly barely noticed this, though, waiting for Charlie to answer.

'Not at all,' replied Charlie. 'Just arrived and I noticed you were standing here staring blankly at the cornfield, all by yourself, *again.*'

'And to think I'd prefer a lifetime of solitude than to share your company,' she lied just as Priscilla bounced up to them, her blonde locks and fairy princess costume perfect in every way.

'What are you doing, Charlie?' Priscilla spat out, suggesting Charlie was more of a belonging than a person. Charlie went the sort of red you go when you are both happy to see someone and disappointed they arrived when they did. Molly then realized that, by some fluke, Charlie had somehow landed the prettiest girl in Majestica. This didn't bother Molly, though, *too much.*

'Hello, Prissy,' said Molly. 'I'm glad to see you've found each other. Now I can spend the night in peace without Charlie following me around like a stray cat.'

'My *name* is Priscilla,' she retorted, casting Molly a dirty look. 'It shouldn't be that hard to remember. I am Princess Priscilla. Nice costume, by the way. What are you supposed to be? A filthy begger?'

Priscilla then cast Charlie an equally dirty look, grabbed him by his sleeve, and dragged him out of sight. Molly was alone, but at least she was now free to see whatever she wanted. She continued at a slow pace, making sure to observe every detail and after getting her fill of the costumes, the magical spider webs, the pumpkins, and the cornstalk skeletons, she worked her way to the middle of the dancing crowd as the tug-o-war contest was sure to take place soon.

Halfway through a jazzy number, the band jumped right into *The March of the King.* All the dancing stopped at once as King Alfred and his trusty steed, Brut, appeared seemingly out of nowhere. Together, the king and his grand horse looked awesome with Majestica's large red and white flag displayed on one side, and a shield bearing the Royal Coat of Arms on the other. The king wore a spectacular suit of armour, so shiny it sparkled in the moonlight, and Brut's saddle was so polished that Molly saw her distorted reflection in it as they walked by.

The crowd hushed and you could hear the clinking of the king's decorative sword against his leg, the creaking of the horse's leather saddle, and the heavy hooves thudding against the ground. Brut came to a quick stop in the middle of the crowd, reared, and neighed as only a large horse can. While Brut was still on his hind legs, King Alfred lifted the face protector on his helmet and shot one triumphant fist in the air.

'*Hoorahh!*' he shouted, and everyone cheered and clapped.

Amidst the excitement, fireworks were set off, illuminating the entire sky with dazzling colours. The crowd cheered louder and louder until they were silenced by a booming voice.

'*WHOSE HORSE IS THIS SPOILING ALL THE FUN?*'

Everyone turned. There was no mistaking the identity of such an immense man. There, standing on the stage in front of the band, was none other than the good knight, Marcus MacDonald. Molly was more than just pleased to see him. She was excited. He was the king's most trusted knight, a man whose reputation of strength and wisdom was known far and wide.

There was only a slight lull before the crowd went absolutely wild. He leapt from the high stage and when he landed, he did not budge, like a statue landing in a pile of thick mud. He took one deliberate step forward, then a second, and the crowd parted all at once just as waves are pushed aside by a ship's hull. He too was wearing his decorative armour, and flung over his shoulder was a very thick rope. He walked past Molly, winked at her, and circled the king and his horse twice before stopping. He stared straight up at the king and the king stared back. *Silence.* In one motion, the king dismounted his horse and hugged Marcus in a way that let everyone know they were the best of friends.

MacDonald removed the rope from his barrel sized chest and began to rig it to the horse's saddle as King Alfred interacted with the crowd. There was a swarm of little girls around the king's legs as they all knew what was about to happen. The king peered around, deeply concentrating, and then turned in Molly's direction. Why was he looking at her? Wasn't she too old for this tradition? As much as she hoped against hope that it could be true, deep down Molly didn't believe she had so much luck. But there he was, looking almost directly at her.

King Alfred paused for a moment and then smiled as he walked directly towards her. Molly instinctively raised her arms to the king, only to be brushed aside for little Ally Topper who was standing behind her. Molly's heart sank again, not so much because she hadn't been chosen by the king, but rather because she allowed her spirits to fill with hope. What was hope, anyway, but a cause for feeling disappointment later on?

King Alfred picked Ally up in his arms as friends *oohed* and her parents waited with suspended breath. Ally was young, maybe only seven, and she seemed very sleepy. She wiped her eyes and yawned a tiny yawn. The king walked over to his horse, opened up a side satchel, rooted around for a bit, and then produced a burgundy velvet pouch tied over with golden twine. He handed it to Ally, motioning her to open it. Her little chubby hand reached into the pouch and pulled out a huge gold coin. At once, Ally's head looked too small for her bulging eyes, and Molly believed she heard Ally's parents finally exhale.

The crowd cheered once again as little Ally Topper threw her pudgy arms around the king's neck. Judging by the smile on the king's face, you'd swear he believed Ally's hug was worth a thousand gold coins. At length, he handed Ally back to her shabbily-costumed parents John and Sally, and turned to face Knight Mac-Donald, who was now tethered to King Alfred's horse with the other end of the thick rope tied fast around his waste.

Brut was a beautiful animal and quite large for a horse. But as large as Brut was, he didn't seem so big next to Knight Mac-Donald. The knight took a couple of steps back and turned away from the horse. The king removed a golden lanyard from around his shoulder and placed it on the ground between MacDonald and Brut. He then took the reins and pulled his horse a few steps forward, making the rope between Brut and MacDonald as tight as a bow string. You could hear the rope stretching under the pressure. MacDonald adjusted his footing, stared intently on the ground in front of him, and shouted, *'MacDonald is ready!'*

With this, the king let go of Brut's reins, stepped to the side, and yelled, *'K'yeaaaaah!'*

Brut quickly took the first step forward and MacDonald stumbled backwards. Before Brut could take his second step, though,

MacDonald leaned forward, and with his feet planted firmly, he forced Brut to stop dead in his tracks. They swayed briefly, with neither Brut nor MacDonald seeming able to move. Finally, Mac-Donald lifted his right leg to step, but as he did, Brut pulled him off balance once more. MacDonald was already a mere foot of the king's golden lanyard and still moving back. The crowd booed. No one really thought the knight would win, but they all hoped he'd put up a better fight.

Now there is something to be said about Knight MacDonald: he gains strength in the face of defeat. He isn't a sore loser by any means, but to say he likes winning is not accurate either. He *loves it,* and hearing the booing was enough for him to dig a little deeper and it couldn't have happened soon enough. Just before being pulled over the lanyard, he found his footing again. MacDonald struck his chest, made a sound not unlike a bull, and leaned forward with all his might. Brut took one awkward step backwards and MacDonald leaned further still. The knight's heavy upper body was so close to the ground, his hands clutched at the grass hoping to find additional leverage. MacDonald heaved again and took another small step forward, followed by another. Brut, against his will, was forced to step back – once, then twice. Again, MacDonald bore down, and with all his strength, he took two more small steps.

Molly worked her way around the inside of the circle so she was directly in front of MacDonald. As she looked up at everyone's faces, she saw all their mouths gaping in pure amazement.

Again, the king struck Brut's trembling hindquarters and yelled 'K'yeaaaaah!' Brut shook his mane, but MacDonald took another step forward. Brut trembled. His hind hooves were almost touching the lanyard.

'K'yeaaaaah!' King Alfred yelled again, with yet another gloved swat.

Old Brut neighed wildly and reared high once more. Mac-Donald leaned over and his right hand reached out in front of him, but he could move no further. Why couldn't he be just a tiny bit stronger? thought Molly.

At this moment, Molly recalled Gabrielle's words: *If you can hold in your mind what you want long enough, you shall have it.*

Molly closed her eyes, hoping and wishing for MacDonald to win. The volume of the rabble seemed to fade away. She then grabbed onto the knight's gloved hand as tightly as she could, and leaned back with all her strength.

She moved! Unbelievably, she moved and with her came Knight MacDonald, and with him came the rope, and with the rope came Brut! The next second took a lifetime, but in that second Molly could have heard a mouse in the forest. And, it is a matter of fact, that Molly *believed* she heard Brut's hoof the very moment it touched the ground on MacDonald's side of the lanyard.

'MacDonald has won! MacDonald has won!' cried the crowd.

Fireworks were set off again and the crowd followed suit in an explosion of cheering. This brought Molly back to the here and now. She opened her eyes and was nowhere near the knight. What had happened? She didn't know how much was real and how much was imagined. It was as if she had just woken from a vivid dream. Her senses were restored fully when she heard Priscilla's voice come screeching through a large blow horn.

'Excuse me!' Priscilla yelled. 'Ex-CUSE-me! It's time for the singing contest.'

The tide of excitement receded in small waves, and Molly was a mere spectator once more. She felt funny and the night was almost over. There was nothing left to do except watch Priscilla win the Majestica Music Award, and then clean up pumpkins, papers, and gob-soaked candy apple sticks with Gabrielle.

Oh! That's right. What was it Gabrielle had said earlier?

Perhaps, thought Molly, the night wasn't over after all.

Chapter Four
- The Lady Gabrielle -

It didn't take the crowd too long to disperse after the singing contest ended. Priscilla was officially crowned the youngest person ever to win the Majestica Music Award, and by the time she finished bowing, and the band had disassembled their instruments, there were only a few admiring stragglers still inside the grounds.

Molly saw Gabrielle right away – she seemed to stand out. As Molly drew near, Gabrielle had just finished assigning all the volunteers their tasks. The last three were the Wortherly brothers – Nic, Vic, and Mick. They'd been assigned the task of cleaning up the horse manure. They didn't seem to mind, though, because they immediately broke into a cheery song, marching away with their shovels in hand: *'Poop patrol! Poop patrol! Three brothers are on the poop patrol!'*

'Well, there you are,' said Gabrielle, handing Molly a woven basket. 'You and I are going to pick up the odd bits scattered about.'

Molly looked around and was pleased to note there wasn't much garbage at all. It definitely wasn't a two person job. Molly hoped that Gabrielle chose this assignment so they would have lots of time to talk, but about what, she could only guess.

It was a tedious chore, though – stepping, stopping, stooping – and it only took a few minutes before Molly grew impatient. What did Gabrielle have to say? Was it simply a matter of Gabrielle asking Molly to volunteer for next year as well? If Molly said yes, then the next time she might not be so lucky. She might be forced to hold the bucket for the Poop Patrol Brothers and Molly knew that job could get quite messy.

Gabrielle appeared to have a lot on her mind, but the silence made Molly want to burst.

'Gabrielle, did you see me during the tug-o-war?' Molly asked, breaking the silence and trying to decipher what had actually happened.

'Yes,' answered Gabrielle. 'You were standing off to the side by Ally and her parents. Did you see how relieved they were when Ally pulled out the large gold coin?'

'Sure, who wouldn't be?' answered Molly. 'But did you happen to see me reach out and grab hold of Knight MacDonald's hand? Right before he won?'

'No, I can't say that I did,' answered Gabrielle.

Molly rethought the whole thing and laughed out loud.

'Phew. It *was* all my imagination. For a moment, I thought I had actually reached out and helped him. How embarrassing would that have been at school?' remarked Molly, feeling rather relieved.

Gabrielle, though, remained quite serious.

'There's nothing wrong with a little imagination, is there?' asked Molly, not knowing how to take Gabrielle.

'Would you be so kind as to tell me what you imagined?' asked Gabrielle.

'S-Sure,' said Molly with a little reservation. 'Well, I remember watching them go back and forth for a while, and I remember the excitement in the air, and I remember really wanting Knight MacDonald to win. It didn't look like he was going to do it, so I grabbed his hand and pulled with all my might. But I guess that last bit was my imagination.'

Gabrielle stooped to pick up another bit of debris, and then looked directly at Molly.

'What if it was *more* than just imagination?' Gabrielle asked.

'What do you mean? Why? What did you see?' asked Molly.

'I saw it going back and forth as well,' replied Gabrielle, 'and then I caught a glimpse of you. I saw you watching cheerfully at first, but then I noticed your face became a little blank, as if your mind had started to wander.'

'That must have been when I was off in my own world,' said Molly. 'I was recently reminded I look kind of funny when I go blank like that.'

'Molly, I want you to take a minute and think about what I just asked,' said Gabrielle. 'What if it was *more* than just imagination?'

Molly was properly confused. After a few minutes of frustration, Molly said: 'I'm sorry, but I'm not quite sure what you're after.'

'Oh, Molly,' soothed Gabrielle, 'do not be sorry. You will never have to stand in judgment for your imagination or for your dreams. No, not in a thousand years will you.'

This warm sentiment touched Molly a little.

'Let me phrase the question another way, then,' offered Gabrielle. 'What if it was *because* of your imagination that Knight MacDonald won?'

Finally, it clicked.

'Oh, I get what you mean,' answered Molly. 'You're asking if I believe my imagination actually helped the knight win, and to that I would have to say no. Perhaps the queen of the Pinkleton Dimples could pull something like that off, but not me.'

'No? Well I would argue that it *is* possible and that is *exactly* what happened,' countered Gabrielle. 'You focused on what you wanted and you got it. True or true? Just like the candy apple.'

Molly didn't have time to answer before she was prodded with another question.

'What about this?' continued Gabrielle. 'Have you ever noticed that those who talk about being poor are the poorest people you know?'

'Sure I have,' replied Molly, 'but that's because all the people I talk to *are* the poorest people I know.'

'What if I were to tell you that the people you talk to *are* poor because they spend all their time talking about it, and they are themselves to blame?' asked Gabrielle.

'Then I'd say you don't know what you're talking about,' snapped Molly. 'My family works very hard and still they are poor. There's no sense lying about it. How silly would we look if we told everyone we are rich, when we are not? We'd be laughed at.'

'Dear, sweet child,' said Gabrielle with such love in her voice it calmed Molly. 'I don't think you'd look silly at all. You see, Molly, there exists something very wonderful in our world, and it is so endlessly consistent, we call it a natural law. To understand what I mean when I say natural law, consider the law of gravity. Rain falls because of it, and if you go outside when it's raining, you *will* get wet, whether you're mean or righteous. Just as the law of gravity does not care one way or the other, *so it is with the law of attraction.*'

Molly had never heard of the law of attraction, but understood the law of gravity very well, having fallen out of many trees. Molly didn't understand the point Gabrielle was trying to make, though, or what all this gibberish had to do with her.

'Do you know how gravity works?' asked Gabrielle.

This seemingly simple question stumped Molly and she shrugged her shoulders in answer.

'So you can appreciate that just because you don't know *how* something works,' said Gabrielle, 'that's not to say that it doesn't. True or true?'

'True,' Molly was forced to agree.

Molly and Gabrielle entered the orchard. With a glance over her shoulder, Gabrielle seemed careful to remove themselves from any listening ears. She then smiled a knowing smile and softly asked, 'What if I am right? What if people are poor *because* they talk about it all the time? What would that mean about being wealthy?'

'*If* what you say is true,' said Molly, 'then rich people are rich because they brag about being rich. But it's not right to brag, and besides, it can't work for everyone anyway because there is not enough money or gold for us all to be rich.'

Gabrielle gestured to the surrounding apple orchard and asked, 'are there enough apples on these trees for every man, woman, and child in Majestica to have a bushel for themselves?'

'Absolutely not,' answered Molly, 'and that proves my point. This orchard goes as far as the eye can see, but it would have to be ten times bigger for everyone in Majestica to have a bushel.'

'Does everyone you know like apples?' asked Gabrielle with a twinkle in her eye.

'Well, no, but that's not the important part of the question,' retorted Molly. 'You asked whether or not there were enough apples for everyone in Majestica to have a bushel, and the answer to that question is *no*. It's just like Dad says, there is not enough for everyone.'

'Oh Molly, but there *is* enough,' countered Gabrielle, 'for everyone who wants a bushel, that is. And that's what makes what I am about to teach you so wonderful. Our dreams are like snowflakes, Molly. No two dreams are exactly the same because we all long for different things. We don't all want apples, just as we all don't want to be queens with our own castles. But the Universe is abundant enough for us all to have what we truly desire. But to get it, Molly, you need to learn the law of attraction. When you do, you'll see real magic and beauty in all things great and small.'

Molly's eyes brightened like a child's on Christmas morning

who has received what they wanted. *Real magic?* For the first time in ages, Molly thought there might be a glimmer of hope. Was there really enough for everyone to be happy?

The moon above, full and as bright as a mirror, slipped behind a cloud and Molly realized everyone else had finally gone home. Molly was content, until she noticed Gabrielle's face was once again creased with concern.

'Are you alr—'

'*Sshhh!*' interrupted Gabrielle.

There was an eerie silence. The wind was no longer blowing through the leaves; the random plopping of over-ripe apples had ceased; the bulldog frogs in the distance quieted themselves, and even the crickets had hushed their midnight chorus as if they were all scared to be heard. Molly looked up to Gabrielle whose eyes were as wide as an owl's. Gabrielle peered around and wherever she looked, Molly looked, too. Gabrielle bent down on one knee and grabbed Molly by the shoulders in a way that made the hairs on Molly's neck stand on end. With the softest, quietest voice, Gabrielle whispered, 'Can you meet me tomorrow?'

Molly immediately thought of a dozen chores she would have to do. Somehow, though, she sensed this was more important and she nodded a silent *yes*.

'We haven't much time,' said Gabrielle, 'and you cannot speak of this to anyone. No, not even if the king himself summons you to the castle and demands you tell him, okay?'

Molly nodded.

'Meet me back here at three in the afternoon,' said Gabrielle. 'Tomorrow I will teach you something I believe you already know. I will tell you all about t—'

SNAP! Gabrielle was cut off by the distinct sound of someone stepping on a dry branch. Both Gabrielle and Molly looked in the direction of the sound, but there was nothing to be seen save some shadows and the black silhouettes of the tree trunks.

'Meet me here tomorrow and I'll tell you about the Go—'

Crack - Fizzle - Crack! An enchanted fairy web sputtered not too far from them. They both looked again, but nothing could be seen in the brief pinpoints of light. Molly froze. Gabrielle picked up an apple, and threw it in the direction of the sound. As it hit the trees, several ripe apples drummed the ground below and there was another sputter and spark from a magic web. Gabrielle's eyes seemed to focus in on whoever or whatever was there. Molly strained to see, but it was hopeless in the thick night.

Gabrielle then heaved a large stone in that direction and incredibly hit her mark. Whatever the thing was, it groaned unnaturally. It must have stumbled as well, because more sparks lit up behind a tree before it fled. Gabrielle and Molly heard its footsteps as it stole away, and they saw its shadow leaping through the orchard with incredible agility. As it manoeuvred through the trees, it set off several of the fairies' spider webs, like an erratic metal stone skipping on a dark pond of electricity. After a few moments, it was gone and Molly found herself out of the orchard and back in the open field. Gabrielle put her arm around her and together they scurried all the way to Molly's home. She wanted to ask Gabrielle what was going on, but knew it was no time for questions. Instead, Molly turned to Gabrielle and gave her waist a big hug. Gabrielle hugged back.

'Molly,' began Gabrielle, 'there was someone else who wanted your company tonight, and because it saw you with me, it knows you are the one. I have put you in danger.'

Molly, having just remembered something more upsetting to her than the shadowy stranger in the orchard, looked up with tears in her eyes.

'I haven't brought father home anything from the Ball,' sobbed Molly. 'I'm going to be punished for sure.'

Molly turned from Gabrielle, entered her home, and tiptoed to bed. As incredible as the Ball had been, and as exciting as her time with Gabrielle had been, she was heartsick. She knew her father would be very upset when he realized she did not bring home any leftovers. She also knew that she couldn't tell him why she had forgotten because Gabrielle asked her to keep their conversation a secret.

Lying there, shaking in her bed, Molly pulled the covers up beneath her chin, and tried desperately to think of happy thoughts. She replayed the highlights of the Ball in her head and, by and by, she remembered walking around the grounds with the woven basket. She began to imagine that she wasn't picking garbage up at all, but that she was stuffing the basket with leftover hams and vegetables and pies and wines and cheeses. In her mind, the basket swelled and the more she added to it, the bigger it grew, and when it was so stuffed with food that it couldn't hold another peanut, she imagined tying it over with a bow. She also imagined seeing the smile on her father's face upon receiving such a basket and with these happier thoughts finally easing her mind, Molly fell fast asleep.

Chapter Five
- *Going to Work* -

As the morning cock crew, Molly awoke feeling quite refreshed. She must have slept very well and been blessed with happy dreams. She jumped out of bed, dressed herself, and went to the kitchen without a care in the world. It all ended, of course, when she saw her father sat at the table looking rather unpleasant. He looked up at Molly over the rim of his glasses, the way he always did when he was upset.

'Good time at the Ball?' he asked with his gruff morning voice.

Molly felt like she had been punched in the belly. Somehow, she had forgotten all about the deal she made with her father the previous night, and now she was left trying to explain why she didn't bring anything home. All of last night's sleepy images of her father smiling as she presented him with a king's share of food had disappeared completely. They were, after all, just the cruel figments of her imagination.

Her stomach knotted tighter and tighter. Even though there was nothing in her belly, she felt like she was going to be sick. She couldn't bear to look in his eyes and she knew she only had a few seconds to think. Surely, he would have looked first thing in the morning for the food from the Ball, and been livid when he found not so much as a crumb. If she didn't come up with an answer quickly, the volcano would explode, and Molly was expecting the worst. Not having anything to give her father was bad enough, but she suspected he'd think she did it on purpose.

She cowered silently in the doorway as he stood up. He looked as big as Knight MacDonald. His eyes still smouldered, but not in an angry way. He walked over to kitchen window, and placed his hands on the counter.

'Tell me, Molly,' he said, 'why don't you help out when you have the chance? Your mom and I are trying, but it's never enough, is it?'

Molly was expecting thunder and lightning, but all she got was drizzle. Her father was quite upset, yes, but he wasn't mad. His feelings were hurt. Molly knew he was disappointed and her heart ached. She knew she'd had a chance to help her parents out and she'd blown it. She also knew her parents worked very hard to provide for her and she knew she didn't do a whole lot to help them in return. Only as much as she was ever told to do.

Molly began to see the other side of the coin. She suddenly understood why they seemed so frustrated and why they were hard on her. It was all because they were poor and they wanted the very best for their one and only daughter. Molly felt sorry for them. She felt sorry they worked as hard as they did and still had very little to show for it.

Molly's emotions swelled within her and in the very centre of her body she felt tiny teardrops form. Then, in the corner of her emerald eyes, two drops emerged, grew, and rolled over her round cheeks. Her father turned immediately upon hearing his daughter's sobs and he wasted no time picking her up in his heavy arms.

'There, there,' he said. 'It's okay.'

Molly hugged him harder than she had in her whole life.

'Well, would you look at the size of this!' exclaimed Annabelle bursting through the door with an oversized basket stuffed with food. 'Molly, I am not sure if you waited till it was over, or if you took it from the king's plate, but my, what an incredible amount of food!'

William spun around, still cradling Molly in his arms, and he couldn't believe what he saw. Annabelle was so excited she was beaming, but even so, she didn't overlook the fact that her husband had Molly in his arms and they both looked as though they had been crying.

Annabelle didn't pry, but instead, heaved the huge basket onto the kitchen table, making its legs tremble under the weight. There was everything Molly had imagined the night before and more. It looked absolutely glorious. There were hams and cheeses and fresh poultry and a wide variety of vegetables. Annabelle pulled a card from the basket and held it briefly to her chest as she smiled at Molly.

William placed Molly back on her feet and gently squeezed her shoulders with approval as Annabelle read the card:

'Dear Molly,
Thanks again for your help after the Ball.
Here is a basket for your efforts last night.
Sorry it wasn't ready when you left.
Your new friend,
Gabrielle.'

All three of them were glowing. William opened his mouth to ask a question, but was unable to get a word out before a knock came at the front door.

Upon opening the door, William saw another basket, larger than the first, hovering in front of him. He could barely see the short squat legs underneath and the chubby fingers trying to hold it up, and he could not see a head at all. From somewhere behind the oversized basket, a man's voice said, 'Delivery for Miss Molly Withers.'

William took the basket from him with ease and placed it on the table beside the first and began to take inventory, oblivious to his surroundings. He didn't even look up when the man said, 'Right then,' and left.

There was so much food in the two baskets it was incredible, but Molly was confused by it. Sure she helped at the Ball, but she didn't collect any of this food. In the end, though, it didn't matter. Molly was happy beyond belief and dismissed the baskets as another funny coincidence in life.

Molly then noticed that the second basket also contained a card. She picked it up from among the mountain of food and read it:

'Molly, you were such a great help last night!
Would you kindly consider becoming my personal
assistant? If this is agreeable with both yourself
and your parents, then please meet me in the

orchard at three o'clock today.
Your friend,
G.'

'Can I, Mom? Can I, Dad?' Molly asked, filling with excitement. Annabelle smiled and then looked to William for his approval. He smiled too.

'Sure you can,' he said, 'but under one condition.' He paused to make sure both Annabelle and Molly paid close attention. 'So long as it doesn't interfere with your chores.'

Molly couldn't believe today was turning out as well as it was. She thought she was going to be punished – perhaps even tortured – but here she was with two overflowing baskets of food and two extremely happy parents. What's more, she had also been offered a position with one of the nicest women in all of Majestica, if even she was a little mysterious. Yes, today was turning out just fine. Molly confirmed her dad's wishes by saying, 'I'll start with bringing in the wood!'

The morning chores seemed to take forever; Molly could hardly wait to meet up with Gabrielle. She was dying to know a little more about the magic and the natural laws Gabrielle had spoken of, and she also wanted to know who had been in the orchard last night watching them. By the time Molly finished all that she had set out to do, there was only enough time to wash up and have some lunch.

But this wasn't a lunch you'd rush. She couldn't remember a time when there had been so much food on the table to eat. Not at Thanksgiving and not at Christmas. Molly, Annabelle, and William ate together and everyone was happy. Molly described everything from the Ball, Annabelle talked about her gardening, and William, true to character, expressed concern about the upcoming winter. There was joking and laughing, and everything seemed perfect.

As the last bits were eaten, Molly asked if there were any other chores to be done after the dishes.

'No,' answered Annabelle, 'but don't you want some pumpkin pie before you go scampering off?'

Pumpkin pie! That was Molly's favourite. Annabelle retrieved the pie and gave Molly a generous slice. She ate it slowly, cherishing each mouthful. When it was gone, she thanked her parents, brushed her teeth, and ran out the door to the orchard.

Molly smiled knowing this was a very first for her. She was going to work.

Chapter Six
- *Keeper of the Magic* -

Molly ran all the way to the orchard and was quite out of breath when she arrived. She saw Gabrielle staring at the cornfield and thought they had something in common. Molly tried to sneak up on her as Charlie had done the night before, but it didn't work. Though Molly was awfully quiet, Gabrielle turned towards her when she was still several feet away.

'Good afternoon, Molly. I trust you received the baskets,' said Gabrielle, motioning them to head in the direction of Town Centre.

'Oh yes,' said Molly. 'Thank you so much. You have no idea how happy you made me today. And my parents, of course, were over the moon.'

'A deal is a deal,' said Gabrielle.

Molly thought she had surely received the better end of that contract. There hadn't been much to clean up and the majority of the time was spent wandering through the orchard.

'It would also seem my proposal is satisfactory to you and your parents,' said Gabrielle.

'Yes, it is, and I am ever so excited.'

'Well, that's good, Molly, but I hope you're not expecting another food basket. Still, I am sure you'll be quite pleased with what I am about share with you. I must stress, though, that what I am about to tell you cannot be shared with anyone. Not your parents, not even the good king, for there may come a time when even he cannot be trusted. Are we agreed?'

'Agreed,' said Molly.

Gabrielle took a deep, deep breath.

'Molly, this may come as a bit of a surprise, but I know you have done a great amount of reading on the Golden Tree of Truth. I have as well, and I have come to know something about it that is going to please you to no end.'

Molly's heart began to quicken, but Gabrielle hesitated. This was great for dramatic emphasis, sure, but stalling at this particular moment was more torturous to Molly than anything she had ever experienced. More torturous than being caned with a bamboo stick. More torturous then being grounded from going outside, or having to watch her beloved forests burn and turn black.

Molly's face quivered, her mouth gaped open, her lungs ached, her muscles knotted, her eyes dried.

'Molly,' said Gabrielle finally, 'the Golden Tree of Truth is real!'

At this point, shock mixed with doubt. Molly couldn't readily believe what she had just heard, but Gabrielle's smiling eyes shone with sincerity. If it was true, then this was insanely wonderful news. This story had been the hopeful seed of Molly's curiosity for as long as she's been able to read.

'A-Are you sure?' Molly asked dryly.

'Yes, Molly, I am sure, and there's something more. There is a magic surrounding the Golden Tree which is as real as the Tree itself, and I am going to show you how to use it.'

A thousand questions exploded inside Molly's head, yet there was one question which was most pressing.

'Why me?'

Gabrielle's eyes sparkled, but there was a hint of tension hiding behind them.

'Molly, there are many people who believe you are very special,' said Gabrielle. 'More special than you realize. We know all about you and your fascination with the Tree, and how you've spent many afternoons reading up on it. We also know that deep down you are still connected to the real magic of the Universe. I guess, in a way, we all sense this magic as children. Tragically, however, most of us are taught to ignore it as we grow older.'

'Gabrielle,' interrupted Molly, 'I don't know any magic. I've pretended of course, waving a stick around as a wand, but nothing ever happened.'

'It's not that kind of spell-magic you've read about where young children are learning to become wizards in grand make-believe castles. Oh no, Molly. I say again that this magic is *real* and it can let you have everything you could ever want. In fact, I've already seen you use this magic.'

'You have?' asked Molly.

'Sure I have. You just didn't understand what you were doing.'

'If you say so,' agreed Molly, doubtfully.

'Did you not get a candy apple last night?' asked Gabrielle. 'Did you not receive two wonderful baskets filled with food? And was it not you, yourself, who has longed to find someone to show you that there is magic left in the world? All these events are not coincidences, Molly; they are examples of you using the the law of attraction.

Molly felt funny. She hadn't given any thought to why she met Miss Sullivan. Despite what Gabrielle said, Molly believed it *was* just a coincidence. All Molly knew was that she introduced herself to Gabrielle because she had to. Molly didn't consider for one minute that Gabrielle was the one person she had daydreamed about meeting; the one person who was going to take her away from her boredom; the one person to prove that there was still magic left in the world.

'Isn't it funny?' remarked Gabrielle. 'Even though we may want something so badly, most times when it arrives we cannot see the thing for what it is. Opportunity knocks all the time, Molly, but it is your responsibility to open the door.'

'I *have* wanted to meet someone who could make me believe there was still magic to be found, yes, but how did *you* know that? Are you psychic?' asked Molly.

'No, I am not psychic,' chuckled Gabrielle. 'It was our suspicion for the longest time, but last night confirmed it. We have been waiting to meet the special someone to whom we are to teach this magic. But, Molly, this is where it becomes dangerous for you.'

'Dangerous?'

'Extremely dangerous,' emphasized Gabrielle. 'You see, this magic has been around since the dawn of Time and it was once passed freely through the generations. Everyone should have access to it, but sadly, the condition of mankind is such that a handful of evil men wanted to keep the magic to themselves. Over time, the magic continued to disappear, until finally, only a few wicked people knew of it. They took all the ancient texts they could find and burned them. A few obscure stories remained, but it didn't matter. The damage was done. Most grownups believe the tales are make-believe, myth, or folklore. But stories such as the Genie and his Lamp, and The Golden Tree of Truth are inspired by this ageless truth. Much of what was first understood is now lost, and it shall remain that way until the Golden Tree is found again. But do not be so foolish as to think finding the Tree will be easy. There are elitist brethren who think it should be known only by men and only the men *they* choose. They have kept it from women's ears for as long as can be remembered.'

'Why?' asked Molly.

'There are many different reasons and theories to explain it,' continued Gabrielle, 'but the root is the same. It is fear. You see, of all the things on this planet where men and women are equal, there is one thing man cannot do. He cannot create life. Perhaps, then, men fear inferiority, and seek a different power in hopes of feeling better about themselves. Bear in mind, Molly, this all began thousands of years ago, but it continues today. The more they learn, the more they keep to themselves. It's the fear of the magic getting out, and these men losing their power, which is behind much of what is wrong with the world.'

'King Alfred isn't one of these men, is he?' asked Molly.

'I certainly hope not,' said Gabrielle, 'but the fear *is* growing stronger. Because of this fear, many people now believe they do not control their own destiny. People live in fear of not being pretty enough, and they live in fear of being hurt, and they live in fear of being weak, and they live in fear of getting sick, and they live in fear of being disliked, and so on, and so on. And what's more, those men who have hidden the magic are gaining control of the world's resources. They have lost sight of what the magic was intended for, and they are coming after those who seek to spread the knowledge.'

'Is that why there was someone in the orchard last night?' asked Molly.

'I can only assume so,' replied Gabrielle.

Molly tried to swallow, but could not. There was very little saliva in her mouth.

'There is an ancient prophecy,' continued Gabrielle, 'that tells of a woman who will find the Golden Tree, become the Keeper of the Magic, and eventually, spread this gift throughout the world.'

Then it made sense. Molly understood why Gabrielle wanted to talk to her. *How simple. Gabrielle was the Keeper and Molly was first in line to hear it. That must be why Gabrielle knows so much about the Golden Tree. She probably already knows where it is. Perhaps that's what she learned when she disappeared after retiring,* thought Molly to herself.

Molly was excited. With any luck at all, Gabrielle would bring Molly along to see it. How grand would that be? Nothing less than a dream come true.

Gabrielle smiled, stopped walking, and looked deep into Molly's emerald eyes.

'We believe,' said Gabrielle, 'that *you* are that woman. It is you, Molly Withers, who is destined to be the Keeper of the Magic and there's something more – you don't have much time to find the Tree. They are coming. They are coming to make sure this doesn't happen, and they will kill you if they must!'

What else could Molly be but overwhelmed? She didn't think she could take another step. Gabrielle must have said it wrong. Surely, this was a colossal mistake. It couldn't be Molly. Molly had never been the keeper of anything. Even keeping secrets was as daunting to Molly as attempting to balance purple elephants on her nose. No, there must be some mistake. How could she find something she knew so very little about? Why, the Golden Tree could be anywhere in the world.

Molly spotted a tree stump just off the path in a thick patch of flowers and without saying a word, waded towards it. As she did, hoards of Pinkletons took to the air briefly before landing again on the delicate petals. Molly hummed the first few notes of one of her favourite songs to see the fairies' wings glitter golden. She had to shoo one defiant fairy from the top of the stump before she could sit down, and as the fairy flew by her ear, it whispered, *'Molly knows the magic!'* It then chuckled and in a tinkling, disappeared into the thick of the woods.

Molly looked at Gabrielle who had waited a few moments before joining her.

'I don't understand,' said Molly. 'Please tell me more.'

'The magic of the Universe,' said Gabrielle, 'is just another natural law; like the law of gravity. I hinted at it last night when we were discussing why some people are poor, but you can see examples of it everywhere. Just as those who speak of abundance are most often wealthy, and those who speak of illness are most often sick, and those who worry about everything are most often troubled by everything, so it is that we *attract* precisely what we focus on. This is the law of attraction, and this is the real magic of the Universe. It's just one of the many wonderful things the Tree has revealed.

Once you know how to use this law, your world will be however you want it to be. Unfortunately, we dismiss too much as mere coincidence, but I must impress upon you that there are no coincidences that do not have a higher purpose. It's not the case that life happens to us, Molly. It's us who happen to life!'

'And those men you spoke of,' said Molly, 'they're willing to kill for it?'

'Yes,' said Gabrielle, 'and they are also willing to die for it. That's a terribly powerful combination. From foreign lands, the fear has been spreading. Some believe it's already begun in Town Centre. Indeed, I'd say whoever was in the orchard last night is proof of it already here. More will come. They will try to fill our hearts with fear and if they are successful, Majestica and its resources will be turned over to the few who are using the law of attraction for their own selfish ends.'

'But Majestica is so beautiful,' objected Molly. 'It just can't happen here. There's never been horrible poverty. My family must be one of the poorest, and even we have our own home and a fire to keep us warm. There's mischief, but no real crime. We haven't ever gone to war and most Majesticans are overjoyed to live here. I'd just die if it were to change.'

'Yes,' agreed Gabrielle, 'everything you have said is true, but Majestica is one of the last places left on earth like this.

Molly thought for a few moments in silence, and a hard truth set in. For the first time in her life, Molly understood that Majestica was subject to change just like everything else in the world.

'Can they be stopped?' asked Molly. 'You have only told me just a little bit and already I am scared.'

'You're simply in a race,' answered Gabrielle. 'You have to lead by example and never let fear take hold of your heart. Once you are able to use this magic, then you will be able to teach others, as many as you can. I doubt it can be done in one lifetime, and I suspect this battle will go on for as long as humans inhabit the earth, but providing we always focus on what we want and show others how to do the same, we will win. We will keep Majestica pure and beautiful. And, if travellers come to us from afar, we will show them our ways so they can take the magic back to their homelands. That's the very best any of us can do.'

'Are you taking me to Town Centre to see evidence of the fear, then?' asked Molly.

Gabrielle nodded. Molly stood up.

'Then we should hurry along,' said Molly. 'I will want to be home by dark.'

Chapter Seven
- *Town Centre* -

There were all sorts of neat things behind the high walls of Town Centre. Molly didn't go to town often, but when she did, she loved it. She could always count on seeing something extra special and today would prove no exception.

Immediately, Molly noticed that it was noisier than she remembered, and there was something else – the common chatter of shopkeepers and customers seemed slightly heavier, as if there was more business going on than friendly conversation. The butchers seemed more interested in carving meat, than they did the customers at their counter. The little old ladies with the fruit and vegetable carts still smiled, but their eyes were not twinkling as Molly remembered. From the children playing in the streets, up to the wealthiest land owners discussing current affairs, everyone seemed just a little less happy than before. Even more noticeable, was the pace at which everyone was going about their errands. They were all in a terrible rush. It was such a difference from Molly's last visit when she heard nothing but laughter and chatter and had seen nothing but smiles, hugs, and the shaking of hands.

'Is everyone okay?' Molly asked.

'Everyone seems content enough, don't they?' remarked Gabrielle.

'Yes,' said Molly, 'but it's different somehow. So much has changed since I was here last.'

They walked on through the narrow streets, and that's when Molly noticed another change. Town Centre was not nearly as tidy as it had once been. She distinctly recalled that before everything had its place, from the cobblestones beneath her feet to the thatched rooftops overhead. Today, though, everything was a little out of order. The chimneys burped out a darker smoke, Molly's feet kicked up dust, there was some litter scattered around, and the smell from the alehouses was offensive. *My,* Molly thought, *look at all the new alehouses!* Many of the fine shops and sweet smelling bakeries had been replaced with stinking alehouses.

Molly and Gabrielle made their way to the square and they saw a man standing on a large box. There was a thick crowd gathered around him and they were all jostling with one another for space.

'Yes, folks, yes folks, step right up. Don't be the last to hear this sad, but important news. Don't be the one left out in the cold!' cried the man.

Instantly, a shiver wiggled down Molly's spine and she turned to Gabrielle who looked equally displeased.

'Oh, Gabrielle, I don't like him, whoever he is.'

'I agree, Molly. He's a Morrukk.'

'A Morrukk!' declared Molly. 'From Nordenburgh? I've never seen one before. They *are* scary.'

'Particularly this one,' agreed Gabrielle. 'It's best you pay close attention to what he is saying.'

Molly listened as she looked on, and though she could barely stand the sight of him, she couldn't look away, either. He was tall; creepily tall, and the curvature in his back was most unnatural. He was also ugly; as ugly a man as Molly had ever seen, in fact. His smile was a snobby smile that showed his crooked, stained teeth. His eyes were as dull as swamp water, and his skin was wrinkly and pale. The top of his head was balding, but around the sides and back was an outcropping of long, wispy, black hair. His face looked as though the life had been sucked out of him. Yes, *that* was it, thought Molly, even though she had never seen a dead person before. This man on the box looked dead.

Adding to the grotesque, his shoulders protruded at odd angles, his arms seemed too long for his body, and on the ends of these arms dangled his bony white hands with nails that were yellow, long, and twisted. One of his gnarled hands gripped a knotted wooden cane that he beat against the side of the box for added emphasis. And it was working. Standing there, in some strange manner of robes, rapping away, he had the full attention of everyone gathered around him.

'Though I come from the poor land of Nordenburgh, do not begrudge me as I am here by your request. Neither begrudge me my ugly shape, but take heed, take heed of my sad, sad news.'

Molly slipped to the front of the circle as only she could do and stared intently at this frightful man.

'We, whom you have counted on year after year after year for a winter's report, have bad, bad news. A hard winter lies before you, but don't be afraid for there's still time. Come. Come, my friends. Stock up, and be prepared. Buy only what you can manage, but buy *as much* as you can manage. If you can afford more, then I'd say buy it!'

Molly noticed behind the raised box was a shorter Morrukk with a large belly and a huge wagon stuffed with all sorts of pelts. There were fox pelts and rabbit pelts, bear pelts, beaver pelts, and even tiger pelts. He couldn't sell them fast enough. The crowd was in a frenzy to get their hands on them. They were almost throwing their money at him, but why?

'Don't be the last, my friends,' said the Morrukk on the box. 'Don't be left out in the cold. Buy warm pelts from me before it is too late. They are almost gone, and when they are, there will be no more. Yes folks, yes folks, step right up. It's going to be a hard, hard winter.'

Molly turned from the man to make her way back to Gabrielle, but the people had closed in around her. Molly pushed as best she could, but no one seemed to notice her. She started to panic. She was suffocating.

'You there, little girl! Leaving so fast?' said the scary voice from above.

Molly stopped pushing and slowly turned back to the man. He stared through her, dropped an awful grin upon her, and then leapt into the crowd. He placed one ugly hand on Molly's shoulder while the other gripped the cane and shielded her from the people as he pushed their way to the back.

'Step aside, step aside, little girl coming through here. Step aside!' he said, hitting the odd person with his cane, and whether they were young or old, it didn't matter.

When they finally pushed through and were in the open, he

stopped and swung Molly around to face him. He got down on one knee and put one hand into his pocket. He searched eagerly for a bit, and then grinned another terrifying grin as he grabbed Molly's hand and placed something soft in her open palm. Molly looked down and was horrified when she saw what she was holding.

'Here you are, my pretty. Can't let you go away empty handed, now can we? A pretty, lucky rabbit's foot for a pretty, lucky girl.'

The rabbit's foot was dyed an artificial pink and it stank like bog. Molly could see the tiny nails sticking out from the end and she grimaced. She wondered if this foot had come from one of the rabbits she had played with in the woods. Molly was terrified staring into the Morrukk's lifeless eyes, and she didn't know what to do.

Suddenly, Molly felt the warm touch of a familiar hand upon her shoulder and she knew it was Gabrielle. Rarely had she been happier to see someone than she was at that moment. The tall lanky man stood upright, sneered, and leaned heavily upon his cane. He placed one hand over his heart (if indeed he had heart) and attempted a bow.

'Mortimer Weedly, at your service,' he said with a smirk, but Gabrielle said nothing in return, nor did she seem displeased with his grim appearance.

It was obvious he was disappointed in Gabrielle's calm expression, and Molly suspected this man loved the sad attention he must have usually received for being hideous.

'Good day to you both,' he said as he turned and limped back into the crowd towards his familiar perch. Before he disappeared into the mass of people, Molly noticed there was something green and stringy peeking out of his pocket. She couldn't make out what it was, but it looked like seaweed.

'Are you alright?' asked Gabrielle.

'I'll be fine in a few minutes,' replied Molly, seeing Mortimer effortlessly leap back up on his high box.

'A little scared, I would bet. I lost you in the crowd. Sorry about that.'

'Can we go now?' asked Molly.

'Sure we can. You have seen what you needed to see.'

They left Town Centre and walked a full mile before either of them spoke again.

'I think I know what you were saying about the fear,' said

Molly. 'It *is* spreading, isn't it? Because of people like Mr. Weedly, right?'

'Yes, Molly, all of what you say is true. Harden your spirits, for it may get worse before it gets better. Mortimer Weedly already has several people worried. He will be back again tomorrow, likely with something else to sell.'

'And all this has to do with the magic?' asked Molly.

'Yes, I believe it does,' answered Gabrielle. 'Mortimer Weedly knows something about the magic, but I don't know how much, or who would have shared this information with him. It is highly protected by the men in power.'

'I would very much like him to leave Majestica and never return,' said Molly.

'Hold on to those thoughts and feelings, and I am sure you'll find a way to get rid of him.'

'But what happens when I become afraid and have negative thoughts that everything is going to go wrong, and what if I say the wrong thing?' asked Molly, flustered. 'Won't I make it come true?'

'We can't help but have horrible thoughts sometimes,' soothed Gabrielle, 'but you can always replace a bad thought with a good thought and the wonderful news is that good thoughts are a thousand times more powerful than bad ones.'

'How will I even know that I am thinking the right thing?' asked Molly. 'How will I know what to focus on? How will I know what I am thinking is going to be for the best?' It stressed Molly to keep track of all her thoughts.

'Follow your heart,' answered Gabrielle. 'It's as simple as that. If you are thinking of something and it makes you feel sad and upset, then think of something else. If, however, you are thinking of something and realize you feel all happy and warm, then *those* are the thoughts to hold on to. You see, your heart will always tell you whether your thoughts are good or bad, because it doesn't think, it *feels*. Your brain does the thinking and your brain is not always your best friend. Any time you think you are poor, or not pretty, or that everything is going to go wrong, that's your mind at work.'

'Do you think it was Mr. Weedly in the orchard with us?' asked Molly.

'I can't say for sure,' answered Gabrielle. 'Whoever we saw was quite nimble, and exceedingly fast. I daresay Mortimer is not so fit.'

'I don't know,' said Molly. 'He limped away, but sprang up on that box easily enough.'

'Either way,' said Gabrielle, 'we have to find out what Mr. Weedly is really doing here. You can rest assured it's not just to sell pelts.'

'How do we find that out?' asked Molly. 'It's not likely he's going to tell us, is he?'

'I think I know who we can ask.'

'Who?' asked Molly.

'Mr. Cayce, of course,' answered Gabrielle. 'He knows almost everything. Tomorrow night, you and I will set out to find him.'

'Tomorrow night! Couldn't we go during the day?' asked Molly, knowing she was much braver when the sun was out.

'No, I am afraid we can't,' answered Gabrielle. 'He mostly comes out at night.'

The sun had just started to set when Molly and Gabrielle returned to the familiarity and beauty of their own little village.

'Is everything okay?' asked Gabrielle, knowing full well that Molly was feeling distraught.

'I don't know the first thing about using the magic,' said Molly. 'Where do I begin?'

'You begin by simply declaring to the Universe what you truly want,' said Gabrielle. 'If you don't declare it, the Universe won't know what to give you. Then, after you've declared what you want, you simply have to *feel* as though you already have it.'

'The Universe? You keep speaking about the universe as if it's alive,' said Molly, 'and I don't understand why.'

'I choose to call it the Universe, but it has been called many different things over the centuries. It has been called God, it has been called our Life Force, and it has been called Mother Earth. Whoever you choose to accept into your life, matters not. You should do whatever feels right for you. If it feels right to ask God for the things you want, then do that. If it feels right just asking the Universe, then do that instead. All of the world's religions have important things to teach us, and they are not as different from each other as some would have you believe. What you really need to understand is that everything in the Universe is connected, and because we are connected, our thoughts affect our very existence.'

Gabrielle reached inside her pocket and tossed what she had retrieved in the air towards Molly. It glinted in the half sunlight, but Molly couldn't tell what it was. It looked like a skinny snake with a fat head flying through the air.

Instinctively, Molly raised her little hands to catch it and as soon as she felt the object hit her palm, her fingers curled around it. She opened her hand slowly and saw a large stone roughly shaped like a heart. It was bound by silver and attached to a leather string. The stone's colour was very intense – a deep blue with a bit of white. It was the nicest necklace she had ever seen in her life and she felt all warm and happy on the inside. Molly loved jewellery almost as much as her mother loved it.

But Molly's joy didn't last longer than a few short moments, as she felt unworthy and undeserving of it.

'It's a sapphire,' said Gabrielle. 'That's your birthstone.'

'How do you know what my birthstone is?' asked Molly, quietly.

'Because I know that your birthday is September seventh,' answered Gabrielle. 'I say again, you are very well-known in certain circles.'

'I wish my birthday was later,' said Molly. 'It often falls on the first week back to school. What a horrible present.'

Molly thought a minute longer and guilt swelled within her to the point where she couldn't stand it. With a lump in her throat, she offered it back to Gabrielle.

'Here,' said Molly. 'I haven't done anything to earn this. Perhaps next time.'

Gabrielle took a quick step forward, snatched it from her fingers, and stuffed it back in her pocket.

'How do you expect to receive gifts from the Universe when you are always telling yourself you are undeserving?'

For the first time, Gabrielle looked a little upset, much like a teacher who becomes frustrated with students who fail to understand a simple concept.

'Now how do you feel?' asked Gabrielle.

Molly knew right away how she felt – *horrible.*

'Mmm-hmm, I see,' said Gabrielle. 'And how did you feel when you were pondering giving it back to me?' asked Gabrielle.

It dawned on Molly that she must have missed something she was taught only a few minutes ago.

'I don't understand,' said Molly. 'I felt bad because I didn't think I deserved it so I thought I should give it back to you.'

'*Think, think, think, thought, thought, thought,*' said Gabrielle. 'These are all things your mind came up with *after* you received it. When you first opened your hand, I'd say you were pretty happy based on that smile you had on your face. Then your mind got in the way and made a mess of things, didn't it? Not really your best friend, is it, that spongy thing between your ears.'

Gabrielle placed one hand on Molly's shoulder and held the necklace up with the other. Her smile returned.

'Listen, Molly, you do deserve this,' said Gabrielle. 'You deserve this and much, much more. You are worthy and deserving of all the gifts the Universe sees fit to give you, no matter what it is that your heart desires. If you can hold on to a thought long enough, you shall have it. Now, take this gift and let it be a reminder for you.'

Molly smiled, placed the necklace around her neck, and gave Gabrielle another hug.

'Thank you, Gabrielle. You're the loveliest lady I have ever met.'

'You are most welcome,' said Gabrielle. 'Now, I must be off, but we'll discuss it again tomorrow. Oh, and be sure to bring some rubber boots.'

'Rubber boots? What for?' asked Molly.

'We are going to Stankwater Swamp tomorrow night. If we have any hope at all of finding Mr. Cayce, it will be there.'

'I don't have any rubber boots. Whenever I'm there collecting cabbage grass for Mother and Father, I wear my old shoes.'

'I will not have you walking around the swamp for hours with wet feet,' said Gabrielle. 'This time of year you'd be apt to catch a cold. No, that just won't do. You have all day tomorrow to get a pair, or I'll go by myself.'

And that was that. Gabrielle turned on her heel and left in the direction of her home. Molly didn't have the slightest idea how she was going to get a pair of rubber boots by the following night, especially knowing she was going to be in school all day. The ten cent piece she saved at the ball would not be enough, so purchasing them was not possible. She wouldn't be able to borrow her father's, either, as they were much too large, and her mother certainly didn't have a pair. Maybe she could make a pair, but out of what?

No, Molly didn't know how this was going to work, but she hoped she'd find a way. Molly suspected this was a test. Gabrielle must have wanted Molly to use the magic to get a pair of rubber boots, so she let her imagination go to work. Later that night, Molly fell asleep picturing herself in Stankwater Swamp looking for Mr. Cayce. She pictured herself wearing a comfy pair of rubber boots. She could see them on her feet as easily as she could see the swamp. Yes, she envisioned finding a pair of boots for tomorrow, maybe even shiny red ones.

Chapter Eight
- *The Hunt for Rubber Boots* -

Molly awoke filled with excitement. She wondered what sort of man Mr. Cayce would be. Would he be tall or short? Would he be thick with muscle or thin and wiry? He would most certainly be old, Molly thought, because all wise men are old.

Breakfast was served and she was off to school. Priscilla was cold, but greeted Molly with a little more emotion than usual because she was still excited with her triumph at the Ball.

'Hey, Molly!' Priscilla called, 'What do you think of my trophy? Pretty nice, wouldn't you say?'

'That is a nice trophy, *Prissy*,' mocked Molly.

'Stop calling me Prissy!' squawked Priscilla. 'I hate it when you call me that.'

Charlie walked behind Priscilla and didn't seem too happy to be there. Molly didn't think they were a good match. She hated to admit this to herself, but she thought Charlie was too good for Priscilla, even if no one else agreed. Charlie was not nearly as wealthy as Priscilla and he definitely wasn't blessed with Priscilla's beauty. Despite being annoying, though, he wasn't as cold as she was.

'Stop gawking at Charlie, would you? He's mine, you know,' said Priscilla, who caught Molly looking at Charlie a little longer than she had intended.

'Go find your own toy,' Priscilla added, as Molly walked by

and entered her classroom.

When the lesson started, Molly's thoughts fell to a greater issue – *boots*. How was she going to find rubber boots if she was trapped in class all day? Already the day seemed to be slipping away.

The morning classes came and passed and everyone was let out for lunch. Molly, like many other students, left the school grounds and walked home for lunch. Halfway there, the skies opened up, and the rains poured down. Molly liked the rain, yet, she found it more amusing today as she remembered what Gabrielle had said about the law of gravity: *whether you are mean or righteous, if you go outside when it is raining, you are going to get wet.*

Molly searched her house just in case there were rubber boots hiding somewhere, but she only found her father's. She tried one on and knew her tiny foot would never fill it. Not even with a thousand pairs of socks would they fit. She searched her heart and her mind and the more she thought about it, the more stressed she became. What if she couldn't find a pair?

Molly caught herself feeling bad, and realized she had to think positively, she just had to. She had to use the magic and make it happen.

She had her lunch and pulled on her old shoes (which were really old because her *new* shoes were also old) and ran back to school. She only ran a few steps before her feet were soaked. All the other kids who had gone home for lunch were now wearing their rubber boots. It seemed everyone had rubber boots but Molly. Even Charlie had a pair. Molly could have just asked to borrow his, but she didn't want to give him the satisfaction of knowing he had something she needed. Plus, she was a little embarrassed she was too poor to have her own pair.

The afternoon went even faster than the morning, and the big, fat raindrops continued to hit the windows until halfway through the last class of the day. At this point, the rain stopped suddenly, the clouds vanished from the sky, and the sun shone full and bright. Excitement ran through the classroom as it always did when the sun appeared after a long rain.

School ended and when Molly walked outside, she saw steam rising from the warm, soggy earth. Molly also noticed many of the students were no longer wearing their boots. Some carried them while others stuffed them in their backpacks.

Just a short distance in front of her, Charlie strolled along, wearing his boots on his hands. He resembled a dog walking on its hind legs. Molly realized if she was going to find Mr. Cayce, she was going to have to swallow her pride.

'Charlie, wait up a minute,' said Molly catching up to him.

Charlie turned to face her without stopping, walking backwards until Molly had caught up.

'Whacha up to?' he asked.

'Just heading home,' answered Molly. 'I notice you have your boots with you.'

'It was pouring earlier, you'll remember,' noted Charlie with a bit of attitude.

The path they followed was beautiful. All around them the grass was tall and perfectly green, the deep rich green you see in autumn. Molly loved autumn and what it did to the landscape with the trees ablaze in fiery yellows, oranges, and reds. Even the sun shone a little differently this time of year. Brighter somehow, and at that moment, as the sun filtered through the waving leaves above, Charlie didn't look so unappealing, *even though he often took his teasing too far*, she thought.

'So, Charlie,' began Molly with much difficulty, 'may I kindly borrow those boots of yours just for tonight?'

'What for?' he asked.

'I have to go back to Stankwater Swamp,' answered Molly.

Molly paused for just a second, not wanting to give Charlie too much information.

'I have to get more cabbage grass,' she added, 'but it's going to be muddy with all this rain.'

'Sure you can,' he said and he held them out for her.

She reached up to grab them thinking this was easy enough, but just as her fingertips touched them, he pulled his boots away.

'So you're telling me then,' he said, 'that there's something of mine you need?'

'Yes,' answered Molly, sheepishly.

'Well, what do I get if I agree?' asked Charlie. 'It's not like you've been overly friendly to me lately.'

'Not very much,' answered Molly. 'I don't want to buy them. I just want to borrow them for tonight, and then tomorrow I'll return them all clean and looking new. Besides, if you want me to be friendlier, you simply have to stop being a brat. Now, what do you say about the boots? Can I borrow them or not? I'm not going to beg.'

Charlie smiled a devilish smile. He had something on his mind, but Molly had no idea what it was.

'I still think I should get something out of this. It's not everyday Molly Withers needs something from little old Charlie Gregg.'

'Like what?' asked Molly rather sharply, wondering why Charlie felt he had the right to ask for anything. His boots weren't special. They probably weren't even waterproof. But they were boots, and they were made of rubber, and that would be enough to satisfy Gabrielle.

'All right, Charlie,' conceded Molly. 'Name your price. Anything you want.'

'Anything?' asked Charlie, his smile growing by the minute.

'Anything within reason,' qualified Molly.

They must have walked another three minutes before he spoke. Molly felt like she was going to burst.

'I know what I want,' said Charlie, finally.

'Well?' asked Molly, nervous he was going to ask for something that she didn't have or couldn't afford.

'I want a kiss.'

'A kiss!' Molly shrieked. 'Are you crazy!?'

Charlie wasn't expecting Molly to be so upset and he tried to change his request to something more reasonable.

'Just on the cheek. What's wrong with that?'

'What's wrong with *that?*' she asked, astounded Charlie didn't see anything wrong with his ludicrous demand.

Apart from being the greatest irritant under the sun, Charlie was also dating the prettiest girl in Majestica. Even if Priscilla wasn't the nicest girl around, didn't she have everything any boy would want?

'Why on earth would you want a kiss on the cheek?' asked Molly. 'So you can embarrass me later?'

'That's for *me* to know,' answered Charlie. 'I want what I want, so if you don't want the boots, then by all means, go marching through Stankwater in your bare feet.'

Molly didn't know what to do. She was flabbergasted. She desperately needed the boots, but she didn't want to kiss Charlie for them. Give her toads, frogs, or slugs and sure, a little kiss would be fine, but not Charlie – not *Charlie*. Surely he had some wretched plan to use this against her. It would come back to haunt her and she'd be scarred forever.

Still, while these thoughts were horrible enough, another thought was growing. Molly couldn't believe her own senses when she realized that she *did* want to kiss him. She didn't know why, but she did – maybe to make Priscilla jealous, or maybe because she simply needed the boots. Or maybe, just maybe, it was because she'd never kissed a boy before, not even on the cheek. How bad could it be? *Maybe it wouldn't be bad at all,* she thought.

'All right, Charlie, you're on. I don't know what fever you've caught to make you want a kiss, but so be it. I just hope I don't get any warts on my lips for kissing such a frog as you.'

'Great!' exclaimed Charlie. 'Whenever you're ready.'

Charlie and Molly stopped in the path and faced each other. They were both nervous, but Molly had made up her mind to get those boots from Charlie and that was that. She took a step towards him and held out her hand expectantly.

'Boots first,' she said.

'Fair enough,' said Charlie and he freely handed Molly the boots. He tapped his cheek three times and said, 'Right here.'

Molly took the final step towards him, stood on her tiptoes, and leaned in. She closed her eyes and, feeling unbalanced, moved slowly. She puckered her lips and was so close to him she could feel the warmth of his cheek. In a moment, she thought, it would all be but a bad memory. *Here goes,* but just before her lips touched his cheek, she heard him move. Molly opened her eyes and was horrified to see Charlie right in front of her. His head shot forward with incredible speed, like a kingfisher snatching a minnow from the water, and he kissed her. Right on her lips!

'Ha ha!' he laughed. 'Gotcha again!'

Molly was mad. She had been upset with him before, sure, but not like this. Never like this. She was hopping mad.

'Molly kissed Charlie, Molly kissed Charlie,' he sang, and he began an annoying little dance. *'What a hoot, and just for a boot! Molly kissed Charlie.'*

Molly was overwhelmed with emotion. She had been betrayed, and felt like she was going to explode. She took a step towards him as he stopped bouncing around. Then, with all the strength Molly had in her little body, she kicked him in the shin. Charlie yelped in agony and fell to the ground, holding his leg. Molly hovered over him feeling proud that she'd finally stood up to this bully.

'Keep your stupid boots,' she said, scowling.

Molly turned, and ran back up the path. As soon as she knew that Charlie wouldn't be able to hear her, she slowed down and cried like she had never cried before. She had cried when being punished by her parents, but never had her heart felt so awful. *Why is Charlie always mean to me?* she wondered. She never said anything to him unless he started it. And to make it worse, now Molly didn't have any boots to wear. She had run out of time. Soon she would be home and she would have to do some chores before dinner. Then they would eat and then she'd have to clean up, and after that she had to meet Gabrielle – without rubber boots. She wasn't going to meet Mr. Cayce after all.

Molly thought she had failed this simple test and assumed Gabrielle would no longer want her around. If she couldn't even come up with a pair of rubber boots, how could she possibly be the one to spread the magic? No, Molly thought, she'd show up in Stankwater Swamp without the boots and she'd hear Gabrielle tell her that she must have made a mistake.

'Yes!' Molly said aloud, suddenly contradicting herself. 'I can do this. I can and *will* find a pair of boots by the time dinner is served.'

For the rest of the way home, Molly told herself over and over again that she would find the boots, and that she'd go to Stankwater Swamp, and that she'd meet Mr. Cayce and he would tell her what Mr. Weedly was doing in Majestica. Though she couldn't imagine how this would happen, she trusted in Gabrielle. She trusted that if she could hold on to the feeling of having the boots, somehow they would appear.

Past the orchard, past the cornfield, past her neighbours' houses, and up her laneway, all the way Molly told herself, *I have the boots, I have the boots, I have the boots, I have the boots.*

The more she told herself this, the more she believed it and her mood improved wonderfully.

'I do have the boots, I do have the boots, I do have the boots.'

She walked through her front door and saw her mother at the counter peeling potatoes.

'Good day to you, Mother,' she said cheerfully. 'I do have the boots, you know.'

Annabelle smiled. 'Of course you do.'

'What did you say, Mom?' asked Molly, still very much in her own world, marching through the kitchen, down the hall, into her dimly lit room, and straight to the window.

'I do have the boots, I do have the boots,' she repeated until she stumbled on something soft and floppy.

Molly opened the curtains and a blinding light washed over the floor. She turned to see what had made her stumble and there, by her bed, was a shiny pair of rubber boots. She was stunned. Molly had never thought that rubber boots could look like anything other than rubber, but the sight before her now was heavenly. They were red and glossy and as shiny as Grandma Jones' apples. Molly picked one up and she could see her distorted face smiling back.

To say she couldn't believe it wouldn't be entirely true. She wanted these boots badly, sure enough, but this seemed more than just a coincidence. This felt *magical*. The law of attraction had worked! It actually worked! Prior to this, Molly had been hopeful it was all true, but was not completely convinced. Sure, the food baskets were lovely, but she had worked for them. This was different. She didn't do anything except picture the boots and hope for them and here they were. Immediately, she wondered if it could work for something small, could it also work for something large? Something like the Golden Tree of Truth?

Molly walked back to the kitchen and placed her shiny new boots by the door.

'Where did these come from?' she asked.

'Your father picked them up today while in Town Centre,' answered Annabelle.

Molly scratched her head, and rolled up her sleeves to help peel the potatoes.

'That's very interesting,' remarked Molly. 'It just so happens that I needed a pair for tonight. Gabrielle and I are going on a hike in Stankwater.'

'Yes, your father mentioned that. He saw Gabrielle in Town Centre earlier, and she told him she was planning on taking you there this evening. That's why he picked them up for you. He didn't want you catching a cold.'

Molly was amazed and sad all at once. She didn't think her father had the money to purchase a pair of boots, especially new ones. Then, as if in response to Molly's concern, Annabelle added, 'There was so much food in the baskets from the Ball, that he hardly had any groceries to pick up today. So with the money he saved, he bought you your rubber boots.'

Annabelle continued to peel potatoes in silence for a few minutes.

'You know, Molly,' Annabelle said, 'he was happy to do that for you.'

Yes, Molly thought to herself. He would have been happy to do that for her. Though she didn't ask for much, Molly knew her parents tried very hard to give her as much as they could. And she definitely was never cold for lack of warm clothes or wood in the fire, and she rarely went to bed hungry. Yes, the magic *was* working as Gabrielle had said it would.

She was ready to find Mr. Cayce.

Chapter Nine
- *Finding Mr. Cayce* -

Supper was served, the dishes were cleaned, and Molly was out the door headed to Stankwater Swamp. She got to the end of the lane when she realized she'd forgotten to do something very important. So she turned around, went back to her house and walked inside.

Sitting at the table, drinking his tea, was her father.

'Thank you, Dad, for the boots,' Molly said. 'Sorry I didn't say it earlier, but I really appreciate it.'

William's eyes lit up, and rightfully so. Though they only take a second to say, *thank yous* leave a warm feeling behind that can last for hours. Molly could tell this was one of those thank yous.

'You are very welcome,' he responded.

Her father smiled a lovely smile that warmed Molly's heart. She had done the right thing.

'Now, don't be too late running around the swamp,' he felt obliged to add. 'You still have school in the morning.'

'I won't, Father,' Molly said with a smile.

With that, she turned and headed back down the lane, through the woods, and to the swamp. Gabrielle was not yet there and Molly was relieved to know she hadn't made her wait. The night had cooled off quickly and the water from the swamp was warmer than the air. This created a thick mist that made everything look bleaker than usual. Molly had been to the swamp hundreds of times before by herself and it had never bothered her, but tonight, alone, and with the sun quickly setting, she was nervous. Crows cawed from their perches, a single vulture circled overhead searching for its next rotting meal, and the grey branches of the trees clacked together like skeletons tapping other skeletons on their shoulders.

'Good evening, Molly,' said Gabrielle appearing from behind the veil of mist with an unlit lantern in one hand.

Molly turned and was relieved to see Gabrielle, smiling as always.

'Are you ready?' asked Gabrielle.

'Yes, shiny boots and all.'

'Great, then lead the way,' said Gabrielle.

'Me?' Why me?'

'We've heard you know the trails around the swamp as good as anyone,' said Gabrielle.

'I know them pretty well, but I don't know where we're going, do I?'

'Well, that's just it, Molly, neither do I,' said Gabrielle. 'I guess we simply have to walk around the swamp as silently as possible and hope we see him. Mr. Cayce will hear us long before we see or hear him, that's for sure. Let's just hope he'll be willing to talk to us.'

'No problem,' Molly said. 'The magic's been working all day. I got some rubber boots, didn't I, and I only had to think about what I wanted and then kick Charlie in the shins.'

'You wanted to kick Charlie in the shins?' asked Gabrielle.

'No, I didn't want to kick him in the shins,' Molly corrected. 'I just wanted his boots...so I kissed him.'

'You kissed him for his boots!?' exclaimed Gabrielle.

'Never mind,' sighed Molly. 'Let's get moving. Father doesn't want me out too late.'

'No, we don't have much time,' agreed Gabrielle. 'And remember: be as quiet as you possibly can. Mr. Cayce and all his kind do not like loud noises. No, not in the least.'

'What's he look like?'

'Sh! Let's go!'

Molly and Gabrielle began walking through the damp night. The mist hung heavy in the air and it wasn't long before their clothes were damp. They trudged along slowly as the thick rain from earlier made the paths around the swamp very muddy, indeed. It was a good thing Molly had on a pair of rubber boots and she wondered how Gabrielle knew it was going to rain today.

As sunny as it had been just an hour ago, the clouds rolled in again with the setting sun. This made the swamp much darker and everything took on shades of grey. The rotten trees leaning against each other for strength were grey; the owls in the trees were grey; the dead vines were grey; the rats swimming in the water were grey; and even the mud was grey.

The swamp was hauntingly silent, too. The crows only cawed here and there. The bulldog frogs, with their puppy ears pinned back, scarcely croaked in answer. Even the crickets were quieter. Yes, Molly thought, all manner of wildlife was a little quieter with the shorter days and longer nights of autumn at hand.

While the night drew ever nearer, Dracufu bats filled the air. Like most things in Majestica, Dracufu bats were legendary. They were frightfully large. To look at them hanging in the trees, like huge black banana bunches, you wouldn't think something so big could fly. They were the size of small dogs, and their large fangs were as sharp as razors. But their fangs would have to be sharp, wouldn't they, for they fed on the blood of Stankwater rats which, of course, were unusually large and leathery.

Molly quivered thinking of the vile creatures that lived in all this putrescence. Still, it was here the sweetest cabbage grass grew. They continued winding through the muddy paths around the swamp for two hours with no sign of Mr. Cayce and no sign of a dwelling. Surely Mr. Cayce would have had some kind of cave, or log cabin somewhere, but there were no lodgings to be found.

Snap! A branch broke to the right of Molly and Gabrielle. They both turned their heads in that direction and immediately saw what it was. A moose! Molly couldn't believe her eyes, and she laughed. She knew there was the odd moose around, but she had never seen one as close as this. Maybe she never saw them because she was always singing, or talking to herself, or throwing large rocks in the water. (Molly generally made noises when in the swamp and she realized that she probably did it to keep herself from thinking about the things that lived there).

Gabrielle lit the lantern as the moose emerged from the woods and walked within a few feet of them. Molly was amazed at how large he was. She knew they were big, but she hadn't realized *just* how big – at least ten feet tall. Its massive body was covered in thick brown fur that smelled dreadful. Even in a place that got its name for being so smelly, here was an animal that smelled even worse. *Wet dog multiplied by infinity* thought Molly trying to remember the nickname for moose she had heard before.

As large as the moose's body was, it was held up on little legs. Even a horse's legs seemed bigger. Molly didn't think these legs were strong enough to keep this animal upright. Its snout was long, like a drooping loaf of dark brown bread, and atop its head was a rack of huge antlers that looked like two mighty trees with flattened trunks. In fact, Molly thought, the antlers looked very similar to the trees in Stankwater – large, hard, and leafless.

His head was low as if smelling Molly and Gabrielle.

The moose stepped closer.

'Swamp donkey!' laughed Molly, finally recalling the nickname. 'Father calls them swamp donkeys.'

'Molly!' Gabrielle stressed. 'You shouldn't have said that.'

The moose took one step back and stomped the ground once with his large hoof. His head rose high in the air and he looked quite imposing. And then it happened. His mouth opened.

'Swamp donkey, *indeed,*' said the moose staring right at Molly before he turned to Gabrielle. 'I am disappointed you've brought me such an insensitive little girl. I am not sure if I care to talk to her.'

Molly couldn't believe it. The moose talked. He opened his mouth and human words came out. There was no one standing beside him or behind him who could have uttered these words. It was the moose.

Gabrielle looked to Molly who was dumbfounded. She couldn't feel her feet, much less move them, and her eyes were fixated upon this massive moose who was talking as if it was an everyday occurrence.

'Mr. Cayce,' said Gabrielle, 'this is Molly Withers.'

'Of course she is. I am the Seer of Things, you know.'

Molly looked up at Mr. Cayce and something came over her. She laughed again. She knew it wasn't appropriate, but she couldn't help it. It felt delightfully awful, like laughing in church. *Swamp donkey,* she thought. That was the most hilarious nickname she had ever heard for an animal. She laughed so hard, her eyes teared up and her belly ached.

'Swamp donkey!' Molly laughed again. 'Isn't that priceless?'

Molly's laugh was so warm that Gabrielle smiled despite herself, and the harder Molly laughed, the harder it was for Gabrielle to keep it in. She too thought the nickname was particularly fitting given the circumstances. Molly kept laughing in a manner that was unbearably lovely and Gabrielle chuckled, too, but it didn't stop there. Gabrielle's chuckle grew to a hearty laugh. It could be said of

Gabrielle that her laugh equalled her smile. Is it not so that few things are more pleasing to the ear than the sound of laughter?

'Oh my,' said Gabrielle with happy tears in her eyes. 'Swamp donkey! Ha! Oh my, Mr. Cayce, I am sorry. Ha Ha Ha!'

With this, Mr. Cayce was drawn into the laughter. If it is true in the land of Majestica that a moose can talk, then it is equally true a moose can laugh; and laugh he did. He laughed and laughed and laughed. All three of them laughed, and even Mr. Cayce himself declared, 'Swamp donkey! Well in all my years I never. Ha Ha Ha!'

Then suddenly, in the midst of the laughter, Mr. Cayce turned and looked down the misty path apparently aware of something that Molly and Gabrielle could neither see nor hear. The way Mr. Cayce moved was impressive; something so large to move so fast, and then to be as still as a stone. Molly and Gabrielle stopped their chorus of laughter and looked in the same direction – lantern raised high and flickering.

There was silence at first, but Mr. Cayce remained focused on the path. He raised his huge head and sniffed the air and then made a sound more becoming of a moose. Something moved just beyond their visibility in the thick mist and then, from the vapour, an image appeared.

'Charlie!' exclaimed Molly. 'What are you doing here?'

Charlie approached Molly and Gabrielle, his eyes fixated on Mr. Cayce.

'Nice moosey,' said Charlie.

'Oh, this is Mr.—' Molly caught herself. 'Pretty tame moose, huh?' she offered, trying to cover up what was going on.

'So tame, it's,' Charlie paused, 'laughable – *heh.*'

Charlie must have heard the three of them laughing. Of course he did. Molly would not have been surprised if all of Majestica had heard them.

Charlie had a pair of rubber boots on his feet, and he also had a pair in his hands.

'I felt bad for earlier,' he said, 'so I thought I'd try to catch up with you, but then—'

'Then what?' snapped Molly.

'Then I got lost. I heard the laughter, and I followed the sound.' Charlie paused for a second and added, 'But I can see you found another pair.'

'What else have you heard?' asked Gabrielle.

Charlie looked up at her and then looked to Mr. Cayce.

'I've heard enough to make me think I'm crazy,' he said. 'Three voices and only two people.'

Gabrielle shook her head, upset Charlie had come to know about Mr. Cayce.

Mr. Cayce stepped towards Charlie who didn't move a muscle. He towered over him and Charlie stared up, wide eyed. Mr. Cayce then lowered his head, observing Charlie up and down. Then he *smelled* him up and down before looking at Gabrielle.

There are no coincidences,' said Mr. Cayce. 'I think he'll do.'

'He'll do for what?' asked Molly.

'Do you think so?' asked Gabrielle.

Mr. Cayce sniffed Charlie one more time, smiled a funny moose smile, and licked Charlie's cheek with his huge sloppy tongue, his wise eyes twinkling.

Charlie wiped the moose goober from his cheek.

'Blech, ick, gross! He soaked me!' said Charlie, quite disgusted.

'What's the matter, Charlie?' asked Mr. Cayce. 'Were you only hoping for a kiss from Molly today?' He then snorted like a moose and added, 'Now let's discuss why you are all here, shall we?'

Suddenly, the mood changed. It was as if, after watching bunnies play in the field for a time, you happen to see the wolf who has been watching them as well. Everyone's smiles melted away, and Mr. Cayce stepped towards Molly, head raised high. His presence demanded attention, and everyone waited for him to speak.

'Molly,' he said finally, 'if you accept this quest to preserve the magic, it will be both wonderful and terrifying. I have no doubt you will get everything you could ever want, but with great success comes great responsibility. Are you certain you are ready?'

Molly was not certain. Not remotely. She was just a girl and everything suddenly seemed unfamiliar and troublesome. Still, she felt this was something she was meant to do. She needed to experience the magic for herself – fully.

'Yes,' Molly said once she was ready. 'I am certain.'

Gabrielle and Mr. Cayce smiled as if relieved.

'But, I won't be able to do it by myself,' Molly added. 'Who's going to help me?'

Gabrielle and Mr. Cayce looked at Charlie in one motion.

'What are you looking at me for?' asked Charlie.

'Charlie Gregg,' Mr. Cayce began. 'Look into your heart and

tell me what it is you want more than anything on earth. But mind your answer. I will surely know if you are telling the truth.'

Charlie thought for just a second, smiled, and declared, 'I want to be a Knight Triumphant!'

Mr. Cayce grinned.

'All knights have to follow their leader with unwavering bravery, you realize, and your very life will be in great danger on more than one occasion. Is this something you are truly prepared to embrace?' asked Mr. Cayce.

'I am already brave,' attested Charlie, 'and I will do whatever the king will have me do. For life or longer.'

'Very good, Charlie,' said Gabrielle, 'but what if your leader is not the king?'

'King or queen, I would obey either,' answered Charlie.

'And what about a princess?' pressed Mr. Cayce.

'Priscilla?' asked Charlie almost horrified. 'If, if I must.'

'Oh no,' said Mr. Cayce. 'Prissy's not the princess I am thinking of.'

Mr. Cayce and Gabrielle looked at Molly. She grinned hearing Mr. Cayce use the word *Prissy,* but she missed the subtle suggestion that had been made.

'Who? Molly?' asked Charlie in disbelief. 'But she's not a princess.'

'Charlie,' said Molly, 'he's pulling your leg.'

'Is it so hard to believe, Molly Withers, that you are destined for greatness?' asked Mr. Cayce. 'All in good time, you will become as I have seen.'

Molly stopped smiling. She was already feeling overwhelmed with supposedly being the Keeper of the Magic, and suddenly, she was also to be a princess. Was Mr. Cayce actually being serious? Charlie was equally confused and skeptical. Less than an hour ago he set out from his home to give Molly some rubber boots and now he was in the middle of the swamp with a talking moose who was suggesting Molly was going to be a princess and Charlie would be her protector.

It was in this uncomfortable silence that something moved in the swamp. Whatever it was, it was big enough to make a swirl larger than any rat could have made.

Mr. Cayce and the others looked over, but the water did not stir again.

'Well, Charlie,' said Mr. Cayce looking back, 'you have to

decide here and now. Are you willing to aid Molly in whatever quests lie ahead?'

Charlie hesitated for only a second and said, 'If it will make me a knight, I will do whatever is asked of me.'

'Good for you, young knight,' said Mr. Cayce. 'So, now our thoughts must turn towards Mr. Weedly.'

'Yes,' Gabrielle said. 'He has been in Town Centre for the last several days, but I am not sure what he wants.'

'Why, he wants what most people want,' said Mr. Cayce. 'Even young Molly here has thought about this and she too wants it for herself.'

Mr. Cayce looked at Molly and she knew exactly what he was talking about.

'The Golden Tree of Truth,' said Molly.

'Precisely. Mr. Weedly is searching for the Golden Tree,' said Mr. Cayce.

'Where?' asked Molly. 'In Majestica?'

'Yes,' said Mr. Cayce. 'We now believe the fabled Tree grows somewhere in our very own backyard. Though I see a good many things, its exact location is not evident to me and, for certain, there will be an unexpected turn of events before it is finally found.'

Molly's thoughts reeled with the prospect of finding the actual Golden Tree. She'd be rich. She had read so much about it, but never fully believed. And to think, all along it was in Majestica. But Majestica was huge – no easy place to find a solitary tree.

'Are you sure you don't know?' Molly asked, and Mr. Cayce smiled as only a moose can.

'I am sure and perhaps that is a good thing,' said Mr. Cayce. 'If you were to find it today, Molly, what would you do? Would you harvest all the Golden leaves for yourself, for your mother Annabelle, and for your father William?'

Molly suddenly felt a mixture of shame and embarrassment. It stung. She had just agreed to become the Keeper of the Magic, but with the first thought of riches, her mind filled with selfishness and Mr. Cayce sensed it.

'They are not entirely selfish thoughts,' said Mr. Cayce. 'It is a good thing to want gold, but gold is only one part of wealth. Never forget that. No, you will find the Tree when your heart is ready for it.'

'Mr. Cayce,' Gabrielle interjected, 'does Mr. Weedly seek the Golden Tree for himself, or does he serve someone greater?'

'We all serve Someone greater than ourselves,' said Mr. Cayce. 'Mortimer may want the Tree for the knowledge it contains, or he may want it for the gold, or both. This I do not yet know, but I tell you he must not find it first. All will be lost if he does.'

'So what if we find it first,' said Molly. 'What good is that unless we can protect it day and night? Eventually, Mr. Weedly will find it too and I am sure he will bring others with him.'

'Yes, Molly, some are gathering in Nordenburgh as we speak,' said Mr. Cayce. 'Mr. Weedly will come, his followers will come with him, and they will eventually find the Tree.'

'So what do we do?' asked Charlie. 'Transplant it?'

'Alas, my good Charlie, even Mr. Cayce, the Seer of Things, cannot see everything. I do not yet know what to do, but I will try to find out.'

'Do you know someone who can help?' asked Gabrielle.

'Perhaps,' answered Mr. Cayce. 'Perhaps.'

'If only Engelbert the Great were still alive,' said Molly.

'Quite right,' said Mr. Cayce. 'You *have* done your research, haven't you? He would be quite old, even for a wizard, but rumours remain that he walks this earth still.'

'Do you know where to find him?' asked Gabrielle.

'No, no I don't, but I know who might.' With this, Mr. Cayce ended the conversation rather abruptly, turned away from Molly, Charlie, and Gabrielle, and trotted back into the misty darkness.

Molly, Charlie, and Gabrielle also left the swamp and within an hour they were almost home.

'Molly,' began Gabrielle, 'I have an idea how to get you out of school tomorrow, but I don't know what to do about you, Charlie. Perhaps you can meet us after school, and I'll tell you all about the Golden Tree. I am sure you are anxious to know. Molly, I will be at your home in the morning to ask your parents if they would be willing to have me as your personal tutor. That should free up your time quite nicely, wouldn't you think?'

'That would be great,' said Molly with eyes so bright you'd swear they were electric frogs ready to leap out of her head.

'Then goodnight to the two of you,' said Gabrielle. 'Charlie, it goes without saying that you are to keep all this to yourself. You are not to whisper a word of this to anyone lest you have a devastating run in with Mr. Cayce's antlers.'

'Yes, Ma'am,' swallowed Charlie.

Chapter Ten

- *Understanding the Magic* -

As the morning cock crew, Molly awoke and readied herself for school, though she was hoping she would be spending the day with Gabrielle instead. Impatiently, she ate her breakfast with her mother and father and just as she stood to clear the dishes, she heard a *knock, knock, knock, knock.*

'Morning Gabrielle,' William said as he opened the door.

'Good morning, Mr. Withers,' replied Gabrielle. 'May I come in?'

'Let her in, Bill,' said Annabelle. 'Can I get you a cup of tea?'

'I'd love one, thanks,' said Gabrielle entering and taking a seat at the table.

'So,' said Annabelle bustling to make the tea, 'what brings you here so early?'

'Molly hasn't done anything wrong, has she?' demanded William.

'Oh, no,' said Gabrielle, 'quite the contrary. To be honest, I was thinking yesterday of how much I enjoyed her company at the Ball, and then I started to think of how much I miss teaching.'

'And?' asked William looking over the rim of his glasses.

'Well, I was wondering if you would allow me to take Molly on as my student,' Gabrielle said with an inviting smile.

Annabelle was pleasantly surprised, but William found the offer rather suspicious. As his brain began to create a whole host of crazy

72

ideas for such an offer, inevitably his thoughts turned to money.

'We don't have any money, you know,' he stated.

'Oh Bill, must you always think of money?' asked Annabelle, feeing embarrassed and awkward.

'Well, Mr. Withers,' said Gabrielle, 'believe it or not, Molly's company is payment enough. It won't cost you a single copper.'

Gabrielle shot an unseen wink at Molly while William remained suspicious.

'I should point out, though,' added Gabrielle, 'with Molly working for me, and being my student as well, she is going to be out quite a bit.'

'What a kind offer,' said Annabelle, but William's face was expressionless. He pondered, and pondered, and pondered some more. His face twitched and he looked at the three girls in front of him observing each of their expressions carefully.

'I suppose it's fine,' said William finally and as his consent floated over the breakfast table, all three girls exhaled with relief, as if they were waiting for his permission to breathe again.

'But the chores better not suffer for it,' he added, 'and I hope you can teach her the importance of hard work, and the unimportance of chasing fairies.'

'Oh and much, much more, I daresay,' comforted Gabrielle. 'Now Molly, is this something that interests you?'

Molly's green eyes were resplendent with joy.

'Oh yes, Gabrielle,' said Molly, 'oh yes.'

'Then it's settled. I am quite looking forward to this,' said Gabrielle. 'Thank you, Mr. Withers, Mrs. Withers. Ah, to be teaching again. I'll inform the school right away.'

Gabrielle finished her tea with the Withers', discussing the sort of topics Molly was to learn: grammar, arithmetic, history, and basic science. She didn't mention today's lesson, however – *real magic.*

After this short discussion, Gabrielle left with Molly at her side and they headed to school where they informed the principal what was going on. As they passed Mrs. Harvey's class on their way out, that lovely teacher looked up from her desk, smiled, and winked at Gabrielle. It was as if Mrs. Harvey knew where Gabrielle and Molly were going.

Gabrielle and Molly made their way to the reading tree and arrived just as the sun began to warm the earth. Charlie, oddly enough, was there too, flinting away. He had a little bag with him which he opened as soon as he stuffed his flint stones back in his pocket.

'Here, I brought us some of my mom's fresh raisin bread,' he said. 'I don't get it often, but it's the best.'

'What are you doing here, Charlie?' Molly asked.

'Playing hooky.'

Charlie gave a piece of buttered raisin bread to Gabrielle and Molly, but they stood there in silence.

'What?' asked Charlie. 'Did you honestly think I'd miss out on today? I have a lot of catching up to do. Besides, I've skipped out to go fishing lots of times.'

Trying to switch topics, he added, 'I have some bread left for later, too.'

His plan worked. What else could be done, really?

Gabrielle spread out a blanket she had brought with her and Molly, and Charlie took a seat beneath the tree. Molly believed all education should happen outside.

Once they were settled, Gabrielle began.

'The Universe is governed by natural laws,' she said. 'Just like the law of gravity. Without fail, these laws work each and every time. The magic of the Universe, Charlie, has to do with the law of attraction. Quite simply, like attracts like. So, whatever you think about and feel about for long periods of time, you will *attract* into your life. Your thoughts, therefore, actually create your surroundings. Does this make sense so far?'

Molly and Charlie nodded hesitantly, and Gabrielle went on to explain that the law of attraction is magical, for it allows everyone to have and be whatever it is they want. She also told them that using the magic can be tricky at times, and that there are three important parts to always keep in mind. First, you must simply declare to the Universe what you want, and it is crucial to be specific. Secondly, you must hold onto the *feeling* of actually having it, for it is this *feeling* that the Universe responds to. Using your imagination is a great way to get that feeling. Then, whatever you are feeling, the Universe will inevitably pull more of that similarity back to you. It works this way because everything in the Universe is connected. We all share the same energy. Our bodies, a rock, a tree, the ocean, the sky; we are all made of the same energy. Therefore, the energy of our thoughts and feelings affects the energy of the Universe and vice versa.

'The final and most critical thing you must do,' concluded Gabrielle, 'can prove quite troublesome. Receiving.'

'Ha,' Molly laughed. 'That part will be easy. When the goodies show up, open your pockets.'

'Easy, is it?' asked Gabrielle. 'You have already tried to return a necklace I gave you, and you offered to work for free. You are very much in the habit of turning away from gifts. The difficulty, if anything, is overcoming your belief that you are undeserving of fine things and greatness. Once again, every time you tell yourself that you don't deserve something, that is your brain at work and you are attracting more of what you don't want. Do you honestly think the Universe cares if you are a carpenter or a king, a princess or a seamstress? Of course not. It takes all kinds to make this world work, and it is up to you to choose who and what you want to be.'

'How do we become good receivers then?' asked Molly, knowing Gabrielle was right about her.

'It is like all things in life,' answered Gabrielle, 'you have to practice.'

'Whoa, whoa, whoa,' said Charlie. 'I'm not sure if I believe any of this. It sounds, I don't know, weird.'

'Just think of a game of catch between your mind and the Universe,' said Gabrielle. 'The ball represents what you want, and you throw it out to the Universe. Trust me when I say the Universe will catch it, make it into a real thing, and throw it back to you. But, you must be in a position to catch it, or it will fly right by. Believe and receive.'

Gabrielle knew Molly and Charlie needed some time to understand everything she had said, so she left them alone to collect their thoughts. Molly and Charlie leaned back and stared up at the tree. The leaves were red, and orange, and yellow, and just enough had fallen to the ground that the warm autumn sun periodically sneaked through, making Molly and Charlie squint.

Charlie's hands were at his sides, as were Molly's. He realized that his hand and Molly's were very close – almost touching. They were so close that he could feel the warmth of her hand on his own. He wondered what would happen if their hands were to touch, but was distracted by a fat bumbler flying around his head. He shooed it once, but the bee returned. The second time

Charlie waved at it, something unexpected happened..

'Ouch! That bumbler just bit me!' cried Charlie.

'Let me see your hand,' Gabrielle said, returning immediately.

Charlie held up his hand and Gabrielle looked in his palm much like a fortune teller.

'Ah ha!' she said.

'What is it?' asked Charlie.

'You weren't bit,' she said. 'You've been stung!'

'I've been stung? By what?'

'A stinger!' noted Gabrielle.

'A stinger?'

'It's like a thorn filled with poison,' clarified Gabrielle. 'Like a wasp, and when the bee gets agitated, it stabs you with it.'

'I know what a stinger is,' said Charlie, 'but since when do bumblers have stingers?'

'Are you sure it wasn't a wasp?' asked Molly.

'No, it was a bee,' said Charlie. 'I know the difference between bees and wasps.'

'I bet it came from Nordenburgh,' said Gabrielle. 'The land of the Morrukks. It's there that bees are rumoured to have stingers.'

'If it's called a *stinger* because it stings,' said Charlie, 'then I suggest we call it a *pain-er,* or a *hurt-er,* or a *throb-er.* Paper cuts sting. This kills.'

'I am almost certain this is all because of the fear,' said Gabrielle gravely.

Gabrielle removed the stinger from Charlie's palm and he stared at the spot wondering how it was possible such a little thing could cause so much pain.

'It's really happening,' Molly said. 'The fear is spreading.'

'Yes,' confirmed Gabrielle, 'and if Mortimer finds the Golden Tree of Truth before us, then Majestica will undergo a horrible transformation. The fear will surely run rampant. We must make sure we find it first!'

'So where do we go looking for it?' asked Charlie, and as soon as these words crossed his lips, Molly silenced him.

'Sh! Do you hear that?'

'Hear what?' asked Charlie.

'Sh!' said Gabrielle as well. 'I hear it, too. Where's it coming from?'

'Listen!' Molly urged.

Molly, Charlie, and Gabrielle listened carefully, and there was nothing but the sound of birds in the trees, and the crickets in the clovers. They listened harder for a minute longer and then they *could* hear something else, something below the sound of the birds and below the sound of the crickets. It was soft; softer than the sound of the wind going through the fiery leaves, but it *was* there.

'Listen,' said Molly again. 'Don't you hear it?'

'No!' answered Charlie.

'It's – it's singing!' exclaimed Molly.

True enough, it was singing. It started so low you'd mistake it for the sound of some insect, but then the sound grew and it was pleasant to the ear. The three of them looked around the tree, and up the tree; everywhere but under the tree.

'Where do you suppose it's coming from?' asked Gabrielle.

Molly looked like the cat that caught the family finch.

'What's that look all about?' asked Charlie.

'I've heard that voice before,' admitted Molly. 'I think.'

'Now that doesn't surprise me,' Charlie said, sucking on his stinging hand, 'you hearing voices.'

'Molly, did you ever see who it was?' asked Gabrielle.

'No, but I—'

'But you *what?*' asked Charlie, growing a little impatient. 'Just say what's on your mind, would you?'

'Well, I used to imagine there were leprechauns inside this tree,' Molly confessed.

'Leprechauns?' scoffed Charlie in disbelief.

'Maybe they aren't leprechauns,' countered Molly, 'but there it is again. Listen.'

Suddenly the singing stopped.

'Be yee friendly folk, who will let me pass?' came a voice from somewhere.

Molly, Charlie, and Gabrielle looked at each other completely surprised. The voice was as clear as day, and they realized it came from within the tree.

'Yes,' Gabrielle said finally, 'it is safe to come out.'

The whole tree shook and as it did, a few more blazing leaves fell to the ground, but that was not all. What once appeared to be a knot in the trunk turned slightly, like a handle, and from the wrinkles in the bark, a door took shape. Slowly, it creaked open, but they couldn't see inside for it was pitch black.

'Are yee sure?' asked the voice from within the tree.

'I swear by the throne of Majestica, no harm will come to you,' said Gabrielle.

Whatever was inside the tree had a foot, for at that moment it appeared out of the darkness. It was a very tiny foot and had a black sock with a dark green shoe and the shiniest gold buckle you had ever seen. The first foot was followed by the second, and out popped a man about two feet tall.

His black socks stopped just below his chubby knees. His shorts were the same green as his shoes and were kept around his small waist by a thick black belt, which also had a shiny gold buckle. Likewise, his shirt was the same colour as his shorts and shoes, and was offset by red suspenders. His chubby hands adjusted the green hat which sat atop a nest of bright orange curls. He bent over, grabbed a fist full of clovers, inhaled their aroma, and stuffed them in his shirt pocket.

'And how be yee all today?' he asked rather cordially.

'No way!' said Charlie. 'You're a leprechaun!'

'Aye, me fine young lad, that I am. But I do have a name, you know. I'm Tommy Troublesome and I am the quickest leprechaun in these 'ere woods, so don't yee tink fer a wee minute about trying to catch me. Just kindly step aside an' I'll be on me merry way.'

Molly, Charlie, and Gabrielle stared in silence without moving. Eventually, Molly turned to Gabrielle and whispered: 'Did you know they were real?'

Gabrielle smiled, and nodded.

'Yes, but I have never seen one,' she said.

Tommy looked to Molly and said, 'Well I'm sure *you* knew we was real. You've heard us at least a t'ousand times before, wit' you being here as much as you are, readin' yerr books as you do, and singin' to the top o' yerr lungs.'

'I'm Molly,' she said, sizing up the leprechaun. She paused briefly and added, 'you don't seem like you're much trouble.'

'Sure, I know who you are. Yerr Molly Withers, and you know the magic. Good for you, good on ya lass. And about me name. It's well earned I can assure ya. Not like I mean to, but trouble's always followin' me around. Harder to shake than me own shadow, ya know.'

No one could have guessed what was going to happen next, but Molly leapt straight at the leprechaun. It was obvious Tommy wasn't expecting it either, as he didn't move. His eyes and mouth opened wide. Molly knocked him over and Tommy was quick to right himself, but before he could get back to the safety of the tree, Molly grabbed his suspenders. He took two more steps, but the suspenders shot him back like a slingshot, right into Molly's arms.

'Aha! Gotcha! Tell me,' demanded Molly, 'is it not true about leprechauns granting wishes?'

'Yes, Yes, Yes,' said Tommy. 'It's true, but I'm not sayin' another word until you put me back on me feet.'

Tommy squirmed a bit, but Molly's grip was like iron.

'How can I be sure you won't run off?' asked Molly.

'Well, yee can't, really, but yee can't force me to grant yerr wish, either, so you'll just have to put me down, and see what happens, won't yee?'

'Fine,' said Molly, and she plopped him down in the thick bed of clovers. He dusted himself off, readjusted his hat, grabbed some more clovers, and mumbled to himself something about *trouble.*

'Now, what is it yerr after, and make it snappy. I surely hope yerr not as daft as other human folk. I don't have the time to wait for yee to make up yerr mind like the other blunderin', blabberin', cryin' fools.'

'Can I ask for anything?' asked Molly.

'Well, of course yee can. Did you not just catch a leprechaun?'

Molly looked at Gabrielle and said, 'I don't know what to ask for.'

'It's your wish,' said Gabrielle. 'You must decide for yourself.'

Molly's thoughts instantly turned to the fabled rainbow and the pot of gold that was to be found there, but she turned back to Tommy and said: 'I want to know how I can find The Golden Tree of Truth.'

Tommy smiled.

'I can honestly say, Molly Withers, that yerr the first person in over a hundred years who hasn't asked me to give em da gold at de end o' the rainbow. It's down right noble of yee, but I'll never understand why yee human folks just don't ask fer more wishes.'

'I didn't think it was allowed,' said Molly.

'Sure, I just told yee that yee could ask for anything. But what's done is done. You want to know *how* to find where the Golden Tree of Truth is. Are yee sure, Molly?'

'Yes, I'm sure,' said Molly without thinking, and Tommy

smiled a mischievous smile.

'Well, I'm glad you didn't outright ask me *where* it is, because I don't know meself. Would've been embarrassin', that. But I can grant yee yerr wish all the same, and tell yee *how* to find it. Simply catch yerrself a Pinkleton Dimple fairy. Though they might not know, either, I guarantee they'll help ya find the Tree.'

'What?' shrieked Molly. 'That's not what I meant, and you know it.'

'Well, it may not be what yee meant, but it's certainly what you asked fer. Next time you'll be sure to be more specific. But don't be sad, little lass. I have granted yee yerr wish. All you have to do is catch a Pinkleton and she'll tell yee what to do next. I wish yee the luck o' the shamrock catchin' one, though. Have a blessed day, now.'

As soon as Tommy said this, he jumped back inside the tree, and the door slammed behind him, becoming part of the trunk once again.

'I am sorry, Gabrielle,' said Molly. 'I have ruined it for us.'

'No, Molly, you didn't ruin anything. If not for you,' Gabrielle said, 'we wouldn't have discovered how to find the Golden Tree. Now all we have to do is catch a Pinkleton Dimple fairy, and that's that.'

'I don't want to be a stick in the mud,' said Charlie cutting in, 'but no one has ever caught a Pinkleton. '

'He's right,' said Molly. 'I haven't even seen one lately. They always disappear this time of year.'

Gabrielle smiled as she always smiled.

'There are still a few around,' Gabrielle said, 'and I might know where to look.'

Chapter Eleven
- Old Man Craggly -

It was already midday when Molly, Charlie, and Gabrielle left the reading tree in search of a Pinkleton Dimple fairy. Gabrielle hoped to find one in the old abandoned cemetery. As a small child, Gabrielle remembered seeing the fairies gather there in the fall, so it seemed like a good place to begin looking.

The road to the cemetery was a rickety old thing that would make your teeth rattle if you were riding in a wagon. They walked for about an hour when they came across some wild cupcake and muffin trees.

'Here,' said Gabrielle, 'you two spread out the blanket.'

Molly and Charlie did as they were told as Gabrielle picked some of the cupcakes and muffins from the trees.

'It's not overly nutritious,' said Gabrielle, 'but these, with the raisin bread Charlie has left over, will do just fine.'

'How much further do we have to go?' asked Molly.

'We have a ways to go yet,' answered Gabrielle.

'I've been to the cemetery before,' said Charlie, 'but I didn't think it was much further.'

'Oh, we're not going to *that* cemetery,' Gabrielle said.

'We're not?' asked Molly.

'No.'

'No?' asked Charlie

'No,' said Gabrielle again. 'We're going to an older cemetery that's no longer in use. I haven't been there since I was a girl, and even then the old church was beginning to sag.'

'I hope it doesn't take too long to get there,' said Molly. 'My parents will be worried.'

'I doubt mine will even notice I'm gone,' added Charlie.

For the rest of the afternoon, they walked the old dusty road towards the cemetery. It was a beautiful walk at first as the sun was shining warmly and there wasn't a cloud in the sky. But then the sun vanished behind a thick blanket of dark clouds and the wind swung round from the North.

Once they passed the common cemetery, the road was completely overgrown and trees became sparse, only providing a bit of protection from the rain which had just begun.

'Here,' said Gabrielle, 'take this blanket and cover yourselves with it. It's not much, but it will keep you both a bit drier.'

Molly and Charlie took the blanket from Gabrielle and pulled it over their shoulders and heads. They had to walk side by side to share it. Charlie thought this was great, but Molly was none too pleased.

Though it wasn't raining heavily, the wind became stronger and cooler and the sky turned a foreboding grey. Gabrielle walked on seemingly unaffected, but Molly and Charlie were chilled.

'Perhaps we should get off the path and stay in the woods until this rain passes,' suggested Molly.

Gabrielle looked up at the dark sky as lightning flashed and a heavy log of thunder rolled over them.

'I think it's going to clear soon,' said Gabrielle, 'and it's not much further now. There will be a place to find shelter when we get there, anyway.'

The three of them marched on in the cold rain. Every few minutes, there was another flash of lightning accompanied by thunder so loud it made Molly jump. The wind intensified and howled through the trees like a confused pack of wolves, so much so, that when they talked to one another, they had to speak a little louder.

'Gabrielle,' said Molly, 'are you sure we're close? I'm terribly cold and my feet are starting to ache.'

Gabrielle didn't need to answer because the path opened up to a large abandoned graveyard with a ruined church on a small hill at the far end.

'This looks homey,' said Charlie.

'This is known as Craggly's cemetery,' said Gabrielle. 'Now keep your eyes peeled for a fairy.'

'Who was Craggly?' asked Molly.

'Old Man Craggly was the groundskeeper here many, many moons ago,' said Gabrielle. 'Kept to himself mostly, but he always came out to help when it was time to bury the dead.'

'That was nice of him,' said Charlie.

'I am not so sure,' said Gabrielle. 'Stories say that he had a morbid curiosity for death, and he worked these grounds without payment to satisfy his dark fantasies. He was a loyal worker and no one bothered him till the bodies went missing.'

'What do you mean, *missing?*' asked Molly.

Gabrielle made no answer as they approached the large metal gate that once separated the trees from the tombs. Molly had never seen anything so creepy. Sure, the decrepit atmosphere of Stankwater Swamp was enough to make brave men uneasy, but it didn't compare to the sight before her now. She thought it was wonderful.

The old metal gate clung to two massive rock and mortar supports that seemed to have stood at attention too long without being relieved. Molly was sure the gates no longer moved, being far too corroded, but fortunately whoever had exited the cemetery last left the gates slightly ajar as if to say *please come in.*

As they squeezed through the opening, the rain, at last, subsided and Molly observed that the rusty old gate continued as a rusty old fence around the entire grounds. It was peeling and twisted and covered with soggy, shapeless vegetation. It circled the cemetery like the half-rotten skeleton of a giant snake. It looked like the cemetery's protector.

'We can stay in there until we're sure the storm has passed,' Gabrielle said, and they walked towards the church.

Molly looked around hoping to glimpse a fairy, but there were none to be seen. There was, however, every manner of tombstone and sarcophagus. Each tombstone was so weathered and surrounded by weeds so high, that Molly could not make out the inscriptions. They no longer stood straight and proud, either, but were crooked and leaning to one side or the other. Several were broken and several had fallen over completely, like an army defeated in battle.

Some of the sarcophagi were partially open with the heavy

stone slabs pushed to one side, far enough that you could reach inside. Molly was curious. Was anything left inside them, like rotten corpses dressed in mouldy clothes? Perhaps they were open because they were looted for treasures like wedding rings or other family jewels. Then again, Molly couldn't help but think they had been opened for another reason. Maybe that's what Gabrielle meant by *missing bodies.*

Looking up at the old dilapidated building that appeared to hover before them, Molly couldn't wait to go inside. The stained glass windows were smashed and the jagged pieces made each and every one look like a hungry mouth with horrible teeth. The window frames were cracked like chapped lips and the paint had peeled off the entire structure, leaving the exposed wood to rot and turn grey.

They walked up the three spongy steps, which Molly doubted could support the weight of a cricket, and approached the mighty front doors. Gabrielle placed one hand on the door handle and pulled, but it didn't open. She placed her second hand on the handle and pulled again, but it moved only slightly.

'Charlie,' said Gabrielle, 'can you help?'

'Step aside, my dear,' he said rather confidently.

Charlie grabbed the long door handle, heaved, and the door opened, but there was high pitched creaking that made Molly cover her ears. Charlie smiled. He felt strong.

The inside was worse than the outside. Almost all of the pews had been removed, save for three which surrounded a large fire pit in the middle of the church floor. It looked like an abandoned campground, but instead of half-burnt logs in the fire, there were the remains of the pews, and crosses, and other pieces of wood from the dismantled altar.

The paint on the high walls was peeled and scabby. Some of the windows were boarded up. The major supports were swollen with moisture and bowed. Yes, the entire church looked like it was tired and might give up the ghost at any moment.

'Are you sure we're safe in here?' asked Charlie.

'Yes,' said Gabrielle, 'for a while, anyway.'

Gabrielle looked at Molly and Charlie and noticed that they were wet and shivering.

'We have to start a fire,' said Gabrielle, 'before you both catch a cold.'

'In here?' asked Charlie.

'Well, I don't see why not. It is clear we will not be the first ones to do it,' said Gabrielle.

'How are we going to start it?' asked Molly.

'I'll be able to take care of that,' said Charlie fishing in his pockets for the flint stones.

Molly took the blanket that was covering her and Charlie, and laid it over one of the pews beside the fire pit. Then they rummaged around looking for things to burn. Soon enough, they had gathered plenty of kindling and odd bits of paper scraps.

'Allow me, my ladies,' said Charlie smiling. In no time, there were sparks flying, and then a tiny flame took shape. Charlie gently blew on it and the little flame began to grow. As it grew, Charlie added larger chunks of splintered wood and suddenly there was a lovely fire and heat. It gave the sort of feeling you get when you come in from a winter's storm, stand by a woodstove, and feel your entire body saying *thank you*.

'Well done, Charlie,' said Gabrielle. 'Now, you two stay here.'

Gabrielle walked up to the altar, apparently looking for something. She entered a closet or a room, which was in the far right corner of the church, and returned holding a large bundle of black fabric.

'What's that?' asked Molly.

'Choir gowns,' answered Gabrielle. 'They are thick and dry. We should put them on until our clothes have dried. We'll put them by the fireside.'

'But there's no privacy to change,' objected Molly.

'We can change in the closet,' Gabrielle said. 'I will go first.'

Gabrielle entered the closet and came out a minute later wearing a choir's gown.

'Very nice,' said Charlie.

Gabrielle placed her clothes on the pew beside the wet blanket and told Charlie he was next. He entered the closet and reappeared donning a gown that was miles too big. He walked to the middle of the dais as if taking centre stage. He raised his hands, cleared his throat, and croaked *Mi Mi Mi Miiiiiii.* He then smiled and bowed.

'Thank you all for coming. You've been a lovely audience,' he said, as he jumped down and walked past Molly who was already on her way to the closet. She noticed that it was very dark away from the fire. It must have been later than she thought, for night was upon them. If she stayed much later, she was going to be in trouble.

Molly turned the old glass doorknob and entered the closet with her new gown. Inside, it was darker still and she wondered how Charlie and Gabrielle could have changed as quickly as they did, especially considering wet clothes have a way of sticking to you.

Once she changed, Molly reached for the door handle, but it wasn't there. She must have gotten turned around inside the closet. She turned to the right and felt the wall, but there was no handle there either. She turned to the right again and again there was no handle. Only one more wall to check, she thought, but as she felt around clumsily in the blackness, she could not find her way out. Molly began to panic, afraid to be in the dark, and she spun in a circle one more time, frantically feeling each and every wall for anything that would let her out, but it was hopeless. Every surface she touched felt flat and shapeless – no doors, no doorknobs – nothing. She became dizzy and the other gowns hanging in the closet touched her face like heavy cobwebs. The walls seemed to close in around her and then, as the panic swelled, she heard a horrible voice beside her whisper: *'Hello, Molly!'*

Molly screamed and jumped back and the closet door swung open. She turned to run, but someone grabbed her so she couldn't move.

'Molly,' said Gabrielle, 'what is it?'

Molly looked up to see Gabrielle holding her, but she got loose and darted towards the fire.

'There's someone in the closet!' she screamed.

'Come now,' said Gabrielle, and she entered the closet to return only a second later with Molly's wet clothes.

Molly was already by the fire, standing close to Charlie, when Gabrielle returned and spread out the wet clothes with the others.

'Perhaps your imagination is getting the better of you?' suggested Gabrielle.

'No, I swear,' said Molly. 'I heard a voice.'

'Here we go,' said Charlie. 'Molly's hearing voices again.'

'It said my name,' Molly pleaded. 'Why would I make this up?'

Gabrielle inspected Molly's face for signs of fibbing or exaggeration, but none could be found. Before Gabrielle could respond, from all around them, they heard something like a large giant taking a quick breath in. Then they heard it exhale and their warm fire was snuffed out like a huge match.

Everything went black.

'Come here!' whispered Gabrielle.

Molly and Charlie wasted no time moving towards Gabrielle's voice, and when they found her, they held her tightly.

The room was as dark as midnight and, in the silence they could feel themselves shaking in their shoes. Then the shaking grew, but it wasn't them at all – it was the boards *beneath* them. They were pulsing like something heavy was stomping across the floor. With each pulse, they heard a noise which grew and grew. Suddenly, all the floor boards were pounding – *thump, thump, Thump, THUMP!* The shaking was so violent they fell and were tossed around as if on a huge bed with giants jumping all around them – *bang, bang, Bang, BANG!*

The whole church shook. The noise was terrifying. The heavy pews shifted, the wood shutters slammed against the windows, sending more toothy glass crashing to the floor, and the soot from the fire pit filled the air. It choked them when they inhaled it.

'What *is* that?' shouted Charlie.

'I don't know!' Gabrielle shouted back.

Molly gripped Gabrielle's gown and her eyes were shut so tightly it hurt. Then, after a terrible moment, it was over. There was silence again, and the fire miraculously reappeared and cast its warmth.

They stood and moved closer to the fire, relieved by its light and heat. They got as close to it as they could without getting burned.

'I want to get out of here,' Molly said.

'Good idea,' said Charlie. 'Perhaps we can look for a fairy tomorrow.'

'There aren't any here, anyway,' Molly said. 'We haven't seen any and there aren't any sleeping close by. We would have heard them.'

As she said this, Molly noticed an odd expression on Gabrielle's and Charlie's faces.

'Something wrong?' Molly asked.

Molly then noticed that Charlie and Gabrielle were not looking *at* her at all, but at something *behind* her.

'Don't look back,' Charlie said. 'Just step towards me.'

Charlie held out his hands to her, but Molly looked over her shoulder and screamed when she saw what was there, *smiling* at her.

It was a ghost of a man floating in front of her and the light from the fire shone through him. He was dressed in ragged old clothes and he looked very old, himself. His eyes were lifeless and his skin was gaunt and transparent. His hair floated in the air as if it were under some invisible water. He held a muddy shovel in one hand and his pants were covered in the same filth. His shoulders were broad, but his whole body tapered towards his invisible feet. His shape was somewhat like a plume of smoke from her father's pipe.

Molly stepped back slowly until she felt the comfort of Charlie's hands upon her shoulders. The ghost hovered in silence, with a grin as horrible as Mr. Weedly's on his face. Finally, his terribly thin lips took shape to speak.

'*I know you've come to catch a fairy, but this old ghost be twice as scary!*'

'Are you the ghost of Mr. Craggly?' asked Gabrielle.

The ghost chuckled.

'*I am the one and yes it's true. I've stolen corpses – one or two.*'

'A pleasure to meet you, Mr. Craggly,' Gabrielle said. 'Sorry to have disturbed your rest. We were just getting warm, but we'll be leaving now.'

'*Should you stay or should you flee, or should you ask about the Tree?*'

'You've heard of the Golden Tree?' asked Molly, feeling braver now that Gabrielle had started a conversation with him.

'*I've searched forever, moved by greed, but have not found that Golden Tree. I hope to catch a fairy kind and ask the fairy what's on her mind. Though, if she only squeaks and cries, I'll have no choice but eat her eyes.*'

'Is that why you are still here?' Gabrielle asked. 'Because you are waiting for fairies?'

'*They used to come here years ago. They came in droves before the snow. But now I've scared them all away, perhaps they'll come another day.*'

'Why haven't you...' Molly didn't quite know how to phrase it...'moved on?'

'*My natural life was dull and poor. I failed to find the Golden cure and now in death against my will, I've lost all hope, though looking still. Oh how much poorer am I now, with all this pain upon my brow.*'

As the ghost of Mr. Craggly spoke these last words, he let out a ghastly cry not unlike a whistling kettle that has come to a boil and demands to be removed from the heat. It was as if his whole existence of sadness was released at once and it momentarily broke his meter. Instead, he spoke with hurried words as if it was *he* who had been frightened.

'As I laid there shivering on my deathbed, cold and alone, I had a strange visitor who asked me if I knew about the Golden Tree, for he had heard it was my life's obsession.'

'Who was it?' asked Gabrielle.

Old Man Craggly grinned.

'*At the time, I could not say, but he came back just yesterday. I tried to scare him much like you. I shook the church, the walls, the pews. But he, you see, was very brave – I could not scare him from my grave.*'

'Who was it?' demanded Gabrielle.

'He introduced himself as one Mortimer Weedly,' said the ghost softly, as if he did not want to say the name too loud.

Molly turned to Gabrielle.

'Surely that can't be the Mr. Weedly we know. Can it?' Molly asked.

'Sh, not so loud,' said the ghost. 'It was indeed the Mr. Weedly you know.'

'But that's impossible,' Molly argued. 'Why, if he saw you right before you died, that would make him, what, how old?'

Old Man Craggly smiled again.

'Simple child, sometimes a crazy obsession stretches one's years beyond what is natural. Look at me.'

'What did he have to say?' pressed Gabrielle.

'*He said he had to find the Tree. He said he'd like to kill you three!*'

Old Man Craggly's face twisted and he become enraged.

'Oh, yes, Mr. Weedly said there would be a young girl who wanted the Tree for herself. A little, greedy, bratty, lying, ugly, frightened girl named Molly Withers. But he promised to bring me some gold if I would help him...you know...eliminate his competitors.'

Mr. Craggly's face contorted into an angry, frightful and pleased expression. His arms reached out towards Molly and he took in another deep breath. His cheeks puffed as he exhaled and again the fire was blown out. Everything went black.

'And now Old Man Craggly is going to eats them up!' laughed the ghost.

'Run!' Gabrielle yelled in the darkness.

Molly, Charlie, and Gabrielle stumbled along blindly. They tripped several times on the debris lying everywhere; it was too dark to see where they were going.

'*Ah, ha ha ha!*' laughed the ghost. '*So sour is a corpse's meats, but yours I bet is surely sweet!*'

Molly, Charlie, and Gabrielle were separated and none of them knew the way to the front doors, nor did they know if Mr. Craggly would be waiting there to devour them.

For a second, Molly stopped scrambling, hoping to be able to make out a shape in the heavy black night, and she felt Charlie's hands on her shoulders. She felt safe for a second until she realized the hands on her shoulders were ice cold. They squeezed and Molly heard a horrible voice whisper, '*Boo!*'

The ghost's frigid breath made the hairs on Molly's neck stand on end. She shrieked and ran until she hit something warm and soft. She almost shrieked again before she knew it was Gabrielle.

'Sh,' Gabrielle said with a soft, soft voice. '*Charlie!*'

Somehow, Charlie found them, and he put his arms around them. They had nowhere to go. Molly strained to see, but it was hopeless. She figured this is what it would be like to be buried alive.

The ghost of Old Man Craggly flew around the room, hitting things with his shovel as he went. He was above them, then to the right, then to the left, then to the right again. There was no order to it, and the chaos was frightening.

Molly closed her eyes and nothing changed – that's how dark it was, but when she opened them again, she saw the smallest, faintest, greenish light from across the room. It flashed for only a second, like a firefly, only quicker. Molly grabbed hold of Gabrielle's gown, and began to walk slowly towards the source of the light. Gabrielle held fast to Charlie who followed. They made it approximately half the distance when Charlie stumbled on something that made a horrible noise.

'*Oh, there you are my clumsy treats, making rackets with your feets!*'

Molly instinctively looked in the direction of the ghost's voice. She shouldn't have but she couldn't help it. When she looked back to find her way, she couldn't determine where the green light first emanated.

'*Now who shall be the first to go, the first to eats, I do not know. Ah, ha, ha, ha!*'

To Molly's relief, the greenish light pulsed once more and it was closer. She began walking again with Gabrielle and Charlie in tow. She was making great progress until she bumped into a wall.

'*Aha!*' said the ghost and immediately the random banging around the walls of the church stopped with a heavy thud upon the floor behind them. It was followed by determined footsteps that were getting louder and closer. He must have been only a few steps away when the green light flickered again. Molly reached out as if to touch it, but it disappeared as the terrible steps were almost on top of them – *stomp, stomp, Stomp, STOMP!*

Then there was silence. Old Man Craggly was right behind them.

'*A little salt and pepper, too. I'll eats you all, yes, this is true.*'

The green light flashed one more time. Molly reached for it and again it disappeared, but she touched something that fit her hand quite nicely – a door handle!

She turned it, pushed, and the door swung open.

'Come on!' she shouted, as she pulled on Gabrielle's gown.

Molly, Gabrielle, and Charlie burst through the door, and in a flash they were in the cool night air. They stumbled down the steps and Molly could now see the green light in front of her pulsing steadily in the darkness.

'Come on!' Molly shouted again, and the three of them were off with Molly leading the way.

Molly didn't know what it was in front of her, but she followed it. She looked over her shoulder once and saw the outline of the church. There were brief flashes of bright light from within as if fireworks were going off. She could see the whole church was shaking violently and she could hear the awful wailing of Mr. Craggly's ghost trapped within.

Molly looked ahead and ran for all she was worth, though it was quite difficult for all of them with the draping gowns playing at their feet. They ran and ran as the horrifying sound of Old Man Craggly disappeared behind them. They continued running till they passed the newer cemetery and until they could see the welcoming lights of their own village in the distance.

Once they realized they were no longer in harm's way, they stopped to catch their breath, but it only took an owl's hooting to get them moving again.

'I've never been so scared in all my life,' said Molly.

'Me neither,' said Charlie. 'And after all that, we didn't even see one fairy. Now we have these stupid gowns. What am I going to do with this?'

'Join the choir,' offered Molly. 'You have a lovely singing voice.'

'You're in rather good spirits, considering,' said Gabrielle.

'I think I saw a fairy,' Molly said excitedly. 'I saw a greenish light which guided me to the door and it continued shining until we were down the path, far enough to know we were safe.'

Suddenly, Gabrielle and Charlie looked at Molly in much the same way they did when Mr. Craggly first appeared behind her. She filled with dread once again and turned around immediately to find a Pinkleton hovering in front of her.

With a voice that was not overly friendly, it spoke to them.

'My name is Lillian and I am the queen of the Pinkleton Dimple fairies.'

Though Molly showed incredible speed when she caught Tommy, her next move was like lightning. Her hand shot forward and, unbelievable to all those who bore witness, Molly caught the fairy.

'No way, Molly, you caught it!' exclaimed Charlie, but as soon as he said this, it disappeared from Molly's hand.

'Where'd she go?' asked Molly.

Suddenly, there were random flashes of green in different spots around Molly's head and specks of green fairy dust fell upon her. You couldn't pinpoint where Lillian was, being in several places at the same time, but you could hear her muttering something about *luck* under her breath.

'I suppose you think you're special,' Lillian said. 'We'll see. Meet me in the far end of the orchard Saturday afternoon, and I shall introduce you to someone you need to meet. As Tommy Troublesome has granted, we will help you find the Tree.'

In a blink, Lillian flew away, leaving a trail of dust behind her.

Chapter Twelve
- *Genevieve Dubois* -

After going their separate ways, Molly crept inside her house as quietly as she could. She hoped her parents weren't up, but there they were, sitting at the table with a single candle burning low. There was a brief moment of relief when her parents saw she was safe, but it quickly turned into an argument. Annabelle fretted over the cold temperature, the rain storm, and the time of night, and William was upset Molly did not have her proper clothes on and suggested it may not be such a good thing for her to spend time with Gabrielle anymore.

'Did Gabrielle not think we'd be insanely worried?' he demanded. 'And where in the blazes are your clothes?'

Molly explained as best she could, and then dragged herself off to bed. She was too exhausted to give the argument much thought, and fell asleep as soon as her head hit the pillow.

Each and every night after that, she dreamt of fairies and horses and leprechauns and the Golden Tree of Truth. She also had unpleasant dreams where Charlie was teasing her and nightmares about Old Man Craggly. She dreamt she was alone in the abandoned cemetery and stuck inside the church with the ghost right behind her. She dreamt she opened the door just in time, but when she ran outside, she could only get as far as the gate before she was somehow transported back inside the church.

Molly awoke exceptionally early one day with the feelings of being chased still in her belly. She was exhausted, but couldn't settle her mind enough to fall back to sleep. Entirely restless, she dressed, packed a few sandwiches, wrote a note to her parents, and headed to Gabrielle's, hoping she might be awake and wanting some company.

As she walked down the road, the sun poked its head over a distant mountain and Molly was glad to see it. Even though only a few days had passed since she was with Charlie and Gabrielle, she noticed the fresh morning air now hinted of winter.

When she drew near to Gabrielle's house, she saw a familiar shape.

'Charlie? What are you doing here?'

'I couldn't sleep very well,' Charlie answered.

'Me neither. Are you okay?'

'I think I'm getting sick,' Charlie said, and no sooner were these words out of his mouth, did he let out a sneeze.

Gabrielle's front door opened and she appeared, still wearing her dressing gown.

'Well, good morning,' said Gabrielle. 'I thought I heard voices.'

'What is it with you two hearing voices?' asked Charlie, with a cheeky little grin.

'I hope this isn't too early,' added Molly.

'Not at all. Come in, come in. Are you hungry?' Gabrielle asked. 'I bet neither one of you has had much to eat.'

Molly and Charlie entered Gabrielle's small home and immediately felt at ease. The heat from the potbelly stove in the corner of the kitchen, the flowers on the table, and the sweet smell of fresh baked bread were as comforting as a hug. Certain homes have another warmth to them that can only be attributed to the loving people who live inside, and this was one of those homes.

'Charlie, have you gone and caught a cold?' asked Gabrielle.

'I think so,' Charlie said with a sniff.

'Here then, let me fix you some tea and after breakfast we'll go straight to the apothecary. No one knows natural cures better,' said Gabrielle.

Molly and Charlie sat at the table and noticed there was an obvious colour scheme to Gabrielle's decor. The walls were a cheerful yellow, the table cloth was orange, and the tea towels were red. Everything was the colour of autumn and Molly loved it.

'Here, start with some bread. The kettle will only be a minute,' said Gabrielle as she placed two thick slices in front of Charlie.

'Mmm,' said Charlie reaching for it without delay, 'this is really fresh.'

'Thank you, Charlie. Now eat up. There's plenty more and we have a long day ahead of us,' Gabrielle said, placing two thick slices in front of Molly.

'Fresh baked bread, I see.' observed Molly. 'First thing in the morning, no less.'

'Perhaps we all had a bumpy sleep,' Gabrielle said, and then looking at Charlie, 'You look as though you have lost your best friend. You alright?'

Charlie didn't realize he looked as glum as he did, and he hesitated before answering.

'I guess I'm still a bit skeptical,' said Charlie thoughtfully. 'If I could just see the magic at work it would be easier.'

The kettle came to a boil. Gabrielle poured three lovely smelling cups of tea as she took a seat at the table.

'It's all around you, sure,' said Gabrielle. 'Listen here. You never have to worry about how the Universe is going to provide you with something. Truth is, what you desire can be provided a thousand different ways, and the Universe will decide what's best. Just be open to different possibilities. If you look around and see nothing but closed doors, then look again. It might be that you have to climb through a window.'

'And what if you see more than one door?' asked Molly. 'How do you decide which one to go through?'

'You use your intuition and you do it quickly,' answered Gabrielle. 'The Universe appreciates haste.'

'*Intuition?*' asked Charlie.

'*Haste?*' asked Molly.

'That's right,' affirmed Gabrielle. 'It's a little feeling on the inside that's trying to get you to act. Whenever you get the feeling you should do something, do it, and do it quickly. There's a kernel of truth in the old saying that says you should always follow your heart. Charlie, did you not follow your heart when you came to Stankwater with the boots for Molly?'

'No,' said Charlie with a smile. 'I followed the path.'

'But what led you to the path?' asked Gabrielle.

Charlie shrugged: 'My heart, I guess.'

'That's right. Your heart led you to the path, and the path led you to us, and look at all that's happened because of it,' said Gabrielle. 'Most people, though, ignore what their heart is telling them and they live regretful lives. These people are the ones you always hear saying: I knew I should have done this thing, or, I knew I shouldn't have done that thing.'

Molly and Charlie split a muffin as Gabrielle sliced off some ham and threw it in a pan on the stove.

'And that's not all,' added Gabrielle. 'The more you listen to your heart, the easier this all becomes. The Universe will reward you for paying attention. That's the law of attraction. You will actually feel as though you are being shown the way and it's wonderful.'

'I still have my doubts,' said Charlie.

'That's fine,' said Gabrielle. 'Molly wasn't convinced right away, either. Sure, she's still not. Not entirely. People become discouraged when they can't see how it's going to work out and they fail to act, but that's not how to reap the rewards of the magic. You simply have to have faith that when you take the first step, the second step will be shown to you. Like walking up a spiral staircase.'

'What do you mean?' asked Molly over the sizzling sounds of ham frying.

'Have you ever walked to the top of a lighthouse?' asked Gabrielle.

'I have,' answered Charlie, 'but only once when our class visited the coast.'

'And were you able to see the top platform when you first began?' Gabrielle prodded.

'No.'

'That's right, Charlie, and that's often how the Universe works,' Gabrielle said. 'Though you may only ever see the next few steps of the path that lay ahead, if you keep stepping, you will get to where you want to go.'

Gabrielle poured more hot tea and served the ham as Molly and Charlie processed this new information.

'Enjoy your breakfast now,' said Gabrielle. 'Take your time. I must have a quick wash up and get dressed.'

Molly and Charlie did not take their time. They finished their breakfast in quick order so they could do what curious children love to do - *explore*. Sadly, adults often mistake exploring for *snooping*, but it's not the same thing, is it?

The most noticeable feature of Gabrielle's small home was the immense oak bookcase that dominated the back wall of the adjoining room. Upon its shelves seemed to be every book ever written, and though the books weren't of any great interest to Charlie, Molly was in paradise. She touched the aging spines and gold-gilded pages of all the volumes before her. In the early morning light, with a fresh day unfolding, each title seemed a grand adventure of mystery and wonder; each author's name a small whisper of friendship.

In the empty spaces on the bookshelf was the oddest assortment of the most curious strangeness. There were peacock feathers, and tiny carved wooden boxes that Molly imagined contained elves' slippers and salty locks of mermaid hair. There were also candle holders shaped like wild animals from far away lands, and tiny teacups shaped like flowers which made you think of summertime, picnics, and all things sunny and warm.

Of all the things on the shelves which caught Molly's eye, however, one particular treasure was undeniably the most spectacular. It was a large Unicorn skilfully carved from wood. It was encased in a glass container atop a tarnished silver base. Though Molly dare not pick it up, she got as near to it as she could to see every detail. Upon closer inspection of the silver base, she noticed a faded inscription: *A-l-k-a-*.

'Find anything interesting?' asked Gabrielle, who reappeared without making a sound.

Molly was surprised and embarrassed, but the smile on Gabrielle's face let her know it was alright.

'Are we ready then?' asked Gabrielle.

Molly, Charlie, and Gabrielle left that warm treasure of a home, walked to Town Centre, and entered a small shop with a weathered sign that read: *Genevieve Dubois - Village Apothecary.*

Immediately, Molly was confronted with a hundred exotic smells, each one more different than the next. Some were pleasant, while others offended. She smelled bergamot, and mildew, and sumac, and rotting parsnips, nutmeg, pine, and fish, and garlic, and wet dog.

From behind the counter appeared a woman almost as beautiful as Gabrielle. She wore a grey sweater and around her shoulders hung a black knitted shawl. Her hair was full, and shiny, and black, and wiry, and streaked with one patch of grey. She was lovely to look at.

'Bonjour, Allo.' she said, 'Ah, Chere Gabrielle, ça va? How are you, my dear friend?'

'I am quite fine, thank you,' said Gabrielle. 'Molly, Charlie, this is my very close friend, Genevieve Dubois.'

Genevieve's eyes fell on Charlie only briefly, but she stared wide and curiously at Molly for an uncomfortable moment.

'Gabrielle,' said Genevieve, 'is this la petite fille I have heard so much about? Why of course it is! And here she is in my humble shop.'

Molly felt funny. She couldn't get used to strangers knowing who she was.

'Yes,' replied Gabrielle, 'this is young Molly Withers, and her friend and protector, Charlie Gregg, who, I am afraid, is not feeling very well today.'

Charlie had never been introduced as a protector before and though he knew Molly did not appreciate the connotation, he couldn't help but smile. He would have continued smiling, too, had he not let out another sneeze.

'Garçon,' said Genevieve pulling her eyes from Molly, 'disease cannot live in a healthy mind. If you chase a cold, you'll come to catch it.'

'I...I...' began Charlie, but he was cut off.

'Perhaps a lesson for another day, non? I shall fix you up the all at the same,' said Genevieve, whose smile rivalled Gabrielle's.

Genevieve disappeared into a back room leaving Molly and Charlie content to explore for the second time that day. Below their feet, was a wooden floor that creaked with every step. There were wooden walls, and a wooden ceiling, and they were all stained dark like a church. There were shelves, and bookcases, and small tables, and it seemed every flat surface had peculiar objects upon them. There were large jars filled with dragon scales, and snake skins, and instruments of some design unknown to Molly. There were piles of different crystals, each one with a placard explaining their uses. There were books on spells, and books on fairytales, and books on love potions, and books on alchemy, and books on astrology.

One entire wall was devoted to the ingredients needed for

remedying common ailments. It looked like a spice rack for witches. All of the tiny brown jars had faded yellow labels describing their contents and Molly was pleased to see that all the ingredients were plant matter. One read *Eucalyptus for Arthritis*. Another read *Rose Petals for Love*. Still another read *Tulips for Courage*.

Everything in the shop piqued Molly's and Charlie's interest. They wondered if perhaps Genevieve Dubois *was* a witch, especially when they noticed that beside the rack of remedies was a very old-style broom. It looked like it belonged in a museum. Perhaps even more convincing was what lay sleeping on the broom's bristles – an immense black cat that clearly did not get much exercise.

'Here we are,' said Genevieve, reappearing from the back room. 'My special blend of garlic and sticklewort.'

She handed the jar to Charlie.

'Just add one teaspoon to a cup of water twice a day,' said Genevieve, 'and you will feel, oh how do they say – *meilleur* – err – better again soon.'

She also handed him a glass that presumably contained the concoction already mixed. Charlie smelled it, grimaced, and drank it down. He looked as though he had swallowed a slug. He also looked a little awkward, wondering if he had to pay for it. Gabrielle smiled at Genevieve who smiled back.

'But of course, this is on the house,' said Genevieve. 'Friends of la jolie Gabrielle need no pennies ici.'

'Thank you,' said Charlie, as he inspected the jar.

'Molly,' said Genevieve, 'it was a true pleasure to meet you, and I hope I shall see you again soon. I wish you great luck in your journey. Bonne chance.'

Genevieve came out from behind the counter, walked past Molly, and retrieved the old broom. The cat had practically squashed it and the sparse bristles were covered with a mat of black fur. Disgusted, Genevieve took up the broom and swatted the cat with it. It did not so much as flinch. *Perhaps it's dead*, thought Molly.

'Snowball! Bad kitty! Scoot! Scoot!' shouted Genevieve and she swatted the cat again. Finally, it stood, glared up at them with burning yellow eyes, and then sashayed beneath a nearby table.

'Snowball?' asked Charlie.

'She's precious, non?' Genevieve said in admiration.

Genevieve returned to the counter, grabbed a cloth, and began to polish the broom's handle. After a few gentle strokes, she methodically removed Snowball's black fur from the bristles. She then retrieved an old bonnet from a hook on the wall, and tied the chin straps down so tightly, you'd swear she was about to face a storm.

'Are you going somewhere?' asked Molly, intrigued by the curious way Genevieve was behaving.

With a grin and a knowing twinkle in her eyes, Genevieve said: 'Not today. I am busy sweeping, of course.'

Molly, Charlie, and Gabrielle turned and exited the shop. Genevieve followed as far as the front step.

'Bonne chance!' Genevieve said again. 'Believe in your dreams, and you shall have them!'

Molly looked over her shoulder one last time and received a wink from Genevieve who took the broom and made a motion of sweeping the step without the bristles touching the wood.

'What a lovely woman,' said Gabrielle.

'Most definitely,' replied Molly.

'Great name for a black cat,' added Charlie.

They proceeded to the town square, and there they saw Mr. Weedly standing on his box with a familiar crowd jostling by his feet. But instead of there being a cart full of pelts by his side, there was a huge pile of what looked like jagged stones that had been blackened by fire.

'Is that him?' asked Charlie.

'Yes,' said Molly. *'He's* the one after the Golden Tree. We don't like him.'

'What's that black stuff beside him?' asked Charlie.

'I'm afraid I may know,' answered Gabrielle, 'but I have only seen it once before.'

'When you left Majestica for all those years?' asked Molly, but Gabrielle did not answer.

'Step right up, step right up,' said Mortimer with a sneer. 'Don't be the last to buy Weedly's fuel. You've never seen the likes of this before. Yes, that's right, this is *coal* and it burns better than wood! Trust me, my dear Majesticans, there will come a day you wish you had your sheds stuffed full of it. Yes, there's a hard, hard winter coming.'

Just off to the side was a small fire burning the black chunks of Mortimer's fuel, and it was giving off incredible heat. Though no one knew what coal was, the crowd was in frenzied, ravenous appreciation. Molly was nervous to see adults pushing and shoving each other. It looked as though things were going to get violent at any moment and Mortimer Weedly enjoyed the tension.

'Yes,' cried Mortimer. 'I say, buy what you can. It's going to be a hard, hard winter. Buy today, while you still can.'

And then it happened – a younger man turned directly to a slightly older man and pushed him to the ground. In that instant, the entire crowd broke out into a horrific brawl. Molly had never seen anything like it. Sure, there had been times at school when boys exchanged the odd punch in the nose to test their courage, but nothing like this. This was ugly. And as ugly as it was, Mr. Weedly continued to pour out his poison. The fear had fully gripped the huddled crowd.

'Everyone stand back!' boomed a mighty voice.

It was Knight MacDonald; he entered the angry crowd without hesitation.

'What's the matter with you?' he asked. 'Have you all gone mad?'

But there were too many people fighting for one man to stop, even for a man like him. Molly's heart pounded and more fear seeped in. Someone was going to get badly injured if this fighting continued.

Without warning, a heavy hand touched Molly's shoulder as another large man walked by.

'Stay back,' said William, striding past his daughter.

What was her father doing here? Though it was comforting to see him, it was unnerving as well. He continued towards the brawling crowd and took a position beside Knight MacDonald. Molly always knew her father was a big man with a big temper, but she didn't realize how large he really was till he stood beside the hulking knight. William was just a bit shorter, but it could be argued his chest was every bit as thick as the knight's.

'I'm here, Marcus,' said her father and the knight nodded.

If you have ever seen a plough go through a field, then you will have an understanding of how Molly's father and Knight MacDonald dealt with the crowd. The fighting and shouting people were being turned over on themselves as these two mighty men cut the group in half. Knight MacDonald went one way, blocking punches and kicks and throwing people to the ground, while

William went the other way doing likewise, only less gently. When William threw these brawling men down, they were slow to get up, if at all. Two men, who went at her father at the same time, received a proper hand washing and Charlie laughed. William's large hands grabbed each of those men's faces and he picked them off their feet! He glared at them briefly before throwing them both to the ground at the same time.

For Molly, it was a terrible comfort to know her father could handle himself this way. Charlie, though, thought this was the best thing he had ever seen.

Then, just as thunder disappears in the distance after a storm, the fighting and the yelling subsided.

'I say again,' said MacDonald, 'what's the matter with you? Have you all lost your minds?'

An old man cried out: 'But winter's coming. We might freeze if not for this...this...this coal.'

Once again, the fear swept through the crowd like a terrible wave upon a shore.

'Stand down, men!' yelled MacDonald. 'Don't be foolish. Have we ever had a really hard winter? Nay, we have not. And if the wind blows stronger this year, do we not have enough wood to burn? Aye, we do. Are you all so quick to bring something so unfamiliar home to your wives and children?'

Knight MacDonald looked up at Mortimer who could not hide that he was pleased with what he had begun.

'Mortimer, get down from there this instant,' said MacDonald. 'You are hereby banished from Town Centre for this rabble rousing and if this mountain of, whatever this is, is not removed in an hour, it shall be confiscated.'

Mortimer remained nonchalant.

'If it be your wish to have these poor folk freeze this winter,' said Mortimer from his perch,' and if you yourself are willing to bury the blue babies, then so be it.'

Mr. Weedly may as well have booed MacDonald for it enraged the good knight. He grabbed Mr. Weedly from the box and slammed him to the ground. But it didn't stop there. He picked him up with one hand, and cocked his other fist to punch him. A punch from such a man would have surely killed him, but Mortimer smiled a devilishly taunting smile.

'He's baiting you, Marcus,' said William. 'It's not worth it.'

Chapter Thirteen
- *Beyond the Orchard* -

Charlie remained melancholy all the way through the apple orchard. It took two hours to walk it, and neither Molly nor Charlie had seen the other side before. Through the trunks of the apple trees, they approached what appeared to be a vast and sudden clearing. Closer still, and they saw that the clearing was a long, narrow and barren field with immense boulders strewn about as if this was once a place where giants had played marbles. The forest on the other side of the clearing looked as tangled as a thorn bush and as inviting as Craggly's bone yard. The clearing was so stark, by comparison, it was as if the apple orchard dare not get any closer to the other side for fear of being consumed by the sprawling dark forest.

'I've never seen woods like that before,' observed Molly.

'I daresay not,' answered Gabrielle. 'That's Bokwus Forest – not a place for the timid, I assure you.'

Once they reached the middle of the clearing, Gabrielle produced a canteen of water, opened it and took a thirst quenching gulp.

'Molly, you're next,' she said.

Molly took several large mouthfuls and passed the canteen to Charlie.

'Take some of your medication,' Gabrielle said. 'Pour it in and swish it around.'

Charlie did as he was told; choking it down as best he could.

'I guess we just wait here?' asked Molly, and Gabrielle nodded. They all sat down in the coarse grass of the narrow field between the great orchard and Bokwus Forest.

Molly retrieved the three sandwiches she had made earlier and gave one each to Gabrielle and Charlie. She then stared at the opening of the forest for a long time, though it made her uneasy. The hole in the tree line looked like a yawning mouth and the path was its dark tongue rolling out to her.

It didn't seem right to Molly that the path was so well worn being so far from town. Where did the path go? Who used it so often? And why were there so many strange tracks in it? Molly paid no attention to this particular detail earlier, but the path had hundreds of fresh tracks alluding to some grand march of animals.

'What are all these footprints?' asked Molly. 'It looks like a stampede has gone through here.'

Then, from the forest's gaping entrance, several chickadees appeared. The tiny birds circled the three humans and one even perched on Molly's shoulder. She was delighted and giggled upon hearing it chirp a little song in her ear. An owl appeared next and claimed a nearby stump for its perch. Then came some grey squirrels with the bushiest tails Molly had ever seen. Next pranced in a lovely red fox with a bushy tail of its own, followed by a beautiful pack of wolves.

'What's going on here?' questioned Charlie, as Molly continued to giggle and clap her hands.

She had always loved animals, but had never seen such peculiar behaviour before.

'Just remain still,' said Gabrielle softly.

Following the wolves, there arrived raccoons and several happy deer. The animals were so close to Gabrielle and the two children you'd believe they were quite used to humans. Molly clapped her small hands again. She only stopped when they heard a great rustling from the bushes where a giant grizzly bear appeared. He too approached them as freely as the other animals.

Charlie was petrified to see the massive hulk of a bear approaching. It lowered its huge head, and sniffed at Charlie's food.

'Good boy', said Charlie with a gulp, as the bear lowered its large rump with a *whump!* into the grass.

There was another crash in the woods and a thrush of white

doves burst from the opening. As they landed and began strutting about, a large moose emerged from Bokwus.

'Mr. Cayce?' asked Molly.

Gabrielle smiled in answer. It *was* Mr. Cayce and as he approached, everyone rose to their feet. Around his head and in and out of his great antlers, a hummingbird flew about. It was manoeuvring so fast you couldn't make out the shape of the small body. Finally, it landed on one of the higher antlers and they realized that this was no hummingbird at all.

'Lillian!' exclaimed Molly.

'Hello, Molly,' Lillian replied with little enthusiasm.

'There she is,' said Mr. Cayce. 'Little Molly Quick Hands, that's what we should call you. Must have the fastest hands in all of Majestica to catch Lillian as you did! Tommy Troublesome too, I hear.'

'Very well then,' said Lillian rather curtly who still seemed a little upset that Molly was able to catch her so easily. 'Time is very precious to us. More precious than you know. It's going to take more than slick hands to save us.'

Lillian took to the air and hovered before Molly, Gabrielle, and Charlie, just inches from their noses.

'Before you meet him,' said Lillian, 'you must first know that he never shows himself to humans. In different times he would have never considered such a meeting, but he needs your help. You should feel very honoured.'

Lillian paused briefly, looking over her shoulder to the opening of Bokwus Forest.

'Are you ready then?' she asked.

They nodded and all three human hearts began beating with a mixture of curiosity and excitement.

'Very well,' Lillian said, and then she disappeared back into the darkness of Bokwus.

The trees trembled suddenly and such a comforting breeze washed over Molly, Charlie, and Gabrielle it would be remembered for all their lives. It was warm and in great contrast to the season. It smelled like honey and sunshine and flowers. It was both the scent of the ocean and of the woods. It seemed to carry the air of being ancient and powerful.

Gabrielle lowered her head and closed her eyes as though trying to commit the experience to memory. Molly did the same. Charlie, therefore, was the first to see what was happening with the animals and said in a whisper: 'Look!'

Molly, Charlie, and Gabrielle watched the animals gathering around the forest's opening in quiet assembly. Then Lillian reappeared and the animals bowed with their eyes cast down in deep respect, for what stepped out of the forest next was the most magical animal to ever exist: a Unicorn.

With all the grace and majesty that Unicorns were given on the day of creation, he entered the clearing and nodded his noble head, acknowledging all the other animals. He was a magnificent, shiny black – as black as midnight. On his chin was a short beard that was also black and it gave the creature a look of old world wisdom. But of course the most notable feature was upon his brow: a long spiralled horn of ebony peppered with golden flecks.

Gabrielle smiled and took a deep breath as though she had waited a long time for this moment.

'I don't believe it!' said Charlie who just finished rubbing his eyes. 'You got to be kidding me. A Unicorn? They're *real?*'

'We are real to those who believe in us,' said the Unicorn in a voice so rich and deep you heard it not just with your ears, but with your whole body.

He stepped slowly towards the humans as if examining their very souls. Lillian hovered close by.

'But I never—' whispered Charlie.

'You may not have until now, young knight,' said the Unicorn, 'but is seeing not believing? I am Alkaios.'

Lillian landed lightly on Mr. Cayce's antlers.

'In the land of Nordenburgh,' Lillian began hurriedly, 'our woodland friends have heard it said that Mortimer covets King Alfred's throne. If Mr. Weedly finds the Tree first, there's no doubting he'll be nestled upon the very seat of Majestica shortly thereafter.'

'It's true,' added Alkaios. 'Mortimer wants nothing less than all of Majestica, and if he finds the Golden Tree of Truth before we do, the land we call home will disappear.'

'But how can we stop him?' asked Charlie. 'Apart from Gabrielle, we are only young, and we don't even know where to look for the Tree.'

'And we don't know what to do with it once we find it,' added Molly.

'Never underestimate the magic of youth,' said Alkaios, 'for in youth there is an innocence and purity of thought that Mr. Weedly has long lost. It is the one characteristic Mr. Weedly requires to find the Tree. As things are now, he is blind. He needs someone to show him the way. Sadly, we already know who that someone will be. Mortimer does as well.'

Alkaios paused. He looked as though it troubled him to continue.

'It is Molly,' Alkaios said gravely, 'who will show Mortimer Weedly where the Golden Tree is.'

Everyone was stunned beyond words. Surely this was a mistake. Before anyone had time to formulate an objection, Alkaios continued.

'Fear not, friends. This path is unavoidable. Mortimer has attracted Molly into his life and once she knows where the Tree is, then so will he. It will come to pass as I have said.'

'Then I never want to know where it is!' said Molly. 'I can't show him if I don't know. I don't care about the Tree and I don't care about the gold. I just don't want anything to happen to Majestica.'

'Be careful with your words,' said Alkaios warmly. 'They may attract the very thing you do not want to happen.'

'Molly, the fear Mortimer spreads will continue one way or the other,' said Lillian, 'so we must find the Tree even though he seeks to destroy it.'

'Why does he want to do that?' asked Charlie. 'Can't he have the throne without killing the Tree? Is it for the gold?'

'No, young knight,' said Alkaios. 'The gold is secondary to Mr. Weedly. He has come to know more about the Tree than we first realized. He knows that when the Tree dies, much knowledge will be lost, and then his ultimate plan will come into play.'

'What plan?' asked Gabrielle.

'He plans to erase the magic from human memory,' answered Alkaios, 'and if this happens, Mortimer Weedly will have ultimate rule over us all.'

'I don't understand any of this,' said Molly.

'Sweet child,' said Alkaios, 'the Golden Tree barely exists as it is, for there are just a handful of people who still believe in it. And, once humans forget about the Tree, then it will fade into story books, just like the race of Unicorns. The strength of the magic in the world has been weakened by humans' fear. Mortimer is moved by the same fear, and he will surely cut down the Tree if you do not reach it first.'

'Don't you know where it is?' asked Molly.

'I am afraid not,' answered Alkaios. 'We had hoped Engelbert the Great would still be alive so that he might help us, but our efforts to find him have not been fruitful so far. There remains only one other who is sure to know, and though I have been searching my entire lifetime, our paths have not yet crossed.'

'Who is it?' asked Charlie.

'Amalthea,' said Alkaios and as this word was carried off on a soft breeze, a peaceful silence fell over all the woodland creatures.

'Well, that's just great,' said Charlie. 'No offence, but if a Unicorn can't even find this person, then how are *we*—'

'It's not a person at all, is it?' interrupted Molly and Gabrielle smiled, knowing where Molly's thoughts had turned.

'Amalthea is a female Unicorn, isn't she?' said Molly, 'and you've been looking for her because she is to become your partner, isn't she?'

'Molly, how very intuitive you are,' said Alkaios with a warm tone. 'Surely, you are the one for whom we have been waiting. Yes, if the tales are true, then Amalthea still exists, and when we find her, we shall find the Tree.'

'Does she stay close to the Tree?' asked Gabrielle.

'She does,' said Alkaios. 'Amalthea willingly guards the Golden Tree and this is a good thing. Only a creature as pure as her has the magic and wisdom to protect something so special. But she, like the Tree itself, is all but forgotten by humans and your disbelief has weakened her terribly. I daresay if Mr. Weedly were to happen upon her now, she would be no match for him.'

'And there's something more, isn't there?' asked Molly.

'Do you know?' asked Alkaios.

Molly thought for a few seconds and nodded shyly.

'You and Amalthea are the last Unicorns left, aren't you?' offered Molly, wishing deep down that she was wrong.

'We are!' said Alkaios. 'Though once upon a time there were countless Unicorns walking this great earth, we have been hunted to near extinction and forgotten by all except your poets and playwrights.'

'I think I understand,' said Molly. 'When humans cease to

believe in all that is wondrous, you, Amalthea, and the Golden Tree will disappear.'

'Yes, Molly, we exist in faith and hope. Without these, we will perish,' Alkaios said.

'Alkaios,' said Gabrielle, 'is there anyone we can trust? Is there anyone who intends on helping us?'

At this point, the grizzly bear let out a mighty growl and swatted the ground several times with his massive clawed paw. This caused a ruckus amongst the animals.

'As you can see,' said Alkaios, 'you have the help of Grizz and every woodland creature known to Majestica. I, too, of course, will endeavour to help anyway I can.'

'Then what are we waiting for?' asked Charlie.

Alkaios turned to Mr. Cayce and smiled.

'You were quite, right, old friend,' said Alkaios. 'Young Charlie here has the heart of a bear, doesn't he?'

Mr. Cayce nodded in agreement. Charlie blushed, and Lillian took to the air once more.

'So, we can all see that we must find the Golden Tree before the wretched Mr. Weedly does,' Lillian said. 'The very existence of Alkaios and Amalthea depends upon it!'

As the words floated by Molly's ears, she was filled with emotion. Suddenly, there seemed to be so much wrong with her world. Still, she wanted something at this moment; something she believed was not permitted. Alkaios noticed right away.

'Molly, if there is something you feel you must say, then you should say it,' said Alkaios. 'From here on in we must be trusting of each other and we must be willing to share all that is in our hearts.'

Molly rubbed her hands nervously, and Charlie realized exactly what was on her mind.

'You want to touch him, don't you?' Charlie said, a little curious himself.

'Is it permitted?' asked Molly.

'It is,' said Alkaios, 'for you, Molly, and your companions here, but should we be successful in our search to find Amalthea, you must realize she is far too pure to be touched by mortal hands. Likewise, a hand must never be placed upon the Golden Tree.'

Alkaios took a step towards them.

'Do you all understand and accept what must never be?' Alkaios asked.

They all nodded and he took another step closer, close enough to be touched. Molly was the first to reach out. Her hand trembled with excitement. Never had she imagined something like this was possible and she was happier at this moment than any other moment she could recall.

Alkaios' black coat shone gloriously in the afternoon sun, and his long, full mane was of equal brilliance. Though he looked as sleek as could be imagined, there was an outcropping of crimped shiny fur on each hoof. He was tall and dense with muscle, but despite being the most powerful creature Molly had ever seen, behind his big brown eyes emanated a feeling of warmth and compassion.

Molly took a breath, and then touched his thick neck. Wonderfully, and instantaneously, her whole being filled with the same warmth and compassion she saw in his eyes.

Charlie and Gabrielle followed suit and were similarly amazed. Simply touching this magnificent animal made them feel so wonderful. But then, as the peace swept over them like a cloudy dream, there was a crashing in Bokwus Forest.

Alkaios took one step back and all the animals faced the direction of the disturbance. Grizz immediately positioned himself between Alkaios and the sound. He then stood on his hind legs and raised his snout to smell the air. When he came down, Molly felt the *thud* under her feet.

Alkaios turned back to the mortals.

'Thank you for coming,' he said. 'Should I or any of the animals find something that will help us locate the Tree, I will send for you.'

'Alkaios,' said Gabrielle, 'what if we need to find you?'

'Use the magic and I will surely come,' answered Alkaios.

With this, Alkaios returned to Bokwus. Behind him followed the large procession of animals, and lastly, Mr. Cayce.

'We will see each other soon enough,' said Lillian. 'I hope you all realize what an honour this was for you. The keepers of all things pure and magical need your help.'

Then, up and off she disappeared into Bokwus Forest.

Molly, Charlie, and Gabrielle returned to the village not knowing their next step, nor knowing for sure when they'd see each other again. All Molly knew for certain was that the following day would be spent with her family and she was quite looking forward to it.

Chapter Fourteen
-The Problem with Cabbage Grass-

The next day Molly awoke and wasted no time getting dressed. She wanted to see something she had not taken the time to enjoy in ages. She made herself a hot cup of her special tea, bundled up warmly, went out to the porch, and settled in to watch one of the most wonderful sunrises she had ever seen.

In the far distance, it was impossible at first to distinguish where the mountains ended and the bank of bluish grey clouds began. As that great orb rose a little higher, the clouds became luminescent, outlined with a strip of bright yellow, while the sky above was an intense reddish orange. The sun climbed further and the deep orange lightened and eventually turned a shade of pink Molly couldn't recall seeing anywhere else in nature. Finally, the intensity of the sky softened and began to take on the lovely blue for which it is famous.

Molly sipped her tea with a smile shining so brightly it would have made the sun jealous.

As the remaining birds that had not yet flown away to warmer climates began their morning song, William joined Molly on the step of the front porch. He coughed deeply as he always did early in the day, lit his sweet smelling pipe, and sat quietly, drawing the smoke in, holding it briefly and then slowly letting it out.

'Father, can I ask you something?'

'Sure.'

'What did Knight MacDonald mean the other day when he asked you about *his royal offer?* Did it have to do with the king?' Molly asked.

William adjusted his position, as if uncomfortable with the question.

'Oh, it was nothing, Molly. The king once asked me if I would do something for him, but I had to decline,' William said.

'What was it?' asked Molly.

'It was nothing of great importance,' was his reply, but Molly didn't quite believe him. Wouldn't anything the king asked be important?

'Doesn't matter now, anyway,' William added. 'That has long passed.'

William stood up, making the entire porch creak, and returned to the warmth of their kitchen. Molly followed behind and upon seeing her mother, knew another headache had taken hold. Breakfast had just been placed on the table and the aroma of toast and bacon wafted lazily.

After breakfast, Molly was asked to spend the morning collecting cabbage grass to place in the natural cellar dug into the ground behind the house. Cabbage grass was an unbelievably hearty vegetable with its thick rubbery leaves and, with a bit of dirt laid over top, it could last as long as a turnip, a carrot, or a potato; long enough to see the spring, provided the winter wasn't exceptionally harsh. For the Withers', though, the best thing about cabbage grass was that it was free.

Molly put on an older pair of pants, and smiled when she retrieved her new boots. Though they already looked well worn from her long march through Stankwater, she was still happy to know her father bought them for her.

It took Molly at least five trips to the swamp to collect enough cabbage grass. Though there was a thick blanket of mist, as was usual, and though it was eerily quiet this time of year, each trip was uneventful. As she stooped one final time to pull the wild vegetable from the soggy earth, she heard a voice so horrible it sent shivers down her spine. She looked up and saw Mortimer Weedly glaring down at her with lifeless eyes.

'I'll tell you the problem with cabbage grass,' he said grinning. 'It doesn't last forever.'

Molly stood slowly and took one careful step back.

'We've never had a problem with it,' she said.

'All good things come to pass, Molly,' corrected Mortimer. 'There's a hard winter coming, you know.'

'I know what you're doing,' Molly said.

'Is that so?'

'You're trying to scare me, but it won't work.'

'Really?'

'No,' Molly said, trying to convince herself. 'It won't.'

'I'd say it's already begun,' countered Mortimer, 'and even at this very moment you're wondering if you are going to see your sick mother and your mean father ever again.'

'Mother isn't sick!' declared Molly.

'But indeed she is,' said Mortimer. 'Almost everyday your mother has a terrible and unexplainable pain inside her brain and it is killing her. Isn't that right?'

'She says it's not that bad,' Molly said.

'Well, I suppose not,' said Mortimer, 'if you believe dying isn't that bad. To fade off into a black nothingness, never to be seen again.'

'She says I have nothing to worry about,' Molly said.

'Stupid child,' chortled Mortimer, with a particular glee in his voice. 'She doesn't want to frighten you. But the truth is this: each day your mother is one step closer to death.'

'No she's not!' screamed Molly and she realized that despite trying to be brave, she was becoming more frightened with every poisonous word that dripped out of Mortimer's grim mouth.

'Oh, but she is Molly, and your father is not that far behind,' said Mortimer grinning horribly over the pain he was causing.

'I suspect,' Mortimer added, 'when it comes time for the undertaker to deliver a pine box for your mother's rotting corpse, he may as well deliver a second for your old man.'

'My father is as big and as strong as a knight,' said Molly, 'and if he were here right now he'd tear your crooked arms from your ugly body.'

'Then why don't you scream for him?' asked Mortimer, already knowing the answer.

This far into Stankwater Swamp, no one from the village would hear her screams, and it was unlikely anyone else was close by.

'Yes, Molly, with each puff of his pipe, he exhales his life force. His coughing and his wheezing all point to a tragic end, indeed,' said Mortimer. 'Why, it just might be that he will fall dead before your sick mother. How positively delightful to think of where you'll be then. Alone. Poor. Ugly.'

'Why don't you just leave me alone?' pleaded Molly.

'Because I want what's in that little head of yours!' cried Mortimer. 'I want the Golden Tree and you're going to help me find it!'

'Never!' shouted Molly, and as she did, Mr. Weedly let out a horrible laugh.

Molly was afraid of her own feelings. She couldn't shake the horrible thought of losing her parents and though she believed they were both healthy, everything Mortimer said made sense. It wasn't right that her mother always suffered from headaches and it wasn't right that her father was always coughing. Suddenly, the Tree didn't seem important at all.

'I don't care if I ever find the Tree,' said Molly quietly to herself.

'Surely you know, Molly, that there's more to the Tree than its golden leaves?' prodded Mortimer. 'There is the answer to every question that you could ever want. But you can't have both! Choose the riches of the leaves or the knowledge of the Tree. If you're wondering, yes, it is true: I want to expand my reign, but Molly, aren't there more important things other than Majestica and money? Some questions you yourself want answered, perhaps?'

Molly sat down in the cabbage grass feeling weak from the conversation. She looked up at Mortimer with despair in her eyes and he fed off it.

'Yes, Molly, I know what it is now, don't I?' observed Mortimer. 'You'd rather have your parents well again than anything else. You could ask the Tree how, you know? And it would tell you.'

What a horrible thing to hang over Molly's head. She wanted to curl up and die that very moment, and she wished someone were there to take her away from his torment.

Mortimer took his twisted cane and poked Molly's side to have her full attention.

'So, here's what I think we should do,' he said. 'You help me find the Tree. When we do, you ask it whatever questions you like, and then you hand it over to me. Agreed?'

Again he jabbed her with his cane.

'Don't! That hurts,' Molly sobbed.

'*What? This?*' he said, and he whacked her arm with his cane and it hurt very much. She tried to move to the side, but he stepped in the way and jabbed her again.

'Don't like this, do you? Just help me find the Tree and you'll never see me again,' he said.

Molly tried moving the other way, but he cut her off, and again he smacked her – harder. Molly fell to the side in a heap and curled into a little ball.

'Molly, there's no escaping old Mort, so just tell me where the Tree is. *TELLLL MEEEE!*' he shrieked.

'I don't know where the Tree is!' Molly said half shouting, half sobbing.

'Oh Molly, but you do,' he countered. 'You know the magic and you know the resting place of that Tree. I can smell it on you.'

Molly was heartsick. She didn't know the magic until she'd met Gabrielle and she didn't know anything about the Tree, apart from what she had read in the library. Why did everyone think she was someone special? She was just a poor, ugly girl and all she wanted was to be home. As a tear rolled across her cheek, Mortimer racked her shin with his cane and she winced. The more she thought she wanted him to stop, the more he kept hitting her.

'Sooner or later, that little brain of yours will remember and when it does, I'll be there. I *won't* be stopped!' he said.

Molly felt horrible, like she was going to be sick, but as she closed her teary eyes, thoughts of Gabrielle, Mr. Cayce, Alkaios, and all the woodland creatures came flooding to her. They were smiling at her and she was happy to see them there in her mind. She wished for just one of them to appear and save her from Mortimer Weedly.

'Molly!' said a voice that didn't belong to the grim man with a cane.

She opened her eyes slowly and saw Charlie on the path, holding a rather large stick. Mortimer looked delighted, believing he now had two children at his disposal. Though Charlie still had so much growing to do, Molly thought he looked wonderfully strong at that moment. Perhaps what Mr. Cayce and Alkaios said of him was true.

'Leave her alone!' Charlie shouted, walking directly towards Mortimer.

He turned to face Charlie, and twirled the knotted cane in his bony hand.

'And look who it is,' Mortimer said. 'It's young Charlie whose lonely heart clings to the king's pretty daughter. My, what a pathetic sight.'

'I *said*, leave her alone!' repeated Charlie just as Mr. Weedly swung at him with his cane.

'Look out!' shouted Molly.

Charlie ducked and came back up swinging his own stick and struck Mortimer in the face. It cut him, but where they expected to see blood, the gaping cut seeped a liquid not unlike swamp water.

Mortimer put his hand to his cheek and smiled.

'Good for you, my boy. You're quick to tap into the fear for strength,' he said. 'Good for you. But you're no match for me!'

With an impossible quickness from such a withered and twisted creature, Mortimer swung his cane three times, and three times he hit Charlie's knees, shins, and ankles. Charlie yelped and fell to the ground beside Molly. It reminded her of when she kicked his shins and it wasn't until this moment that she regretted doing it.

Mortimer raised his cane and his eyes narrowed in on Molly, but before his cane struck her, Charlie shielded her from the blow. But it wasn't just one blow. Mortimer must have been amused to see this act of young chivalry, for he laughed and continued striking Charlie's ribs and back.

'Someone help us!' shouted Molly as loudly as she could, but her tiny voice was swallowed up by the swamp's vastness.

'*Someone help us. Someone help us,*' mocked Mortimer, still pummelling Charlie with his cane.

From behind Mortimer, something large and shaggy appeared from the swamp's mist. It was a grizzly bear and Molly was certain it was the same bear from yesterday. It stood on its hind legs and silently observed what was transpiring. Mortimer raised his bony hand again. With this, the bear growled fiercely and Mortimer spun around in horror.

Who's to say what went through his mind when he looked up and saw the grizzly bear's frothing mouth, large stained teeth, and its massive front legs held ready at its sides with huge paws and deadly claws, but Mr. Weedly actually struck the bear with his cane. Perhaps it was an uncontrolled response; perhaps it was because Mortimer was so defiant, or perhaps it was from pure panic. Either way, Mortimer swung a second time, but his hand was met mid air by one of the grizzly's paws. The cane fell to the ground and Mortimer sank to his knees, writhing in pain.

Mr. Weedly flashed his wounded arm. Molly and Charlie were horrified and looked to the ground. There, alone and twitching, Mortimer's white knuckled hand still clutched the cane. The bear had swatted it clean off.

'You'll pay for this,' Mortimer hissed.

Grizz growled, came down off his hind legs, and repeatedly smacked the ground with his paw. Everyone could feel the vibrations. Mortimer snatched up his severed hand and scampered off deep into the swamp. A peace descended upon them. Without paying any attention to Charlie or Molly, the bear turned and went in the other direction, so slowly you'd imagine he was off to look for honey.

Charlie stood, turned to Molly, and helped her to her feet.

'Are you okay?' he asked with sincerity, and Molly's answer came in the form of an unexpected hug. It lasted only long enough for Molly to whisper a thank you in his ear.

Now whether it was because of this thank you, or because he was in a lot of pain, Charlie wanted to put his arm around Molly's shoulder, but he feared embarrassment. Plus, he didn't want to give Molly the wrong idea. Instead, he carried Molly's cabbage grass home for her. He tried to keep his thoughts from wandering, but he could not. Mortimer's hurtful words continued to sting and he seriously wondered why he was dating Priscilla. In fact, for the first time since he and Priscilla started seeing each other, Charlie wasn't remotely nervous she would show up and see him with Molly. *Perhaps that would be a good thing,* he thought.

'You're awfully quiet,' observed Molly. 'Are you in pain?'

'Only a little,' he answered.

'I thought that was wonderfully brave of you, Charlie, if even you did act a little nuts.'

Charlie wasn't used to getting compliments, but when he did, like most people, he was happy to receive them.

'Sorry I wasn't there sooner,' he said.

'You arrived just in time, I'd say.'

'Are you going to tell your father what happened?' asked Charlie.

'No, I don't think so. He worries enough as it is. This is for me to sort out.'

'I'd tell him if I were you,' said Charlie. 'That way you won't have to worry about the Tree.'

'What do you mean?'

'Your father would hunt Mr. Weedly down and rip his legs off if he knew what he did to his little girl,' said Charlie enthusiastically.

Molly chuckled nervously. She recognized the truth in what Charlie had just said, but she really didn't think it was the least bit funny. Molly hated violence, and as much as she wished for Mortimer Weedly to fall from the face of the earth, she did not want to see him hurt. If everything about the magic was true, then somehow Molly could find a way to resolve this whole thing peacefully. Still, she suspected that because of the fear, violence would also take root no matter how positive she kept her thoughts. Hadn't it already? Mr. Weedly beating them with his horrible cane, and then losing his hand, the brawl in Town Centre, and even the stinging bumblers all seemed to point to something very horrible, and something very present. These thoughts made her heartsick and she didn't want her parents involved.

'No,' Molly reaffirmed, 'I'm going to keep it to myself this time.'

'Fair enough,' said Charlie. 'You have to do what you have to do, and so do I.'

'Sounds like you have something in mind,' said Molly.

'Troutin',' said Charlie.

'Trouting?' asked Molly.

'Fly fishing. You know, for trout!' said Charlie becoming more excited. 'Yes, I am going to take my pole down to the river and try to catch me a meal of 'em.'

'My father used to fly fish,' said Molly, 'but he has long since lost interest in it. I'd love to join you, but I have to go for dinner. Who knows, maybe I'll walk by the river afterwards to see how you're making out.'

'I'll be in the Studies,' said Charlie. 'You know. The same path you'd take to go to that old tree you like, but not nearly as far.'

'Oh, you mean Gidot? Sure, I know it,' said Molly.

'Great! I'll see ya if I see ya,' said Charlie.

'Charlie?'

'Yes,' he answered as they arrived in front of Molly's home. 'Thanks again.'

Molly turned and walked up the laneway to her home. When she reached the top step, she set the cabbage grass down, and did her best to brush herself off so as not to look like anything had gone wrong.

Molly placed one hand on the door, but for some reason she didn't open it straight away. She didn't know what she was waiting for, but she found herself unable to walk through the door. Instead, she looked over her shoulder at Charlie walking away, and was pleasantly surprised to see, at this precise moment, Charlie was looking back. He was smiling, too, which made Molly blush, and spurred her to escape inside.

Charlie continued smiling all the way home and his pace quickened as he went. Though he longed to be a knight, he didn't think anything was more enjoyable than running down to his favourite stream and wetting a line. Charlie liked to say: *a bad day's fishing is better than a good day of school.*

Chapter Fifteen
- *Subterranean Abode* -

Mr. Weedly continued down the path through the very heart of Stankwater towards Nordenburgh. He was moving as fast as he could without succumbing to the pain, but he had lost much blood and was on the brink of collapsing. All the while, he was followed by a vulture soaring overhead who thought he'd found himself his next meal.

Mortimer's small heart pounded dryly inside his chest as he shuffled along, and from his stump, a nasty blood-like fluid continued to ooze. He stammered and spat as he went, and though you would guess his endless rant was of the most profane nature, it was not.

'I am healed, I am healed,' he said over and over again while ambling over rotten tree stumps and stepping in rank puddles.

After venturing one hundred times further than Molly even knew existed, he slowed his pace. In front of him was a small hill. It looked as though something was beneath the earth trying to get out.

Standing crookedly atop the hill was a tree so frightful that even the following vulture flew away. If a tree could have arms, then this tree had them – two major branches that drooped out at either side. Each arm bore two knots which looked very much like elbows and two larger knots which formed its swollen palms. On the end of these wart-like hands were long thin branches that comprised its twisted arthritic fingers. There was no head to speak of, but another mass of bulging knots situated where you'd expect the head to be. Still, if you stared at it long enough, the suggestion of a face appeared.

Mortimer climbed the hill and was so exhausted once he reached the top that he leaned against the tree for support. Had he not been such a despicable specimen, you may have felt sorry for him at that moment.

'Dark Lord,' he called with a weak raspy voice. 'Let me in. *Quickly, Lord!*'

There was a sudden rush of air and the earth beneath his feet swelled as if the mound he stood upon had taken a deep breath. Mortimer fell in a pathetic heap and lay motionless for several minutes gasping for air, like a goldfish that had fallen out of its bowl and landed hopelessly on the floor.

'Have you found the Tree?' asked a slow angry voice that seemed to come from everywhere; a voice too deep and frightful to be human.

'I haven't,' sobbed Mortimer. 'But I'm close. So close! Please let me in.'

'You ask for too much!' yelled the voice.

'She doesn't know yet,' gasped Mortimer, 'but when she does, I'll find out. I promise.'

'You bring me nothing, and here you are on Death's doorstep once more.'

'Please!' whispered Mortimer.

Whoever was speaking to Mortimer on that small hill let out a devilish laugh which somehow sparked the ugly tree to life. Its mighty arms creaked at its bulging shoulders and knotted elbows, while its arthritic fingers splayed out. It reached for Mortimer and picked up his limp body. The tree raised Mortimer high in the air as if offering up a sacrifice.

The suggestion of a face in the knots at the top of the tree took on a more apparent shape. From the grooves in the bark, angry cheekbones formed, as well as long, deep, dimples. Then the furrowed form of a forehead appeared. A mouth grew somehow and opened up, large and black. What appeared to be the tree's jaw shifted in jerky movements, like a snake preparing to eat something rather large.

Mortimer's body was brought to that gaping mouth and then stuffed inside. The tree swallowed him whole, and although it had no decipherable eyes, it somehow noticed Mortimer's severed hand abandoned on the ground. With a great creaking, the tree picked up the hand and tossed it in its mouth – the last delicious morsel. The tree let out a thunderous burp and Mr. Weedly slid into its wooden belly.

It was tight at first, wet, and rank with rotten cabbage grass, but Mortimer picked up more and more speed as he continued downwards. Eventually, the tunnel opened up, and Mortimer landed with a groan on a massive pile of decaying vegetation and old garbage. His hand arrived next and hit him on the head before bouncing off to the side.

It was an incredibly large space and was filled with all sorts of things you would not expect to find below Stankwater Swamp. There were many little wooden tables that had been carved by good hands of the trade. On the tables lay rare books that Mortimer had scoured for knowledge of the Golden Tree and for the lost treasures of the seas. What he wanted to know most of all, though, was how to keep the power of the magic in the hands of a few and away from the many.

There was also an odd assortment of jewellery from the towns Mortimer had visited, preaching his lies about his special coal and hard winters. He would smile his crooked smile as old men gave up their treasured keepsakes and women forfeited their wedding rings for small scraps of coal that Mortimer promised would warm their loved ones more than their vain, monetary trappings.

There were also gold coins aplenty stuffed in fine velvet sacs. Mortimer touched and sang to them often. He loved knowing that he had wealth while others suffered; that he enjoyed abundance while others lacked.

Mr. Weedly also had the largest collection of fine chocolates as could be boasted anywhere. It was strange to see such a dark and twisted creature unloading his latest candies from around the world. He would giggle and snort and cram handfuls of the rich chocolates into his mouth, making quite the mess with his chomping and drooling. He would gorge himself until his belly was round and full and he became drowsy, almost intoxicated.

But, there was another collection in that dark lair more horrible than the others. Adorning the walls and shelves and heaped upon the floor were the heads of countless animals that he himself had taken the pleasure to stuff. Lifeless faces of lions, foxes, birds of prey, and bears stared blankly at him, and he stared back. Mortimer despised animals and how they seemed to live so carefree in the world. In fact, Mortimer hated everything to do with nature and that was why he chose to live in the belly of the earth. To him, sunshine was a glaring detestable thing; bird songs were a dreadful pain to the ears, and the colour green? Why, to him, green was the worst colour imaginable.

Apart from Mortimer's prized collections, the cavern was as decorative and as organized as a garbage heap. There were huge piles full of random artifacts Mortimer had stolen along the way. These piles were composed of forgotten dolls and wooden spoons, and the clappers of bells from churches that had fallen down into dust throughout the centuries. There were the lids of clay pots without the pots themselves, people's left shoes (many whom must have puzzled over their whereabouts), clock faces without minute or hour hands, fine gold chains that attached nothing to nothing, and clumps of grey sheep's wool that looked as though it had been carted around for decades without a hope of ever seeing a spinning wheel.

Mortimer rolled off the heap and slowly got to his feet. He looked around frantically, and snatched up his severed hand. He scanned the candlelit cavern and breathed contentedly, for though it all belonged to the Dark Lord, Mortimer lived there and he was relieved to be *home.*

'I am healed,' he said, heading directly to a particular wooden cabinet. Inside was a strange assortment of threads and needles and zippers and buttons. He placed his dismembered hand in his mouth and retrieved one large needle and a spool of thin black twine with his good hand.

With his hand dangling from his mouth, he brought the needle and thread to an old, weathered table. He sat at its chair and spat his hand out, making it land on a shiny plate. He took the needle and pressed it into the table so it stood on its own. Once prepared, he took the loose end of the black thread and soaked it in his mouth to collect the frayed bits into a tidy group that he could put through the eye of the needle. Once threaded, Mortimer sighed and began his horrible task.

He put his stumpy arm on the table, and then placed his severed hand close enough to pass the rusty needle through both body parts. He then took the needle and pierced the skin of his dead hand and continued through the skin and tissue of his stump. He winced upon first puncturing live skin, but with each circular pass, it became more and more numb. After every three stitches, he tightened the string, drawing his severed hand closer to the stump.

Once he finished the underside of his wrist, he flopped the whole fleshy work over to sew the top side. It didn't take long before the final stitch was in place. He pulled on the string one last time, and everything came together nicely. Two final passes through the flesh were made for good measure. He tied a knot and cut the string with his rotten teeth. He raised his arm off the table, but his reattached hand dangled lifeless at his side, as animated as a pork chop.

With his last bit of strength, Mortimer rose from the chair and rummaged through various piles of junk. Random items were being discarded left and right, but when he happened upon a jar marked: *Crushed Pinkleton Bones,* he smiled grimly. He took this jar to a muddy wall that constantly dripped from the swamp above. There was an exposed root that channelled the dripping muddy water like a spigot. Mortimer held the jar beneath it and began to count as he collected each scummy drop.

'One, two, three, four,' he said with a twinkle in his widening eyes. 'Eleven, twelve...and...and? Precious thirteen.'

After collecting this final drop, he placed the jar in his armpit. He looked around as if there might have been someone else there watching him, but being content that he truly was alone, he stuck his long twisted finger inside the jar to stir its contents. When he removed his finger, it dripped with a runny white liquid that had the consistency of curdled milk.

'Mmm,' he said as he suckled his finger clean and then swallowed the rest of his concoction.

'Nothing heals like fairy bones,' he snorted, tossing the jar to the side without caring where it landed, and as he did, the horrible voice from above shook the cavern.

'Fool! Have you forgotten what I have taught so soon?'

Mortimer cringed and cowered.

'Believe you are healed. Know you are healed. Feel you are healed and it shall be so!'

Mortimer nodded to himself and faced the largest heap of junk in his subterranean abode. He smiled to see such an enormous pile of rubble, and of course, the thing that stood atop it: his throne. Mortimer approached the mountain of filthy collectibles and began ambling up one side. Pitch forks and rocking horses and broken church pews shifted, but Mortimer had mastered climbing this pile. Even though he only had one working hand, it wasn't long before he reached the top.

He stood there a moment or two admiring his throne. He believed it was the most wonderfully crafted masterpiece in creation and he was very proud that he had made it himself. The legs of the chair were the bones of a bear he had slaughtered earlier that year. Each leg still had the bear's clawed paws intact and Mortimer grimaced at the irony. The armrests were cleverly crafted using a fat and blood glue to secure hundreds of wings. There were robin wings, blue jay wings, dove wings, owl wings, eagle wings, and vulture wings. Though some of the wings had lost their feathers, exposing the skeletons underneath, Mortimer still thought it was beautiful, artsy even. These feathery armrests sat upon the ribs of forgotten family pets, and where Mortimer's palms rested, he had attached two highly polished wolverine skulls with gaping, fanged jaws.

Mortimer had made a small hole in the top of each skull through which he fed some string. Above the skull, the string was tied to small finger bones. This ensured the string didn't slip through the skull, for the other end of the string was attached to the skulls' lower jaws. This way, Mortimer could pull on the strings and make the jaws clack and snap shut like two dreadful puppets.

The pelt which covered the seat and the backrest was a leopard's and projecting out to the left and the right behind the furry backrest were the racks of countless deer. The top of the backrest was crowned with huge moose antlers and this gave the throne a powerful and distinct appearance. But, as much as Mortimer loved his bony throne, he longed to sit in one wrought with gold; one such as King Alfred's, and he would not rest until he had both the throne of Majestica and the Golden Tree for his own.

'You will have to do for now,' said Mortimer stroking the wolverine skulls, 'but when the time comes, I'll find a special place for you.'

At the base of his throne, Mortimer noticed a white clown's mask speckled with silver flakes that was taken from a foreign circus ages ago. It gave him a most horrible idea. He chuckled with delight as he finally sat himself down and after adjusting himself repeatedly, moving sharp edges this way and that like a pig in fresh straw, he sighed a deep contented sigh and closed his eyes.

'I am healed,' Mortimer said one final time, and the dark voice from above answered: *'Yes.'*

He placed his good hand on his belly, and it wasn't long before Mortimer Weedly began snoring. Then, unbelievably, as he drifted off into a deep, deep, sleep, his recently attached hand twitched with life!

Chapter Sixteen
- *The Studies* -

Apart from his parents, very few things stood in the way of Charlie's fishing. Walking up the path to his house, he stepped as quietly as he could. He opened the front door as quietly as possible, and this was no small feat considering how loudly the rusty springs screeched. Charlie snuck inside and made it all the way to his bedroom without being seen. How ironic. Most of the time Charlie felt as though his parents didn't notice him, yet here he was trying *not* to be seen.

In the far corner of his room rested his fishing gear which he cherished more than anything else he owned. Though his father did not fish, Charlie's Uncle Cecil was a legendary fisherman. It was this uncle who taught Charlie how to fly fish and who had given him his first fly pole. Charlie still had that bamboo pole and he loved it.

'Fly fishing is a special kind of fishing, and a fly fisherman is a special kind of man. They are one with Nature for they appreciate the importance of the tiniest forms of life,' his uncle would say. Merely hearing these words made Charlie feel special, too.

He also remembered his uncle saying: *'A good fly fisherman can out fish any other fisherman,'* and it was true. Though a fish will go after a worm dangled in front of its nose and yap at something shiny like a lure, at the end of the day, fish eat bugs more than anything else. Like an aspiring entomologist, Charlie taught himself all about the insects which fish most often eat and then he learned how to tie imitations using small hooks, bits of fur and feather.

Charlie collected his pole, his hat, his flies, his creel, and he fluttered back outside his home as silently as a dusty miller. Once free, it wasn't long before he was running down the road, and he didn't slow his pace until he was well into the winding dirt path that led to his favourite stream. But his heart did not slow so easily. Such was his excitement, even though Charlie knew from experience this late in the year he had almost no chance of seeing insects that only hatched in the warmer months.

All the same, Charlie enjoyed every little detail of his trek down to the river, and as he focused on the scenery around him, thoughts of Priscilla faded away. Even Mortimer's sharp words softened, quieted, and disappeared. Soon, Charlie would be submersed in the smooth metronomic casting of fly fishing, and all his worrisome thoughts would forfeit their ability to dampen his spirits.

Strolling along, Charlie reluctantly observed the bare trees swaying this way and that. Only a handful of the strongest leaves clung defiantly to their branches, and in the absence of the summer song birds, the near silence was deafening. Fall was in full vigour and the undeniable sign that fishing was almost done for the year was in the song he missed the most – the trill of the red-winged black bird. Overhead, though, came a constant honking from *V* after *V* of Canadian geese who were heading south for the winter. Charlie closed his mouth rather quickly, recalling important advice from his uncle. *'Unless you want a horrible surprise, never go bird watching with an open mouth.'*

'It's going to be a good day!' Charlie suddenly blurted out with thoughts of the magic and the law of attraction popping into his head. Simultaneously, a beautiful breeze touched his face and it reminded him of the honey sweet air that accompanied Alkaios. It was a breeze that seemed to whisper hope, and Charlie hoped it would be warm enough to cause at least a bug or two to hatch. Yes, reaffirmed Charlie, with a warm breeze on a sunny day it would be warm enough. He *was* going to catch fish this day. The more Charlie thought about this, the more he believed it to be true.

The path opened up a bit and the smell of moss filled his soul. He had arrived at the Studies. It was a bit of a marshy place, not swampy, and it smelled lovely and green. The river originated some place in the mountains running cool and quick over stones and through a dense forest, but eventually it poured out here, which, for the most part, wasn't rocky at all. Nor was it shallow, or fast, or bright. It was slow, very slow, the colour of tea, and the trout who lived here were much darker than their mountain cousins. It was also quite deep – so deep, that when Charlie took his long fly pole to see if he could touch bottom, he could not.

It was much more open closer to the river, with only a few scattered trees; just enough to hide behind. There were grasses, weeds, and shrubs, but nothing major to get in the way of a fly fisherman's long graceful casts. It was perfect, but as perfect as this place was, it could also be very dangerous. The banks of the river were undercut further than any other river Charlie knew. In fact, the ground you walked was more like a floating mat than anything else. The roots of the grasses, weeds, and shrubs were so tightly interwoven, that it was suspended on the water below. It was sturdy enough to hold you up in most places, but there were other places that were so soft they would swallow you up should you step on them. You'd sink, for sure, and you'd continue to sink unless someone was there to pull you out. *'This is not a place to fish by yourself,'* Charlie's uncle warned, but what else could Charlie do?

Charlie saw his uncle step into one such hole and disappear before his very eyes. He was just a young boy at the time without the strength to pull him out. Crying, Charlie frantically reached into the hole, but he felt nothing except the cold water and some loosely woven roots. Fortunately, Uncle Cecil didn't panic, and he was able to make his way to an opening in the river without tying himself up in the grasping, clutching roots. Charlie remembered the relief upon seeing his uncle emerge, pole still in hand. But ever since then, Charlie was extra cautious while fishing here.

Charlie looked intensely at the river and to his surprise, he saw a few happy flies dancing just above its surface. Charlie smiled and stared upon the mirror smooth water until he finally saw it – the most glorious sight imaginable. There, just off the far bank, a fat trout came to the surface to gobble down a fly who landed irrecoverably on the stream's surface. The swirl the trout left behind did wonders for Charlie's heart.

Charlie hurried to put his pole together. He propped it under one arm and opened his fly case. Though he had dozens of flies to choose from, today there was one in particular that had to be used

- a Majestic Coachmen. It was just buggy enough, with the right red, white, and brown colour combination to fool a trout – a favourite with fly fishermen all over.

Charlie took his tapered leader and threaded his Majestic Coachmen. He tied a trusted knot, and snipped off the excess line. He removed his pole from his chicken wing, placed his hand firmly on the cork handle, peeled off some line with his free hand, and began the metronomic casting. *Flick, flick, flick, flick.*

The casting was quick at first with only a little line flying through the air, but as Charlie let out more, the pace slowed. *'You must have patience,'* Charlie recalled. *'The more line you have out, the longer you must wait before each flick.'*

To reach the part of the river where the trout had risen, Charlie paid out twenty feet or so. As the line carrying the Majestic Coachmen soared in a figure-eight motion, the rhythm became more relaxed: *flick----flick----flick----flick.*

Charlie finally let his pole drop forward and, in so doing, his fly nestled gently on the water's surface *exactly* where he had seen a trout rise a few moments ago. Charlie held his breath. Had the trout moved on? Did it really come up for a fly? Perhaps it wasn't a fish at all, but an otter.

With the pole in one hand, and the line in the other, Charlie twitched the floating Coachmen ever so gently, just enough to have the fly shift on the water's surface and create the tiniest rings imaginable. *SPLOOSH!!*

The hungry trout returned and bit his fly. Charlie laughed and set the hook. His pole arched as the trout danced and danced trying to shake the fly hook from his mouth. Charlie kept the line tight and pulled the trout to the bank. He then heaved up on his pole, and the trout came flopping out of the water and swung right into his hand.

What a fat and glorious trout this was! It must have been at least thirteen inches long and its colours were magnificent. Along the back of the fish was a dark bank of green peppered with black dots. The rest of the fish's body was a perfect dark silver, save for a colourful rosy band on each side with hints of purple and blue. Charlie thought of all the trout names he knew; this trout's name was the most fitting. It was a rainbow trout, and though there was no pot of gold to be found on one end or the other, it was a treasure all the same.

Charlie admired the trout for only a brief moment and then removed the barbless hook from its mouth. Charlie felt a little sad for the trout knowing that its pumping gills were failing to get oxygen. It would die if not put back soon. As much as Charlie enjoyed a meal of pan fried trout and as much as he knew in the grand scheme of things there was nothing wrong with taking the odd one, most often Charlie let them go. So, as had happened countless times in the past, Charlie kissed it and slipped it back into the cool water to be caught another day.

But that's not to say Charlie was done fishing – no, not in the least. Charlie walked the Studies for the next three hours and he caught too many trout to count. Had someone else told Charlie that they had caught this many trout this late in November, he would have dismissed the tale as another bit of fisherman story telling.

After quite some time of peaceful fishing, Charlie heard a tiny voice growing in the woods. Though Charlie generally didn't like any distractions while fishing, today it was quite comforting. Molly's voice was as buoyant upon the breeze as was his fly upon the water. She appeared and smiled to see Charlie already looking in her direction.

'Be careful where you step,' warned Charlie.

'How's the fishing?' Molly asked.

'You wouldn't believe it if I told you,' said Charlie.

'Can you really believe anything a fisherman says?' asked Molly playfully.

'I was just thinking that,' said Charlie, 'but it's true. The whole way here I was concentrating on a great afternoon's fishing, and it happened. I've let them all go, but I kissed each and every one of them first.'

'You've kissed a bunch of slimy trout?' asked Molly. 'You're gross!'

'Sure have,' said Charlie as he turned back to the river. 'Just watch.'

Charlie began casting again, but whereas just moments ago he couldn't keep his fly on the water without a trout going after it, suddenly there was no action. No, there was not so much of a hint of a fish for a full twenty minutes.

'I don't get it,' said Charlie to an exceptionally patient Molly. 'I've been catching trout since I got here.'

'Sure you have.'

'No, I have. I really have,' said Charlie.

Another ten minutes passed, and still there was nothing to speak of. There were no fish breaking water, and the bugs had disappeared.

'Maybe I'm bad luck,' offered Molly.

Charlie stopped casting and turned to her.

'You're not bad luck at all, Molly. You're the luckiest and sweetest girl I know.'

Charlie was horrified; he didn't mean to say *sweetest* as well, but he did, and there was nothing he could do to take it back. *Nothing.* His face grew hotter and hotter.

'First you save me from Mr. Weedly, and here you are paying me compliments,' Molly said with a smile. 'What's gotten into you, Charlie Gregg?'

This was the second time Molly tested a theory, but what sort of answer she was hoping for, she didn't quite understand. Even, if she did understand the obvious, she was not ready to admit it.

Charlie didn't have an answer, so he resumed casting. He was entirely embarrassed. Had he been able to divine a reason to run away, he would have, but that too would have been obvious.

'I didn't mean anything by that,' said Molly, wanting Charlie to turn back to her. 'I was just teasing.'

Charlie did not turn back, and Molly felt bad. She didn't like making people feel awkward, nor was she one to tease others. Usually *she* was the one being teased and she knew how it felt.

'Ya, ya, ya. Whatever,' was all Charlie offered, noticing for the first time that it's not nice when you're the one being teased.

'I wasn't—' Molly started to explain, but she cut herself off.

She knew she had touched a nerve, but she also knew that there was nothing she could do or say at this moment to make him feel better. Silently, she turned and walked away, and as she left, she seemed to steal the warm air of the afternoon. Charlie noticed it immediately. He looked around almost befuddled that the temperature could change so rapidly, but he dismissed this thought knowing cold weather was more typical for this time of year.

Charlie cast once more for good measure, but the mirror smooth surface now churned because of a sudden increase of wind. Though his exposed hands were now bit by the cold, he twitched his fly along the water's surface this final time hoping to entice the bravest trout in the stream.

A small droplet fell upon one hand, and Charlie noticed that the blue skies had made way for grey clouds. They didn't look like rain clouds, though. They were meaner, greyer, almost like steel, and appeared as though they were stuffed with snow. Charlie couldn't believe it, but that's exactly what it was: the droplet upon his hand was a melted snowflake. Here and there, like dandelion seeds carried upon a breeze, Charlie saw that it was now snowing quite heavily.

Charlie reeled in his line and bit off his fly. He placed it carefully in the case, broke his pole down and, though these tasks took but a few minutes, the sporadic snowflakes had already brought their friends and family, and the ground was turning white.

Charlie took one step and heard the ground crunch beneath his feet. *Impossible*, he thought to himself, but it wasn't long before many of the countless miniature puddles were frozen entirely. He tied up his cardigan to slow the wind's attempts at getting in and two more frost crackling steps later, Charlie saw his breath. He was chilled and he covered his aching ears with his hands. His knuckles felt the punishment immediately, and he had the full length of the river to walk before he reached the safety and cover of the path. Minding his steps, he rushed as best he could.

Overhead, the sky darkened still and the wind and snow increased its intensity. Though once the unexpected flakes were fanciful, the current conditions rivalled any storm Charlie had ever seen. He could have said it was now snowing sideways, and not been called a fibber.

Charlie quickened his pace, but as he leapt over a small patch of frosty moss, both his feet broke through a thin layer of ice and he instantly sank to his waist. As he fell, he threw his rod off to the side so he wouldn't land on it and break it, but this left him with nothing to pull himself out. The ice cold water seeped into his boots and through his pants. He kicked frantically, but this only proved to suck him further down. He looked around again for something – *anything* – to use to pull himself out, but there was nothing. Not a tree, not a shrub, not even so much as a branch was within his grasp. Further, further, further he sank till his arms were the only thing preventing him from slipping under completely.

'Molly!' he yelled, hoping she hadn't made it too far down the path.

'M⊖LLY!' he yelled even louder, praying to hear her respond, but her comforting voice had long since disappeared.

If only he hadn't been embarrassed earlier or too proud, then perhaps he would have been listening to Molly sing a Christmas carol instead of sinking to his death. But, the only sounds he could hear were the heckling winds and the older trees crying as their arm-like branches snapped off.

The freezing water gripped Charlie's body. He shook violently and his teeth rattled in his head. He could feel the roots beneath the surface clutching at him like the fingers of a scaly monster trying to pull him down. Further he sank and his grasping hands slid towards the hole, leaving perfect furrows similar to ploughed fields. Whether he squirmed to keep his head from dipping below the icy surface, or whether he remained perfectly still, Charlie continued to sink, and the moment his chin touched the frigid water, he lost all hope.

He was moments away from drowning, but just as his mouth and nose dipped below the surface, a hand reached out to him. Charlie looked up, and there, standing before him with a fiendish smile, was a Morrukk. Charlie only recognized him as a Morrukk because of the unmistakable height and lanky limbs, but this freakish shape was dressed in a clown's costume and its face was painted – red circles on the cheeks, black teardrops below its masked eyes, and a characteristically large foam nose that bulged forward as if hoping to fall off.

Charlie thought he must have been hallucinating, but the long skinny hand grabbed hold of Charlie's frostbitten fingers, and began to pull. For the briefest of moments, Charlie was relieved until he heard a horrible sound behind him. Charlie turned his head a little and saw another Morrukk clown – laughing. It continued laughing, as a third appeared. Then there was a fourth, a fifth, and like a nightmare too horrible to describe, Charlie was completely surrounded by Morrukks. How positively frightful they looked. They all wore seemingly happy costumes, but no amount of make-up could hide their terrible expressions.

This wasn't joyous laughter, though, not like a child's laugh. It was darker and spoke of hate and fear and anger and jealousy. Charlie looked up to the Morrukk whose hand he still held, and eyes as lifeless as Mr. Weedly's stared back from behind the silver-speckled mask.

Suddenly, the masked Morrukk let go of Charlie's hand and he once again began to sink. He arched his head back to lift his mouth, prolonging the inevitable for a few seconds longer, but the Morrukk towering over him stepped on Charlie's head with his large clown shoe. He stuffed him down into the hole with such force that even Charlie's outstretched hands were submerged.

Charlie had taken a large breath, but he believed it to be his last. There, under the water, he exhaled as slowly as he could. After what seemed to be an eternity, he sensed vibrations which he guessed were the Morrukks leaving, now satisfied with their awful murder. Charlie let out the last bit of air in his burning lungs and made one final attempt to grab something solid. And there it was – suddenly, there *was* something there! Something like a branch. Though Charlie was on the brink of death, he grabbed hold and tried to heave himself towards the light above, but he could not. He was too weak. Somehow, though, that branch began to move and Charlie held on for dear life. Up and up it moved and Charlie felt the underwater roots loosening their twisted grip as he neared the surface. He continued to hang on until his hands became even colder, as if exposed to a wind.

It *was* the wind, for no sooner did his hands feel it, than his arms did, too. Then the draft hit the top of his hair, his forehead, and then his eyes, cheeks and chin. Charlie coughed violently upon being able to breathe again. He tried to understand what was happening, but he could discern nothing but the blurry white of the storm and a massive dark shape attached to the branch he still grasped.

Charlie continued to hold on until his chest, stomach, legs, and feet all cleared the hole. Though he was breathing, another danger loomed imminent. He would surely freeze to death if left in the cold much longer. Shivering uncontrollably, Charlie whispered *thank you* and then all that was bright around him faded to black.

Chapter Seventeen
- *A Special Breakfast* -

Charlie didn't know for how long he had blacked out, or where he was when he first awoke, but he did know the first sound he heard upon awaking was the one he wanted to hear most of all.

'Charlie?' said Molly, noticing he'd moved a bit in his sleep. 'You awake?'

'Uhhn,' was all Charlie could say at first, but as his eyes opened, and as the room took shape before him, he mustered an 'uh-huh.'

'How do you feel?' asked Molly, tucking the blankets around Charlie.

Charlie looked around the room and didn't recognize anything, until he saw a pair of shiny red rubber boots in the corner.

'Am I at your place?' Charlie asked.

'Yes, you are.'

'How did I get here?'

'Oh, Charlie you won't believe it,' said Molly. 'I was behind my house, closing the cellar to keep the snow out. Then from the forest came a thrush of birds followed by Mr. Cayce. I asked him what he was doing, but before he could say anything, from behind *him* a bear appeared. It was that grizzly bear who cut off Mr. Weedly's hand. Anyway, on the back of Grizz was *you!*'

'What?' asked Charlie, still feeling foggy and confused.

'Grizz carried you back from the river,' reiterated Molly. 'Mr. Cayce pulled you out of the hole and the bear carried you back.

Isn't that incredible?'

'Mr. Cayce was there?' Charlie asked.

'Yes, and he told me all about it. He arrived as the Morrukks were standing around waiting for you to drown, but he and the bear chased them away.'

Charlie sat up in the bed a bit and as soon as the covers fell from his shoulders, Molly pulled them back up over him.

'You must stay warm,' Molly said.

'How did I get out of the hole?' asked Charlie.

'I told you already: Mr. Cayce pulled you out.'

'Can't be,' refuted Charlie. 'Someone stuffed a branch in the hole, I held on, and then they pulled me out.'

Molly laughed gently.

'That branch was Mr. Cayce's antler,' she said.

'Humph,' tutted Charlie. 'Pretty clever.'

'Pretty clever, indeed,' said Molly. 'Mr. Cayce saved your life and I am ever so happy for it.'

Molly looked at Charlie as if she had something to add, but his kind eyes interjected to reassure her all was well. His silent smile said he was no longer embarrassed over what he'd said in the Studies. Charlie knew Molly was the nicest person he had ever met and he realized it was better she know it than not, but the kind look faded as quickly as it had come. At that moment, Charlie recalled the frightful smiles of the Morrukks dressed as clowns.

'I've told Gabrielle about what happened in Stankwater, too,' Molly added.

Molly stood up to leave. She wanted to leave him alone with his thoughts, but she only made it as far as the door before Charlie spoke to her.

'Where are you going?' he asked.

'Nowhere,' answered Molly. 'Just giving you time to rest.'

He didn't want to admit it, for what knight would ever admit to being scared, but he *was* scared by his memories of those awful smiles on those painted faces. He didn't want to be left alone.

'Don't go,' he urged. 'Not yet.'

Molly returned to the stool by her bed.

'Do my parents know where I am?' he asked.

The question, which was more than fair and a little late in coming, made Molly uncomfortable. She knew the answer, and it was hurtful. She knew her mother had gone to Charlie's as soon as possible and Molly also knew his parents didn't seem to care, so long as he was at least alive. No wonder he fished as often as he did.

'Well, as long as they know I'm here,' said Charlie, 'then I guess I won't get in trouble.'

'Oh, Charlie, I thought I had it rough,' said Molly. 'I am so sorry.'

'That's okay,' replied Charlie, sitting up in the bed to get her full attention. 'None of it will matter when I am a famous knight defending Princess Molly,' he said brightly.

He was stronger than his circumstances. Such a simple gesture, and yet, as reassuring to Molly as anything else he could have done.

'How about it, Molly?' Charlie asked. 'Would you sing just one song for your knight?'

'Of course. Ahem. Lord Gregg, of the order of the Knights Triumphant, tell me thy favourite song and may I be blessed with an angelic voice to do it justice.'

Charlie and Molly chuckled as he pulled the covers up to his chin.

'Whatever, you pleaseth,' struggled Charlie, 'so long as it maketh his royal, err, um, highness sleepethly soundly.'

Charlie's Old English dialect, though rough upon the ears, made Molly smile. As Charlie closed his eyes, she began singing and she didn't stop until her brave knight fell fast asleep. There wasn't a babe in all Majestica who slept as well as he did that evening.

It was not until late the next morning that Charlie awoke from his slumber. Where yesterday there was but a small stool and a singing princess beside him, today there was a larger, more comfortable chair with a sleeping Molly.

As if on cue, Molly woke a few moments later, stretched, and yawned, oblivious to the fact that Charlie was observing her every move.

'Good morning, sunshine,' said Charlie. 'How are you feeling?'

'How are *you* feeling?' she countered.

'Couldn't be better,' Charlie said, 'but I am awfully hungry.'

'I'd say you are. You slept the whole day yesterday,' said Molly. 'Don't worry, though, I'll fix you up.'

In an instant, she was up and scurrying around the kitchen. Charlie was a little slower to rouse than she, but once he had shaken off the cobwebs, he ventured to the kitchen and smiled to see Molly preparing breakfast, for *him*.

'Here,' she said pulling a chair out from the table. 'I've been instructed to make sure you're still taking Genevieve's cold remedy. Want some of my special tea to wash it down?'

'Special, is it?'

'Why yes it is,' confirmed Molly. 'Of my own creation, no less. Are you sure you're feeling all right?'

'Couldn't be – *eckh* – better,' forced Charlie, gagging on Dubois' concoction, shooting his eyes to Molly hoping her tea was ready.

Charlie sat as Molly poured the boiling water over her special brew, and within a minute, she presented it to him. Though it was still quite hot, Charlie lapped at it without delay to get the awful taste out of his mouth.

'So, I've been here a day and a half?' asked Charlie.

'You have,' Molly said.

'Any word from my folks?' asked Charlie, surely believing that after another day they would have asked about him, but the hesitation in Molly's response was all the answer he needed.

His parents had not called on him and his heart suffered for it.

'Now, we don't have much, but I can offer you ham, eggs, and toast with jelly if you like,' said Molly as pleasantly as she could, trying to prevent Charlie's thoughts from wandering.

'Is it raspberry jelly?' Charlie asked.

'Of course it is,' answered Molly, placing some toast directly on the woodstove, several slices of ham in a frying pan, and scrambling a few eggs all at the same time.

Shortly thereafter, she put the meal on the table, and Charlie dived in as if it was the first breakfast he had ever had the pleasure of eating.

'Can I get you anything else?' asked Molly

'No fanks,' mumbled Charlie with a ham-stuffed mouth. 'Viss's de-wicious,' he added stuffing toast in as well. His cheeks swelled like a peanut-hoarding chipmunk.

There were very few words spoken during the meal, but Molly continued providing more tea, toast, ham, and eggs, even though every time she offered, Charlie politely said *no fanks*. Nevertheless,

Charlie devoured all that was made for him originally and all that was made for him thereafter. When he could not force in another crumb, he leaned back, and rubbed his belly, which now protruded a wee bit.

'Full?' asked Molly, observing his new little potbelly.

'Couldn't eat another bite if my life depended on it,' he answered.

Charlie knew that Molly's folks didn't have much money and still she had given him everything she could. Charlie was a little worried her father might scold her for giving Charlie so much of the precious groceries, yet despite this concern, he was flattered. He was flattered that Molly didn't send him home right away; he was flattered and impressed with how generous she was; and, most importantly, he was flattered that she took the time to cook him a meal and brew her special tea.

'Are you sure I can't get you anything else?' Molly pressed, 'because as soon as you have your strength back, I am to take you to the circus.'

'What circus?' asked Charlie, again recalling the dreadful clown clad Morrukks that stood around him laughing as he slipped into the icy black abyss. He already knew the answer. He just needed to hear it.

'The Morrukks have come to town with a large circus,' confirmed Molly, 'and they've set up games, and exhibition tents, and food vendors, and the whole works. They're calling it the Nordenburgh Circus and all of Majestica is in a frenzy to see it.'

'When did this happen?' asked Charlie.

'The caravans and tents and horse-drawn spectacles all arrived the evening they almost...well...you know, but everything wasn't set up until yesterday. Gabrielle said we should go today, but if you're not up for it, I'll tell you about it when I return.'

Charlie stood and looked at Molly as if to say *yeah right*.

'Thanks so much for taking care of me,' he said, 'and thanks for this special breakfast. It was fit for a king.'

'Or a knight!' returned Molly and then she quickly tidied up.

She then retrieved one of her father's toques and a sweater so Charlie wouldn't freeze on the way to the circus. She thought he looked adorable in the oversized clothes.

Once they were both dressed for the weather, which had only slightly lifted after the original storm, they walked out the front door. They almost tripped over themselves, though, when they saw who happened to be walking by at that very moment.

'So *there* you are, Charlie,' spat Priscilla standing on the roadway dressed in her perfect, white winter furs. 'Spending more time with Molly, I see.'

Charlie was surprised at first, but even more surprising was a new found confidence. Where and when he came across this, he didn't know, but he looked Priscilla straight in her pretty eyes.

'Yes, Priscilla,' he began coolly, 'I *have* been at Molly's since nearly drowning, and she and her family have cared more for me in the past day and a half, than you have in our entire—'

Charlie cut himself off. He could see Priscilla already knew what was coming, and he didn't want to be too hurtful.

Molly stood in silence. She was somehow comforted by Charlie's words, but she didn't show it. After all, Priscilla had a heart like anyone else. Molly knew this must have been terribly painful for her. Perhaps even more so considering Priscilla must have grown accustomed to getting her own way.

'Are you thinking of breaking things off with me?' hissed Priscilla in a most disbelieving way. 'For *that*?'

'Oh no, Priscilla,' Charlie said calmly. 'I'm doing this for me.'

Priscilla was beside herself. Behind her outward anger was an inevitable heartache, and she ran off hoping her streaming tears would remain unseen.

Molly stood for another moment without saying a word. She wondered if Charlie doubted his decision and if he had thought about it beforehand. If he had thought about it before, then why did it take him so long to make up his mind? Molly suspected she knew the answers – it had to do with fear. Fear of what, she did not know, but she did know this: Charlie was much better at facing his fears than she was.

'Come on, Molly,' said Charlie without hesitation. 'We've got a circus to go to.'

Chapter Eighteen
- *The Nordenburgh Circus* -

The walk to Gabrielle's was a frosty one, but beautiful all the same. The snow that had fallen for the past two days left Majestica blanketed in a white freshness. Each and every branch on each and every tree was covered, giving their former bleak and skeletal arms a white, soft flesh, not unlike a baby's. The evergreens, too, were all sagging under the weight of the sticky snow. The ground was so covered that small shrubs and logs had all but vanished, leaving only subtle mounds to prove they still existed. Molly loved the snow; it made her think of Christmas, the happiest holiday of all.

They arrived at Gabrielle's and she emerged from her warm home before they could even knock.

'Perfect timing,' Gabrielle said. 'You gave us all quite the scare, Charlie. How are you feeling?'

'Oh, I'm doing okay,' Charlie said. 'Thanks to the princess here.'

If Molly's cheeks weren't already rosy red from the cold, you would have seen her blush from his compliment.

'Good,' said Gabrielle. 'We're off, then.'

The three of them walked to Town Centre enjoying nature's splendour and they were not alone. They were joined by hoards of Majesticans all heading in the same direction and they were speaking in excited tongues.

'My, I haven't heard of anything like this before.'

'I just can't wait to see it.'

'I'm told they have the most remarkable oddities.'

'Surely, this is the best thing to have happened to Majestica.'

'Guess we all had the Morrukks wrong. And to do it all for free. What generosity!'

The crowd entering Town Centre was thicker than a herd of cattle. Despite Molly's sense of foreboding, she could not help but be amazed with what she saw before her. As large as the town square was, it seemed small with the countless people and barbeques and tables and tents which were hung in fantastic colours. Set against the snow's perfectly white background, these tents, striped in reds, blues, greens, and purples, were dazzling to look at. Equally impressive was the glorious smell of foods they'd never before tasted; it was as if you could actually pull the aromas out of the air.

Morrukks were handing out fresh popped popcorn, exotic chocolates, sausages, and sweet wine with the promise of tantalizing everyone's taste buds. Here and there, smoke billowed from various tents and there were countless fires contained in little stoves that attracted those silly enough to venture outside without mittens or gloves. As the trio walked by one such fire, they noticed it had a unique smell, but it wasn't wood that was burning, it was *coal*, and those gathered round were speaking highly of the heat it gave off.

All throughout the square, men laughed and women giggled, passing one friendly face after another. To Molly, it felt like Christmas. Such was the overall joy, companionship, and high spirits of the crowd. Even the terrible Morrukks seemed filled with contentment. To see them with their bright costumes and happy painted faces as they juggled, walked on stilts, breathed fire, and played various instruments, you would not believe that a solitary one of them had any purpose other than bringing merriment to Majestica.

Molly smiled despite herself and Gabrielle seemed distant, as if a spell had been cast over them. Charlie, alone, seemed immune. He did not so easily forget the Morrukks stuffing him down the frigid hole, and was disappointed Molly and Gabrielle could have been so easily distracted.

'Excuse me, but aren't you two forgetting something?' asked Charlie.

'Quite right,' Gabrielle said softly. 'I'm sorry, Charlie.'

'Me too, Charlie,' said Molly. 'I am sorry. I have just never seen anything like this.'

'Look it,' continued Charlie, 'these Morrukks didn't come here to entertain us. They are after the Tree and they are working with Mortimer Weedly. Any of this ring a bell?'

'Yes, Charlie,' agreed Gabrielle, 'you're right. I think it best if we split up to see as much as we can.'

'Well, I'm not leaving Molly's side,' said Charlie. 'One of them almost got me two days ago and I am not about to let them try anything on her.'

Gabrielle and Molly smiled at once.

'What?' asked Charlie, wondering why his last, perfectly realistic comment brought about those smiles.

'Oh nothing,' said Gabrielle. 'That's a wise decision. You and Molly see what you can see, but be careful.'

Gabrielle headed towards some tent which caught her attention, while Molly and Charlie jostled through the crowd. They walked by a Morrukk on enormous stilts and Charlie had a mind to trip him. They walked past the Juggler, the Puppeteer, the sausage stand and all seemed quite right with the world. Everyone was truly happy and it was hard not to get drawn into the excitement that filled the air.

'Want some candy?' asked one Morrukk, holding out two glorious bundles of joy.

'Is it poisoned?' scowled Charlie, pulling Molly away from the pink clouds of sugary goodness.

All the vendors and acts were around the outside of the town square, but the exhibit tents were in the middle, and they all promised to dazzle the audience with some curious oddity. Each tent was adorned with a wonderful canvass painting attesting to the intriguing treasures inside, and each tent had a happy Morrukk bidding the passersby to enter.

One canvass read: Howling *Wolf Boy Dances to a Timberland Drum*. Another read: *Singing Merman from the Aegis Sea*. There was another which read: *Giant Brothers of Wesdenburgh Stand Eight Feet Tall*, while still another promised: *Chupacabra Capturado y Vivo – an Old World Monster*.

Though Molly was anxious to take it all in, she suddenly sensed something was very wrong. The energy of those entering the tents was nothing less than incredible, but upon exiting, they appeared to be in some sort of stupor. It was as though everyone had consumed a toxic drink inside that sucked the energy out of them. The expressions of those leaving the tents were not entirely vacant, though, for they bore shadows of shock, amazement, horror, and dulled delight. Molly couldn't quite tell what these people were feeling or thinking, but there was one thing for certain: after a few short sobering steps, as mindless as tumbleweeds, they fell towards the next attraction.

'Charlie, if we are truly going to find out what this circus is all about, we are going to have to see what these people are seeing,' Molly said. 'So take a look, pick one, and we'll both go in.'

Charlie looked around, and the sign reading *The Giant Brothers of Wesdenburgh* caught his attention more than any other.

'Imagine that, Molly, eight feet tall! It's the shortest line, too.'

Molly and Charlie joined the line which seemed to be the natural starting point for all the others. Within ten minutes, they were inside and it was much warmer – not due to any fire, but because of the crowded living furnaces emitting their own heat.

At the front was a makeshift stage with wonderful red curtains sewn with golden threads. Not being able to see anything right away increased the excitement. To the right of the stage was a Morrukk dressed more modestly than those entertaining outside.

'Gather round,' he said. 'Make room for those behind you. Come in. Come in. Come in and see the Giant Brothers of Wesdenburgh.'

People packed themselves together like porcupine quills, but Molly and Charlie were able to weasel their way to the front. The jostling spectators made Molly and Charlie recall the crowd eager to buy Mr. Weedly's coal.

'Draw near. Show's starting in three minutes,' said the Morrukk. 'Draw near, draw near.'

The tension was building.

'Come in, come in. Show starts in two minutes.'

The people behind them continued to jockey for a better vantage point and in so doing, pushed Molly and Charlie closer to the stage.

'Draw near, draw near,' he called again more passionately. 'Draw near to see the Giant Brothers of Wesdenburgh. The show starts in one minute!'

The pushing eased off a bit as someone, somewhere must have finally come to their senses, and prevented anyone else from entering the small tent. Molly thought the seams were about to blow apart as this final minute passed painfully slowly.

'Sh, now,' soothed the Morrukk and suddenly a wave of hushing swept though the tent until all was eerily silent. The lanterns dimmed and only the stage before them had a light upon it.

'Ladies, and Gentlemen, boys and girls, thank you for coming to our humble circus,' began the Morrukk. 'I promise you will not be disappointed for you are about to see something most spectacular. I can tell by looking at your faces that many of you do not believe it is possible, that a human frame can grow to such a freakish stature, but behold, I give you the Giant Brothers of Wesdenburgh!'

With this, the Morrukk pulled a rope dividing the curtains in front of the stage, and there they were: two men who were two feet taller than the tallest man in Majestica. If not for seeing them, no one would have believed it to be real. The two giants wore some sort of foreign hunting outfit and they both carried a mighty bow with a single arrow. Molly took particular notice of their colossal bows – massive, yet proportionate to the two men holding them. Molly didn't think even Knight MacDonald would be able to draw one of these back to fire it.

Suddenly, the two brothers placed the arrows in the guides and began to pull the bow string back. The thick bows creaked so loudly, it sounded like they were about to explode under their own pressure. Further and further they bent until they were fully cocked and aimed towards the heavens. Even for two men such as these, Molly could tell they were straining as their arms began to tremble and beads of sweat appeared upon their brows.

Without warning, both brothers changed their stance and pointed their bows directly at Molly and Charlie: a deadly arrow for each of them. Molly's and Charlie's eyes locked with the heckling black orbs of the gigantic brothers. Then, as the freakish men stared back at their would-be victims, their full-lipped mouths curled slightly on one side, giving a hint of smile.

Some people gasped behind Molly and Charlie, but no one moved to intervene. Everyone was frozen with fear. The two brother's faces then shone with the largest smiles imaginable. Still staring directly at Molly and Charlie, the two brothers winked at exactly the same time and released their arrows. Molly and Charlie didn't have time to turn, run, or even close their eyes. Instead, they saw the bows snap back to their former shape with an unmistakable *twang*. They instinctively looked to their chests, expecting to see the back half of the arrows sticking out of their bodies, but they did not.

Whirling with funk, Molly and Charlie looked up to the stage and the two gentle giants were smiling warmly and holding out a fistful of red carnations. The arrows had somehow turned into bouquets – gifts for Molly and Charlie from the Giant Brothers of Wesdenburgh.

All the spectators exhaled together causing an audible *whoosh*. Cheering ensued immediately, as the two brothers took one step off the stage and stuffed the flowers into Molly and Charlie's shaking hands. In an instant, they were back on the stage posing in ways that accentuated their stature. Behind a startled Molly and Charlie, the Majesticans went from cheering to commenting, and then from commenting to insulting.

'My goodness, they are rather large, aren't they?'

'Oh yes. Too large, I'd say.'

'That's just not right.'

'I wonder what they eat.'

'I don't know, but there must have been a lot of it,' and a chorus of laughter swept across the tent.

'What freaks!' said a fourth, loud enough that the brothers heard. The giants looked sternly in the direction of the gentleman who said it. There was an uncomfortable pause in the laughter, but then, unbelievably, both brothers smiled. Molly thought this was quite peculiar. You'd think that such comments would have been hurtful, but the giants were unaffected. To the contrary, the comments were well received and suddenly there was a rash of insults.

'Ha!' laughed another and another. 'They *are* freaks! *Look!* Ha, ha, ha!' The more comments that were made, the more the Wesdenburgh Brothers smiled, the more they laughed, and the more they posed.

Charlie looked to the Morrukk and saw he loved the spectacle as much as anyone. Charlie grabbed Molly's coat sleeve, pulled her to the other side of the tent, and then back outside to the white, fresh, coolness.

'Well?' said Charlie. 'How about it?'

'I don't know what to say,' answered Molly. 'I don't feel good inside, and yet I'm curious to see what's in the other tents.'

'I didn't like that stunt they pulled,' said Charlie. 'I thought I was done for. The crowd sure seemed to like it, though.'

Molly and Charlie shuffled along in the snow unaware their feet were guiding them towards the very next tent.

'I wonder what it means?' asked Charlie.

'Maybe we should see just one more,' offered Molly.

'Just one more then,' agreed Charlie.

They looked up simultaneously and found themselves in another line up. Molly looked past the queue, towards the tent, and saw the words: *Singing Merman from the Aegis Sea.* Her eyes lit up as she devoured the life-size canvass that was painted with all the colours of the rainbow. Sitting upon a long, finely carved chair in front of an amazing sunset, the merman had a vibrant green tail and fins painted in such a way that the canvass still looked wet; his muscular torso was bronzed, and his long brown locks of hair lay full on his wide shoulders. It was glorious.

'This can't be real, can it?' asked Molly.

'There's only one way to find out, isn't there?' remarked Charlie.

Molly and Charlie were inside the tent before too long, and as before, they positioned themselves in front of the curtains. The excitement at this exhibit was twice what it was in the last, but there was no Morrukk bidding people to enter, nor announcing when the show would begin.

The lights dimmed as before, and the audience quieted themselves. There was nothing remarkable for five minutes, and the crowd grew impatient, but as soon as their irritated voices rose, another sound descended upon them. It did not seem to be a human voice, and from where it came could not be determined – like a sea monster's haunting cry bubbling up from the abyss.

Molly had no other experience to compare it to, but this musical wailing gave her goosebumps. It reminded her of a storm coming across an ocean. The painful notes swelled momentarily, and then softened, only to swell a little bit higher the next time, carrying tense anticipation.

Suddenly, the curtains fell to the floor and there upon the dimly lit stage was the source of the horrible song. What Molly saw was nothing like the painting. The fine chair was little more than an old weathered box; the sunny background was, instead, a burlap sheet, and the merman himself was thin, gaunt and fettered. There were two grisly scars where you expected to see ears; his hair was dry and matted, and oozing sores covered much of his grey upper body while the rest of his skin was flaky, scabby, and crusted from dried sea salt. Even his tail and fins were dry. Charlie understood what this meant moreso than Molly. He recognized that the sloughing scales, beaten fins, and dull colour were all signs of early decay. The merman's pumping lungs heaved with each strained breath and Charlie knew the merman would surely die if not returned to the sea soon. *SPLOOSH!* An unseen hand pulled a release, and a bucket of water poured from overhead, drenching the merman. Someone laughed off stage.

It was not long before Molly felt tears swelling within her. She couldn't help herself. It was't just Molly who felt it, though. No one was immune to the power of his suffering, and Molly heard crying all around her. Even Charlie had a solitary tear rolling down his cheek.

The sorrow of the distant storm had arrived, and the merman's thunderous tones now cried out anger and hatred. Molly's tears subsided instantly. If you were not there to hear it, you would have dismissed the notion that any voice could so sway people's emotions. His voice was both the cry of dolphins and the angry blow from Triton's conch.

Everyone stood in complete horror as he continued to call out his chorus. He couldn't offer a solitary pleasing note, yet there he sat with tears upon his cheeks singing as hard as he could. Everyone pitied him. It was as if he sang of his former beauty – before he was drudged up from the deep, robbed of his ears, and put on display.

Suddenly, he raised his hands upward as if pleading for help, and then as mysteriously as the curtains had dropped earlier, so up they rose to the ceiling. His very last note filled the air for what seemed to be an eternity. Finally, it softened ever so slightly, and then it was gone with the cracking of a whip and a cry of pain!

The crowd inside the tent silently ushered themselves back outside, but the haunting voice still resonated in their perfect ears. They could not shake the image of the merman whose pain was beyond compare.

Molly and Charlie moseyed along in silence trying to make sense of the two bizarre exhibits they had just seen. It perplexed

Molly to no end. What could it possibly mean? The Morrukks entertaining around the town square were still as happy as children on Christmas morning, but the exhibits inside the tents were horrible, and still people seemed to be enjoying them both equally. Perhaps the general gaiety of the town square somehow made the exhibits tolerable. Perhaps such a contradiction of good-natured joy set beside ill-conceived exhibitions was the way of the world outside Majestica. Perhaps, thought Molly, it was a way to spread the fear.

The more Molly considered the circus in this light, the more sense it made. Not only was it a way to spread the fear, it was the *perfect* way. *But fear of what?* questioned Molly. It didn't seem to have anything to do with the Golden Tree; still, she knew in her heart it must be connected.

'So how are things going?' asked a familiar voice.

Molly looked up and saw Gabrielle smiling down at her. This was just the person Molly needed to see.

'Oh, Gabrielle! I've seen the most horrible things!' said Molly.

Gabrielle looked at Charlie and saw he too was upset. Neither one of them had been ready to see what they had seen. No one in Majestica was ready for it. Still, the excitement continued to grow as the sun set on the Nordenburgh Circus. Only time would be able to explain what it all meant, and time was not on their side.

Chapter Nineteen
- Lost and Found -

The next day was darker than the day before and the white snow had been muddied along the roads and laneways of Majestica. Molly, Charlie, and Gabrielle met after breakfast and headed back to Town Centre. They hoped to see more exhibits before discussing the previous day, but the circus had packed up and withdrew in the middle of the night. In its wake, there was nothing left behind but confused and frustrated Majesticans. Some citizens couldn't make it the day before for one reason or another and complained it wasn't fair their friends saw the circus and they did not. Still others were so stung with intrigue and curiosity, they returned to see it all again today. All of them were uncharacteristically agitated and many were grumbling and stomping around like spoiled children who have been too finely doted upon.

In the middle of the town square was an abandoned horseless boxcar with a sign that read: *A storm has hit Nordenburgh. We must return to our homes.*

Upon reading it, most Majesticans expressed incredible displeasure and some even cursed the good name of Marcus MacDonald.

'That storm will come to Majestica. Just you wait.'

'Can't say Mr. Weedly didn't warn us.'

'I hope we have enough wood to last us through.'

'If not for that crabby MacDonald, we wouldn't have had to

worry about wood.'

'Whatever are we going to do?' cried an elderly lady.

The atmosphere was positively dismal, and it was obvious to Molly, Charlie, and Gabrielle what had happened. The Nordenburgh Circus came, planted a seed of fear, and left the weeds behind to grow and flourish and choke out hope and happiness.

After a few moments of contemplation, Molly, Charlie, and Gabrielle headed back home.

'I am so very confused,' said Molly. 'I have a thousand different thoughts whirling in a thousand different directions and yet the one thing that keeps coming back to me is Alkaios.'

'Alkaios?' remarked Gabrielle.

'Yes,' said Molly, 'I want to see him again.'

As if in response to Molly's request, a plump chickadee landed on her shoulder, whispered something in her ear, and flew off.

'What was that all about?' asked Charlie.

'She said we're to follow the path beyond the orchard,' answered Molly.

'Into Bokwus Forest? Great. I can't wait,' replied Charlie.

'Alkaios is there waiting for us,' answered Molly.

'Did she say when we're to go?' asked Gabrielle.

'Immediately!'

The three were off to pack for what they expected to be a long day. Only an hour or so had passed, and they met up in the orchard to begin their trek to Bokwus Forest – further than they had ever ventured from home.

They reached the small clearing where they had seen Alkaios before and continued into the yawning mouth of Bokwus on the far side. It was a good thing they brought their warmest winter clothes because the moment they left the orchard, the weather turned again. The wind did not have the same bite in the cover of the woods, but soon the snow fell in great droves.

'I wonder how much further we have to go,' asked Molly.

'I don't know, Molly,' Gabrielle replied.

They walked and walked and walked some more. Everything was strange to them and the woods were frightful. There was a constant babbling under the wind, like a stream, but they came across not even a creek. The odd sound was soon dismissed, though, as the path before them vanished with the heavy snowfall. There was no one to point them in the right direction and it wasn't long before they realized they were lost. Making things worse, they were very cold.

They continued walking in what they thought was the straightest line possible. Someone walking behind them though, like a huntsman or a tracker, would have been able to point out that they were hardly making any progress at all. Molly wanted one of her woodland friends to appear from the snowy background and say: *follow me,* but there was no such luck. No signs of hope.

They walked for another mile or so and Molly got an idea; a most wonderful and glorious idea. Why she hadn't thought of it before, she didn't know. Why any of them didn't think of it, in fact, was a bit of a mystery, but suffice it to say, it is easy to forget about the magic when things are looking down.

'Aha!' exclaimed Molly.

'What are you *ah ha-ing* about over there?' asked Charlie, who was the coldest as his winter clothes were the oldest and most worn.

'Why can't we use the law of attraction to find our way?' asked Molly. 'If it can be used to give us everything we want, then why can't it work for this?'

'It should work,' said Gabrielle, 'but it hasn't yet. I've been trying.'

'Have you captured the feeling of it?' asked Molly remembering that it is the *feeling* of having what you want that is most important.

Gabrielle knew the answer, and it was *no*. She couldn't hold on to the feeling because she was focusing on the cold, the snow, and the Morrukks at the circus.

'No,' confessed Gabrielle, 'I have not.'

'What about you, Charlie?' What are you thinking about?' Molly asked.

'I was thinking of how cold I am,' answered Charlie, 'and how much trouble I am going to get in if I get sick again.'

'Well no wonder,' said Molly. 'We have no idea where we're going and our thoughts are all willy nilly. Now listen. It's not that cold out. In fact, if you think of blue skies, flowers, and all things summery, you'll find it's quite tolerable, really. Just think about it for a few minutes. Imagine all this and imagine Alkaios galloping out of the woods up ahead. He's all sleek and black and looking beautiful against the snowy background. Just imagine it and I bet we'll be saved in no time.'

Gabrielle and Charlie did their best to do as Molly said. They trudged on a little further holding on to the feeling of seeing Alkaios appear from the snowy woods, but it didn't last. Their hopes had turned to ice. All except for Molly's, of course. She remembered Alkaios saying that should they need him, all they would have to do is use the magic, and she believed it. Under her breath, so softly she could not be heard, she said Alkaios' name over and over and over again. As she was saying it, she held on to the feeling of seeing this beautiful creature appear in the midst of the storm. She expected it to happen any minute.

'This isn't working at all,' grumbled Charlie, breaking her concentration.

'It isn't working because you don't believe in it,' said Molly coolly.

'Come on, Molly. Do you really think that Alkaios is going to come trotting out of the woods?' asked Charlie. 'Let's face it – we're lost, and we should turn back now and retrace our steps before it's too late.'

The three of them turned to look at their tracks and saw that they were already covered with snow.

'What are we going to do?' asked Charlie. 'I can't feel my toes.'

'We must keep walking,' said Gabrielle. 'We'll freeze to death if we stop, but Molly is right. We should still focus on what we want.'

'Why don't we light a fire for now?' asked Molly. 'Maybe that will help us focus.'

Instantly, Charlie rummaged through his pants, but he was not so quick to find his favourite flint stones this time. His hands were numb and his pants were rigid from the cold.

'Don't you have them, Charlie?' asked Gabrielle.

'Hold your horses. Hold your horses,' he said. 'Just gimme a minute. My hands are frozen.'

He searched and searched, but the more he searched, the more frenzied he became.

'They have to be here,' he said. 'They just have to be.'

'That's okay,' said Gabrielle as gently as she could. 'You must have forgotten them. Let's just keep—'

'What do you mean *I must have forgotten them?*' interrupted Charlie, still fumbling through his pockets. 'Did you ask me to bring them?'

'That's not what I meant—'

'Did *you* ask me to bring them?' asked Charlie, now scowling at Molly.

'No—'

'Then as far as I can tell,' snapped Charlie, 'I didn't forget anything.'

Charlie was cold, and his spirits were down. He continued searching his pockets as he began walking again. His pace was faster, though, as if he was trying to outrace Time, or in the very least, get away from Gabrielle and Molly.

'Magic, smagic. Why hasn't he come for us?' he asked himself, speeding along. 'Doesn't he know what it's like out?'

'Charlie, wait up,' called Molly as they hurried after him.

It was all Molly and Gabrielle could do to keep up. Charlie was fit and he marched through the deep snow as if it were grass beneath his feet.

'Charlie,' called Gabrielle. *'Charlie!'*

It was no use. He quickened his pace until he was just a speck in front of them.

'Don't leave us, Charlie!' cried Molly after him in the howling wind, but he continued on.

Molly and Gabrielle were forced to slow down, and then he was gone.

Despite not having a fire, Molly insisted on sitting down and taking a break.

'But we mustn't,' stressed Gabrielle. 'We'll get too cold.'

'Didn't I just say it's warm out? Please just give me five minutes,' Molly pleaded.

Molly *was* cold, but she didn't give in to it. Her thoughts continued to bend towards that warm day when she first met Alkaios. She rocked back and forth, whispering his name. Her eyes were closed, but where you'd think you'd find a crinkled face holding fast against the bitter cold, there shone a smiling, glowing expression instead. Wherever Molly's thoughts were at that moment, she was happy inside them.

Five minutes turned to ten and ten turned to an hour. All the while, Gabrielle paced trying to keep warm, yet respecting Molly's good intentions. Suddenly, there was a distant footfall. Gabrielle thought it was Charlie returning, but Molly knew otherwise.

Through the snowfall's swarming veil, a black figure appeared before them and approached with all the majesty for which it was known.

'Alkaios!' exclaimed Gabrielle. 'You've found us!'

Gabrielle turned to Molly expecting to see her jumping for joy, but she simply sat there looking upon Alkaios as content as ever. To say Molly's expression spoke of relief would not be completely untrue, for she was relieved. More accurately, Molly expressed a *knowing*, a knowing that she had used the magic, and it had worked.

'Come friends,' said Alkaios with his warm voice. 'Let us get you inside.'

'But Alkaios,' began Gabrielle, 'Charlie ran ahead of us, and we have no idea where he is. We'll have to form a search party.'

'Charlie is fine,' said Alkaios calmly. 'It was he who let us know you two were lost. From our shelter, we didn't know the storm had progressed so.'

As Alkaios turned, he heard a *plopping* behind him. Molly had fallen upon trying to stand. Gabrielle lifted Molly to her feet, but she was very shaky.

'I can't walk. My legs must be asleep,' lied Molly. Her legs were not asleep. They were severely frostbitten from sitting in the snow for so long. They were so cold they felt as though they had been burned with hot shards of glass. 'Please wait just a few minutes.'

'Can *you* walk?' Alkaios asked of Gabrielle.

'Yes,' Gabrielle replied, 'a little further.'

'Good,' said Alkaios, 'then help Molly onto my back and I shall carry her the rest of the way.'

'Oh no,' objected Molly. 'You mustn't. It's not right.'

Molly pulled her hand away from Gabrielle and rubbed her thighs gently, but this made them burn even more. She attempted another step, but the result was the same. She fell to her knees. She could no more stand than she could bear the thought of Alkaios carrying her. Why, he was the most pure and magical animal in ever all the world. Molly thought to climb upon his back would be to place the mule upon its owner. But as these thoughts coursed through her, she felt a soft warm nudge on her watery cheek. It was Alkaios gently pressing his face against hers. She felt his warmth and it was more comforting than she could describe.

'Molly Withers,' said Alkaios with the same compassion that

accompanied all his words, 'I would be honoured.'

Molly looked up into Alkaios' eyes which poured out Love and Hope and Warmth. She was overwhelmed with joy. She felt so very special inside that she couldn't handle it. It is often the case that true happiness, if having long been absent, will bring a tear when it is experienced again, like seeing a loved one rise briefly from the grave to remind you how much you mean to them. Such was Molly's joy.

She felt Gabrielle's hands once again and once again Molly was lifted to her feet. Gabrielle locked her fingers together as a stirrup and Molly put a tiny foot inside. In one quick motion, Molly pushed off as best she could and found herself upon him – *a Unicorn!*

Chapter Twenty
- *The Congregation* -

What strange sensations Molly experienced as she laid her head against Alkaios' thick strong neck. Faster than what seemed possible, his warmth passed through her to rejuvenate her tired body. She felt renewed strength in her legs, and within a few minutes, the pain had completely subsided. Though her eyes were barely open lest the wind find a way in to sting them, she could see hues of red, and yellow, and orange. She opened her eyes a little wider figuring the hues would disappear, but they did not. The white and grey forest, though surely unchanged in the physical world, had indeed changed in her eyes. The reds, yellows, and oranges remained and she fancied she could even see ghosts of summer flowers floating among the trees. Even the falling snow was not white, but rather a storm of falling petals. It was wonderful to behold and lasted until Alkaios came to a stop.

Molly looked up and saw before her something which scarcely resembled a door on the side of a huge hill. It was not a normal door as you would think, with a handle and hinges, but was instead composed of knotted roots, small trees, and hanging vines. It was so natural in appearance you would certainly miss it if you did not know where to look. Then, from some silent and magical command, it opened much like a curtain. Alkaios and Molly entered with Gabrielle following close behind; a wave of warmth washed over them. It was lovely and comforting and so thick with the smell of

Nature's goodness, it was as if they had walked into a summer's afternoon.

The earthy corridor twisted this way and that, and as they passed through it, the summer smells intensified and mixed with the distinct aromas of a grand meal. If you have ever been fortunate enough to dine with the king and queen in their grandiose castle at Christmas, then you will have an idea of the lovely airs which now tickled Molly's nose. It made her hungry. She imagined seeing piles of freshly baked breads, great wheels of cheeses, thick pots of lentil, and cabbage and bean stews. Everything must have been flavoured wonderfully for the scent of rosemary, sage, thyme, pepper, and other popular Majestican spices like goosenuts, wineblossoms and saffomar all danced deliciously in the air.

While each new aroma was inviting, Molly found her thoughts returning to the law of attraction. She wondered if she had anything to do with Alkaios coming to them, and the more she thought about it, the more she doubted it. After all, it was Charlie who first found this cave and notified Alkaios of their dire situation. Molly's thoughts continued to spiral until her brain convinced her it was all just another coincidence.

'Molly,' said Alkaios, 'there is no such thing as a coincidence.'

'I'm not so sure,' said Molly, aware that he was reading her thoughts.

'Never question the workings of the Universe,' he said, 'for it always knows the most efficient and benevolent way to provide you with what you need. You asked for me, and I came. No coincidence. That's attraction. People push the magic away, though, because they are picky with the manner in which things are provided. It's like discarding a Christmas gift because you don't like the giver's name upon the tag or the wrapper in which it came. Doesn't make sense, does it?'

They arrived at the end of the passageway and entered a vast opening which glowed red from a huge fire situated in the middle of the cavernous room. There were several smaller fires as well and each one had its own pot with its own tasty something cooking away inside. Charlie was standing over one such pot, stirring the contents; he waved when he saw Molly and Gabrielle. He felt a little embarrassed having lost his cool in the storm, but was quite proud of finding the secret door.

Molly slid off Alkaios' back, whispered *thank you* to him and absorbed the details of the room. To her right was a great long wooden table with what must have been one hundred narrow chairs at its side. It was all blustery above the table like a snowstorm, but it wasn't from snow, of course. They were fairies. Pinkleton Dimple fairies. They were whirling around so fast you could not make out their shape and it was unclear what they were doing until you watched the table. The salt and pepper appeared to come from out of nowhere, as did the plate settings, the goblets, and the cutlery. Item after item arrived in a blur as the fairies set the table faster than the eye could track.

Other sorts of wonderful goodness then arrived on the table in a *poof*. There were bowls of carrots, corn, sugar snap peas, and sadly, yes, there were even some Brussels sprouts. There were potatoes, too, served as many ways as you could imagine: whipped, mashed, roasted, riced, baked, and scalloped. There were also piles of grapes, pears, oranges, and apples.

'Do not forget our guests,' called Alkaios and in a similar fashion, three large chairs and ten medium sized chairs appeared.

Molly reasoned the larger chairs were for herself, Charlie, and Gabrielle. The others, though, left her quite puzzled. Whomever they were for, thought Molly, must have been considerably larger than a fairy, yet considerably smaller than a human.

Situated directly in front of the table was a huge, yet oddly shaped throne. It wasn't designed very well for a human; it had rounded armrests that swooped down and then up again. Despite its odd shape, though, the whole work was wrought with gold. It also had a very high backrest with a masterfully carved tree. So finely sculpted were the golden leaves on this tree, they fluttered with the slightest draft. Finally, the seat itself had a huge red cushion adorned with golden tassels.

'Let us take our seats,' called Alkaios as he strode up in front of the great throne, took two steps backwards, and sat upon the red cushion. *Of course*, thought Molly to herself.

Molly and Gabrielle were the next to be seated. As Charlie joined them, Molly looked at him, smiled, and winked. Charlie was already flush from standing so close to the fire, but even so, his cheeks turned rosier still.

In another whirlwind of activity, all the remaining items were brought to the table and it took no less than five fairies to carry the oversized pot of bean curd. It was placed in front of Molly, and then with a tinkling, another fairy poured the hot chocolate around the table more speedily than could be followed. In fact, Molly saw the same fairy at two different mugs at the same time, and not a drop was spilled.

From another entrance in the cavern, there began a chorus of cheerful singing accompanied by the distinct sound of marching. Suddenly, a band of leprechauns appeared, led by none other than Tommy Troublesome. They approached the table and waved at Alkaios in sequence as they all marched past him. Molly was more than happy to see them. She was surprised.

'Where's the swillers?' demanded Tommy with a glorious smile, and then with a kind wink just for Molly, he quietly added, 'Didn't think we'd let yee go it alone, did yee now?'

Tommy and the leprechauns took their seats as Alkaios bowed his head.

'Dear Maker of all things Magical and True,' began Alkaios, 'please bless these fine foods set before us today.'

Alkaios raised his head, as did everyone gathered round the great table, and so began the wonderful meal. Food was passed around in quick order, and everyone must have been very hungry for the mounds shrank quickly. It wasn't long before the bowls and plates were scraped clean, the last of the swillers was drank by parched leprechauns, and the flock of fairies disappeared from the table. In a likewise manner to the table being set, it was unset, but every empty bowl and plate that was removed was replaced by a glorious dessert. There were yogurts, and cakes stuffed with jam and cream cheese, and every kind of freshly baked pie imaginable. After everyone had their fill of all things tasty and sweet, they turned their attention to the matter at hand.

'Thank you everyone for coming,' said Alkaios. 'I wish you were here before me today to receive great tidings, but I have little to give. The Nordenburgh Circus, as I am sure everyone is aware, was successful in spreading fear throughout Majestica and we should assume this is one small piece of a much larger puzzle. Furthermore, confirmation has reached Town Centre of a great storm hitting Nordenburgh and from accounts given to us by our woodland friends, it's gaining strength and heading towards us. Surely, the heavy snow outside, which almost swallowed up our guests of honour, is proof of this.'

'And what of the Golden Tree?' asked Tommy Troublesome.

'Or news of Engelbert the Great?'

'Still none,' answered Alkaios gravely. 'I suspect he has finally moved on.'

Molly's heart sank. She feared she would not be able to see this quest through to the end.

'Molly, this quest is not yours alone,' said Alkaios wisely. 'Everyone present has vowed to help you any way they can. The Golden Tree and Majestica are important to all of us, are they not?'

There was a brief, but loud cheer from all the leprechauns and fairies, but Molly's heart was unmoved. The void of doubt consumed her.

'And it's not just those gathered here,' Alkaios continued. 'Every animal in Majestica is on your side, Molly, and they are our very best source of knowledge. They listen to the words of humans without causing alarm.'

'I'm so very confused,' said Molly. 'I can't help it. Sometimes I feel as though the magic is mere coincidence. No matter how hard I try to believe, and no matter how hard I try to focus on the good, I can't. I can't stay positive. I can't. I am so sorry.'

'It's okay, Molly,' said Charlie rubbing the small of her back.

'Well, fancy that,' said Tommy. 'Our wee Molly doesn't believe in the magic. Now with all due respect, Alkaios, are yee sure yee picked the right lass for the job?'

Alkaios' answer did not come in words, but rather in a stern glare that pushed Tommy back in his place.

'I'm very sorry, Molly,' said Tommy. 'I didn't mean anything by it, but we're all just a little concerned for Majestica. Just assumed from the prophecies you'd be a wee bit bigger is all. And older, maybe.'

'Was it not Molly who caught the speedy Tommy Troublesome?' asked Alkaios, 'the quickest leprechaun in all Majestica?'

There was a soft eruption of laughter from the other leprechauns who had all heard Tommy brag endlessly about his speed.

'And was it not Molly who also caught Lillian, queen of the fairies?' Alkaios added. Naturally, the Pinkletons joined the chorus of laughter until Lillian shot them an icy stare.

'I have no doubt Molly is the one whose coming was foretold all those moons ago,' said Alkaios commanding attention, 'and I think her tender age is perfect. That and her vivid imagination, for it is the imagination of children which is the purest and most magical. Molly has not yet forgotten the importance of dreams, and she clings to the hope that magic still exists in this world. That's what's important – Hope. So long as hope remains, fear will not win the day. Even in Majestica, the place on earth where the magic is the strongest, many citizens have already cast aside hope, and the notion of Unicorns, magic, and the Golden Tree, but not our Molly. She still hopes to find that which we all want.

'You must mean swillers,' declared Tommy, taking another long draft. 'Tickles me heart like nothin' else.'

'Happiness, Tommy,' corrected Alkaios. '*Happiness* is our heart's desire. Below the desire for rewards, and grand castles, and beneath the longing for strength and recognition, there is only happiness. But once we forget that we are the creators of our own happiness, we dismiss good fortune as mere coincidence and we hold others accountable for our sad circumstances. Circumstances, I might add, that we ourselves have attracted. This is the most horrible thing that can befall us, for it is at this point we unknowingly, yet willingly, become the puppets of those who use the magic for selfish purposes. This has happened to the greater parts of the world outside Majestica, and it was only a matter of time before we too were tested by the likes of Mortimer Weedly.'

'What else, Alkaios?' asked Gabrielle.

'Sadly, there is more troubling news,' said Alkaios, 'and that's why you've been summoned.'

Suddenly, there was a rash of noise at the table with each fairy and leprechaun expressing their own concerns and opinions.

'Quiet!' demanded Alkaios. 'It comes to this: our woodland friends have heard secret conversations in the heart of Nordenburgh. They report Mortimer Weedly has formed a formidable army. He has always had a handful of loyalists, but now there are faithful Morrukks too numerous to count. They will follow Mortimer to their graves as willingly as marching to their beds. Many were here with the circus, and they won't be long returning.'

Again there was an outburst of discussion at the table. Everyone was terribly worried and in their disbelief that such a horrible thing was possible, they argued over who was to blame.

'Do we know how much time we have?' demanded Molly over the ruckus, silencing the gathering as Alkaios had done.

'Precious little,' answered Alkaios, 'and we have to accept that the magic is just as available to Mortimer as it is to us, and that makes him a worthy foe. Indeed, our woodland friends advised us Mortimer has already used the law of attraction to heal his severed hand.'

'What!' exclaimed Charlie. 'That's impossible.'

'Believe it, Charlie,' urged Alkaios, 'for the magic works just as well when it comes to attracting health to the body temple. Yes, our threat is very real and we are in a deadly race. Should Mortimer and his army find the Tree before us, he will use the magic to steal the throne of Majestica. After which, he is certain to destroy the Tree, the grandest symbol of something so great, and then even the memory of Hope will be vanquished from the minds of Majesticans.'

Everyone now expected the very worst. Even Alkaios seemed dismayed with the news of Mortimer's growing army. Molly, Charlie, Gabrielle, the leprechauns, and all the fairies sat in silence pondering these dark times.

'Though things seem bleak,' Alkaios said, 'have faith. Everything will unfold as it should, and we owe it to ourselves to continue with the things that bring us joy. In so doing, we will attract more of what we want.'

Alkaios seemed to cut himself off now listening to a sound coming from the outer entrance. He smiled as only a Unicorn can.

'Well, here they are now,' he said.

At once, everyone was aware of a sound of rushing wind, and suddenly Genevieve flew in upon her broom.

'So you *are* a witch!' exclaimed Charlie, as Genevieve, and two others landed in a *whoosh* beside Alkaios.

'Je m'excuse,' said Genevieve, 'we did not mean to be so late. The weather outside is, how does one say, pas bien. We had a hard time finding this place.'

The other two witches dismounted their brooms and shook out their snowy cloaks. One witch raised her hand and somehow beckoned three wine glasses off the table. Up they lifted and flew directly into each of the witch's outstretched hands.

'Allo Gabrielle. Ça va?' asked Genevieve as she raised her hand, summoning the wine carafe to fly from the table and pour itself into their glasses.

'Fine, thank you,' answered Gabrielle.

Genevieve and the other two witches relished a long mouthful of wine, smiled, and then cackled briefly to themselves.

'Nathalie, Janine, this is Molly, Charlie, and Gabrielle,' said Genevieve. The two witches bowed graciously.

'What news,' Genevieve asked, turning to Alkaios. 'Is there more from our furry critters in the North?'

'Not yet,' Alkaios answered.

'Then let us prepare for a joyous night,' she said. 'We should remember the importance of keeping high spirits, non? Does like not attract like?'

'That is the law,' agreed Alkaios.

'But first,' Genevieve said raising a glass to the table. 'Here's to our future Princess Molly and her brave knight Charlie. May we all find the courage to help them in these troubled times. Happiness and health. Santé!'

'Here, here!' shouted Tommy Troublesome, and as soon as he did, so too did the other leprechauns, and the swarm of fairies.

'To Molly and Charlie,' affirmed Alkaios.

'Now, let us leprechauns strike up some joyous music for yee all to enjoy. May we never forget this night and may we never go thirsty, neither,' said Tommy, opening another bottle of swillers he'd hidden in his clothes.

The fairies took to the air as before and all the chairs were placed around the great fire in the middle of the room, while a collection of instruments were provided to all who knew how to play. Molly, Charlie, and Gabrielle were escorted to the fire and once everyone was gathered round, Genevieve began to play a harp. It was a lovely song that Molly knew very well: *The Roses and the Daisies*. The fairies' wings flickered gold with the harp, but once Molly joined in during the second chorus, they shone as brightly as could be imagined, lighting up all the dark corners of the cavern.

For the next three hours, there was singing and dancing and clapping and all manner of merriment. Molly knew it was a night not to be forgotten, but as the horrible clock marched on, and as more and more fairies retired for the evening (snoring as loudly as ever), she also understood it could not last forever. Even the leprechauns, who had laughed and sang the loudest, were quiet now and eventually the last song was sung, the last story was told, and the instruments were set aside.

'Come now,' said Genevieve. 'We'll take you all home.'

'What? On those?' asked Charlie looking at the well-preserved brooms, and for an answer, the three witches smiled.

'Won't we be cold?' asked Molly.

'Oh no,' replied Genevieve. 'Not with *us.*'

Suddenly, the brooms came to life, and the three witches mounted them. Nathalie winked at Charlie, so he was the first to climb aboard. Gabrielle was the second, joining Janine. Molly naturally rode with Genevieve.

In another *whoosh,* all three witches, along with their passengers, took to the air, flew down the earthy corridor, and headed straight towards the knotted door. Charlie, on the first witch's broom, noticed it was still closed and they were heading for it terribly fast. *Perhaps it won't open in time,* he thought to himself. He held on to Nathalie for dear life, but just before they ran straight into the closed door, she snapped her fingers and it opened.

It was still snowing heavily outside and though the wind was quite strong, they did not feel the cold. By some trick or hex, Molly, Charlie, and Gabrielle were kept warm while they were whisked away to their homes. Genevieve landed softly in front of Molly's home, but took flight the moment Molly dismounted. Molly felt the cold attack her immediately and as she rushed inside, she heard a faint *Bon soir!* in the distance.

Chapter Twenty-One
- *A Private Confab* -

Molly awoke the next morning, and felt uneasy as soon as her eyes opened. It was already light outside, which meant she was late for *tutoring* with Gabrielle. *Why didn't someone wake me?* Though still a little groggy, Molly began humming as she jumped out of bed and rushed to the kitchen. With one look, Molly could tell that her mother was suffering from another headache, having seen the telltale signs for so many years. Her mother's hair was dishevelled, one eyelid drooped, and the rooms were dark.

'Would you like me to stop?' asked Molly.

'Oh no, Molly,' replied Annabelle. 'When a mother hurts the most, the need to hear her child is greatest.'

'Bad one is it?' asked Molly.

'Oh I am fine,' answered Annabelle. 'Just a little headache.'

'What time is it?' asked Molly.

'Just after ten o'clock, but you needn't worry,' said her mother. 'The school is closed because of the weather, so your father and I thought you should stay home as well. We've already told Gabrielle.'

'Is the weather that bad?' asked Molly peering out the window.

'What is it you do with Gabrielle?' asked Annabelle, ignoring Molly's question.

'Huh?'

'Come now, Molly,' said Annabelle, 'I somehow think there's

more to you two than meets the eye.'

Molly had promised Gabrielle that she would keep everything about the Tree a secret, but it was about to come to an end. If Mortimer could heal his hand, then why should her mother have to suffer? Because of a promise?

'Where's Dad?' asked Molly.

'He's out clearing the snow from the woodpiles,' Annabelle replied.

If there was a parent Molly thought she could trust with all this, it was Annabelle. It would be such a relief to tell a parent and in so doing, hopefully gain a little support. Molly also knew her mother loved it when her daughter confided in her. What mother doesn't? In fact, Annabelle had already poured two cups of tea, and one of them was *not* for William.

The time had come for a private confab.

'Have a seat, Mom,' said Molly.

'Certainly,' Annabelle said sitting at the table without delay.

'Mom, do you promise to keep everything I say to yourself and not even tell Dad?' Molly asked.

'You're not in some kind of trouble, are you?' asked her mother.

'Do you promise?'

'Are you?' her mother pressed again.

'No, of course not,' answered Molly, 'but unless you promise to keep this a secret, I can't tell you anything.'

'I promise.'

Molly looked at her mother in a way that asked the question one final time.

'I promise. *I promise,'* assured Annabelle.

Molly believed her. There was no turning back.

'Have you heard of the Golden Tree of Truth?' Molly asked.

'Why, sure,' Annabelle replied. 'That story is as popular as any other fairytale in Majestica.'

'What if I were to tell you that it wasn't just a story?' Molly asked.

Annabelle shot a look of disbelief at Molly, but Molly's eyes shone sincerely.

'Mom, the Tree does exist and it's somewhere in Majestica,' Molly said in a whisper. 'But I've learned its worth is not in gold, but in its knowledge.'

'Molly, you don't really expect me to—'

'Yes, I do expect you to believe me,' Molly said a little louder. 'This is serious, Mom. Everything I have been learning lately has to do with the Golden Tree and the law of attraction.'

'The law of attraction?' asked her mother.

'Yes, and I'm telling you it's just like magic. So long as the Tree exists, the knowledge can be shared with others, but if it falls in the wrong hands, it will all be lost forever.'

'Oh Molly, you sure have an imagination,' said Annabelle.

'It's *not* my imagination!' Molly exclaimed louder than she intended. 'It's as real as the leprechauns and the fairies and Mr. Cayce the talking moose.'

'Leprechauns?' asked Annabelle doubtfully. 'Talking moose?'

'Why not?' retorted Molly. 'Look, Mom, if you don't want to believe in leprechauns, and talking moose, that's fine, but I think I've learned how you can feel better.'

'Oh, there's nothing wrong with me,' countered Annabelle, rather routinely.

'But it's not right that you have headaches all the time,' insisted Molly.

Annabelle sipped her tea and stared blankly at her cup for the longest time. She had given up the hope of feeling better ages ago. She had tried every remedy and seen every healer in Majestica, but no one had been able to help her. Still, Hope is a funny thing for it can reappear with the slightest suggestion.

'I think I can help you,' continued Molly, 'but you have to believe in this. You have to believe there is something inside of you that you have forgotten. I can't tell you everything yet, but I can tell you this: if you can come to believe that you are healed, if you can remember the time when you did not suffer from headaches, and if you can just hold onto this *feeling* of well-being, then the Universe will make it so. That's the law of attraction. That's the magic Gabrielle has been teaching me.'

'It's been so long, Molly,' said Annabelle with tears brewing somewhere inside, 'since I knew what it was like to go even a couple days without a headache.'

'But that good feeling is still inside you,' urged Molly. 'Do whatever it takes to find that feeling once more, and hold on to it, and I promise your headaches will melt away like a candle. It might be tough at first, but I have seen miracles happen these past weeks and it's all because of this natural law. But, I can't do this for you. No one can. This is something you have to do for yourself.'

Annabelle's tears finally burst and rolled down her cheek. She loved her daughter with all her heart. If there was ever someone who could lift her spirits, it was Molly.

'You are such a sweet, sweet child, Molly. So very caring.'

'I know I am. You're lucky to have me,' said Molly rather cheekily and this brought a smile to her mother's face.

'Do you know—'Annabelle paused.

'How it works?' said Molly finishing the question, and her mother nodded hesitantly. 'Not exactly, but I know you shouldn't focus on *not* having headaches.'

'But I *don't* want these headaches,' Annabelle objected. 'I haven't ever wanted a headache.'

'That's just it, Mom, you bring into your life what you focus on, so if you focus on *not* wanting headaches, that's what you're going to get – more of not wanting headaches.'

'And Gabrielle taught you this?' asked Annabelle.

'Well, not that part,' replied Molly, 'but it's all true. I've seen it with my own eyes.'

'Oh, Molly,' said Annabelle, wiping her eyes. 'I am truly blessed to have a child like you. Though I'd love to know what you're still not telling me, I'll try.'

'It works for money, too' added Molly, 'but I am no longer convinced money makes us happy. It's only part of it, I think.'

'At what point did my little child become so wise?' Annabelle asked herself.

The tea was finished in silence. Molly walked back to her bedroom doubting she had fully convinced her mother of everything, but it was a step, and she felt lighter for sharing what had been going on.

Molly dressed in her winter clothes and made it as far as the front door when something wonderful came to mind.

'What day is it today?' Molly asked.

'November twenty-fifth,' Annabelle replied, still sitting at the table holding her empty teacup. 'Christmas is one month today.'

'That's right!' exclaimed Molly.

Where had the time gone? Molly wondered. Why, only four weeks till the happiest day of the year. Molly couldn't believe how much had happened since first meeting Gabrielle at All Hallows

Ball.

'Thanks, Mom,' Molly said as she walked outside as content as ever.

Though it was absolutely freezing, it was also wonderfully white again with a fresh dumping of snow. Molly could tell that it must have blown something fierce while she was sleeping. The snow was two feet deep everywhere, but where there was an object to cause a drift, the snow was twice as deep.

Her father had shovelled much of the front porch, and there were great mounds of snow up to the handrails all the way around. Molly thought it would be best if she jumped in. So, as the young do (and those young at heart) she climbed up on the rail of the porch, steadied herself for a moment, and scouted out the best place to land. She took a deep breath and launched herself into a particularly plump drift. Molly giggled upon landing and whirled her arms and legs in whichever direction she fancied. Snow went everywhere. It was lovely, and exciting, but she wasn't done. Oh no, for she remembered that she had not made a snow angel in a full year. Many girls her age had already outgrown making snow angels, but not Molly. She loved it.

Molly examined her front lawn for the best place. It looked like a fresh piece of paper, or better yet, a canvas. Yes, her snowy lawn was a canvas, and *she* was the artist. She marched to the middle of the page, and fell backwards with her arms outstretched like the letter T. The snow whirled in a cloud and gently settled back around her. It took Molly quite some time, sweeping her arms and legs like horizontal jumping jacks, to make the shape of the angel, but once she was convinced it was just right, she slowly and carefully rose to her feet to observe her artwork. It was perfect – a masterpiece.

Once she'd had her fill of playing in the snow, she continued on to Charlie's. Though Molly thought it was a beautiful day, the adults out shovelling their laneways were not so impressed. Many were grumbling, but it didn't bother Molly one little bit. Christmas was coming: the time of year when everyone is the happiest.

Ha! thought Molly as she began singing Christmas carols softly to herself. This is no coincidence. People are happiest this time of year because they make the greatest effort to be. The more you focus on spreading love and goodwill, the more you receive.

Molly continued on and noticed that horse buggies were

sidelined for sleighs. What a sight! The horse's breath steamed out of their flaring nostrils as they trotted by with shiny polished jingle bells. It put a smile on Molly's face all the way to Charlie's where she wasn't surprised to see him out shovelling.

'Pretty, isn't it?' asked Molly.

'Pretty deep,' said Charlie looking a little sad, 'but once this is done, I'm going to go tobogganing, and then have some hot chocolate.'

'You have hot chocolate?' asked Molly. 'That would be just the thing right now, wouldn't it?'

'Sure would,' said Charlie looking up at his seemingly uninhabited house, and then back to his shovel. 'But I don't really have any hot chocolate and I don't really have a toboggan. You know that. I sure hope all this changes soon. It will, won't it, Molly? I won't be my parent's slave forever, will I?'

'Of course not,' answered Molly. 'Hey, maybe you'll get a toboggan for Christmas. You never know. Just remember what Alkaios said: *everything will unfold as it should.*'

Molly didn't linger any longer. She knew when Charlie wanted to be alone, so she turned and walked back home, as freezing snow pellets fell and stung her cheeks. She walked inside and saw her mother and father sitting at the table with toast and tea. Molly loved the smell of toast, and was surprised by another glorious smell.

'Is that hot chocolate?' asked Molly, trying to contain her excitement in case her brain was playing a trick on her.

'Sure is,' replied William, taking an exaggerated slurp from his mug.

'That's so funny,' said Molly. 'I was just thinking about hot chocolate.'

Molly winked at Annabelle hoping her mother understood this was an example of the magic. Annabelle winked back, and poured Molly a large mug of chocolaty goodness. Molly retrieved a book from her room and returned to the kitchen table. She loved reading, and reading by a fire on a snowy day was almost as good as reading by an oil lamp during a summer's thunderstorm.

All afternoon Molly read, but every hour or so she got up to stretch her legs and look out the window.

The snow continued to fall heavily well after supper and Molly was certain, if it kept up, she'd not be able to see outside the windows come morning.

Chapter Twenty-Two
- *Storm of the Century* -

Molly fell asleep thinking of Christmas, and awoke to another snow day. It was exciting. The school children would still see each other, but it would be on the hills and *not* in the classrooms.

William came in from outdoors, coughing as usual, and a deathly draft accompanied him. He was covered with a mixture of sawdust and snow, and he carried a scuttle of wood.

'I sure hope this doesn't last much longer,' he said. 'It's only been a few days, and we've already gone through a lot of wood. Three times that of last year at this time.'

'It's just a storm,' said Annabelle. 'It will pass.'

'It's not just a storm. It's the storm of the century,' William stated. 'Everyone is talking about it.'

'I think everyone's making a big deal out of nothing,' Annabelle said.

'Well, I hope you're right,' said William and he went outside to assess his wood stores – *again*.

This day went much the same way as the day before. Molly read, and the storm grew. She poked her head outside only once and saw four feet of snow in most places and, though it looked pretty, she was a little concerned.

So it was for the next three weeks: each day Molly arose to find out that the storm had continued and tutoring had been cancelled as no one wanted to venture far from home. She also noticed with each passing day that her father was more and more stressed by his diminishing wood piles. It wasn't just William who was stressed either; all of Majestica was anxious. In every small home and in every shop, there were lengthy conversations over the lack of wood. The time approaching Christmas was blanketed by the growing fear in Majestica. With everyone focusing on the lack of wood, Molly wondered if the law of attraction would propel the storm until all the wood was burned up.

Molly saw Gabrielle and Charlie only once or twice in those long three weeks, but there was no news about the Golden Tree. Gabrielle hadn't heard from Alkaios, Mr. Cayce, or the fairies. It was as if they had gone into hiding with all the woodland animals. Even winter birds like chickadees were nowhere to be seen.

Molly awoke on Christmas Eve morning suffering from cabin fever. She'd been cooped up for so long that she was desperate to get outside. She'd been hoping the weather would lift at least on this day so she could leave her house and see some different faces, but there was no such luck. Today was the worst day yet.

During the night, the heavy droves of snow made way for a storm of freezing rain; the likes of which Majestica had never seen before. Everything was covered with an impenetrable layer of thick ice, and there was a littering of broken branches that had fallen under all the extra weight. But worse than this, Molly's home was much, much colder than normal.

Molly went to the kitchen and saw pain etched on her mother's face: another headache. William came in from outside with the scuttle only half filled with wood.

'Sure is cold here,' said Molly innocently, but it was not well received.

'Haven't you been paying attention?' growled her father. 'We're all but out of wood. I am already into next year's supply, but it's green and it doesn't burn right. Wear two sweaters if you have to!'

Molly didn't know what to say. She didn't mean anything by it, but she knew she had touched a nerve. Her father took pride in keeping the house warm and if he said that he was running short of wood, you could be certain it was true.

William removed his coat and sat at the table. He was more than concerned. He was scared. The kind of scared you get when you can't see how things are going to turn around. Molly knew this and tried to respect his space, but she was sick in her heart. Each day was a little worse than the day prior. Her mother's headaches worsened each day. Her father's temper worsened each day. Her own fears about Mortimer and Majestica grew each day as well. Though all the snow had once been so lovely, Molly hated it now. With the tension in the house, it didn't seem like Christmas Eve at all. There weren't even any decorations around the house – the surest sign that all was not well.

'Are we going to have a Christmas tree this year?' Molly asked without really knowing her mouth had opened and words had poured out. She couldn't believe she asked such a question, but there was nothing she could do.

'No, we're not, Molly!' yelled her father, 'we're not having a Christmas tree this year. If I could cut down one of those frozen trees, I'd bloody well burn it. Do you want me to risk breaking my neck for a damn old tree? Take a look outside!'

'I'm sorry, Father,' was all Molly could say.

Tears formed and she ran off to her room to cry.

She couldn't help but want a tree and she didn't think asking about it was such a crime. Even though there were never presents underneath it like the other children's trees, it was still a lovely thing to look upon and such an important symbol of the season. How could you have Christmas without a Christmas tree?

Molly's thoughts whirled around, but it was at this point she came to fully understand the importance of the Golden Tree. It was as Alkaios said: a symbol of something greater. Yes, thought Molly, what was a Christmas tree, but something you could touch and smell and look upon to remind you of the true meaning of this great holiday? At this moment, Molly knew the Golden Tree of Truth must be preserved not for the Tree itself, but for the wonderful things it represented – Hope and Happiness.

Molly heard the front door slam and knew it was her father heading back outside to get things off his mind. He'd smoke, for sure, and contemplate how he could make things right for his family. She knew he was quick to anger, but she also knew it subsided just as quickly.

Molly didn't want to be in sight when he came back, so she decided to stay in her room. She lit several candles, grabbed another book, jumped into bed, and wrapped up in her blankets content to spend another day reading. After a few hours of solitude, she heard the door slam again. Within a couple of minutes, she heard her mother and father talking, but she couldn't make out what they were saying. Yet, Molly could tell by the sound of the conversation that her parents were not arguing. Arguing has a very distinct sound. *No*, thought Molly, what she heard right now actually seemed joyful. In fact, there may have even been a short chuckle. Had the storm passed?

Molly sat up in her bed and listened for all she was worth. She wished she had her mother's hearing; nothing could be whispered within a mile of their home without Annabelle hearing it.

'No, *you* go get her,' Molly thought she heard her mother say and then she recognized her father's unmistakable heavy footsteps in the hall. He knocked twice and opened Molly's bedroom door.

'Molly, can you please come to the kitchen for a minute?' he asked gruffly.

Molly hoped he had good news, but waited for him to walk back to the kitchen before she got out of bed. She felt like a mouse that had a close run-in with cheese in a trap and was now weary to try it again. Cautiously, she walked into the hall trying to hear signs that things were safe. Everything was silent, but suddenly, Molly met the most recognizable and perfect smell; a smell only present inside her home once a year.

She ran to the kitchen, and there, propped up in one corner where it stood every year, was the most glorious Christmas tree Molly had ever seen. Though it wasn't yet decorated, it was still beautiful. It was round, fat, the full height of the ceiling, and it filled the kitchen with the smell of evergreen. Molly laughed and giggled and clapped her hands together and once she was able to pull her eyes from the tree, she saw that her parents were smiling proudly. Molly ran to them and hugged them both at the same time.

'Thank you!' said Molly, and she meant it.

'You are most welcome, Molly,' said Annabelle. 'Now let's decorate it and have some hot chocolate, shall we?'

It was a home where apologies most often came by way of unexpected acts of kindness and Molly came to know this was just as meaningful as words. That Christmas Eve was one of the loveliest Molly would remember in the years to come. There was singing and sweets and joking and laughing and hot chocolate and games, and the feelings of love and happiness filled their home that night like never before. And, when it was finally time for bed, Molly fell asleep believing everything would work out, *somehow*.

Chapter Twenty-Three
- *The Invitation* -

Christmas morning arrived. Years ago Molly would have been the first one up by several hours, but today, unbelievably, she was the last. Molly smiled to herself thinking *I must be getting old.*

By the time Molly was dressed and made her way to the kitchen, breakfast was almost ready. The smell of toast, bacon, and eggs was in the air and it tickled her soul. Although the kitchen was warm, William was stuffing more wood in the stove. Annabelle put breakfast on the table and poured three cups of tea before she noticed Molly standing there.

'Well, Merry Christmas, Molly,' she said. 'Come give your mother a hug.'

'Merry Christmas, Mother,' replied Molly, as she buried herself in her mother's apron and squeezed for all she was worth.

'Merry Christmas, Father,' added Molly.

'Merry Christmas, Molly,' he said warmly, as he stood, smiled, and patted her on the head.

Molly stared at the Christmas tree for a long time, intentionally squinting. This blurred the candle lights and decorations and the effect was heavenly. The whole tree shone with a tinkling, glowing aura. Molly then turned her attention to her stocking resting on the stove's mantle; it was swollen with treats.

'May I, Mom? Is it too early?' Molly asked.

'Go on,' Annabelle replied and Molly retrieved her stocking

and joined her father at the table.

Molly dove into it without delay and relished every item. There was a huge shiny red apple which would have made Grandma Jones proud, a large orange, a few Clementines and an assortment of walnuts, chestnuts, almonds, and peanuts. But, at the very bottom of the stocking, was her favourite treat of all – macaroons. She loved the chocolaty coconut. It was, she believed, a match made in heaven.

After a quick look, Molly found nothing else in the stocking. Usually there was at least a small *something*, but not this year, and she knew the pennies must have been extra tight. This was the first Christmas that she received no gift, but she brushed off her disappointment. *I'd rather have a Christmas tree than a gift, anyway.*

'Thank you! Thank you!' Molly said with as much enthusiasm as she could muster.

'Missed anything?' asked William, trying not to let his eyes sparkle.

'I don't think so,' replied Molly, kneading her stocking for some yet-to-be retrieved trinket and then looking inside just to be sure.

'No?' asked her father peering over the rim of his glasses in the direction of the tree.

Molly's head spun like a top. To her astonishment, there, beneath the tree, were two presents wrapped brightly and adorned with bright red bows. How could she have missed them? Molly looked back to her father and saw him smiling ear to ear. She then looked to her mother, who, if it was possible, wore an even grander smile.

Molly knelt in front of the tree and looked at the two gifts – they had to be opened immediately. They were wonderfully wrapped, and though she knew you shouldn't judge a book by its cover, she couldn't help but admire the colourful paper and bows. She picked one up, the smaller one, and flipped the tag over to verify its ownership. It read: *'To Molly, Love Mom and Dad.'*

Her excitement was spilling over now, but still she did not want to risk damaging the bow and paper. She untied the knot on the underside of the gift and the bow fell freely to the floor. She picked it up and carried it to the table ceremoniously and placed it beside her stocking treats. She rushed back to her gift and methodically removed the paper off one side, then the next, and as carefully as she could be with her excited, shaky hands, she preserved the entire wrapping in one piece. She would have carried this back to the table, but she wasn't yet ready to relinquish her wonderful gift: a book. And it wasn't just any book. She recalled seeing it in the library and wanted one for her own: *The Golden Tree of Truth: the Myth and the Magic* by Benton Wolford. He was a famous Majestican author who Molly hoped to meet one day.

'Your mother picked it out,' said her father, still uncertain it was a good gift, but whatever doubt was in him melted away the very instant Molly gave him a huge hug.

'It's perfect, Dad. You have no idea how perfect!' and as she said this, she let him out of her grasp and went over to her mother to give her a hug.

'Do you like it?' asked her mother, 'because I can take it back if—'

'Of course I do. It's the best gift ever!' said Molly earnestly.

'There's still one more,' noted her father and Molly returned to the tree having rested the book on the table with her stocking stuffers, bow, and paper.

The next present was much larger than the previous one and, upon picking it up, Molly realized it was much heavier as well.

'She said to be very careful with that,' warned her father. 'It's fragile.'

'*Who* said?' asked Molly.

She inspected the tag and was pleasantly surprised with the inscription: '*To Molly, my most treasured pupil, Gabrielle.*'

'*Gabrielle,*' whispered Molly to herself, and she removed the wrapping as ritualistically as before.

Molly was so surprised with what she saw that she almost fell over. She couldn't believe it. It was a wooden sculpture of a Unicorn: the same sculpture Molly fell in love on Gabrielle's bookshelf. It was brilliantly carved by some master craftsman's hands for the detail was beyond description. Molly pored over every curve and every knot, but most importantly she now had time to inspect the inscription she had only glimpsed before. There, holding it in her hands without the worry of being caught snooping, Molly deciphered the faded letters: *A-l-k-a-i-o-s.*

In the midst of her wonder and excitement, a gentle knock came from the front door and Annabelle saw to greeting whoever was there.

'Merry Christmas, Charlie,' said Annabelle opening the door. 'Come in. Make yourself at home.'

'Merry Christmas,' replied Charlie, and Molly smiled to hear his voice.

Charlie entered with a fierce draft of icy coldness riding piggyback.

'Merry Christmas, Charlie,' said William. 'How goes the battle?'

'Oh fine,' answered Charlie. 'Merry Christmas, Mr. Withers.'

Molly, unable to control herself, gave Charlie a great big hug. Unknown to her, though, at that precise moment her father and mother exchanged winks as if they had just been permitted to stand by the cauldron to watch where spells are brewed.

'Merry Christmas, Charlie,' said Molly. 'It's so good to see you. I've been cooped up for ages.'

'Me too, but look, you won't believe what I got for Christmas,' said Charlie excitedly.

Charlie opened the door to show Molly what was resting against the rail on the porch.

'You got a sled! I knew you would!' Molly said, quickly closing the door again.

'Maybe later on we can try it,' suggested Charlie, 'if it's okay with your folks.'

'Of course it is,' Annabelle said.

'And you said your parents didn't like you,' noted Molly, but she was off the mark.

'What's the matter, Charlie?' asked Molly.

'It's from Gabrielle,' answered Charlie and it was clear to Molly that he didn't want to discuss it further.

It was also clear to Molly that Charlie was out and about so early on Christmas day because he didn't have the love in his house that Molly had in her home. He likely didn't have a Christmas tree and the sled was quite possibly the first gift he'd ever received. Molly's heart went out to him and she looked at her mother in a way which asked a question. Annabelle smiled and nodded.

'Why don't you come in and have breakfast with us, Charlie?' Annabelle asked.

'I'd like to, but, uh, my parents are expecting me back shortly,' said Charlie. 'I'll see you later.'

'I can't wait,' said Molly as warmly as she could.

'Merry Christmas,' Charlie muttered one final time before walking outside, retrieving his sled, and heading off in the direction of some famous hills which were *not* in the direction of his house.

Molly closed the door and went back to her gifts knowing they were even more special than she'd originally thought, but within a minute, there was another knock at the door. Molly suspected she knew who it was, and therefore mouthed the word *Charlie* to her father who was concerned that his precious heat would escape their home once again. Annabelle went to the door and opened it expecting to see Charlie.

'Uh...I don't know what to say,' Annabelle mumbled.

'Merry Christmas is usually customary on this day,' said a muffled, yet familiar voice.

What was Charlie up to? Molly wondered.

'Why yes it is. Meh – Merry Christmas, Sir,' Annabelle strained to say.

'You're letting in the cold. Has he changed his mind about breakfast?' asked William, winking at Molly.

'Merry Christmas, Bill,' said the voice.

Annabelle stepped back from the doorway and in entered Marcus MacDonald wearing his best regalia, though it was covered with soot. Molly thought he looked so handsome: big and powerful and as silent as snowfall. He held a large bucket of black chunks, which, though no one was certain what they were, must have been the source of all the soot.

'I have some news,' began MacDonald. 'News deemed so important the king himself has asked me to do my best to personally pass it along to as many noble citizens as I can.'

'What you got in the bucket, Marcus?' asked William, mesmerized by the round black chunks of a familiar *something*. 'Is that *coal* again?'

'Why this, this is supposedly the answer to all our prayers,' answered Marcus.

'Is that really coal?' asked Molly who was equally curious.

'Yes, this is Mortimer's coal,' said Marcus, 'and all that he had said is true. It burns better than wood.'

'It looks messy,' remarked Molly.

'Better you say?' asked Annabelle.

'It appears so,' replied the knight. 'It burns longer and hotter.'

'Seems you may have changed your tune,' noted William, rather skeptically.

'To be truthful,' confessed Marcus, 'I've been told to change my tune.'

'By the king?' pressed William.

'Aye, and who am I say otherwise?'

'Where does this coal come from?' asked Annabelle.

'From the bowels of the earth,' answered Marcus.

'Never been to the bowels of the earth myself,' said William.

'Neither have I,' agreed Marcus, 'but the Morrukks have, and a full procession of caravans all stuffed with coal are continuously arriving in Town Centre. Mortimer Weedly is to thank. He heard of our situation in Majestica and he has come to help.'

'To help or to hinder?' asked William.

'Who's to say, for sure? Every man is entitled the opportunity to improve himself, I suppose. Especially here in Majestica,' said Marcus.

'He brought this to town once before,' added William, 'and it cost a pretty penny. *We* can't afford it, that's for sure.'

'You can today,' countered Marcus. 'The king confided that Mortimer refused a fat purse of gold and apparently apologized for causing the ruckus before. He has promised to bring more coal tomorrow, enough to see us through this storm and all for free. Can you believe it?'

William believed it, but sensed Mortimer was up to something. William was a wise man and a great judge of character. Molly knew very few tricks could be played over on her father without him knowing it.

'And there's enough for everyone?' asked William.

'It appears that way,' answered Marcus. 'This is just a sample, but this afternoon you can come by Town Centre for more. Merry Christmas to you.'

And with this, Marcus placed the huge bucket by the stove, turned, and saw himself out the front door.

Nothing good would come of this, thought Molly, and her father had his doubts as well. He was relieved to have the warmth and threw a chunk in the fire right away, but it troubled him nonetheless. What was coal? Where did it *really* come from? How long would it be free?

Christmas morning passed and after lunch, William was out the door heading to Town Centre to see if what MacDonald had said was true. Molly accompanied him with the same intention, but she stopped by Charlie's to see if he might come along as well. Charlie was just leaving his house when Molly arrived and she couldn't help making a snowball. He hadn't seen her yet.

'Do you have to fill *that* with coal?' Molly asked, launching the snowball at the same time. Just as Charlie answered 'Yeppers, peppers,' the fluffy snowball hit his coat and Molly giggled triumphantly. Charlie smiled too, but did not retaliate. Instead, he lifted the handles of the enormous wheelbarrow and began pushing.

'Don't you have, umm, a smaller one?' Molly suggested.

'Nope, but this is better, anyway,' said Charlie. 'I'd rather do it in one trip.'

'I see,' replied Molly, admiring Charlie's ambition, but doubting he'd have the strength to push it even half filled.

On the way to Town Centre they encountered swarms of Majesticans, many who had wheelbarrows as well. They seemed quite happy and were relieved with the supposed good news. The Wortherly brothers, along with some other children, were there too, with empty Christmas stockings to stuff with coal.

'Coal patrol, coal patrol. Three brothers are on the coal patrol.'

Shuffling through the snowy paths, Molly and Charlie finally made it to the heart of all the excitement. There, piled mountainously high in the middle of the town square was Mortimer's coal. All around the base of the huge pile, the snow was black and dusty with countless dark trails spiralling out from it like a painted spider web.

Mortimer was standing on a box, waving his hands in the air addressing the crowd much like he had done before.

'Step right up. Step right up,' he cried out. 'Come and get your free coal, a new source of energy from Nordenburgh. Step right up.'

'I'm really worried about this,' said Molly.

'Me too,' agreed Charlie. 'When my dad told me I had to come today I wanted to throw-up. I can't believe I have to take something of Mortimer's to my house, even though our house is as cold as an ice box.'

'Let's just get it and get out of here,' said Molly. 'I'll help you.'

As Molly and Charlie approached Mortimer and his huge pile of coal, they saw King Alfred, Queen Claire, and Priscilla walking in the same direction. The royal family made it there first and Mortimer jumped off his box to greet them. As soon as his feet hit the ground he received a royal procession of hugs. Yes, the king, queen, and princess all embraced him and he smiled wildly upon receiving them. Instinctively, Molly and Charlie veered slightly to the right. They wanted to hear the conversation, but wanted to do so unnoticed. Charlie positioned his wheelbarrow by the edge of the pile, and he and Molly began filling it with coal, slowly. They had to strain to hear and though they couldn't make out everything, what they did hear sent shivers down their spines.

'Mortimer Weedly,' said King Alfred, 'I cannot thank you enough. Please reconsider accepting some token for your troubles?'

'Kindly no,' said Mortimer. 'Don't think anything of it. Why, it's Christmas Day, of course.'

'Well, there must be something we can do,' offered Queen Claire.

'In time, fine lady, there might be something. In time.'

'You'll simply have to name it,' said King Alfred, 'and I will do whatever is in my power to get it.'

'You are far too kind. Too much generosity for just an old dusty pile of coal, which—'

Mortimer cut himself off here rather cleverly, for it sparked the king's curiosity.

'Which, *what?*' asked the king.

'Oh nothing. Far be it from me to spit out any words against your gallant Knights Triumphant, especially on this day.'

'Speak to me, friend,' said the king. 'It sounds as though you have something on your mind.'

'Well, surely you know I was here once before. It's just too bad Knight MacDonald threw me out of Majestica before I could explain to your good people about this coal. My intentions were always honourable.'

'Yes, it's too bad indeed,' said King Alfred. 'Perhaps your intentions could have used some polishing that day. We're not receptive to panic mongering around here. No one has heard of coal before and uncertainty can cause fear, you know.'

'And for that I am heartily sorry. I did not mean to stir the emotions of your citizens so. I just wanted to help, but when you look—'

Again Mortimer cut himself off, pretending to be caught up in his own emotions.

'Speak,' said the king again. 'You are safe to share with me whatever is in your heart. When you look, *what?*'

'With all due respect, your Highness, when you look the way we Morrukks look, not so kind upon the eye, then you become accustomed to people ignoring you and fearing you. I was only trying to help.'

Mortimer Weedly normally looked as dry as a cracker, but somehow, from his dried out old body, he managed to squeeze out a single tear upon his cheek and it fooled Queen Claire completely.

'Come now,' she began, giving Mortimer another loving hug. 'Perhaps we can forgive each other and move on.'

Mortimer faked a sob, and the queen was compelled to make it right.

'Al, I won't stand for this man to return to Nordenburgh empty handed,' she said. 'Let us at least invite Mr. Weedly to be a part of our Christmas feast this evening.'

'Marvellous idea, Claire,' agreed the king. 'Mortimer, we will accept no refusal.'

'How kind you all are! Who am I to go against the invitation of such a stately family?'

'Then it's settled,' said the king. 'I shall notify my attendants at once. It will give us the perfect opportunity to discuss this coal of yours. I am very interested in learning all about it.'

'Very well, your highness. I have never been to a royal feast before, but if I may be so bold, I'd like to ask for just one thing.'

'Name it,' said the king.

'This night, let us heat your castle with coal,' said Mortimer trying to suppress his evil smile. 'The proof is in the pudding, they say.'

'We'd be honoured,' said King Alfred. 'Tonight we will dine as our souls are warmed by the gift from Mortimer: the most generous Morrukk in all of Nordenburgh.'

King Alfred, Queen Claire, and Princess Priscilla turned and walked by Molly and Charlie who, by now, had the wheelbarrow piled so ridiculously high with coal, it would have taken a horse to move it.

Priscilla paused, casting a hateful glare in Molly and Charlie's direction.

'Did you get all of that?' hissed Priscilla.

'Did we get all of what?' asked Charlie.

'Don't play dumb with me,' she hissed again. 'I know you were listening to every word. Too bad you won't be joining us. Our Christmas meals are always the best. And to think, Charlie, you could have been right there with us. Instead, you'll spend your day with Molly shovelling coal.'

Priscilla didn't give Charlie time to answer before bouncing merrily off to catch up with her parents. Molly and Charlie looked to Mortimer and he was looking directly back at them. His smile was more horrible than ever. He could barely contain himself and like the twisted old wretch that he was, he waved limply with his once-severed hand.

'Step right up,' he said climbing back onto his box. 'Free coal from the land of Nordenburgh. Let the homes of Majestica glow hot tonight!'

Charlie was fuming and, in an unbelievable display of strength, he grabbed the handles of the over-stuffed wheelbarrow, and picked it up.

'Come on, Molly,' he said, and he pushed the heavy wheelbarrow through the snow all the way home without once stopping to catch his breath. Molly couldn't believe it. Charlie was stronger beyond his years.

Just as Charlie heaved the wheelbarrow up and over, tipping the coal by his front step, a familiar plump chickadee landed on Molly's shoulder, whispered something in her ear, and flew off in the castle's direction.

'What did it say?' asked Charlie. 'Any news from Alkaios?'

'No,' answered Molly. 'She said she would spy on Mortimer tonight in the Castle, and for us not to worry.'

Chapter Twenty-Four
- *Advisor to the King* -

King Alfred arranged for Mortimer to be picked up at Town Centre in the royal sleigh. It was large and black, trimmed with gold filigree and had a large calligraphy style '*M*' on each door. The black horses pulling this coach numbered six and each horse was adorned with golden reins and a black feathery headdress. Mortimer was pleased the whole ensemble was the colour of midnight, preferring to believe it was not so much a sleigh, but a hearse.

As he was transported up the hill to the castle, Mortimer dangled out the window, smiling with his recent success. Through his lies and show of false sincerity, Mortimer had convinced the king to invite him to the royal feast. Everything was going according to his malicious plan.

'Only a few seeds left to plant,' chuckled Mortimer, 'and I'll have these pathetic Majesticans turning against themselves, I will.'

Mortimer closed his eyes and rocked back and forth.

'I want to sit upon the throne. I want to sit upon the throne. I *will* sit upon the throne,' he said to himself.

Once he was close to the grand castle, Mortimer opened his eyes and relished every detail. Situated on top of a hill, the castle appeared bigger than it actually was. But that's not to say that it wasn't large. It was huge in fact, dwarfing any castle in all the surrounding kingdoms, but it appeared even more imposing because of its strategic location.

The castle shone glorious and bright, as it was made from pure white stones which were quarried in far away lands. During the winter, the white castle was particularly serene for it blended in with the frosty landscape, as if it too were made from snow and ice. In the summer, with the grass and the surrounding gardens in full bloom, however, the castle looked like an iceberg floating on a sea of assorted jewels. But it was most beautiful in the fall, for embedded in the white stones were millions of tiny crystals. When the rays of the autumn sun touched the stones at just the right angle, the castle walls blushed with all the colours of the rainbow. The outer walls were covered with statues of white angels, white knights, and white animals, but Mortimer knew as soon as he ruled Majestica, they would all be replaced with beastly grey gargoyles who had fangs and claws and were dense with stony muscle.

Mortimer arrived and as his coach door opened, so too did the portcullis of the outer entrance. Waiting just beyond was King Alfred who insisted on greeting his guests in person.

'How now, Mortimer?' asked the king. 'Come in, come in. The castle is warm and the feast is almost ready.'

'Did you receive the coal?' asked Mortimer.

'Oh, yes,' answered the king. 'Every fireplace in every room on every floor is burning it now. Thank you for your generosity.'

'Thank *you*,' Mortimer said and they entered the massive double oak doors.

One could spend a lifetime describing all the wonderful artifacts, furniture, paintings, and fabrics decorating the inside and still not account for everything. The castle was like a museum whose air carried the very essence of Majestica. Each new spectacle shouted its historical importance to Mortimer, but he was deaf to it. He intended to throw the lot of it out as soon as he secured the throne.

The empty shells of the Knights Triumphant armour would be replaced with grotesque statues of fabled monsters and demons. The paintings of Majestica's royal lineage would be burned and in their place would hang pictures of Mortimer. The wonderfully sewn draperies would be taken down to make room for Mortimer's huge collection of stuffed animal heads. The richly stained furniture would be smashed to bits and replaced with piles of rubble. Mortimer loved his filthy mounds of refuse beneath the earth and he longed to turn this beautiful and orderly castle into a cluttered hall of junk.

The king discussed every item, and Mortimer seemed enthralled with the castle's history, but he was not. Inside his scheming brain, the wheels spun as he rehearsed his plans. He was crafty, to be sure, and could fool anyone of anything. It could be said of Mortimer that he was a great actor upon the stage of life.

They soon entered the Great Hall to find it hung with all things Christmas. There were wreaths and ivy and holly and the largest Christmas tree imaginable, decorated with silver and gold. There was also the smell of the feast working the air, but what made Mortimer hunger the most were the golden thrones raised up at the far end of the hall. He drooled when he saw them, and he coveted one throne in particular: the king's. Mortimer ached with envy and longed to sit in it and the king noticed his guest staring intently in their direction.

'Wonderful, aren't they?' remarked the king.

'Oh, I agree,' said Mortimer. 'You're quite the lucky man. I'd give anything to sit upon it. If even just for a minute.'

'Luck had a lot to do with it, but so did hard work,' corrected the king.

'I've been working hard, too,' said Mortimer. 'The coal we're enjoying didn't come easy, and—'

'Yes, yes, yes,' interrupted the king. 'I am eager to hear all this and more, but not on an empty stomach.'

It galled Mortimer to be interrupted. He wasn't used to anyone cutting him off and those in Nordenburgh who did so paid with their lives. If Mortimer didn't have grander schemes, he would have jumped on the king at that very moment and strangled the life out of him, but he could do nothing. Not yet. So he choked down his pride as easily as swallowing broken glass.

'Are you hungry?' asked the king.

'So hungry I could eat you up,' replied Mortimer and they both laughed.

'Then let us be seated.'

King Alfred naturally took the seat at the head of the table where there was a wonderfully carved armchair much larger than every other. He gestured to the foot of the table for Mortimer who immediately pretended that it was *this* end that marked the place of recognition.

Queen Claire arrived and took the seat directly to Alfred's

right.

'Hello down there!' she called, for it was truly a long table. 'Merry Christmas, Mortimer.'

'Merry Christmas,' he replied, attempting to fake some manners. He vaguely remembered it was proper to stand when a lady joins the table.

'Pri-scil-la!' called King Alfred with a booming voice that resounded throughout the entire castle. 'Come down here, please.'

Priscilla arrived shortly thereafter and she flounced up to the left of the king wearing her new Christmas clothes.

'Merry Christmas, Priscilla,' Mortimer said standing once again. 'You look very pretty tonight.'

'Do you like?' asked Priscilla with a quick twirl. She always looked for compliments, if even the person giving the compliments was as ugly as she believed Mortimer to be.

'You look like an angel,' Mortimer reassured.

Next to join the table was Marcus MacDonald and his wife. It was slightly uncomfortable for the good knight who had wanted to kill Mortimer the last time they had met, but he made a good show of it.

'Merry Christmas,' Marcus said. 'This is my wife, Elizabeth.'

'My, my, my,' said Mortimer standing once again and placing one hand over his heart. 'This table is peopled with those who are entirely beautiful, isn't it?'

Everyone laughed; Elizabeth blushed at the compliment, and took her seat.

Then MacDonald's children, Andrew and Stephen, came racing in and they were followed by the other knights and their families. Everyone's spirits soared, but none were so happy as Mortimer. He could barely keep his enthusiasm inside and he wanted nothing more than to jump up on the grand table and yell: *Fools!*

'Are we ready to eat, then?' asked the king once he believed everyone had greeted each other with kind holiday words. 'Very well.'

King Alfred clapped his hands twice, and there was a rush of activity around the table. A team of royal attendants and servants arrived in a flurry, while a familiar chickadee took the opportunity to fly in unseen. She perched atop a large family banner while the attendants delivered everything imaginable for the royal feast. First were the mashed and roasted potatoes, followed by huge gravy boats that actually looked like boats. Then there was every sort of vegetable steamed perfectly and a variety of freshly baked breads, buns, croissants, and Yorkshire puddings. There were also three different kinds of stuffing: one made with sage, one made with savory, and one made with saffomar.

Though everyone gathered round the table *ooohed* and *aahhhed* as each new platter was delivered, what came next pleased Mortimer most of all – the meat. There was a huge, perfectly bronzed turkey, but there was also a prime rib roast so large it could have easily fed everyone by itself. There were hams aplenty and beef ribs and pork ribs and quail and duck and pheasant and smoked salmon. It was true Mortimer hated animals, but he loved to eat them. Why, the only other pleasure animals afforded Mortimer was stuffing them to put on display.

'Ladies and gentlemen,' said the king standing and raising his glass. 'To friends at Christmas, and to Mortimer Weedly, our very special guest. The most generous Morrukk in Nordenburgh.'

There was a chorus of declaring *Hear Hear! To Mr. Weedly! Merry Christmas and Happy Holidays!* heard round the table as once again everyone gave each other festive cheer. The royal feast had begun and everyone dove into the bounty set before them.

Mortimer preferred to eat with his hands. He snatched up some juicy ribs and stuffed them into his gaping mouth. He enjoyed sucking the greasy fat from his fingers as much as he enjoyed sucking the meat from the bones. He made an awful racket while eating, but was excused for such poor manners because everyone believed he didn't know better. With the same reasoning, he was likewise excused for ignoring the traditional fork and knife when he opted to eat the turkey and prime rib with his hands as well. But he did know better. He just didn't care. The MacDonald youngsters found his manners quite funny and giggled to themselves.

It was a wonderful meal, and as everyone discussed how they could not eat another bite, trays of desserts were delivered. Mortimer couldn't believe his eyes. There were chocolate cakes, chocolate chip cookies, chocolate biscotti, triple chocolate brownies, hazelnut chocolate fondues with fruit, and his very favourite – chocolate truffles. Mortimer gorged himself with shameless gluttony. It wasn't long before his fingers, hands, and face were covered with the chocolaty sinfulness and he continued to stuff himself till he could hardly move.

Once he and the others had filled themselves to the point of being uncomfortable, everyone exited the Great Hall except for King Alfred and Mortimer.

'Full, Mortimer?' the king asked, giving Mortimer a healthy slap on the back.

'Yes, indeed, sire. Never have I had the pleasure of such a meal as this. You have a lovely family and I am honoured to be here with you all today.'

'Come now, Mort,' said the king modestly. 'May I call you Mort?'

'You may call me anything you wish.'

'Come now, Mort,' repeated the king, 'it was the least we could do for you, but now that we are both satisfied, having slain the wolves of hunger and thirst for another day, let us have that chat.'

'Most certainly, king, but first I have another small gift for you and your family.'

'You've given more than enough to Majestica already,' said King Alfred.

'Dear sire, if you insist on refusing, you deprive me the opportunity to give. Hardly customary, given the holiday.'

'Very well spoken,' said the king. 'If you feel as though you wish to give something else, I gladly accept.'

'Thank you,' said Mortimer and as a smile grew upon his face, so too did some sound of strange jingling from another room. Suddenly, thirteen Morrukks clad in clown costumes marched into the Great Hall. The king, with his eyes instantly bright and dancing, turned to Mortimer.

'Is this what I think it is?' asked the king.

'The circus *was* cut rather short, King, so I thought you and your family may want another taste.'

With a smile that seemed to go all the way round his head, King Alfred stared on in amazement. Some played instruments, while others juggled. Still others sang and danced around. Directly behind the Morrukks were the children falling over themselves to see what all the excitement was about. They whooped and clapped and laughed, and though Mortimer despised the sound of laughing children, he intended this gift to be a success.

Claire, Priscilla, and the other knights joined them and all were delighted with Mortimer's surprise. Soon, the great table was pushed off to the side to accommodate this smaller version of the

Nordenburgh Circus. The children and grownups alike gathered round the Morrukks to enjoy the entertainment. One Morrukk made animal balloons. Another brought a small table and played the role of magician and another read palms while another, the one drawing the largest audience, spoke of the strange human oddities that travelled around with the circus.

'Quite noisy, isn't it?' Mortimer said weaving his web.

'Too much so,' agreed the king, 'for a civil conversation, that is. But where can we go?'

The king looked around thoughtfully for a minute. He was eager to learn about Mortimer's coal, but he didn't want to miss anything either. For him to see what he wanted, while still being able to hear Mortimer without straining, left the good king only one option.

'Looks like your wish is about to come true,' said the king looking in the direction of the thrones.

'What?' asked Mortimer knowing full well what the king was suggesting. 'Where?'

'Let's sit on the thrones,' said the king. 'I'll even let you choose, though I suspect I already know which one you'll pick.'

'Surely, this is the greatest surprise of the day,' lied Mortimer.

'Are we not both leaders in our own lands?' observed the king.

King Alfred took his wife's throne without further discussion and Mortimer, the conniving imp that he was, sat in the king's. Mr. Weedly was beside himself with pleasure, but he tried to hide it lest the king become suspicious. In a blink, a dancing Morrukk pirouetted up to Mortimer and King Alfred and presented them with two goblets and a bottle of wine.

'What's this?' asked the king reaching for the wine and taking one goblet for himself. 'There's no label on this bottle.'

'That's because a wine this good cannot be named,' boasted Mortimer.

'Ha!' laughed the king. 'Well, it is known there are no greater wines than those of Majestica.'

'Forgive me for saying, Alfred,' Mortimer played, 'ahem, may I call you Alfred?'

'All right, *Mort,*' chortled the king.

'Forgive me for saying, Alfred, but you have yet to taste my wine. Seems rather unfair of you to pass judgment without first putting it to your lips,' said Mortimer.

'Perhaps another night,' declined the king. 'I have already made myself rather merry.'

'Then I will take that as bowing out of my good natured challenge,' Mortimer replied.

'Not so fast, Mortimer,' said the king pouring up two glasses.

After handing one glass to Mortimer, the king inhaled his own and was impressed with the wine's warm bouquet. He swished it around his goblet and took a healthy swallow. He smiled.

'Not bad, Mort,' admitted the king.

'Merry Christmas,' said Mortimer and he clinked his goblet against Alfred's. 'So, where shall we begin?'

'Let us be frank with each other,' said King Alfred. 'I have heard nothing but praise about your coal. Reports have been pouring in all day from the furthest reaches of Majestica and I am interested in acquiring as much of it as I can.'

'That's straight to the point, isn't it?' observed Mortimer.

'Who knows how long this storm will last,' said the king. 'I need to know if there is enough coal in Nordenburgh to see us through the winter and I need to know how much it will cost me.'

'We have mined enough for Majestica,' answered Mortimer. 'You needn't worry about that, but I am not interested in taking your money.'

'What *are* you interested in then? I am wise enough to know everything comes at a price. Are you prepared to make a business proposal?' asked the king.

'I'd like to think of it as a partnership,' clarified Mortimer. 'Nordenburgh will give Majestica all the coal it needs for a lifetime.'

'And in return?' asked the king.

'In return,' Mortimer said in a whisper, 'you help me find the Golden Tree of Truth.'

'The Golden Tree!' King Alfred said louder than Mortimer wished him to speak.

'Sh,' Mortimer urged. 'Yes, the Golden Tree.'

'That's nothing but a myth,' scoffed the king.

'Is it?' Mortimer asked as patiently as he could.

The king looked at Mortimer and saw he was deadly serious.

'I dismissed the silly notion of that tree ages ago,' said the king, 'but if it does exist, what makes you think I can help you find it?'

'Because,' continued Mortimer smoothly, 'there are Majesticans who know where it is and I have it on good authority they are close to finding it!'

'Who? Where?' demanded the king. 'Is this some sort of Christmas game?'

'This is no game,' corrected Mortimer. 'It is rumoured the Golden Tree grows somewhere in Majestica, and the least suspecting citizen knows where it is. Molly Withers.'

'Molly Withers?' said the king incredulously.

'Yes, yes, yes. Molly Withers. William Withers' daughter. You know William. I believe you had a falling out with him years ago,' said Mortimer.

'How do you know about that?' King Alfred asked, quite surprised.

'Come now, Al,' said Mortimer. 'It's no secret you once asked him to be your chief advisor and he refused.'

The king adjusted himself in his queen's throne seemingly disturbed by the turn in the conversation. He poured himself and Mortimer another glass and looked out across the hall to all his family and guests who were having a wonderful time. He smiled a half smile.

'I suppose he had his reasons,' said the king with a heavy sigh.

'Did he? Who would turn down such an offer? Why I'd give anything to be your advisor,' said Mortimer.

'He said the timing wasn't right,' said the king, recalling the disappointment of William's refusal.

'And then he renounced his knighthood too, didn't he?' Mortimer pressed. 'But that's not all, is it? When you turned to Marcus MacDonald with the same offer, he too refused. They may as well have slapped you in the face and told you they didn't want you as their king!'

'I'd trust Marcus MacDonald with my life,' said the king feebly, as cloudy thoughts began filling him with doubt, 'and William too, believe it or not.'

'Be that as it may,' said Mortimer, 'you've done without the council of a chief advisor for all these years. Too much of a burden for one man to carry, if you ask me.'

'Yes, Mortimer, that much is true,' agreed the king. 'It is a heavy load, but the things you speak of happened so long ago, I had all but forgotten about them.'

'Perhaps you chose to forget?' Mortimer suggested.

'I didn't realize anyone remembered, nor that anyone cared to remember. That was long before Majestica was the kingdom it is today,' said the king.

'You know what else I heard?' Mortimer prodded.

'What else can be said?' asked the king.

'I heard that you, William Withers, and Marcus MacDonald were all young knights at the same time,' said Mortimer. 'I also heard when *your* righteous leader, King Adalbrecht Elfinstone, appointed you heir to his throne, William Withers became quite jealous.'

'Now that I did not hear,' said the king. 'How is it you came to know all this?'

'Things are very hard to keep secret,' said Mortimer. 'Trust me.'

'I wonder whatever became of Adalbrecht,' said King Alfred. 'Everything I am today, I owe to that man, even though he was a chaser of dreams like you.'

'Sire, I don't mean to pull you from your youthful thoughts,' said Mortimer, 'but I have to impress upon you that Molly is a greater threat than you think.'

'She is just a child,' said the king dismissively. 'What can one little girl do to a king such as myself? I think this is all a bunch of poppycock anyway. You have no proof that Tree exists, and if it does, then let her find it. I hope it makes her happy.'

'What if it *does* exist? Would you not rather protect it and keep it safe, as opposed to letting it become a plaything for some bratty little girl?' asked Mortimer.

'Bratty, is she?' questioned the king, sensing Mortimer's urgency. 'What is it you really want, Mr. Weedly?'

'I want the gold,' said Mortimer only confessing a partial truth. 'I believe I have earned the right to sit on my very own throne, one as nice as this one even, and what's wrong with that? Surely, once upon a time you shared the same passion that courses within me now?'

'Yes,' agreed the king, 'but I didn't go around chasing fairytales to get here, you know.'

'You have your ways, and I have mine, but I don't know what all this fuss is about. It would seem to me that this is a win-win situation for you. I am asking you to help me find something you don't even believe in. Whether I find it or not, you are still guaranteeing Majestica will have an endless supply of coal. So what do you say?' asked Mortimer.

The king had consumed too much wine by this point in the conversation and his thoughts were fuzzy. He didn't believe in the Golden Tree and was therefore convinced he had nothing to lose. He had also received much criticism for not buying the coal the first time round and he wanted to make sure it never happened again.

'What do you say?' asked Mortimer again, holding out his ugly hand to the king.

'Deal!' declared the king as he grabbed Mortimer's hand and shook it.

'You've given me your word then? You promise to help me find the Golden Tree?' asked Mortimer.

'My word and my honour are one and the same,' said the king. 'Even though I think you're wasting your time, if there is anything at all I can do to help you find the Tree, I will.'

'Anything?' demanded Mortimer.

'Anything'!' asserted the king.

'That's a very wise decision,' said Mortimer cooly. 'First thing tomorrow I shall call for my strongest Morrukks to help disperse your coal as far as you wish. Perhaps you could give them lodging somewhere in the castle. Just until the storm subsides.'

'Tha' won't be a problem,' slurred the king.

'I'll insist they build sheds to keep the coal dry, of course, wherever your citizens wish,' continued Mortimer as he poured the king yet another glass of his potent wine. 'I'll send them back as often as is necessary. You've made a wise decision, Al. Your people will never go cold again. I'll take care of all your fears.'

'You know, Mor'imer, I have a mind to make you my chief advisor,' said the king. 'Especially if iss true what they say. You've travelled far an' wide, 'ave you?'

'What *me*?' replied Mortimer with as much modesty as he could stomach. 'I've been here and there, seen a thing or two, sure, but I'm just a Morrukk. Apart from matters of coal, what can I advise you, a great king such as yourself?'

'Are you refusing me as well?' asked the king having become sad with too much of Mortimer's wine infiltrating his veins and having recalled two previous rejections from William and Marcus.

'Never, sire. I would never refuse you. I promise to advise you anyway I can,' said Mortimer slyly.

'Then iss settled,' said the king.

King Alfred, though a little wobbly, stood up and pulled Mortimer to his feet. He cleared his throat and his mighty voice shook the hall.

'Ladies an' Gen'lemen,' he said demanding silence. 'I haff won'erful news. I've juss appointed Mr. Mortimer Weedly as chief advisor to the king – *ahem* – which is me of course.'

A chorus of cheers erupted in the Great Hall, and the plump chickadee flew out of the room unnoticed. She headed straight to Alkaios while everyone else clapped and whistled and called out congratulations to Mortimer. Everyone, that is, save Marcus MacDonald who was visibly displeased with such a random decision. King Alfred's eyes fell upon Marcus at this precise moment and the king suddenly felt the slightest bit threatened.

Mortimer knew his plan had worked brilliantly. *Only one more seed to plant,* he thought.

Chapter Twenty-Five
- *The Inquisition* -

King Alfred arose the next morning feeling a little worse for wear. The effects of the wine had mostly worn off during his slumber and his thoughts quickly returned to the decision to appoint Mortimer as his chief advisor. *Perhaps it's just what I need,* thought the king initially, but thoughts of *perhaps not* also went through his head. The king was a good judge of character and he reconsidered Mortimer's motives. Unable to determine if the previous night's decision was favourable or foreboding, he sent word to have Mortimer summoned.

Within an hour's time, Mortimer arrived at the castle and met with King Alfred in the Great Hall as they had done the night before. Only this time, the king seated himself in his own grand throne and set out a lesser chair for Mortimer below the raised dais.

'Come in,' said the king pointing to the chair.

Mortimer took his seat, disappointed he could not at least sit in the queen's throne at King Alfred's side.

'You called for me, sire?'

'Mortimer,' began the king, 'it would seem last night I made a hasty promise under the influence of your dreadfully tasty wine.'

Mortimer didn't know what to say having fallen asleep the night before confident everything was going his way.

'Does that mean you wish to retract your oath sworn to me upon Christmas Day?' asked Mortimer.

'It means,' continued King Alfred authoritatively, 'you have to present something more substantial than a fine grape to make me trust you as my chief advisor. If last night's discussion was founded in honesty and purity of intention, then surely you will be able to speak comfort to me now.'

'If comfort you need,' said Mortimer calmly, 'then comfort I give. Ask what you will, but if you ask about the Golden Tree, be warned. I doubt you will like what I have to say.'

'Why not?' asked the king.

'May I speak freely, as was the offer last night?' asked Mortimer.

'Go on,' said the king, leaning forward in his throne.

'I believe and accuse a select few of your devoted citizens of having committed heresy!' declared Mortimer.

'Heresy, Mortimer?' remarked the king without concern. 'Heresy is not so much a crime in Majestica as it is in other kingdoms. I have always encouraged the people of Majestica to think freely without fear of punishment.'

'If that be the case, said Mortimer, 'then I too must be exempt.'

'Naturally,' confirmed the king and Mortimer, stood, bowed, and cleared his throat.

'Your good Majesty,' said Mortimer, 'there are those around you who seek the Golden Tree for themselves.'

'Molly Withers? You mentioned her last night,' recalled the king.

'Namely, Molly Withers, but there are others,' answered Mortimer.

'And they are?' pressed the king.

'Charlie Gregg is one,' said Mortimer.

'What? Another child?' scoffed the king. 'Surely this is not the threat you spoke of.'

'Oh, a threat they are,' countered Mortimer. 'Whether you believe it or not, the Golden Tree of Truth exists, and Molly has been spending day and night looking for it these past months.'

'With whom? Who other than Charlie?' asked the king.

'Gabrielle, the retired school teacher, and there are others,' said Mortimer gaining confidence in the tale he was brewing.

'Who else?' demanded the king. 'Tell me everyone whom you believe is looking for that old twig and tell me why I should be remotely concerned. I have seen many a man waste away chasing such nonsense.'

'If it is a list you're after, then a list I shall give,' said Mortimer. 'Molly, Charlie, and Gabrielle are the cunning key players, but by strength of family ties and old grudges, I can only assume William Withers is very close to this conspiracy as well. Perhaps Marcus MacDonald, too? Now I don't know that for sure, but he certainly looked upon you rather disapprovingly last night when you honoured me with such a noble appointment.

King Alfred recalled that look from MacDonald, and it stung a bit.

And of course, there are the three witches,' continued Mortimer hurriedly, 'all buzzing around this sad scene.'

'Witches in Majestica? Rubbish!' said the king. 'The only known witches are those found in Wesdenburgh, and even they have not been seen in nigh a hundred years. I am growing impatient, Mortimer.'

'Oh, sire, indeed there are witches, and they are as real as the Tree itself,' said Mortimer. 'If you need to know their names, allow me to share that Genevieve Dubois, the apothecary, is certainly a witch and nightly she flies with her fellow demons of the sky, Janine, and Nathalie.'

'Witches, Mortimer? Please, mere children of nature. I have visited Genevieve myself when feeling poorly, and would personally vouch for her character,' said the king.

'Then vouch away,' said Mortimer growing equally impatient, 'but the indisputable fact is this: these people you deem to be of no threat to you will soon find the Golden Tree, and when they do—'

'And when they do *what?*' demanded the king, leaning further forward in his throne while glaring down at Mortimer.

'And when they do, the power you currently enjoy will be stripped away,' Mortimer declared.

'Ha!' laughed the king. 'Give them an orchard full of golden trees, and *I'll* still be king!'

'It's not the gold they're after,' Mortimer said hesitantly.

'What then?' asked the king.

Mortimer only had a few seconds before the king demanded an answer.

'What then?' growled the king again.

'There is much they want,' answered Mortimer. 'But first, help me to understand. As king of this great land, how much have you heard of the Golden Tree?'

'I've heard enough,' King Alfred said. 'Folklore. Myth. Rubbish. Nothing more than a bedtime story. I've heard enough to know this – you're obsessed with it and you're not the first.'

Mortimer suspected King Alfred scarcely understood the importance of the Golden Tree. The king didn't know its worth was not in the gold, but rather the knowledge it contained. The king didn't know about the law of attraction. The king didn't know the magic, and he especially didn't know that it should be kept a secret as Mortimer believed.

'If I am obsessed then it's with good reason,' said Mortimer. 'Now, you will either believe what I have to say or you will not. That is up to you, but know my *obsession,* as you call it, comes from years of exploring. I have seen many parts of the world and the legends shared with me are as varied as the creatures of the Aegis Sea. Some believe in abominable snow men, while others believe in werewolves. Still, some believe in vampires, leaving others to believe in mummies. This is not the case for our Golden Tree, though. It is ubiquitous. In one form or another, this story was once cherished in all the known lands. Think about it. If all cultures shared this common myth, might we not presume it contained a kernel of truth?'

'Perhaps, but not necessarily,' said the king. 'Perhaps the tale was forgotten because there was no truth to it. Tell me, Mortimer: what is it about the Tree that has you so intrigued? Share with me what you *really* know.'

Mortimer realized he would have to shed some light about the Tree or the king might not help him find it. Yes, thought Mortimer, but not without twisting things a bit.

'It comes to this,' Mortimer concocted. 'The Golden Tree equals power. *Your* power, even.'

'My power? I doubt that,' said the king.

'Even you are not immune to the laws of the universe,' said Mortimer, 'and there is one law you should pay particular attention to.'

'Go on,' said the king beginning to show some interest.

'It is the law of attraction,' said Mortimer, 'a universal law that can give you everything you could ever want. I don't know exactly how it works, but I do know if we were to find the Tree, the answers would be made clear to us.

Since it was first discovered, rulers around the world have fought to keep this power protected. They have shrouded it and disguised it as folklore and myth and fairytales. All the great kingdoms around the world have convinced their simple-minded citizens that the Golden Tree is, as you have said, nothing more than a bedtime story and this is a good thing. It must remain a secret! Yes, there were some rulers foolish enough to share the law of attraction with their people, but I assure you, they lived to regret it.'

'How so?' asked the king.

'They believed,' lied Mortimer, 'that there is enough of everything for everyone.'

'And is that not the case?' asked the king. 'Majestica seems abundant enough.'

'Sadly, there is not. I wish there was,' countered Mortimer. 'Those rulers did too, until, with teary eyes, they witnessed their kingdoms crumble around them. And yours will too if you do not mark my words.'

'Go on,' urged the king, 'I'm listening.'

'You don't have to look far to see that lack and limitation abounds,' said Mortimer. 'If there were truly enough for everyone, do you not think everyone in Majestica would have their own castle? They most certainly would. Why should *you* be the only one? There are those with and there are those without, and that is that. Life was intended to be this way and in all truth, it's *safer* this way.'

'Safer? Explain yourself,' said the king.

'Not all of us were born to be rulers,' answered Mortimer. 'To give power to everyone would be dangerous. You may as well hand a sword to a babe and ask him to swing it in battle. But, those of us who can wield it, those of us who are brave and calm and command attention and can make decisions in the blink of an eye, why, we come to govern those who cannot govern themselves, don't we? Without people like us, our kingdoms would be overrun with chaos. We keep the order when others cannot. We give harmony where there is confusion. We build towns and roads and irrigation because we have the will to do it, as burdensome as it is. But, in payment for these loads we carry, so we are rewarded with wealth and prestige. It's the way it was meant to be.'

'Part of me agrees with you Mortimer,' the king said beginning to digest Mr. Weedly's toxic words.

'Why, you yourself told me just last night that you worked hard to make Majestica the kingdom it is today,' Mortimer stressed.

'And that I did,' agreed the king, sitting back dopily in his throne.

'Now,' said Mortimer, 'just suppose there is truth in the legend of the Golden Tree, and suppose that Tree has the ability to give you whatever you want. I tell you, once it is found by the commoners, there will be castles popping up everywhere, cluttering your countryside. Do you think it's fair for any old person to happen upon the Tree, and *poof*, they have a castle? What of discipline? What of hard work? Well, this certainly doesn't seem fair to me.'

'Nor I, but I do believe we were all meant to be happy,' said the king, slowly filling with emotion.

The heavy words and false omens had taken root in the king's mind and he was the sadder for it. Mortimer was great with words. He used them like an evil warlock uses poison to concoct a deadly brew. Each vowel was arsenic, each consonant, cyanide, but stirred together his words smelled sweeter than almonds and made unsuspecting throats eager to swallow it down! Such was the effect on the king now. It all sounded logical to the king and he had long forgotten that there is more to the universe than logic – there is *Magic!*

'Noble king,' soothed Mortimer. 'We are all meant to be happy, yes, but rulers, no. This is why we must find the Golden Tree. This is why we must learn the laws. This is why we must keep the power to ourselves: to protect the very thing you have worked so very hard to accomplish. Don't let them steal it from you.'

As wise a man as King Alfred was, Mortimer had filled him with fear. He had drunk of Mortimer's brew and his eyes became as the morning dew.

'Come to me, Mort,' said the king raising his arms to Mr. Weedly.

'Don't let them take it from you,' whispered Mortimer again, approaching the king and giving him a hug. *'Don't let them.'*

'Mortimer, you have opened my eyes to a sad truth,' sobbed the king. 'I asked for you to speak comfort to me, and you have.

Yes, you have.'

'Do you wish me to remain your advisor then?' Mortimer asked gently.

'Advisor and friend,' said the king. 'I am sorry to have questioned you.'

The king released Mortimer from his desperate arms. Mortimer slid himself down in the queen's throne and pressed on.

'Though it pains me to even suggest this at such a tender time,' said Mortimer, 'I think you should summon those I spoke of immediately. No need to live with doubt. Question them as you have questioned me and see for yourself if all what I have said is not true.'

'Do you think that wise?' asked the king absently.

'I do indeed,' answered Mortimer, 'and should you find any falsehood in me whatsoever, do with me what you will.'

The king wiped his eyes, cleared his throat and clapped his heavy hands thrice. Suddenly a guard entered the hall.

'Yes, King?' asked the guard.

'Before any other task is done in this castle,' called the king, 'summon Molly Withers. Tell her I have...err...*ahem*...a gift for her.'

Mortimer continued to pour poison in King Alfred's ear for the three hours it took to summon Molly. She was ushered through the great corridors feeling suspicious and as soon as her eyes fell upon Mortimer poised in the queen's throne, her suspicions were confirmed.

'Come in. Come in,' said the king as jovially as he could.

Molly approached them slowly and Mortimer's eyes flashed at her and then to the king.

'Notice how slow she walks?' whispered Mortimer to the king. 'She certainly carries a heavy conscience, for upon her brow is written the word *greed!*'

'A little closer,' the king urged. 'A little closer.'

Molly's heart pounded as she sat in the chair Mortimer escaped just a few short hours ago.

'How's the weather?' asked the king. 'Still blowing, is it?'

'Yes, sir,' answered Molly, her skin beginning to perspire.

'Do you know why I have sent for you?' asked the king.

'I was told you have a gift for me and though I wanted it to be true,' said Molly rather bravely, 'I think perhaps a fib was told.'

'I, I do have a gift, but we'll get to that in a minute,' waffled the king. 'There's something I wish to discuss with you first. Do you know what that might be?'

Molly knew it had to do with the Golden Tree, but she didn't know what she should say.

'No, Sir, I do not,' she finally answered, all the while looking straight at Mortimer.

'How rude of me,' said the king. 'This is Mortimer Weedly, my newly appointed advisor. Have you met?'

Molly still didn't know if she should lie or tell the truth, and it weighed heavily upon her. She wanted to run away, but she could not. Part of her wanted to tell the king everything, but she suspected he'd dismiss her story of talking animals, Alkaios, the ghost of old man Craggly, and the witches, as lies. If he couldn't believe that much, Molly reasoned, he wouldn't likely believe what Mortimer had done to her and Charlie either.

'I say again, have you two met?' asked the king.

'Yes, sire we have,' answered Mortimer. 'The first time I came to town selling pelts. I gave her a lucky rabbit's foot.'

'Is that so?' asked the king.

'Yes, sir, but I didn't keep it,' corrected Molly.

'Was that the last time you saw each other?' the king asked of Mortimer.

'Not quite,' Mortimer replied and the king raised a brow. 'We saw each other when I brought the coal as well. The day I was so rudely thrown out of Town Centre by her father and that Marcus MacDonald.'

'Is that it?' the king asked turning back to Molly.

'Once more, sir. I saw him again yesterday at the coal pile,' said Molly.

'Very good,' said the king content at least this much was in order. 'Well Molly, it just so happens that Mortimer here has told me about the Golden Tree of Truth. Have you heard of it?'

If only Molly knew if she should tell the truth or not. Molly's brief bravery sputtered and was extinguished like a candle's flame between two wet fingers. An internal battle raged on, and despite being warned several times by Gabrielle to keep it a secret, she buckled under the pressure.

'Yes, sir,' Molly answered as quietly as a mouse, 'I have heard of it.'

'So you *have* heard of it?' repeated the king, now believing there was some truth in what Mortimer had said.

'But only in storybooks,' added Molly.

'You lie!' Mortimer cried out.

'Mortimer, be quiet,' demanded the king.

'Why are you asking me this?' asked Molly, fighting back the tears.

'Molly,' said the king more gently, 'it's best if you tell me the truth. Have you been searching for the Golden Tree?'

Molly looked to her feet.

'Yes,' she finally replied. She had given up hope that things would work out as they should.

'I told you! I told you!' Mortimer said. 'Didn't I tell you?'

'And with whom?' asked the king.

Molly's heart was broken in two. She felt to answer this question was to betray Charlie and Gabrielle utterly. Her guilt consumed her.

'Just me,' she answered weakly.

'SHE LIES!' cried Mortimer again. 'What about Gabrielle and Charlie? Are you so quick to forget about your fellow treasure hunters?'

'Tell the truth now, Molly,' added the king. 'Are you sure you've been looking for the Tree all by yourself?'

'I *am* telling the truth,' Molly tried to say convincingly, but it did not work.

'Just look at her,' Mortimer squeaked. 'The little brat's not capable of telling the truth!'

'Mortimer!' said the king with his mighty voice. 'Not another peep!'

'Sorry, sire,' said Mortimer, almost trying to hide in his seat. 'It just pains me to see you deceived so.'

'Where did you learn about the Tree?' the king asked roughly.

'From books mostly,' answered Molly.

'From books *mostly,* or from books *entirely?*' pressed the king.

'Entirely,' Molly replied and Mortimer squirmed in his chair trying to bite his tongue.

With every question he asked, the king grew more impatient with Molly. He suspected she was not telling the truth, and Molly realized there was no going back.

'Don't lie to me, Molly,' said the king leaning forward in his throne once again.

'And a little from Gabrielle,' Molly added.

'*See?*' said Mortimer just above a whisper.

'And what would you do if you found the Tree?' asked the king.'

'I would share it with the world!' declared Molly truthfully not expecting this answer would displease the king as much as it did.

With every word falling awkwardly out of her mouth, the more she made it seem Mortimer had told King Alfred the truth.

'Do you know where it is?' asked the king eagerly.

'No, sir,' answered Molly.

'I can't stand all these lies!' cried Mortimer as he stood pointing one long ugly finger at Molly. 'You know exactly where the Tree is, don't you? You've likely known all along. You, the hag Gabrielle, and that coward Charlie have found it, and you're just waiting to steal it in the middle of the night? Aren't you?'

'Mortimer!' shouted the king. 'Sit down!'

Mortimer did as he was told, but the damage was done. King Alfred didn't know how much of what Molly had said was fact or fiction. He also didn't know what to make of Mortimer, except that this Morrukk knew that things had been going on in Majestica behind the king's back.

'Forgive me, gracious King,' said Mortimer in a whisper too soft for Molly to hear, 'but you know in your heart this girl is lying. Why, she's hardly spoken a truthful word on her own free will. You've had to pull each answer out of her like a rotten tooth. If nothing more, sire, surely you now have grounds to call the others in for questioning and I advise you to do this before they steal the Tree out from under you!'

The king clapped his hands again and the same guard reappeared.

'Yes, King?' asked the guard.

'Send for William Withers, Charlie Gregg, and Gabrielle Sullivan at once!' boomed the king.

'NO!' Molly cried out, and she stood and bolted towards the door.

'Detain her!' called the king and just as she was about to reach the door, the guard caught her and held her fast.

'*Only the guilty run,*' whispered Mortimer in the king's ear.

Molly kicked and screamed and bit the guard's hand. Though he yelled out from the pain, he didn't let her go.

'King Alfred, you're making a big mistake!' Molly cried as she stomped the guard's toes, sending a lightning bolt of agony through his foot. 'It's Mortimer who wants the Tree. It's Mortimer, I'm telling you!'

'What should I do with her?' asked the struggling guard who'd had his fill of Molly's squirming.

'Throw her in the dungeon!' yelled Mortimer. He had always wanted to say such a thing.

'But,' replied the guard awkwardly, 'we don't have a dungeon,'

'Just put her in a guest room for now,' said the king, 'but see to it that she is kept comfortable, warm, and fed. She's being detained for questioning and, as of yet, is guilty of no crime.'

'Yes, King,' replied the guard as Molly chomped into his other hand.

The guard spun her around and raised his hand as if to hit her. Mortimer smiled ear to dirty ear.

'Halt!' yelled the king, but it was too late. The guard had swung his hand round, and struck Molly across her face. She fell to the floor and covered her head.

'She bit my hand!' shouted the guard.

'I don't care if she bit it off,' countered the king. 'If you act out like that again, if you so much as lay a piece of dust upon her, I'll see you whipped for it!'

The guard dragged Molly out of the Great Hall, past a spying Priscilla, down a long corridor, and into a guest room where he threw her to the ground so hard that she scraped her knees.

'Bite *my* hand, will ya?' he spat as he locked the door on his way out.

Molly sat there for a short time sobbing and holding her knees. They were bleeding and stinging and she found it hard to straighten her legs. But Molly was strong and not just for a young child. She soon stood on her shaky legs and looked around the room trying to devise a way to escape. It was a lovely room and under different circumstances, Molly would have loved to have been a royal guest. She had only been in the castle once before on a school trip, but she didn't get to see as much as this.

The room was large and beautiful and the only obvious thing it lacked was a grand bookcase. There was a large soft bed with a knitted quilt and three huge pillows. Even given her current circumstances, Molly could no more ignore a bed such as this, than she could turn away jumping in a snow bank. She climbed up on it and, after several moments of dejected contemplation, she jumped once, then twice. Oddly enough, her knees felt improved the instant she began jumping and Molly was reminded of all she had learned. Doing something that brings you joy pushes away troublesome thoughts. Just like Charlie and his fishing. It was as if happiness and sadness cannot be felt at exactly the same time. You can look forward, or you can look back, but you can't look both ways at the same time. It was up to you which way you look, and Molly was currently looking at her feet leaving the bed with each gigantic leap.

The last bounce saw Molly lying flat on the bed. She was amazed at how very comfortable it was and also how very tired she was. Hardly aware of what she was doing, Molly snuggled under the covers and fluffed up a pillow. She then closed her eyes and, though her thoughts continued to whirl about, she fell fast asleep.

Upon waking, Molly noticed the light outside the window had changed. It must have been long past suppertime, she figured, and her thoughts were made the truer when her belly grumbled. She climbed out of bed, walked straight to the locked door and began knocking.

'Hello? Is anyone there?' Molly called out.

After a few minutes of knocking and calling out, Molly heard quick footsteps far too little to be the guard's. She hoped it was someone to let her out.

'Hello?' Molly whispered.

'You better enjoy this,' Priscilla's voice spat beyond the door. 'This is the closest to being a princess as you'll ever get.'

'Prissy, please let me—'

'STOP CALLING ME PRISSY!' she screamed. 'Why won't anyone listen?'

Molly knew the answer: the more you yell at something to go away, the more you attract that very thing into your existence.

The little footsteps scurried off, and were replaced by heavier steps and the jingling of keys. Molly knocked again.

'I'm hungry!' Molly cried as the heavy steps stopped just outside the door.

Molly took a few steps back and the door swung open, revealing the horrible guard from before.

'How's your hand?' Molly asked, noticing it was wrapped in a bandage.

'Not bad,' he said with a shrug. 'How's your cheek?' The guard's face wrinkled with delight and without saying another word he gave Molly a silver platter.

'I want to speak to my father,' demanded Molly, and the guard's face brightened.

'Your father will be here soon enough,' said the guard. 'Oh, they are in trouble, aren't they? He, Charlie, and Gabrielle have proved a little more difficult to find than you, but we'll find 'em. Oh yes, we'll find 'em.'

The guard turned, laughed, and locked the door behind him.

Molly took the silver platter back to bed, removed the cover, and ate up everything inside. It was quite a delicious meal considering she was a captive. She took special care not to spill any food on the bed's fine linens and was amused to recall what Priscilla had said a few minutes ago. There *was* a small part of Molly that felt like a princess and she tried to hold onto these thoughts as she climbed out of bed to look around. Perhaps there was a secret passage, or a hidden key to let her out.

On one side of the bed was a small, but beautiful chest of drawers. The top drawer was completely empty, the middle drawers had nothing more than a few forgotten nightgowns, but Molly couldn't open the bottom drawer at all. It was stuck, or locked. Molly took a step back, placed both hands on the handle and gave a hard tug. All at once, the front part of the dresser splintered and cracked as the drawer flew open with a momentum that sent Molly flying – taking the drawer with her. Now she had done it. The front of the fine dresser was ruined, and there wasn't even anything inside the drawer. It was dusty, though, except for a clean rectangular spot.

A book! thought Molly. But what book, and where did it go?

Molly dragged the drawer back to the dresser and that's when she spotted it. On the floor inside the cavity of ·the dresser, underneath where the bottom drawer would go, Molly found a very old book covered with dusty cobwebs. There was also a massive, shiny, black spider standing beside it as if it was the book's guardian. It stared defiantly up at Molly, but she shooed it without delay and snatched the book up in her hands. *Majestica's Popular*

Folklore by Engelbert the Great. Molly couldn't believe her eyes. Engelbert the Great!? Was it really possible Molly now held a book bearing the name of the great wizard who planted the Golden Tree? If real, this was surely one of a kind.

Molly opened it immediately, flipped through the pages, but saw nothing of great significance until she returned to the inside front cover. Scribbled with horrible penmanship was a brief inscription:

> *'Dear Alfred, Perhaps someday we'll meet again*
> *and I'll be able to tell you the Truth.*
> *I have no doubts you will make a great King.*
> *I must find what I have lost.*
> *A.E.'*

Who is A.E? It's not the author's initials.

Molly was convinced this had something to do with the Golden Tree. Everything she had experienced from first meeting Gabrielle led her to this precise moment and she believed she was locked in this room on this day for some important reason.

The book contained both stories and pictures of dragons, knights, fair maidens, leprechauns and sea monsters, but that was it. Nothing extraordinary. Molly flipped through it one final time and happened to notice the book began on page 7. She checked again and, sure enough, pages 1 through 6 were missing. They'd been torn out, but by whom? And why? What story in *Majestica's Popular Folklore* had been removed? Maybe the missing chapter was about the Golden Tree. Perhaps King Alfred had found this book, and wanted to find the Tree for himself. Maybe he was like other selfish rulers outside Majestica.

Molly brought the book to the other side of the bed where there was an ornate chair with a matching vanity. On the vanity lay combs, brushes, a small personal mirror, and two finely carved wooden boxes which Molly knew *must* be opened.

Molly set the book down, and upon opening a drawer in the first box, her eyes were flooded with a glorious twinkling. It was a jewellery box over-stuffed with the most breathtaking jewellery she had ever seen. There were golden necklaces and golden earrings and golden rings aplenty. There were also rubies and diamonds and pearls not attached to anything, but piled in different compartments.

Molly couldn't resist touching it all. One particular silver necklace caught her attention and she placed it round her neck, knowing her mother would do almost anything for jewellery as fine as this.

Her eyes scoured the vanity once more and fell upon the second carved box. She opened it and smiled curiously. There were powder brushes, mascaras, and lipsticks galore. Having never had the chance to wear makeup before, Molly couldn't resist snatching up the small mirror and applying a little lipstick and a little rouge on her cheeks. Once complete, she looked up to the vanity's huge golden framed mirror to take it all in, but where she expected to see a picture of beauty, she instead saw a very plain girl looking back at her. She didn't seem to match the jewels, the makeup, the room, or the castle. Even though Molly recalled Gabrielle telling her that our minds are not often our best friends, she felt unworthy of wearing such fine things and as a tiny tear rolled across her cheek, she heard something hit the large window behind her.

Molly carried the chair over to the window, climbed on it, and when she looked outside she saw a full moon shining above a thicket of leafless trees. She must have been in the rear of the castle that backed on to a forest. Again something hard hit the window, but she could not see where it was coming from. It was too dark. Molly lifted the latch on the window wondering why she hadn't tested this earlier. It opened easily and Molly was surprised the guard could have been so careless and she could have been so oblivious. Molly stuck her head out in the cool with the intention of jumping. She could scarcely make anything out, but when her eyes adjusted, she realized the guard hadn't been careless at all. The ground was at least fifty feet below.

'Molly!' she heard an unseen man whisper urgently from somewhere beneath her, but she didn't recognize his voice.

'Molly!' she heard again and her heart raced. 'Did you find it?'

Molly instinctively pulled her head back inside and heard a double thud against the wall followed by repetitive creaking. Molly jumped off the chair and took one step back. The creaking grew louder and then the face of a very old man appeared in the window.

He had a long white moustache with long white hair spilling out from under a rather old hat. If Molly was forced to say what she was looking at, she would have guessed a magician. He had a very kind face, but his eyes expressed urgency.

'Molly,' he whispered again, while scanning the room.

'Yes?' she replied and his face lit up like a shower of fireworks.

'I must get you out of here,' he said. 'Have you found it?'

Something about him seemed trustworthy, but Molly wasn't completely convinced. This sort of man appearing at her window to save her was the last thing she was expecting.

'Have I found what?' asked Molly just as the man's face fell on the book left on the vanity.

'You did, you did,' said the man. 'Hurry now. Alkaios has sent me for you. Grab the book and let's go!'

'You know Alkaios?' asked Molly, partially relieved.

'Yes,' the man answered. 'He is waiting for you. They are all waiting for you.'

There was a sudden horrible sound of familiar jingling and from behind Molly the locked door flew open. Molly expected to see the guard once again, but it was Mortimer Weedly. His eyes penetrated hers and she froze.

'Quick Molly! Grab the book!' urged the man in the window reaching out to her, but Molly couldn't move.

Mortimer must not have noticed the man in the window at first, but upon hearing him speak, Mortimer's head snapped in his direction.

'*It's you!*' Mortimer sneered.

Mortimer then observed the broken dresser, the open jewellery boxes and the silver necklace Molly had around her neck. He smiled.

'THIEVES!' Mortimer shrieked. 'There are thieves in the castle! THIEVES IN THE CASTLE!'

Molly looked back to the window and the man's arms still reached out to her.

'Hurry,' said the man again and Molly felt a rush of energy pass through her body.

In an instant, she retrieved the book and returned to the chair as her rescuer disappeared below the sill. With a speed that suggested a lifetime of window escapes, Molly had her legs through the opening to follow the man down the ladder, but her dangling feet were unable to find the rungs.

'Thieves! Thieves! Thieves!' Mortimer shrieked again, storming the window.

Molly's legs flailed frantically, but she could not find her footing until a warm hand grabbed her ankles and directed each spastic foot to the ladder while thunderous footsteps grew within the castle. Molly began her descent, but just as her fingers slid over the sill, Mortimer grabbed one of her hands and she dropped the book inside.

'Gotcha!' Mortimer said triumphantly, knocking the ladder to the ground with his other hand.

'Little snooping brat!' hissed Mortimer. 'Where's the Golden Tree?'

Molly was transfixed by his horrible eyes and devilish face.

But then she noticed the very hand which held her own had stitches all the way round its scarred wrist and this gave her an idea as horrible as any of Mortimer's own divination.

If you have ever seen a cat swat a moth out of the air, you'd have an appreciation for the speed in which Molly reached up and clawed frantically at the stitches on Mortimer's wrist. Three stitches broke instantly, and that's when Molly noticed something else. Hidden inside Mortimer's sleeve, were several rolled up pages peeking out at her.

Though Molly didn't know what would come of her falling to the earth below, if she had to die it would *not* be in the arms of Mortimer. Molly grabbed his once-severed hand with both of hers and shook violently. Instantly, they both heard a horrible tearing sound and Molly felt sick as she saw Mortimer's remaining stitches come undone, one by one. As each stitch tore open, so too did the wound and a nasty ooze poured over her slipping hands.

Mortimer desparately tried to hold on to his own hand, but it was too late. With one final yank, Molly pulled it clean off, and just before falling back, she released Mortimer's again-severed hand and snatched the papers from his sleeve.

Molly plummeted for what seemed an eternity with Mortimer's hand following her down. She closed her eyes and random memories flickered in her mind. She thought of her mother and her father, Charlie and Gabrielle, and then recalled how all the woodland creatures bowed their heads for Alkaios. So followed thoughts of Genevieve and her smiling face the first time the two of them met. Molly recalled how Genevieve helped Charlie with one of her potions inside her strange shop, her black cat Snowball, and the old broom that was never meant for sweeping. Molly also recalled each wrinkle that framed Genevieve's kind eyes and when she said...

'Bonjour, Molly,' said Genevieve. 'That was a close one, non?'

In a whirling of wind and snow, Genevieve cut through the veil of the dark night upon her broom, and caught Molly just before she hit the ground. Molly came to her senses and held on tightly as Genevieve steered her broom in such a way that she was able to scoop up a handful of snow. With Molly still in her safe grasp, Genevieve shot straight back up the wall of the castle, whizzed by the open window and threw the snowball inside smacking Mortimer squarely in his face.

'Molly Withers lives!' Genevieve cried with a joyful cackle as she zipped back down to safety.

Genevieve landed beside the old man with kind eyes just as Janine appeared with Charlie in tow.

'Charlie!' exclaimed Molly.

'Nice necklace! Trying to impress Mortimer?' asked Charlie smiling as Nathalie arrived solo. Nathalie hovered beside the man who looked like a magician, gestured to the rear of her broom and said, 'If you please, Monsieur.'

As powdery snow eddies upward with the slightest wind, so did the three witches take to the air with their passengers Charlie, Molly, and the one they all hoped was Engelbert the Great. Looking over her shoulder as the castle shrank in the background, Molly wondered if her father had been captured.

Chapter Twenty-Six
- *A Stranger Speaks* -

They soared through the air at top speed. Over the castle, over the orchard, and over Bokwus Forest, eventually returning to Alkaios' hidden lair. Approaching the door of twisted roots, Genevieve snapped her fingers; it opened, and they entered in a *whoosh*. Once they made it to the inner cavern, the witches landed and everyone dismounted. Already seated round the table were Gabrielle, Tommy, and the leprechauns, with Alkaios on his grand throne.

'Where are Lillian and the other fairies?' Charlie asked.

'Keeping an eye in Bokwus,' answered Gabrielle.

'Has anyone heard f—' began Molly.

'Everyone, please take a seat,' Alkaios beckoned and they all did except the mysterious man from the castle.

'By now,' said Alkaios, 'I suspect you are all very anxious to meet the strange face among us. Indeed, he has an interesting tale to tell.'

'I don't mean to interject,' said Molly, 'but d—'

'Your father is locked inside the castle,' answered Alkaios, 'but he is safe for now.'

'Then we have to—' continued Molly.

'I am sorry, Molly, but we do not have the time,' said Alkaios, closing the subject as gently as he could.

As much as it pained Molly, she agreed with Alkaios. The Tree must be found first. After a few difficult moments her eyes expressed renewed determination. The strange man took his cue, stepped forward slowly, and removed his old hat.

'Despite your hopeful eyes,' he said slowly, 'I am *not* Engelbert the Great.'

Everyone gasped in disbelief.

'Well, who be yee?' asked Tommy Troublesome.

'I am Adalbrecht Elfinstone,' he said.

His initials instantly registered in Molly's mind and she blurted out: 'So you're A. E. Of course! You wrote a note inside *Majestica's Popular Folklore* for King Alfred, didn't you? That's the book I found!'

'For certain, I did,' agreed Adalbrecht, 'and where is it? You did get it, didn't you?'

'I did,' Molly hesitated, 'but I dropped it inside the castle when Mortimer grabbed me. But...hang on...I...'

Molly suddenly recalled snatching the rolled papers from Mortimer's sleeve, but she didn't know where she put them. The leprechauns and fairies grumbled with impatience, while Molly looked around frantically. She knew she had them – *somewhere*.

'What are you looking for?' asked Charlie.

'I grabbed some papers from Mortimer just before I fell, but I can't find them,' answered Molly. 'I must have dropped them. Now I don't have the book, and I don't have those papers. Whatever they were, they must have been important to be up Mortimer's sleeve like that. I bet they were the—'

'Oh, Molly, Je m'excuse,' said Genevieve reaching inside her cloak. 'How forgetful. You dropped these when you fell out of the castle.'

Genevieve passed Molly the rolled pages and she slowly opened them. Everyone held their breath.

'Now wait just a wee minute!' said Tommy looking around at everyone. 'Before we look at those, shouldn't we let this man 'ere explain himself, or did yee all miss who he said he was?'

Everyone's hopes were dashed and they seemed too confused to think clearly.

The stranger smiled: 'I say again: my name is Adalbrecht Eflinstone. I am the true founding king of Majestica, but you will only find my name in the very oldest of history books.'

'That's what I thought you said,' declared Tommy with glaring eyes. 'What sort o' sham is this? Where's Engelbert? We weren't lookin' for an old decrepit man sufferin' from delusions of grandeur, as pleasant as yee are, I'm sure.'

'Alas,' said Alkaios, 'it has finally been confirmed – Engelbert the Great has been dead these many years, but this man before you is who he claims to be.'

There was an explosion of *What do you mean?* and *Who did he say he was?* and *I can't believe it?* from the leprechauns and fairies and witches.

'Excuse me for rantin' an' all,' added Tommy above the noise, 'but am I the only one here who is confused as all blazes and, forgive me for sayin', a wee bit more than just skeptical?'

'*Si-lence!*' commanded Alkaios standing up from his throne and all mouths slammed shut. 'Do you think I would bring a fraud before you at such a time as this? The truth *is* as Adalbrecht says. It was *this* man – this man here today – who ruled Majestica before King Alfred all those years ago. Now, without interruption, listen to what he has to say.'

From his long cloak, Adalbrecht produced a much larger and much older book than the one Molly tried to take from the castle. Curiously, the book Adalbrecht held was bound closed with a golden lock!

'This belonged to the real Engelbert,' said Adalbrecht, 'the man in which you have placed all your hopes. It is the *Diary of Magic* which Engelbert himself had written.'

'Well, that's a fine book now, isn't it?' said Tommy.

'This isn't just any book,' said Adalbrecht.

'So what is it, then?' asked Tommy unable to control himself. 'Some light after tea readin'?'

'After planting the magical seed,' continued Adalbrecht, 'Engelbert the Great spent his lifetime writing down all the answers the Golden Tree had given him, and he locked them inside this diary. Whatever happened to him, or the key, no one knows for sure, but centuries later, it chanced that this diary found its way to me by way of a weary traveller who asked to lodge with me one stormy night. The payment for my hospitality was what you see here. Of course, I asked the traveller who she was and how she came by it, but she said she couldn't tell me to protect her own safety. The knowledge contained within these pages, you see, is nothing less than the workings of the Universe. All the natural laws which govern our entire existence and everything you ever wanted to know about love, and happiness, and power, and peace are captured in these pages.'

'So what have you been doing all these years?' asked Tommy. 'Hoardin' it to yerself, I s'ppose?'

'No,' Adalbrecht answered, 'I haven't even opened it. I do not possess the key. No, Tommy, I've been running – running for as long as I care to recall.'

'If you don't mind me askin', running from whom?' asked Tommy. 'I am sorry for saying, but you don't look like a runnin' sort at all. And if *you* don't have the key, who does?'

'I don't know, Tommy. The traveller didn't tell me. Perhaps she herself did not know. Well, time passed and certain men came to know that I was in possession of Engelbert's diary and they have been hunting me ever since.'

'The Morrukks?' asked Molly.

'Yes,' said Adalbrecht. 'The Morrukks are one group of men, but there are others. They must believe I also possess the key, but I do not.'

'So that's why you wanted the book from the castle?' asked Molly. 'Because they were both written by Engelbert the Great.'

'Right again, Molly' Aldabrecht confirmed. 'But don't worry. Though you left *Majestica's Popular Folklore* behind, I somehow suspect you found what we are looking for all the same. Were you not thinking *there are no coincidences* when I found you?'

Adalbrecht's knowing eyes twinkled, and Molly slowly unrolled the papers in front of her. After a brief, but thorough inspectioin, Molly didn't see anything extra special. It was nothing more than a six page story called: *The Golden Tree*. Molly flipped through the pages, but the only noteworthy characteristic was that the story began on page 6 and progressed to page 1.

'I don't get it,' said Molly.

'Well, I'm glad I'm not the only one,' added Tommy. 'What does it say, Molly?'

'It's just a short story on the Golden Tree,' answered Molly. 'I haven't seen this particular one before, but I've read countless others just like it.'

'Oh no, Molly, you haven't read *any* story quite like this,' Adalbrecht warmly contradicted. 'Somewhere in those papers you hold is the precise location of the Golden Tree. Don't you see? These are the very pages missing from *Majestica's Popular*

Folklore!'

Molly began reading it right away, as Adalbrecht continued:

'The traveller and I talked all that night and into the early morning, and she shared with me the story of the Golden Tree – *that story* – and why it was to be protected for all times. I was so excited and intrigued with this traveller's tale, I believed it was my duty to help anyway I could. She then warned me of the danger. She told me how Engelbert the Great prophesied there would come a time when the magic of the earth would all but disappear and violent men would seek to destroy the Tree forever. Then, and only then, just before a great battle, a riddle would be decoded by the princess of the land...and here she is.'

'But I am not a princess,' declared Molly softly, noticing she was still wearing the royal silver necklace. She tore it from her neck, and threw it on the table. 'I'm no more a princess than you are a–a–*magician!*' she added a little louder.

Everyone looked to Molly while she turned her attention back to the story. She read it quickly, but didn't find anything at all that spoke of the Tree's location. She felt as though a boulder had been chained to her ankle, and she had been thrown into the sea. Trying frantically to swim back to the surface, she plummeted further and further, fathom by fathom, each inch bringing more pressure than the last.

'Come now,' said Adalbrecht. 'It would seem to me that you *are* the very princess whose coming was foretold all those years ago. I am not the wizard that you were hoping to find, but that does not mean I cannot do magic.'

Adalbrecht raised his hands and the silver necklace came to life, rose, floated before Molly's sad eyes and then fell in her hands.

'Never once did I call myself Engelbert,' continued Adalbrecht, 'but having spent a lifetime in hiding protecting the diary, only to surface now and again looking for you, people began calling me Engelbert. You see, it's not the name which makes us who we are, but our actions, and I have no doubt when the time comes, you'll decode this riddle and save the Golden Tree.'

Charlie placed one hand on the small of Molly's back, and rubbed it gently.

'We all believe in you, Molly,' said Charlie. 'It's time you believe in yourself.'

'Ah, now that's a fine story, Adalbrecht,' said Tommy. 'Yee

got me all misty eyed, but how can yee be certain the riddle's in that story Molly's got in her hands, and not some other book?'

'Because there are no coincidences,' answered Adalbrecht softly.

'But I don't even see a riddle here,' objected Molly scanning the pages again and then stuffing it in Charlie's hands.

Charlie had a quick look, and then passed it on to Gabrielle who read it without luck and then placed it on the table.

'Perhaps we witches should have a look,' offered Genevieve. 'We are very good with riddles, non?'

Nathalie and Janine nodded their own praise.

The three witches looked over Gabrielle's shoulder, but they could not find the riddle either. The leprechauns were next to read the story, followed by Adalbrecht, but no one was able to come up with the answer, and as the night grew terribly long, everyone fell asleep. All except for Molly and Alkaios.

'What am I doing wrong?' Molly asked quietly looking once more at the story.

'You aren't doing anything wrong,' answered Alkaios. 'Sometimes things just come to us when we least—'

'Wait a minute,' interrupted Molly. 'I think I found something.'

'What is it?' asked Alkaios.

'Look, the first word on page 6 is *Beyond,* and the last word on that page is *Where,*' said Molly shuffling the pages, 'and the first word on the fifth page is *Land* and the last word on that page is *Floats.* Isn't that a little odd?'

'Maybe a little. Go on,' encouraged Alkaios.

'I think this is it,' said Molly. 'See? The first word on page 4 is *On,* and the last word is *Tea,* so together it reads: *Beyond Where Land Floats On Tea.*'

'I see,' said Alkaios.

'But there's more,' said Molly hurriedly. 'The first word on page 3 is *There,* and the last word is *You.* The first word on page 2 is *Will* and the last word is *Have.* The first and last words on page 1 are *To* and *Dig,*'

Molly looked up Alkaios – her eyes shining brightly – and then she arranged the pages on the table one final time.

'You just have to follow the page numbers! That's why they're backwards!' declared Molly. '*Beyond Where Land Floats On Tea*

There You Will Have To Dig!'

'That's it, Molly. I knew you were the one,' said Alkaious warmly. 'Everyone up! Everyone up! Molly has found the riddle!'

'So, what is it?' asked Charlie with a yawn.

'Beyond where land floats on tea, there you will have to dig,' said Molly. 'This must be it, but I have no idea what it means. Do you?'

'Not a clue,' answered Charlie. 'Never been good with riddles.'

'Where land floats on tea?' remarked Tommy, wiping his eyes. 'Too bad it weren't beyond the land that floats on swillers. Now that'd be something worth lookin' for. I sure hope yee have something more than that. How do we even know it's in Majestica at all?'

'We can only hope,' said Alkaios, 'that Engelbert the Great, who lived in these lands one thousand years ago, planted it close to his heart and home.'

'Fine thing that is,' remarked Tommy. *'Hope.'*

Suddenly there was a draft, and Lillian arrived in a great panic.

'Get up! Get up! Get up!' cried Lillian.

Those not yet awake jumped up with her tiny cries.

'What's the matter, Lillian?' asked Alkaios.

'Majestica is turning black!' cried Lillian.

'From what?' asked Gabrielle.

'From the coal!' Lillian declared. 'People have been burning it relentlessly and every chimney in every home and shop is belching out a thick black smoke day and night. It rises, and then falls again. It's everywhere. It's in the streets, it's on the trees, and it is spreading.'

'What else?' asked Alkaios.

'The Morrukks are in Bokwus Forest,' panted Lillian. 'They are led by Mortimer and the king!'

'Now who in their right mind would've t'ought mighty King Alfred would have turned as fast as he did?' observed Tommy. 'It's a cryin' shame, that.'

'Fear is a very powerful force,' replied Alkaios, 'and Mortimer is as cunning as they come. Allow the king his weakness. We all have it to a greater or lesser extent.'

'How many Morrukks are there?' asked Adalbrecht.

'So many they cannot be counted,' said Lillian.

'And the Knights Triumphant?' asked Adalbrecht, 'do they ride with the king?'

'No. They cannot be found,' answered Lillian. 'Majesticans believe they have fled.'

'The knights would never flee Majestica,' countered Charlie rather forcefully.

'How far away are Mortimer and the others?' asked Alkaios.

'Five miles, or so,' answered Lillian. 'Not much further and they are heading this way.'

'Now, how'd they know where we are?' asked Tommy. 'Maybe they'll pass us by.'

'We can be certain of this,' said Alkaios, 'even if he passes by once, sooner or later he will find us. We must go!'

'But where?' asked Tommy. 'We haven't the foggiest idea where the Tree is, and you an' Molly have been studying the story all night.'

Halfway through a yawn, Charlie looked at Tommy with an odd expression on his face.

'What did you say?' asked Charlie stretching his arms.

'I said, they've been studying the t'ing all night, and we're no further ahead. Sure, she only just found the riddle,' said Tommy. 'And I'm not too sure she's done that much!'

'I don't believe it,' said Charlie suddenly wide awake.

'Yee don't believe *what?*' asked Tommy.

'Beyond where land floats on tea, there you will have to dig,' said Charlie repeating the riddle. 'Tommy, you said it - *study!*'

'Thank you,' said Tommy, 'but, uh, what for exactly?'

'Does this mean something to you?' asked Gabrielle.

'I don't know about the digging part, but I know where land floats on tea. Or does in the summer, anyway,' said Charlie.

Charlie looked at Molly and smiled.

'You've been there too, Molly,' he said.

'I don't think so, Charlie,' Molly said doubtfully.

'I don't mean to be knockin' yerr first date or yerr first kiss,' interrupted Tommy, 'and though this surely seems like a sweet moment an' all, do you mind sharing with us what yerr t'inkin'?'

'Where land floats on tea!' said Charlie again. 'That's the Studies!'

'I didn't say a t'ing about studyin', did I?' asked Tommy looking blankly at the other leprechauns.

'The Studies?' asked Gabrielle.

'Of course,' said Charlie. 'The Studies. I fly fish there. *You* know Molly. Where the Morrukks almost got me.'

'Oh, that's right!' said Molly.

'The water there is the colour of tea,' reiterated Charlie. 'It looks just like it, and the banks are undercut like you wouldn't believe...you may as well say the whole thing floats.'

'Does it make sense that you'd dig there?' asked Tommy. 'And who goes diggin' fer a tree, anyway?'

'I said I didn't know about the digging,' said Charlie, 'but I'm sure the first half of the riddle is the Studies.'

'And we don't dig *there*,' added Adalbrecht. 'The riddle says we're to go beyond that.'

'Charlie,' asked Alkaios, 'can you take us there?'

'Blindfolded, but it's quite the hike from here, especially in the snow,' said Charlie.

'Then it is time to call for our woodland friends,' said Alkaios rising from his throne.

Alkaios closed his eyes and the room fell peacefully silent. Everyone stared intently upon him and noticed the air around his great black horn changed somehow, as if it were suddenly warmed. After a moment or two, Alkaios opened his eyes again and smiled.

'To Bokwus Forest!' Alkaios commanded.

Chapter Twenty-Seven
- *The Golden Tree* -

There was urgency in Alkaios' voice like never before and soon everyone was outside running towards the Studies with Charlie leading the way. The air was still incredibly cold, but the snow had stopped and in its place fell black soot from the fires of Majestica, darkening the sky and the snow.

Charlie had a great sense of direction and though he had only been through this part of Bokwus once before, he found his way back to the barren clearing by the orchard with hardly an upward glance. From here, he figured he knew a shortcut to the Studies.

Molly, Adalbrecht, and Gabrielle were on the witches' brooms and could have gone on forever, but Charlie was tired from running.

'I have to take a break,' he said huffing and puffing.

'Well, it's about time,' said Tommy. 'Our legs aren't as long as yerr gangly pins, don't ya know.'

As the entire party caught their breath, a faint sound grew. It was muffled and eerie and its origin could not be pinpointed. Though it was undecipherable at first, soon it was plain to everyone that Mortimer, the Morrukks, and the king were close behind.

'We must keep going,' said Alkaios.

'One more minute,' pleaded Charlie. 'I can't keep this pace.'

No sooner did these words cross his lips than there was another sound. But it was different. It was softer, like a pattering, and it came from the orchard.

'They're in front and behind us!' Gabrielle exclaimed.

'I don't like this,' said Molly. 'What is it, Alkaios?'

'You'll see,' Alkaios replied calmly.

Suddenly, the tree-line of the orchard came to life as a force of Pinkletons arrived with all the woodland creatures. The foxes, the wolves, the owls, the doves, the chickadees, the deer, the rabbits: all that they had seen before and more. They gathered round their heroes as lovingly and protectively as any family pet. Then, with a *snort*, out trotted Mr. Cayce.

'I've gathered all I could,' said Mr. Cayce, 'but Grizz did not want to be disturbed.'

'Is he not coming?' asked Alkaios quite surprised.

'Oh yes,' said Mr. Cayce. 'He's coming, but he is one grumpy bear.'

There was another breaking in orchard and out sauntered Grizz. He was a little thinner than in the fall, having lost weight during hibernation, but this only proved to articulate his massive bulging shoulder blades as they moved beneath his shaggy fur. Grizz walked right up to Charlie.

'He came for you,' said Mr. Cayce.

'Huh?' remarked Charlie.

'For you to ride, brave knight,' added Mr. Cayce as Grizz lowered his forward haunches.

With great respect, but without hesitation, Charlie jumped on Grizz's back.

'Come on, old boy,' said Charlie with his hand pointing not towards the path of the orchard, but on an angle to the right which he believed was the direction of the Studies.

The leprechauns mounted the deer, the witches took to the air, and all the woodland friends followed Charlie and Grizz as the noise of the Morrukk army grew behind them.

There was no path to follow from here, but at least it wasn't Bokwus. Still, it was all the witches could do to steer through the timber maze at this speed. Grizz simply smashed through all but the larger trees. The smaller animals darted this way and that way. Mr. Cayce was also light on his feet, though his antlers were as large as could be imagined. Everywhere he ducked his head, the branches miraculously accommodated his great size as if they dared not get in his way. Those that stood defiant were severed on the spot.

They charged on and on while the sound behind them intensified. Somehow, King Alfred, Mortimer, and all the Morrukks were gaining on them. Molly wondered if some black spell had given them unnatural speed.

If you have never been chased before and if you have never been in fear of losing your life, it is hard to appreciate the heightened keenness of your senses. Everything seems to slow, as if Father Time draws near to his own end, and certain things you don't think you'd observe become as obvious to you as if you had a lifetime to look upon them.

Molly's eyes began to see in this way. Such was the detail of each barren branch sauntering by her head. Such was the curly loose thread dangling from Genevieve's cape. Such was each droplet of drool falling from each of the wolves' stained canines. Such was each colourful feather on each winged animal at her side. Such was each distinct footprint made in the snow. Such was each steamy breath from the animals' nostrils captured for an ocean of time in the air. Such was the solitary pulse of the fairies' beating wings. Such was Molly's echoing breaths and her own *lub-dub, lub-dub* heartbeat inside her small frame. Such were all the infinitely subtle details of her surroundings while the horrible sound of their enemies grew behind them.

The sound was so great that Molly came to understand that some of the Morrukks must have been riding horse-back and mixed with their pounding hooves was the clanking of metal against metal. Molly imagined that the Morrukks had fashioned some heavy armour in the dark land of Nordenburgh and were also armed with cold, cruel weapons – not rusty, but not polished either. Such was the clanking and crashing resonating in Molly's ears.

Still, as clear as all these sights and sounds were, they vanished the instant she heard Charlie's voice.

'We're here!' exclaimed Charlie breaking out into a small clearing that followed the river. 'I've never been on this side, but this is it. This is the Studies.'

'I don't see any tea,' said Tommy, 'nor any floating land.'

'Trust me,' said Charlie, 'the water in this river is the colour of tea. Why, even the fish in it are darker here, and though it looks solid, everything we are on now floats like a raft of weeds.'

'And where do you suppose we go from here?' asked Tommy.

'I don't know, *Tom,*' answered Charlie rather curtly.

The thundering hooves and the clanking Morrukks drew nearer. They were shouting and grunting and calling out the most hideous things. Only a few more minutes and they would arrive.

'Molly,' Alkaios said, 'do you understand the nature of this riddle?'

'No! I don't understand anything,' said Molly pushing the answer away from her.

'Quiet your mind,' Alkaios said with his warm steady voice. 'Attract the answer to you.'

'How can I quiet my mind at a time like this? We're about to be overtaken by an army of Morrukks,' said Molly struggling to maintain her balance on Genevieve's hovering broom: 'Here, let me off this thing.'

Everything was so confusing. Molly was more frightened in that moment than any other she could recall. Everyone was looking to her for answers, but with the Morrukks advancing, the leprechauns arguing amongst themselves, the fairies buzzing around, the witches chanting incantation after incantation, and all the animals growling and pacing about, it was impossible to think.

No, thought Molly again. It just wasn't possible to quiet her mind.

'It *is* possible,' whispered Alkaios.

Molly caught Alkaios' loving eyes as he said this, and a small flame of hope ignited within her.

She knew what she had to do.

She had to ask for what she wanted.

'Q–U–I–E–T!' Molly yelled.

Mighty Alkaios reared high in the air, neighed gloriously, and by the time his hooves hit the frozen earth, the entire party was as silent as the falling ash.

Alkaios lowered his great head to Molly's and their cheeks touched one another while her arm caressed his stooping neck.

'I believe in you,' whispered Alkaios so softly, only Molly heard. 'It's time to let your fear go.'

For the longest time Molly and Alkaios did not move, though their party grew restless with the noise of the approaching army growing stronger and stronger. Molly closed her eyes and suddenly felt at peace. The dark thoughts of Mortimer faded away. He was just a man, after all, and he belonged to a race of men who became ugly because they focused on what they did not want. Greed paled their skin, jealousy muddied their eyes, and anger twisted their bones.

There in that quiet moment, Molly understood the Morrukks were no different than any other people. They too wanted to be happy and to feel loved. For one reason or another, they had simply lost their way and if given the chance, Molly would forgive them. Much too often people do not allow themselves to forgive, for they focus on the pain that others have inflicted, but this way of thinking only attracts more pain. *Yes*, realized Molly; if ever in all the world there was a way to feel lighter, it was to forgive people their trespasses.

Molly's mind was at peace. Her fear melted away and as is often the case when the heart is at ease, Molly had a moment of intuition.

'Charlie, can you take us to Gidot from here?' asked Molly.

'Gidot?' asked Tommy.

'Huh? The tree students visit with Mrs. Harvey?' asked Charlie.

'Who's Mrs. Harvey?' asked Adalbrecht.

'Yes, Charlie,' answered Molly. 'Can you take us there?'

'Not to be interruptin' another trip down memory lane,' Tommy said, 'but who in the name of green clovers are Mrs. Harvey and Gidot?'

Even though the magnificent tree, Gidot, was long dead, Molly was compelled to go there, to follow her intuition, to let the Universe show her one step of the lighthouse at a time.

'Can you take us there?' Molly asked again urgently.

'Of course I can,' answered Charlie.

'May I?' asked Molly turning to Alkaios who smiled, knowing both the question and the answer.

'Of course, Molly. Whatever you need,' answered Alkaios. 'Mr. Cayce, would you be so kind?'

'Certainly,' said Mr. Cayce lowering his huge head. 'Hold on, Molly.'

Molly sat herself in the cradle of his great antlers and was lifted astride Alkaios. In an instant, she leapt from one to the other, and sat upon *him* – the Unicorn – her hands gently grabbing his flowing mane.

'Lead on, Charlie,' Molly called and her company of friends set out with great haste.

They ran along the river for a good length and then Charlie directed them into a thicket, through a field, over a frozen creek, and they eventually arrived in another clearing.

The running stopped and everyone stood still, looking at an old tree a teacher had named Gidot ages ago. Molly slid off Alkaios and stared at it. As dead as it was, Molly believed it looked beautiful – so twisted and knotted.

'Sure is a pretty tree,' remarked Tommy with much sarcasm. 'Wouldn't it look nice in me front yard?'

Slowly, everyone approached the old tree. The fairies and birds perched upon its branches. All were unsure why Molly had taken them there, but no one had the courage to ask. No one, of course, except for Tommy.

'I don't see a single scrap o' gold on this ole t'ing,' said Tommy. 'Molly, are yee sure here's where ya want to be?'

'And we fairies have been to this tree before,' added Lillian buzzing in front of Molly. 'I think you've made a mistake, Molly. Surely the Pinkleton Dimple—'

'Did you ever look for it and believe you'd find it?' asked Molly.

'Well, no' answered Lillian,' but—'

'So you have never asked it a question, either,' said Molly.

'Of course not,' answered Lillian. 'It's only a tree.'

'Then maybe you were never meant to find it! Or maybe you're just too arrogant to see it!' said Molly. 'I am just sure I was meant to come here.'

'Meant to come here 'cause you missed the tree?' asked Tommy, 'or because yee t'ought it'd be a great place to stop for spot o' tea and a crusty bannock?'

'Not another word,' said Alkaios.

'If Molly was moved to come here,' said Adalbrecht, 'that's good enough for me.'

With this, Adalbrecht produced a shovel from his long cloak and began to dig.

'Beyond where land floats on tea,' Adalbrecht repeated to himself, *'there you will have to dig.'*

'I've never gone diggin' fer a tree.' said Tommy. 'Seems every tree I've seen has been, you know, kinda stickin' out o' the ground.'

'Perhaps we have to dig to find the next clue,' countered Adalbrecht sweeping the snow to one side. 'I believe Engelbert would use such a tree as a sign, so if you are quite finished with your jokes, then maybe you'd like to help.'

'Sure, that ground's froze harder than diamonds,' said Tommy. 'You'll never so much as scrape the frost off it.'

'Do you have any better ideas?' asked Mr. Cayce.

Tommy did not answer, as a crashing in the woods pierced the air. The Morrukks were closer now than ever before. Molly didn't have much time before they arrived. The riddle had to be deciphered. Molly closed her eyes and thought of all the things she had come to know.

Molly knew she was there, by Gidot, at this particular moment in time for a reason. Though her fear had all but left her, she struggled with the final piece of the puzzle. What did it all mean?

I know the answer, I know the answer, I know the—

'To dig, to dig, to dig,' complained Tommy, while everyone else was now on their knees sweeping the snow away. Even the animals scratched at the frost with their hooves and talons and paws.

'We'll dig till we're blue in the face,' said Tommy, 'and the Morrukks will arrive and wonder what in the blazes we're doing.'

Molly looked up at Gidot and saw all the fairies in the tree with their green wings. There, in the dead of winter, this tree alone looked as though it were still alive.

'Dig, dig, dig,' continued Tommy. 'This has to be the most backwards way to look fer a tree as ever I have heard.'

And there it was! Molly understood. The Universe answered the riddle through Tommy for the second time.'

'Tommy's right!' shouted Molly.

'I know I'm right,' said Tommy. 'We're not uncovering a solitary t'ing on this good day, I'll tell yee!'

'But we have! We've uncovered everything,' said Molly. 'Beyond where land floats on tea, there you will have to dig.'

'If you've not been watchin' em,' said Tommy, 'they have been diggin'.'

'But as you've said, we have it backwards. There you will have to *dig*, but it's not to *dig*' said Molly, 'it's to dig backwards. Just like the story's pages were backwards. There *are* no coincidences!'

'A pleasant thought, I'm sure, but I'm not sure if I know how to dig a tree backwards,' said Tommy.

'Don't you see? *To dig* backwards spells *Gidot!* This is it!' exclaimed Molly. 'This has to be it! Gidot is the Golden Tree and we're just not seeing it.'

'But Molly, this tree is as dark as mud,' said Tommy. 'How in green clovers do yee figger this is it? There's nary a single scrap o' gold to be found, I told yee.'

'Are you sure, Molly?' asked Charlie.

'I *am* sure,' said Molly, expecting it would turn to gold any second.

And then it did.

From behind Tommy there was a great birth of wonderful golden rays as if, at midday, the sun had risen for the second time.

'Look!' exclaimed Molly.

Tommy and all the others turned to face Gidot in pure amazement. It was shining bright and golden, but *not* from any golden leaves. Perched upon its branches, the wings of a thousand fairies had lost their green hue and instead shone a wondrous gold. The whole Tree was illuminated as were the faces of all the leprechauns, witches, humans, and animals. No one had ever seen anything that could rival the Tree for brilliance.

'It *is* Gidot,' said Molly. 'This is the Golden Tree!'

'Sure that's not real gold,' said Tommy, but there could be no doubting that Gidot was nothing, if not the Golden Tree of Truth.

'How is this possible?' asked Gabrielle. 'There's no singing. What's making their wings gold?'

'Only one other thing on earth can,' said Alkaios.

And then, from behind the Tree, there appeared the only other creature who equalled Alkaios for beauty. It was Amalthea, the mare Unicorn, the protector of the Golden Tree of Truth, and she was as white and as pure as fresh fallen snow. Whereas Alkaios' horn was black with flecks of gold, Amalthea's was white with silver. She was Alkaios' exact opposite in colour and yet they were the perfect match.

Standing there with more magic than any other creature under the sun, Amalthea appeared to glow as if there was a light within her shining brightly. To merely look upon her, was to have your heart warmed.

Amalthea approached Alkaios in complete silence. They

swooned for each other. Molly couldn't believe the awesome power of this moment. Never before had she seen such a display of love, affection, and beauty. Who else, in the history of the greatest love stories ever told, were as destined to be together as these two?

Amalthea turned her attention to those who swore to protect the Golden Tree and, though she spoke no words, everyone felt her say *thank you*. It resounded within them so thoroughly they forgot all about King Alfred, Mortimer, and the army of Morrukks. Instead, they remained speechless, respecting this long-awaited union, oblivious to all else.

'THERE'S THE TREE!' screeched Mortimer, breaking out in the clearing with King Alfred and the rest of the Morrukks. There were hundreds of Morrukk soldiers, some on horse, some on foot, and they were all heavily armed.

'They're taking it, they're taking it!' cried Mortimer.

'Charge!' yelled the king.

The Morrukk foot soldiers unsheathed their weapons and charged at the king's command. Mortimer, the true schemer, stayed behind with King Alfred and the Morrukks on horseback, waiting to see how the first wave would fair.

'We have no weapons!' shouted Charlie. 'What are we going to do?'

'Get Amalthea out of here!' cried Genevieve.

'There's too many of them,' added Tommy as the dreadful Morrukks drew closer. 'We can't beat them. Not that many, we can't.'

Molly thought for only a second, and she knew what they had to do.

'We must forgive them and love them,' said Molly.

'Yee must be mad,' retorted Tommy 'I don't love a damn t'ing about 'em.'

'But you must!' cried Molly.

Closer still the Morrukks came.

'She's right,' agreed Alkaios.

'But they have weapons,' countered Tommy and the other leprechauns grumbled in agreement. 'Some of us should stay back.'

'These Morrukks deserve our love,' said Molly and she left the safety of her group to greet the advancing army.

'She's gone mad!' Tommy yelled, but Molly kept walking.

She wasn't alone, though. Charlie, her brave young knight

jumped off Grizz, rolled up his sleeves, and caught up to her without hesitation.

'Him too,' added Tommy. 'Have they both been sippin' on the swillers?'

Molly and Charlie marched on until they met the Morrukks halfway.

'I believe in you, Molly,' Charlie whispered to her.

The Morrukks were properly confused. They did not know what to make of their willing victims. So baffled were the Morrukks, in fact, they stopped dead in their tracks as if their feet had become one with the earth.

'Kill them!' cried Mortimer from far behind the ranks. 'KILL THEM!'

But the Morrukks did not move. They stood staring at Molly, grunting, and panting just as Gabrielle joined the brave youngsters.

'I knew all along you were the one,' said Gabrielle.

'We all did,' said Alkaios now standing to one side of Molly, Amalthea holding fast on the other.

There in a silent stand off, Molly, Charlie, Gabrielle, Alkaios, and Amalthea looked deep into the Morrukks' eyes and saw great pain and suffering, but they also saw a deep-rooted longing for love and happiness. The Morrukks, looking into the eyes of their unarmed adversaries, found this love and it overwhelmed them. Their hearts softened. Their hands dropped to their sides.

'Kill them!' cried Mortimer again. 'Kill them, you ugly, worthless, idiots!'

Despite Mortimer's commands, the Morrukks did not budge, but rather dropped their weapons to the earth. Molly and the others had quieted the hearts of their foes. Instead of seeking war, the Morrukks now sought forgiveness and redemption. Such was the miracle of the moment. The soldiers fell to their knees and wept.

'This is a new beginning for you,' said Molly to them.

Alkaios approached the kneeling Morrukks with his head hanging low. He walked by each of them so they might feel the love and magic for themselves. Some were too shy to touch such a glorious creation, while others were too wrought with guilt to even look up; still others reached out to lay their hands upon him, smiling like they had never smiled before. But, as each Morrukk hand touched Alkaios, he seemed to grow weaker.

'Fools!' cried Mortimer. 'Second rank, charge! *CHARGE!*'

The Morrukks riding horseback, those filled with the most hate, charged towards the peaceful battlefront with their weapons drawn. They intended to do the bidding of their master having gone far behind the hope of redemption. But before they could get any momentum, there was a clamorous noise from the woods behind the Golden Tree.

Molly turned to see her father William upon a giant steed leading the Knights Triumphant. They wore their historic armour and waved the great red and white flag of Majestica. Unlike any time known in history, though, the knights now carried swords. Quickly they approached and stood strong beside their young heroes. William looked down only briefly, winked at Molly, and then stared intently upon the charging Morrukks.

'My fellow knights!' William commanded, and in unison they all raised their swords.

'They're Knights Triumphant!' cried one of the advancing Morrukks and, like a flock of birds who changes direction at once, so too did the Morrukks flee into the woods.

An uncomfortable silence fell across the clearing. The kneeling Morrukks stood, and filed away with their comrades in the woods. Mortimer and King Alfred were left alone – defeated. Far off in the distance, they appeared to be arguing, pointing angry fingers of blame at each other.

'Leapin' leprechauns!' shouted Tommy from behind. 'We've won!'

There was a chorus of cheering and Molly and the others turned back to see the leprechauns and witches dancing for joy.

'You've done it!' said Charlie placing his arm around Molly.

'I have a little explaining to do,' said William smiling down at Molly, who was too overjoyed for words.

'Congratulations, Molly,' said Gabrielle.

There was hooting and hollering and shouts of jubilation as Molly and her followers returned to the Tree to rejoice. The celebration was so loud, that no one heard Mortimer approach.

'You little brat!' shouted Mortimer.

Molly turned and was horrified to see Mortimer Weedly right on top of them. He smiled his devilish smile. Then, with his one hand, he hoisted his dull sword high in the air. Charlie leapt to intercept the deadly blow, but Mortimer threw him aside with ease. Mortimer's target was not Molly, though, it was Amalthea, and he drove his rusty sword into her pure heart.

'*Noooo!*' cried Molly.

Mortimer laughed as Amalthea staggered twice and fell to the earth.

'The Tree is mine!' Mortimer squeaked, and in a flash he bolted past the knights.

Molly slumped down beside Amalthea, crying, while her father spurred his horse into a lightning gallop. She didn't see Mortimer fight off the leprechauns, elude the witches, jump over Alkaios, and continue towards the Tree. She didn't see King Alfred come to his senses as though he had just woken up from a horrible nightmare to discover the world was a cruel place. She didn't look up, in fact, until Mortimer had reached the Tree and groped it wildly.

He leapt up and down, swiping hopelessly at the Pinkletons as if to catch one, and that's when he realized there was no gold at all.

'Where's the gold?' he shrieked hurriedly. 'Where's the gold? Where's the gold? This can't be. *WHERE'S MY GOLD!?*'

Mortimer laughed nervously, but the laughs turned to sobs. He did not understand that with the loss of one opportunity, another, more glorious, opportunity was bound to appear.

William drew his sword, raised it high in the air, and let it fall just as Mortimer turned to him with tears in his eyes. He looked up at William, sobbing, but William was too wrought with anger to feel the least bit of remorse. His sword continued to fall towards its mark as Mortimer mouthed the words 'forgive me' to him.

'*No!*' yelled Molly unable to endure the sight of murder. She'd never be able to look at her father again, but his sword did not falter from its course and severed a lock of Mortimer's black hair.

'If you are as clever as you think you are, Mortimer, you will not cross my path again,' said William leaving Mortimer to wallow in his own misery. But, at the precise moment William offered a stay in the execution, Grizz's teeth sunk deep into Mortimer's neck, and he was dragged off into the woods, convulsing and shrieking and begging for mercy.

Then, there was silence.

'What have I done?' sobbed King Alfred now standing over Molly and Amalthea. 'Forgive me. However can I put things right?'

Everyone gathered round Amalthea who lay shivering in the

snow and ice. She struggled to breathe, and as each drop of her blood fell to the earth, a tree in the distance came into bloom.

'Look,' said Charlie noticing the trees surrounding the clearing were exploding with colour one by one.

'It's her love,' said Molly. 'Her love for us is making this happen.'

And, it was true. As Amalthea's life drained from her body, everyone filled with love as did the very Earth beneath the snow and all that it connects. So much, in truth, that spring was born that very moment.

'This can't be happening,' said Molly. 'It wasn't supposed to end this way.'

William placed his hand upon his daughter's shoulder, but she shrugged it off. A sadness captured her and bound her utterly. The pain of the loss was too great to endure.

'It wasn't supposed to end this way!' she cried again.

Alkaios gently nuzzled Molly's cheek. Though his heart suffered the most, he still sought to comfort.

'You've done your best,' said Alkaios. 'No one here could have asked for more.'

'I am so sorry,' cried Molly looking into his dark brown eyes. 'Is there nothing else I can do?'

All those around Molly, Amalthea, and Alkaios felt it best to leave them alone. They returned to the Tree, gathered round it, and held hands. By and by, each wing on each fairy turned from gold back to green until there was not a glimmer of hope left. They knew Amalthea had surely passed away.

'The Tree is dead,' said Tommy. 'Mortimer's cursed hand has killed them both.'

As he said this, the massive trunk seemed to exhale and sag while several large branches fell to the earth sending the fairies to other branches. Everyone believed they had failed, but none more so than Molly who sat caressing Amalthea's lifeless body.

'Can she not heal herself with this magic?' whispered Molly to Alkaios as another branch drummed the earth. 'What good is it then?'

'Sometimes, Molly,' replied Alkaios, 'the wound is too much for the body and spirit to overcome. We cannot have miracles every time.'

'My life for hers,' sobbed Molly. 'If I could give my life for hers, I would do it. There must be another way. Tell me you can bring her back, Alkaios.'

Molly laid her head upon Amalthea and placed one little hand upon the wound hoping to reverse the horrible march of Death, but she could not. It looked as though she were clutching a river of rose petals.

'But we've found the Golden Tree,' sobbed Molly. 'There must be an answer for this.'

'There is no answer for death, but death itself,' spoke Alkaios softly. 'It is every bit a part of life.'

'Not today,' Molly whispered even too quietly for Alkaios to hear. 'Not today.'

Molly closed her eyes and in a rush of white light, she saw the image of her smiling mother. There was another rush of white light, and in a second memory Molly recalled her mother's horrible headaches and how often Molly had stopped singing in case it made it worse. Finally, there was a third rush of brilliant white and she recalled her mother's words: *When a mother hurts the most, the need to hear her child is greatest.*

Molly didn't realize it, but at this very moment she began to humm. She hummed the song her mother loved the most. It had no words, but a melody as heavenly as any on earth. Softly, the sad, beautiful notes drifted through the air, over the heroes, and high up to the branches of great Gidot. There, the fairies heard the sweet music and one by one, their wings flickered and sputtered gold.

'Look!' said Charlie. 'It's starting again.'

Everyone stared at the Tree, but Molly paid no attention. She continued to humm to herself. Her voice grew and as her sweet song filled the hearts of the fairies, the Tree glowed gloriously once more.

'Molly,' said Charlie, 'look at what you're doing.'

But Molly did not look until Alkaios nudged her shoulder.

'Let her go,' he said softly.

Molly rose to her feet and with one quick and determined motion she pulled Mortimer's rusty sword from the poor body of Amalthea and then cast it to the ground. She then looked up and saw the Golden Tree glowing in all its splendour. Molly was strangely drawn to it and she joined her circle of friends – all staring in stunned silence.

'It still glows,' whispered Tommy, 'but—'

'Just enjoy it,' interrupted Gabrielle.

'And that I am,' said Tommy, 'but Molly's stopped 'er singing.'

Tommy paused, wondering why no one else shared his curiosity, but he couldn't keep quiet long.

'Anyone know why's it still glowing?' he asked softly.

Molly hadn't offered a note since standing. She *couldn't*. She may as well have tried to swallow the moon, for the lump which had risen inside her throat had choked her voice off completely. Still, the Tree shone more and more brilliantly.

How can this be? Molly wondered while she and the others basked in the glory of the Tree. Then, as curiously as could be imagined, Molly's sad song was heard again, faintly. Molly had not opened her mouth, but the music had returned all the same, carried upon a warm breeze rich with the smells of spring. It was as though choirs of angels had been so touched by Molly's depth of feeling, they felt it only right to breathe life back into her sad song.

Then, from behind Molly, there was a weak and awkward stumbling.

Molly was almost afraid to turn around, but turn she did. Hoping for Hope she turned, and when she saw what was happening she fell to her knees. Standing shakily, but standing all the same, was Amalthea leaning against her loving Alkaios for strength. She was alive! Somehow, some way, she was alive! It was a miracle on the grandest level and it wasn't long before Amalthea stood on her own – as full of life as ever!

Slowly and silently, Amalthea and Alkaios approached Molly, bowing their heads low so Molly's trembling hands could touch the miracle she had helped create. And, it is no falsehood to report, the instant Molly laid her hands upon the Unicorns, she felt them say: *'We will never forget Princess Molly, the one who saved us with her Faith and Love. Thank you.'*

Chapter Twenty-Eight
- *In The End* -

And finally, everything unfolded as it should. King Alfred admitted to hiding *Majestica's Popular Folklore*, but could not explain how Mortimer came across it to tear out the story: *The Golden Tree*. The king promised, however, to never again forget its teachings. He also apologized to William, Marcus, and especially to Molly. He even allowed her to keep the silver necklace she had innocently taken from the castle, but this was no surprise to Molly. She believed all along she would be allowed to keep it, and when it was official, she gave the necklace to Annabelle one day over tea while retelling her everything she had learned. This time, Annabelle listened a little more closely, and eventually her headaches all but disappeared, for she began each day telling herself she was healed.

By and by, William shared all of his adventures as a young knight with Molly. He also rekindled his friendship with Marcus and King Alfred who offered him the position of chief advisor once more. William accepted, and along with Marcus and the other Knights Triumphant, they swore an oath to defend the Golden Tree until the end of their days. They also promised to pass on their wisdom to the next great band of knights so the Tree's protection would be for all Time.

After the *Majestican Miracle*, as it came to be known, Adalbrecht felt a little empty. Having waited for the Tree's salvation for half his life, he now felt as though he had lost his purpose. He and King

Alfred spent much time together for several weeks, but Adalbrecht's feet became itchy before too long, and he left Majestica hoping to find the key which would open Engelbert's diary. Before leaving, though, Adalbrecht entrusted King Alfred with the *Diary of Magic*. Even without the key, this ancient text was too precious to be left unguarded, and the king agreed to keep the diary locked inside the castle until Adalbrecht returned.

Majestica continued to flourish and the black mess from the coal was, in time, sponged away leaving the kingdom as pristine as ever.

Tommy Troublesome and his fellow leprechauns made themselves scarce to humankind, but they told Molly the next pot of gold hidden at the end of the rainbow would be in honour of her. So it was that one spring day, after a warm rain, Molly and Charlie went to the reading tree to see if, per chance, Tommy might be there. Sure enough, Tommy Troublesome appeared from within the tree and with his sparkling mischievous eyes looking upon the glorious rainbow, he said: 'Come along wit' me, and be light of foot. I have somethin' to show yee.'

With the earth awake after her long winter slumber, the land was in full bloom and the rivers ran bright and fast. There you'd find Charlie fly fishing as always, kissing and releasing most of the trout to be flashes of brilliant colour another day.

Molly, of course, continued to sing and play in the woods as much as possible and though she loved spending time with all her woodland friends, she longed to see Amalthea and Alkaios one more time. All summer she called out their names, yet she never once caught sight of them. But, that's not to say she did not see a Unicorn, for one day she happened to spy the most adorable colt Unicorn running across her path and she knew very well to whom it belonged.

Gabrielle left Molly to enjoy the summer with the other school children on holidays. Then one afternoon, as the days were suddenly much shorter and a cooler breeze spread news of autumn's returning reign, Gabrielle knocked on Molly's door. Together they walked towards Town Centre.

'Have you enjoyed your summer?' asked Gabrielle.

'Very much,' answered Molly, 'but I am looking forward to the fall. If you'll teach me again, that is.'

'Of course I will,' said Gabrielle.

Molly's eyes shone with renewed excitement. She wondered what else Gabrielle would teach her. She also wondered what would become of the Golden Tree and if Adalbrecht Elfinstone would ever find the key to Engelbert's *Diary of Magic.*

'It's not over, is it?' asked Molly with a sudden sense that something was wrong.

'No, Molly, I am afraid it may never be over,' answered Gabrielle. 'The evil force behind Mr. Weedly still exists.'

'The fear?' asked Molly.

'Yes, but you needn't worry about that now,' said Gabrielle. 'When the time comes, you'll know what you must do.'

'I am sure I will,' said Molly. 'Everything I have learned this year, about myself and about the Universe, I owe to you.'

'You wouldn't have learned a thing if you were not who you are,' said Gabrielle. 'Sadly, not everyone believes their dreams can come true – not everyone opens themselves up to the magic.

'Do you really think *magic* is the right word to use?' asked Molly.

'I don't know,' answered Gabrielle. 'I'm not really sure it matters what word we use.'

'Oh, Gabrielle, I still have ever so many questions to ask,' said Molly.

'Such as?' asked Gabrielle.

'Isn't it funny how Mrs. Harvey named the Tree Gidot?' Molly asked with her curiousity stirring once again.

'Just coincidence, I guess,' replied Gabrielle.

'But *you* said,' noted Molly right away, 'there's no such thing as coincidence.'

Gabrielle smiled that knowing smile of hers and Molly knew her questions would just have to wait.

Molly took a step in front of Gabrielle, turned, and gave her a great big hug.

'Gabrielle' said Molly. 'I feel as though I never properly thanked you.'

'Sure you have,' said Gabrielle. 'If not for you, today's conversation would be quite, quite different I daresay. It is *I* who needs to thank *you,* and there's someone else who's been waiting to thank you, as well.'

'Who?' asked Molly.

'You'll see.'

Molly then happened to notice there was an uncharacteristically large number of people walking in the same direction and they were all speaking in hushed, excited whispers. Molly and Gabrielle continued on and upon entering the town square, there was an immediate sounding of trumpets and a chorus of cheers.

'What's going on today?' asked Molly, but Gabrielle did not answer.

The cheering was so loud it seemed the entire kingdom was in attendance. But what was the occasion? Molly saw a greatly decorated platform raised up at the far end of the square which was adorned with the red and white colours of Majestica. Standing in the middle of the platform were King Alfred, Queen Claire, and Princess Priscilla. Right of the royal family stood William and all the Knights Triumphant wearing their best armour. Standing awkwardly to the left of the royal family were Annabelle and Charlie.

'What *is* this?' asked Molly again, but the only answer she received was Gabrielle's smile.

'MY PEOPLE!' began the king with his big mighty voice that quieted the crowd. 'Behold, Molly Withers!'

Again, the cheering erupted. Molly didn't know what to do or say. She didn't understand.

'This is for *you*,' said Gabrielle unable to contain her excitement any longer. 'This celebration is for you, Molly!'

'I, I don't know what to say,' Molly said above the cheers, and then a little quieter: 'Gabrielle, does everyone know what happened?'

Suddenly, several small children, all holding up books and pencils, spilled out of the crowd and nearly knocked Molly off her feet.

'Sign mine, Molly! Sign mine!' they cried out, jostling before her to be the first.

Molly took one of the children's books and inspected the title on the cover: *Molly Withers and the Golden Tree* by Benton Wolford.

'What is this?' pleaded Molly.

'The king commissioned Mr. Wolford to write a book about you!' whispered Gabrielle into Molly's ear. 'These children want your autograph!'

'Benton Wolford?' Molly said to herself. 'I don't believe it. He knows me?'

Trumpets sounded again as Molly absently signed two or three books. When she looked up next she saw the crowd had parted, creating a path to the decorated platform. *This is how I pictured a wedding should be,* she thought to herself. Upon receiving a gentle nudge from Gabrielle, Molly's feet finally moved, but with every step more and more children poured out of the crowd with their books. They slowed her progress terribly, but eventually Molly made it to the bottom of the carpeted stairs that led up to the dais.

Molly looked at Charlie for an answer, but he simply shrugged his shoulders and clapped with the others. Molly then looked to the king and his beckoning eyes convinced her to ascend. Once at the top, Molly turned around and again the crowd roared with delight.

The king raised his hands and the ocean of cheers ebbed.

'My People,' said the king, 'may I present to you the Keeper of the Magic and honourary Princess of Majestica – Molly Withers!'

King Alfred presented Molly with a small but beautiful coronet and as he placed it upon her head, he whispered: 'You're quite the special girl, Princess Molly. The citizens of Majestica are in your debt, and none more than I. Thank you.'

The king faced the crowd and raised his hands once more. 'And to Charlie Gregg,' boomed the king, 'I present to you this shield bearing Majestica's Royal Coat of Arms.'

William handed King Alfred an authentic Knight Triumphant shield. Charlie stood as expressionless as a stone. He wasn't expecting this.

'The youngest man in Majestica to ever be ordained a Knight Triumphant!' declared the king.

Predictably, the crowd's joyous cries burst out again, but even so, Charlie's face expressed nothing but shock.

As the king handed Charlie the shield, he spoke softly: 'Charlie Gregg, you're the bravest young man I have ever met. I see nothing but great things for you.'

Marcus hoisted Molly upon his shoulder, while her father did the same to Charlie. This snapped Charlie out of his dazed state. He smiled widely, and shot one triumphant fist in the air.

'Molly Withers and Charlie Gregg!' declared the king, 'Majestica thanks you!'

Molly and Charlie were happy beyond belief. Both of them

received what they had always wanted through the knowledge of the Golden Tree. Charlie became a Knight and Molly became an honourary Princess. More importantly to Molly, though, she came to know that there was real Magic left in the world.

And one fine day not long after the celebration, Molly and Charlie went for a walk in the woods and recounted the incredible events of that year. They also talked about what the next year would bring, wondering if they'd ever see Grizz again or ever find out what happened to Mortimer. As much as Molly was relieved he was gone, she felt a little sad that his body was left to rot away with not a single friend to mourn his passing. Charlie, though, believed Mortimer got just what he deserved, but he was touched by Molly's caring. An unexpected appreciation suddenly tickled his heart as Charlie looked at Molly with her lovely green eyes and brown hair shining in the sun. He opened his mouth to speak, but was interrupted by a sudden *snap - crack - snap* on the path behind them. Molly and Charlie spun round to see who or what could have been there and were quite relieved it was only Gabrielle.

'Molly, Charlie, I am glad I found you!' said Gabrielle, sounding a little out of breath – her brow creased with concern.

'What's going on, Gabrielle?' asked Molly.

'You must come quickly,' Gabrielle answered hurriedly. 'The *Diary of Magic* has been stolen!'

The End